A FATE SO CRUEL

FAE OF ALASTRÍONA

J. E. REED

Books by J.E. Reed

The Chronopoint Chronicles

Running with the Wolves
Rise of the Wolves
Feral Magic

The Fae of Alastriona series

The Divine and the Cursed
The Revered and the Pariah
A Fate so Cruel

PRONUNCIATION GUIDE

Characters:

Aila - EYE-luh
Alana - ah-LAN-uh
Alec - AL-uhk
Avalon - AV-uh-lon
Callum – KAL-um
Caol - KAY-ul
Cara - CAR-uh
Eimear – EE-mer
Fin - fin
Foley - FOH-lee
Liam - LEE-um
Lillian - LIL-ee-uh-n
Orla - OR-lah
Rion - REE-on
Saoirse - SUR-sha
Seàn - shawn
Selina - suh-LEE-nuh
Vaz – v-AE-z

Places:

Alastríona - al-as-TREE-na
Ashling - ASH-leen
Brónach - BRO-nah
Fernsworth - FERNS-worth
Fiadh - FEE-ah
Levea - Le-VEE-ah
Móirín - MUY-rin
Nàdair - nay-DEER
Pádraigín - PAH-druh-geen
Púróg - pure-AHG
Whiteridge - WHITE-ridge

HUMAN LANDS
ASHLING
PÁDRAIGÍN
RUADHÁN
PÚRÓG
FIADH
MÓIR

ALASTRÍONA
EN SEA
NÁDAIR
VILLAGE
BRÓNACH
FERNSWORTH
WHITERIDGE
LEVEA

A FATE SO CRUEL

J. E. REED

THE CURSED FAE AND A MOTHER'S LOVE

CHAPTER ONE

The steady, loud drumming of a woodpecker stirred Rion from a dreamless sleep. Gooseflesh rose on his arms and the brisk air in the small cabin room stung his cheeks. His nose was already numb.

He curled in on himself, hiding beneath the warmth of piled blankets that smelled of cedarwood and lavender.

Finches sang outside the window and he heard their little feet scrape against wood as they leaped between branches and onto the feeder his mother had put out last night. A cardinal called from above. Another answered in the distance.

Rion shifted the blanket so his ear poked out despite the cold. His mother had taught him to listen. To identify the birds and plants and all the animals that roamed the forest. From the tiniest insect to the great mountain cats. He liked to make her proud.

Rion finally cracked one eye open and found that she'd draped another blanket over his thick comforter. It smelled like her.

He listened beyond the bird's excited chatter and shifted his attention inside.

Pay attention, his mother always said. *Listen. Know what's in a room before you ever set foot in it.* Sometimes Rion felt those lessons were more important than his schooling. She always praised him when he got things right.

Rion listened now. He pulled his head out from beneath the covers and rested it on the soft down pillow. His breath clouded slightly in the air before him, but Rion closed his eyes again, concentrating on the living room just beyond his door.

A fire crackling in the large hearth and a slight clink of a glass told Rion his mother was awake. Hers was the only heartbeat in the house. Which meant the others had left without him. Again.

His father always said Rion was too young to accompany their morning training sessions. Rion had begged Saoirse to try to change their father's mind, but she always gave him a playful smile. He knew what that smile meant. Their father's mind was a fortress that couldn't be changed by anyone save for their mother.

Rion rubbed the sleep from his eyes and sat up. The cool air hit his back and he shivered again. The sun had barely risen and still hadn't quite crested the treetops.

Another clink of glass from the living room told Rion his mother knew he was awake, and that she was pouring a steaming cup of her favorite tea just for him.

She always knew. He pursed his lips. He'd never succeeded in sneaking up on any of them. Maybe he'd be able to once he got his magic. Maybe then they wouldn't treat him like such a little kid.

Rion slid from the bed with the blanket still tucked around his shoulders and hissed at the cold floor beneath his feet. His mother had told him to bring his slippers in last night and he hadn't listened. He was regretting it, just like she said he would.

The door creaked as he opened it and his mother turned at the sound. Her bright smile greeted him, as it did every morning.

She set the steaming mug back on the counter and bent with open arms. Rion ran into them and she scooped him up as if he were as light as a feather.

He was seven now. Too old, his father said, to be coddled the way he was. But his mother didn't listen to their father. She was probably the only Fae in all of Brónach who got away without listening to the High Lord.

His mother just held him and stared out the large window that overlooked the snow covered land. Rion tilted his head to look with her. A fox played in the distance and after a few minutes, he watched another join it. Not Fae, but animals enjoying the winter snow before spring came to melt it all away.

His mother said this would likely be the last bit of snow they'd see for the year. He didn't mind. He didn't hate the snow, but winter prevented him from swimming in the nearby lake. He couldn't wait for summer.

Rion buried his head back into her shoulder and listened to her steady heartbeat. Her hair tickled his nose. Red, just like his. And beautiful. It flowed past her waist. At home, she always had it tied up around her head, but out here, while they visited the lake house, she let it hang down in soft waves.

His father liked it, too. Rion often caught the male running his fingers through it. It was only with their mother that Rion ever saw a gentle side to his father. Not that the High Lord was ever mean to any of his children. Their mother wouldn't allow that. He was just . . . scary. Stern. He didn't smile easily, and his mother always told Rion that he had his reasons.

Maybe Rion didn't want to join his father, Saoirse, and Alec for training after all.

Holding him with one arm, Rion's mother grabbed the tea tray with her other hand. She didn't even shake. Not like some of the half-breeds did when they tried to carry heavy things.

Half-breeds weren't allowed here.

His mother ambled toward the fire and set the tray down on a small wooden table stained with rings. She re-wrapped the blanket around his body, then seated herself in the rocking chair closest to the fire.

Between the flames and his mother's warmth, Rion stopped shivering.

She rocked back and forth in silence, rubbing one hand up and down his back in slow, methodical strokes. This was his favorite part of the morning, and he never wanted to be too old for it. He wanted his mother to hold him forever.

But whenever he said as much, she'd just laugh and a sad smile would cross her face. He'd pestered her endlessly about what that meant, but she'd never tell him.

A small laugh rumbled through her now. "You're just like your father. Thinking too much before the sun's even come up."

Rion didn't sit up. He hated being told he was anything like his father. He didn't want to grow up cold and stern. Rion wanted to be more like his mother. A kind Fae the citizens nearly worshiped.

"Why don't you ever go out with them?" he asked. Never once had she left him in the cabin alone.

She held him a little tighter. "Because I want to be here with you."

"But didn't you used to go? Before me?"

She chuckled again. "I did."

"Do you miss it?"

She leaned her head against his. "I'll miss this more. One day you'll be all big and strong and I won't have my little Rion to snuggle."

He pursed his lips at that. "I don't want to grow up then." Another laugh. "Will you go when I'm older?"

She brushed a hand through his hair. "I'd miss my tea. Your father wakes up far too early for my taste."

"Then I'll stay here, too."

"I thought you wanted to join them?" He had, but—

"I don't want you to be here by yourself. That doesn't sound like fun."

She shifted and he sat up to stare into her green eyes. The same eyes that looked back at him through the mirror whenever he brushed his teeth. "Tell you what," she said. "When we come here, I'll make sure you're allowed to stay with me every morning."

A smile spread over his face. "You promise?"

"Promise."

His brows scrunched. "Won't Father be mad?"

She poked his side and Rion doubled over, trying not to laugh. "You let me worry about your father."

He pushed her hand away. "It's a promise, then. Forever."

Her face shifted at that and something like pain crossed her features.

Rion pushed. "You'll always be here, right?"

She pulled him back into her shoulder and squeezed tight. "I can't always see the future, little one."

Rion didn't like the acrid scent coming off her. He'd learned to recognize it for what it was. "Liar."

She chuckled again. "Just remember, the future isn't set in stone. It can always change."

He sat up again. "What do you see in my future?"

"Great things."

"Like what?"

She flicked the tip of his nose and he swatted her hand away. "If I told you everything, it would ruin the journey."

He pouted. "You tell Father things."

His mother studied him, then lowered her voice to a near whisper. She glanced around as if someone could be hiding in the shadows. "I don't tell him everything."

Rion leaned closer and lowered his voice as well. "Really?"

She smiled again and it reminded Rion of the sun's rays now streaming through the window behind her. "Really. Like today, for instance."

Rion waited, then bounced on her lap. "What happens today?"

She gave him a mischievous grin. "Would you like to find out?" Rion nodded vigorously, his heart racing with excitement. "Then go get dressed and I'll show you."

Tea and the cold forgotten, Rion leaped from his mother's lap and ran for his room. He threw on the first pair of clothes he could find and was back out in the living area before his mother had even emerged from her room.

Rion pulled on two pairs of socks, threw his coat around his shoulders, and pulled on the hat he hated to wear. But he'd do it without argument today. When she finally emerged, he was standing by the door, thoroughly bundled. He'd even grabbed his gloves.

She shook her head. "I should tell you secrets more often."

Rion bounced on his toes. "Come on, come on, come on."

She pulled on her own coat, hat, and gloves, but bent down to his level before she opened the door. "We have to be very quiet for it to work. Once we enter the trees, you can't talk or they'll hear you. Do you think you can do that?"

Rion nodded again. He was more excited now than he'd been to get his presents on the winter solstice.

"Take a breath," she commanded. "Slow your heart and remember to listen. You can tap and point and I'll do the same."

He did as commanded and willed his body to relax. Then his mother turned and Rion climbed up onto her back. She exited the warm cabin and though she left prints in the snow, Rion could hardly hear her footfalls.

He clung to her, listening as she'd instructed him. The wind bit into his cheeks and he shivered suddenly, glad he'd opted to wear his hat.

His mother often claimed the wind could be a valuable weapon on the battlefield. If one were mindful enough, they could use it to hide their scent while trying to sneak up on their enemies. She hadn't exactly told him what they were doing out here, but Rion suspected they were sneaking up on Saoirse and the others. He wondered if their father would hear them, though. Nothing ever surprised him.

His mother stopped, scanned the trees with a careful eye, then moved farther north before entering the forest. Her hands kept his legs in place. Strong hands that would never let him fall.

They crept through the trees in silence, Rion watching every move his mother made. He scented her magic as it sprang from the ground at her feet. Leaves unfurled from the cold snow and flowers trailed behind her wherever she stepped. He could smell them, but realized the wind was blowing back toward the house. Which meant if Saoirse, Alec, and their father were ahead, then the sweet aroma wouldn't give them away. He wondered if his mother did it on purpose or if her magic was so great that she couldn't contain it.

Rion also wondered if his magic would be like that. He wasn't sure he wanted flowers trailing him wherever he went.

The birds stopped calling overhead, a sign of a predator in their midst. A survival instinct that told Rion to be on guard. Then again, maybe his mother was the predator they feared.

His mother backed up a step and pressed her body against the bark of the wide oak tree at their left. Alarm flared through him, but his mother's smirking face set his fears at ease. They waited like that for several minutes. She drew his attention, then set him on the ground. Rion was careful of his footing. He didn't want to step on anything that might alert the others.

His mother peered around the tree, pressed a finger to her lips, then pointed.

There was Saoirse, moving through the trees hunched over as

she searched around the trunks and through the barren branches above. Rion was certain she was looking for Alec or their father. They were training, after all.

Another moment passed, then faster than his young eyes could see, a blur of color. The sharp ringing of metal filled the air. Rion clutched his mother's sleeve as he watched Alec and Saoirse exchange blows. Their magic flew up around them, ripping the ground and snow up in a flurry of quick movements he couldn't follow.

His mother didn't move and her smile didn't wane despite the violence between her two eldest children. If anything, she looked . . . proud.

Rion's chest swelled at that. He wanted his mother to look at him with those eyes, too. Maybe he would join his siblings after all. Once they let him, of course. They were all strong. He wanted to be strong, too.

Another shift of rapid movement and their father appeared, vines and trees all seamlessly following in his wake.

His mother ducked behind the tree, then urged Rion to climb onto her back. He did. Then she was off, sprinting at breakneck speeds.

The High Lady of Brónach was as fast and swift as a deer. Faster. Rion swore her feet barely met the forest floor as she darted between the trees. His weight didn't hinder her movements or magic in the slightest.

His father's head whipped toward them, but his mother's magic was already moving, rising in a tide of living plants that blocked the others from view. Then his mother was on the other side of that wave, giving Rion a clear view of his father's shocked face. Roots and trees rose to defend the High Lord and collided with the surge of his mother's magic.

Bark exploded and the crushing sound of the impact had Rion

wanting to cover his ears, but he didn't dare let go of his mother's coat for fear of falling.

Another cascading wave of roots and branches, then his father's surprised face turned to one of smirking challenge. Alec was next to strike out against the magic surging for him and his sister. Then Saoirse joined in, moving around the branches that reached out like clawed fingers.

A vine tied down Alec's leg, then another caught one of Saoirse's arms, rooting both siblings to the ground. They ripped free and snarled, a fierce sound that might have had Rion cowering were it not for the person he clung to.

No. He could be brave for this. He wanted to join them in their training exercises. A thrill of excitement went through him. He was here. Watching. Participating. For the first time, he wasn't told he was too little. His mother was allowing it, going against his father's wishes.

A broad smile spread across Rion's face as Saoirse launched her own sea of greenery toward them. His mother didn't cower away. She stood her ground and, without her even moving, the world came alive at her feet. Trees shot out to block Saoirse's magic, blooming as if they couldn't help themselves despite the unfolding chaos.

Another wave formed, this one thicker and stronger somehow. Alec.

It only managed to make it halfway before everything fell, as if his mother had commanded it with her mind.

Alec snarled, then their father's rare boisterous laugh echoed through the trees. His mother patted Rion's leg and she emerged from the torn branches and brambles that now coated the once soft forest floor. She leaped easily over a large trunk, and Rion's two older siblings relaxed their pensive stances.

"Enjoying yourself, Eimear?"

She let Rion slide down from her back, then took his hand. "I can't always let you have all the fun with our children."

"You knew I wouldn't see you coming."

"Naturally, though Rion played a large factor in that. There were about a dozen ways he could have given us away."

His father scented the air, studied his youngest child, then stepped forward and ruffled Rion's hair. "You did well." Rion had never felt prouder than in that moment.

"He wanted to join you all, so I brought him along."

"He could have gotten hurt," Saoirse said, her breath still ragged.

"Not with your mother guarding him," their father replied. He stared at his mate fondly, eyes swimming with emotion. "Shall we call it early today and head back for breakfast?"

"Yes," Eimear said without hesitation. "I'd like to enjoy our last few days. The snow will melt tomorrow."

Eimear met Rion's gaze and offered him a sweet smile that she extended to her other children. She held her free hand out to their father and the male interlaced his fingers with his mate's. Saoirse joined at Rion's other side, smiling down at her little brother while Alec followed at their father's far side.

Rion took Saoirse's hand and the two females lifted him over the chaos they'd created in the forest. But even as they walked away, the trees were righting themselves, rising up to new heights. Fresh flowers bloomed and vines took over the places where branches were scattered and torn. Within moments, it looked as if the landscape had never been disturbed.

His mother's magic. A magic full of life. A magic he couldn't wait to explore for himself.

Rion looked at his mother again and his smile widened when he saw the floral path that opened before them.

It hadn't been a coincidence. She'd already known they would head back this way as a family and she'd carved a beautiful path to lead them home.

THE CURSED FAE AND THE FIRST LOSS

CHAPTER ONE

*I*n the span of what seemed only a few minutes, the world had erupted into absolute chaos.

Alarms blared across the darkening horizon, the sun having already dipped behind the tall redwoods that circled and protected the great city of Nàdair. Smoke rose from rooftops in the distance, giving the air a hazy glow. Slaves and servants raced down the hallways, their arms full of various supplies.

Voices echoed. A shrill scream. A barked command. Weapons and armor clanged together and Rion swore he could hear the soft whine of blades being dragged over whetstones three floors down.

Rion's small fingers gripped the window's ledge as he pushed up onto his toes and observed the mayhem below. He'd been thrown into the study, left to do nothing but watch as the world turned various shades of red and gray and black.

Bodies littered the normally beautiful cobblestone path that led out the side garden doors. The immaculate white peonies were stained with crimson. Statues were broken at jagged angles and the treasured dogwoods had been uprooted and strewn across the freshly cut lawn.

No one bothered cleaning any of it up. Even the bodies.

A small group, he'd overheard a Fae female whisper. *It shouldn't have been possible*, another argued. *How did she fall prey to them*, a meek voice asked.

Her. That's all anyone said. No name. No title. As if they were afraid saying the words out loud would make it real.

No one had answered his questions, either.

Rion had been playing with a wooden chess set in the grand library when he'd felt his father's frantic pulse of wrathful magic. It had raised the hairs on the back of his neck and Rion's stomach had flipped as if he were plummeting from a hundred foot drop.

He'd never experienced anything like it. Neither had the library staff, if their uncertain and fearful expressions were anything to go by.

Two guards had burst through the library's intricately carved doors seconds later and had escorted him here on Saoirse's orders. They'd supplied him with everything an eight-year-old might need, then had positioned themselves outside the closed door to stand watch.

Rion chewed his bottom lip, eyed the items they'd brought in, and turned away from the offering. He wasn't a normal eight-year-old and he hated the thought of being trapped anywhere. Especially in a small room where he couldn't ask anyone questions.

Fed up with trying to tiptoe, Rion grabbed a chair and scooted it toward the window, making as much noise as possible. He wanted them to burst in, if only so he could pester them for answers.

He climbed up and unlatched the top locks before jumping down again and shoving the heavy glass panes open.

Rion recoiled from the thick, acrid air. He covered his face with one hand and his eyes watered as he took in the gruesome scene on the ground again.

Listen, his mother's voice coaxed. *Be aware of your surroundings. Access the situation and be patient. Don't act unless you're sure of your intentions.*

Rion tilted his head and strained to hear anything that might prove useful. He just wanted a name.

The voices were still too muffled. Most were drowned out by guards as they instructed civilians to take shelter beneath the palace itself. He'd seen the safe rooms before. Cavernous halls surrounded by thick rock that promised refuge.

Someone mentioned an attack. They whispered to a companion about their fear of an entire enemy fleet wreaking havoc on their beautiful city. Rion identified the tremors in their voices. They weren't warriors, nor were they in charge or informed. He loosed a sigh of relief. It was little more than fear that drove them to believe such things.

Rion focused again and tried to sift through the noise for the voices that were steady. That's where he'd get answers.

One guard worried about allowing civilians inside at all, claiming that whoever was responsible for the attacks might try to seize an opportunity to destroy the structure from within.

Another quelled that male's fears, assuring him the villagers would remain isolated below the central hall. There were only two ways in or out of the underground rooms, and neither led directly into the palace.

Were they truly worried about an invasion or was their caution just standard protocol?

Rion's head whipped toward the door and he glared at the brass handle. They'd used the key to turn the lock after pushing him inside.

But why? Were his mother and Saoirse safe? And if so, why hadn't either female come for him yet?

Rion looked back out over the chaos, doing his best to pretend the bodies were nothing more than mounds of dirt. He overheard the word "abduction," but the rest was too muffled to make out.

Rion's heart beat faster. Who? What had happened and why couldn't he know about it?

Rion looked toward the door again, then his gaze drifted to the old woven rug beneath the heavy bookcase in the far corner. He wasn't sure how many knew about the trap door underneath.

Saoirse had instructed him to only ever use it in the event of an emergency. She claimed if he feared the dark tunnel passage, then he wasn't scared enough to use it.

But fear for himself wasn't the emotion that had Rion tearing books from the shelves. It wasn't what drove him to brace his feet against the wall and scoot the shelf inch by inch until the rug could be folded over.

Rion listened for those outside the door. Surely they would have heard all the noise. But maybe it wasn't enough to warrant an investigation. He was a child in a locked room, after all. How much trouble could he possibly cause?

Rion lifted the hatch and stared into the darkness. The light from the room illuminated the floor below. Nothing but bare boards coated in dust and cobwebs.

He glanced at the door one final time before jumping inside. Rion had to crawl on his hands and knees to avoid busting his head on the floor above.

He wasn't sure what he expected to accomplish. He was too small to be of any use in a fight. And he still didn't possess a drop of magic. Both were valid enough reasons why he should have stayed where Saoirse put him. But he had to know.

Cobwebs coated his hair and stuck to his face. He crawled slowly, afraid the boards beneath his weight might creak and alert the guards. Then the passage just . . . ended.

He'd expected it to stretch halfway across the palace. Maybe even end at the back wall where he'd be forced to climb down a steep rickety ladder.

Instead, Rion's fingers searched for the interior latch. He pricked his index finger on a splinter, muttered a foul word Saoirse had told him to never use, then wrapped his hand around a smooth metal surface.

Rion turned it, then pushed up.

The door didn't budge.

He tried again, bracing his whole body against the wooden frame before it finally popped open. Almost as if a seal had been broken.

A rug prevented him from searching with his eyes, but Rion knew no one occupied the space above him. No heartbeats. No gasps of shock. No ruffling or movement.

He kept pushing the door open an inch at a time, hoping to prevent anything from falling over in the process. The leg of a table scooted against the hardwood floor and Rion froze to listen, hoping the guards wouldn't come rushing in before he finished shimmying his way out from beneath the rug.

His foot slipped, and the trap door slammed shut with a loud thud. He cursed again and waited for the bedroom door to burst open.

Nothing.

Some guards they were.

Rion inhaled a familiar scent and found himself standing in Saoirse's room.

He came in here often, especially when he woke from savage nightmares. A map sat on top of the small table he'd scooted while crawling out from beneath the rug. The trinkets holding it in place—a candle, a figurine depicting a forest sprite, a book, and an empty mug—had all toppled over. Miraculously, none were broken.

Swords and knives rested on a shelf beside the bed, some with jewel-encrusted pommels. A bookcase stood against the back wall, lined with their histories and endless texts he didn't yet understand.

Saoirse had sage green drapes around her window and the same shade bedsheets with little vine designs embroidered along the seams.

A bit of relief washed through him. Everything was orderly and intact. No sign of a struggle or that she'd left the room in a hurry. But that didn't mean she was safe. Especially with how the side garden path now looked with—Rion shook the images away.

He crept toward the door and paused to listen once again. He didn't even hear their heartbeats anymore. Hadn't for a while now. Had they just . . . left?

Rion silently reached for the handle and turned it carefully. The hinges were blissfully silent. No guards stood on the other side. He wished his own door was just as quiet, but Saoirse always seemed to know whenever he made an attempt to sneak from his room. All for the kitchens, of course, and midnight snacks.

But right now, he wasn't sneaking out for cake or pastries.

Rion eased his breathing, just as his mother had shown him, and peered out into the hall. He crept over the lush rug, debated heading straight for the stairs, but paused when curiosity got the better of him.

Guards. There were supposed to be guards. But he didn't scent their presence. Nor did he hear . . . anything.

Rion peered around the corner and hesitated before stepping into the hall. No one stood before the door of the study or the door to his room. He carefully ventured down, keeping his footsteps quiet as he went, and peered around the corner toward the staircase. No one was there either.

Puzzled, Rion returned to the study's door and reached for the handle, only to jolt at the sound of hushed voices.

He sprinted back around the corner near Saoirse's room and worked to keep his heart from beating too hard as he pressed his back against the wall.

They'd lock him inside with a guard next and while he could ask plenty of questions, it would prevent him from finding the truth for himself.

Rion glanced down toward the other side of the hall. If he was quiet, he could reach the stairs without them knowing, but he'd never successfully snuck past Saoirse, so the chances of sneaking past them . . .

"Be quick about it," a nasally male voice hissed. Rion paused, curious, and scented the air. They were from Brónach, but definitely not the guards who'd been stationed to his room. They smelled like fire and . . . blood. Why was there blood on their clothes? Had someone broken in? Is that why the guards had left?

"You do it," another demanded. The previous male scoffed and the hairs rose on the back of Rion's neck when a blade slid free of its sheath.

Danger, danger, danger, a voice inside him warned.

Rion's breathing turned shallow.

"I don't want a child's blood on my hands."

His heart lurched in his chest. Rion dared a quick glance around the corner.

Four individuals stood close together.

One male with dark hair that hung in front of his eyes was kneeling before the door's lock with a pair of long objects in his hands. Rion didn't know what they were called, only that he'd seen Saoirse use them before to pick a lock.

Another stood with his back against the wall, flipping a knife in his hand as if he hadn't just suggested killing someone. The other two watched the opposite staircase.

Rion leaned back slowly before they turned his way. He counted the steps toward the stairs nearest to him. Twelve, if he sprinted. He chewed his lip, then centered himself. He hadn't trained like the others, but his mother had worked with him enough that he could keep himself calm. *Think*, her distant voice chanted. *Your mind will be the thing that keeps you alive.*

Rion took a steadying breath and waited, counting the seconds.

The latch clicked.

He didn't move. Not until the door swung open and the first male stepped inside.

Rion took off sprinting down the hall, pushing his legs as fast as they would go.

He'd barely reached the top step when four sets of heavy boots thundered after him.

Panting, Rion took the stairs three at a time, clinging to the smooth railing for balance. His heart was in his throat, choking him as he jumped from step to step to step.

Faster.

He was rounding to the second flight when a vine shot past his ear and exploded through the wall before him. Rion cried out and cursed and tried to ignore the biting sting on his right cheek.

Another mesh of green whipped out at him from within the side wall. It sliced into his forearm and Rion tripped, rolling down the final three steps. Bits of plaster and marble bit into his flesh, but he ignored their sting and shoved to his feet to race down the final flight.

Almost there.

Just a little further and people would be waiting to intervene. He hoped.

Please, please, please.

A dark root ripped from the floor and grabbed Rion's ankle, yanking him hard enough that he lost his balance and his chin cracked on the final step. Stars shot across his vision, but he shook them away, desperate to break free of the thorny plant now embedding itself into his leg.

A guard rounded the corner, his weapon already drawn. Their eyes met. The world stilled. Then shouting from above had it all moving too fast again.

The warrior lunged and Rion closed his eyes, bracing for a blow, until the roots around his ankle slackened. He scrambled away from the staircase and the males standing on the platform just above.

"Get to the safe room." It was a command and Rion obeyed, limping his way down the hall that seemed far longer than it ever had.

A series of growls and snarls had Rion moving faster, his heart beating so hard he was sure it would stop. His head was dizzy and everything was a blur of voices and scents and sounds. His throat burned. His arm ached and tears pricked the corners of his eyes from the pain radiating up his leg.

Clashing steel echoed behind. A whimper escaped his throat, but then the set of double doors to his left burst open. He could have sobbed from seeing the crest of their uniforms. Might have also seen it on the other guard if he'd been paying closer attention.

One look was all it took for recognition to flash across their faces. They drew their weapons in unison and ran to his side, ready to protect their young lord.

One kneeled. Rion couldn't remember the male's name but knew him to be someone important to his father. He was always attending meetings at his side. His mother seemed to like him, too.

"What happened?" he asked, his voice gentler than Rion had ever heard it.

Rion opened his mouth to answer but his throat had closed up. Tears welled in his eyes then his lips trembled and his throat burned from the effort of trying to hold them back. He pointed and six guards took off without another word.

Another guard approached, gently took Rion by the arm, and guided him through the door.

Rion's knees quaked and the fear sinking through his gut wouldn't subside. His stomach rolled.

Breathe, his mother's voice urged. *You're safe now*. But he needed her arms, not her voice.

Inside looked like the main room of a cathedral. It *was* a cathedral, he realized. At least an old version of one. Stained glass covered the upper walls in a way that had Rion wondering if they'd once been windows. Perhaps an old High Lord had built around the structure rather than destroying it. Or maybe it would have been sacrilegious to destroy an old place of worship.

Statues of the gods lined the side walls with depictions of the Fairy Folk dancing around their bodies.

A few benches stood at the front of the space. If there had been others, they'd been removed long ago.

The space was . . . open, and he wanted to run to a corner where he could put his back against the wall and hide away from the world. To try to calm his mind from what had just happened.

Had it happened? Were the last few minutes even real or—Rion ran a delicate, trembling hand over the cut on his forearm and a single step had pain radiating up through his leg again.

Real. Oh so real. As were the Fae seated in various clusters throughout the space. Several younglings clung to their mothers, their faces frozen with fear while others played quietly in the center of the room, shifting puzzles and blocks.

Their fear hit him, then Rion vomited all over the floor.

He heaved, struggling to catch his breath. Had strangers just tried to—his breath was too shallow, his lungs too empty. Air was gone, sucked out of the space. He couldn't breathe, couldn't breathe, couldn't—A light hand touched his shoulder and Rion leaped back, his heart pounding so hard he could feel it in his throat.

His mother. He needed to find Saoirse and his mother and—

"Breathe." It was a simple command, yet he found it difficult to obey. An adult female with sky-blue eyes kneeled before him, offering a reassuring smile as she draped a warm blanket around his shoulders. "You're okay now, little one."

A lump rose in his throat. He knew her. The eyes, the long sand colored hair. Liam's mother. His friend must be here, too.

As if a single thought summoned him, Liam appeared from around his mother's side. Or maybe he'd already been standing there.

Rion's lips trembled again and a sob escaped. Liam's mother pulled him in, holding him close while his chest heaved. She rubbed light circles along his back and whispered in hushed tones, telling him over and over that he was safe. He was safe. He was safe.

When he could breathe again, Rion pulled away and wiped the tears from his face. Liam's mother gave his arm a gentle squeeze. He winced. "Shall we get you cleaned up?"

Rion gave a subtle nod, unsure what else to do with himself. She guided him with a hand at his back and Liam ran up to his other side.

"Are you okay?"

Rion wasn't sure how to respond. Liam had his father's eyes, a deep chestnut brown, and his mother's hair that hung too far over his face. He'd pushed it to the side twice already.

Liam had been his best friend for as long as he could remember.

They'd met in the first year of grade school and had been inseparable since. "I don't know." Rion's voice shook and everything felt strange. Like he was experiencing the world from outside his body.

"Don't crowd him," Liam's mother coaxed with a gentle tone as if she were speaking about an injured animal.

They entered a large bathroom foyer and Liam's mother instructed Rion to sit on one of the unoccupied sofas.

The room smelled of sterile cleaning supplies and too much blood. A female sat across from him, wincing as her companion pulled a needle and thread from a case.

Rion turned away from it, hoping his arm wouldn't need stitches as well.

He was in a room full of noble males and females, he realized, but even they hadn't been spared from whatever had happened downstairs.

Liam's mother had her hair tied back when she returned and settled on the floor before him with a bowl of water and clean cloths. She went for his shoe first.

Rion winced and she muttered apologies as she undid the laces and carefully pulled it away from his swollen foot.

It was twice the normal size and had already turned various shades of blue and purple. Liam leaned over his mother's shoulder and made a face. "Is it broken?" Rion hoped not. He'd never had a broken bone before.

Liam's mother prodded at the tender areas and Rion flinched and hissed in response. "I can't tell. We'll wrap it tight and keep you off of it until one of the healers can check the bones."

His mind was finally calming. Clearing. "Where's my mother?" He didn't want a healer and he couldn't care less about getting cleaned up.

Her jaw tightened and she turned to dip a rag into the bowl of steaming liquid. Not just water, not from the scent wafting toward him.

"There's no need for you to worry, she'll be all right."

His heart leaped into his throat. Not an answer. It was never good when a Fae didn't answer. "Where's Saoirse?" He tried again.

Liam settled on the bench at his side and patted Rion's shoulder. "They'll be okay. My dad is with them. He'll keep them safe."

His father. Rion had always envied Liam for his father. One of the High Lord's personal guards. He seemed stern too, but Rion had seen the male playing and laughing with Liam. Something Rion's father never seemed to have time for. It sent a pang of jealousy coursing through him.

Rion opened his mouth to ask another question when the bathroom door slammed open and crashed into the back wall. Everyone in the foyer jumped and the female seated across from him cursed when the needle went through her arm at the wrong angle.

A male, his body covered in blood and dirt, searched the sea of faces before his copper eyes locked with Rion's. Rion stiffened and gripped the bottom edge of the bench when the male marched toward him.

Liam's mom stood and placed her hands on her hips. "Callum, you're going to scare the life out of the younglings."

The male paused at that, seemed to take himself in, then glanced back at Rion and Liam who were both sitting ramrod straight, ready to bolt at the slightest movement. Not that Rion would get far with his ankle the way it was.

Callum cleared his throat. "Apologies. I overheard what happened to the young lord and came to see if he was all right."

Rion looked him over again and recognition finally sparked. This male was also part of his father's personal guard. A unit of elite whose responsibility was to guard the High Lord and his family.

Liam's mother's relaxed. "He's a little banged up, but nothing that won't mend with the help of a healer."

Callum sighed. "Thank the gods."

"What happened? I thought he was under your care?"

Shame flashed across the male's face. "He was. We were careless. Four assassins tried to—" he stopped himself and glanced at Rion again. His gaze fell to Rion's swollen ankle and he grimaced. "They dispatched two of our guards and broke through our line. It won't happen again."

"And the others?" Rion perked up at that, his heart beating just a little faster with the possibility of news on his family.

"Things are . . . precarious."

Liam's mother cast a glance at Rion, then her son. "Will you stay with him for a moment?"

Liam nodded, but Rion jumped from the bench, careful to keep weight off his injured joint. "I want to know." Precarious meant things were bad. He understood the word. His private tutors had always complimented him on his ability to remember things. "Where's my sister?"

"She's in the field with your father and Alec." A bit of tension left Rion's shoulders. Nothing would hurt Saoirse with those two at her side.

But Rion's worry returned two-fold when the male didn't continue. "Where's my mother?"

The male shifted on his feet and Liam's mother shook her head in warning.

"Tell me," he insisted, even as grief flooded his heart at the possibility of his next words.

"We're still looking for her."

CHAPTER TWO

They stayed in the safe room for the rest of the night, Liam's mother keeping a watchful eye on Rion and his injuries. Callum found a healer and the female made quick work of Rion's smaller wounds before wrapping his foot and instructing him to stay off it.

It wasn't broken.

Worry took over as the hours passed. He'd barely slept and couldn't stomach a single bite of his food. Even the sweets. Liam happily ate his portions.

Sunrise didn't bring any news, but it did allow him a bit of freedom.

Callum and his unit of warriors declared the city secured. The civilians were instructed to return to their homes and Rion was allowed to wander the palace. With an escort, of course.

The healer had brought him a pair of crutches and he'd used them to limp from room to room before he'd finally settled in Saoirse's bed. Rion used one of her pillows to prop his leg up and stared out the window.

We're looking for her.

The male's words wouldn't stop repeating in his head. Rion tried to convince himself everything would be okay. He wanted to believe nothing bad could happen. His mother was strong. Just as strong as their father. She could fight her way out of anything.

But his stomach was a pit, empty and void.

Rion's good leg bounced. He stared out Saoirse's window, watching the breeze glide through the fruit trees on the outskirts of the garden path. He wasn't leaving Saoirse's room until she returned.

Rion's gaze drifted toward the trapdoor in the floor. The guards had discovered it, of course, and two were also stationed at the entrance of the study, just to make sure he wouldn't try to escape. And to ensure no one else came to finish the job.

Rion shuddered. He'd never had to run for his life before. He'd been lucky, or maybe the gods had watched over him. His mother prayed to them a lot.

Rion rested his chin on his knee, folded his arms around one leg, and waited and waited and waited.

CHAPTER THREE

aoirse didn't return that week or the week after. His ankle healed. He attended therapy. Liam tried to keep him occupied. And the staff throughout the palace tried to cheer him up to no avail.

He visited the messenger room every morning. No one sent a letter. No one had an update. His entire family was out on a mission to find his mother and Rion was left to wander the halls while his mind conjured the worst possible scenarios.

She's strong. She's strong. She's strong.

He wasn't.

Life resumed in a somewhat normal fashion. He attended school, paid attention to his studies, and even took up a more advanced level of combatives. No one denied him anything.

He received extra treats and attention from the cooks, and his father's assigned warriors followed him around wherever he went. Were it not for his healing foot and the tender tendons, he would have tried to outrun them. Might have even enjoyed it were it not for the aching pain in his chest.

Gods, he missed them.

Even with all the activities to keep him occupied, Rion saw the way the adults exchanged uneasy glances. The worry in their eyes when he didn't finish his meals and chose to spend his spare time staring out the large window, hoping someone, anyone, would walk down the cobblestone path with good news.

It was a stormy afternoon when the palace halls finally came alive. It started with a rushing slave, followed by several others sprinting down the hall.

Then the guards' boots echoed, their voices shifting into a frenzy of whispered noise. The nobles stopped what they were doing and crowded before doorways, curious and wary.

Rion's heart crawled into his throat and he barely dared to hope. He sat a little straighter, wondering if there had been another attack instead. He inched toward the doorway and two words had him bolting past the warriors who guarded the hall.

"They're back."

Rion had never run so fast in his life. He ignored a desperate voice that called after him, dodged a pair of gloved hands that reached out, and downright refused to acknowledge the pain shooting through his ankle as he sprinted through the halls.

The ankle gave out once but Rion bit the inside of his cheek to ignore the pain.

Tears fogged his vision as soon as he scented her. Saoirse. She was okay. She was alive and here and—Rion blasted through the final doorway then skidded to a sudden stop.

His sister, Alec, and their father all stood just inside the foyer. All were coated in weeks of mud and blood and sweat.

But it wasn't the smell or the way their clothes were torn and hair disheveled that froze him in place.

It was the haggard look on their faces. The absolute defeat.

Saoirse just stared at the marble floor as though she were lost. Alec silently unbuckled his sword belt and handed it off to a slave.

And their father—Rion could scent the rage spilling off him from here. His fists were tightly clenched and his body shook as if he couldn't contain himself.

Someone tried to speak to him and the male's face snapped up so suddenly that the warrior stepped back and quickly bowed their head.

Then his father's fist flew into the nearest pillar. The marble splintered and cracked, a line racing all the way toward the ceiling.

And then the High Lord of Brónach hit his knees and wept.

Rion's throat swelled shut and he stepped back. He tried to clear it, tried to breathe.

Breathe, breathe, breathe.

Saoirse looked up at him then. Looked at him with those empty green eyes that confirmed the one thing he feared above all else.

Their mother was gone.

The Cursed Fae and a Secret Refuge

CHAPTER ONE

Rion bounced on his toes, eyes darting from one colorful stall to the next. Saoirse kept a tight hold on his hand. She never let him go far, even if he was practically dragging her down the crowded street, eager to see the performers who were scheduled to arrive within the hour.

"We still have time," Saoirse giggled, letting Rion pull her through the throng of Fae enjoying the festivities. Many offered kind smiles in passing, while others outright laughed at his sister's predicament.

He didn't care. He wanted to be the first in line to see the performers balance across the tightropes and juggle fire. He'd spent the past week reading every book he could find on them. He'd even tried to juggle a few things himself. Much to his sister's amusement.

Sweat rolled down the side of Rion's face. Saoirse had mentioned something about humidity. He just knew it was hot. But the heat brought the summer solstice. A night he'd been especially looking forward to this year.

Lanterns lined the streets, casting a pleasant glow over the lines of Fae moving from one stall to the next purchasing all manner of trinkets. Jewels reflected the light in a myriad of colors. Wooden boxes and carved statues promised luck and fortune to those who believed in them. And the smell of food wafted through the air, beckoning patrons toward those stalls.

He wanted to visit them too, but only after seeing the performers.

The pleasant aroma of burned cinnamon floated toward him and Rion's mouth watered in response. He paused, staring longingly at the pastries dripping with sugar.

"We have time," Saoirse repeated. "Do you want one?" Rion glanced down the street again, his heart torn. He knew the stall wouldn't run out anytime soon, especially with the festival lasting the entire week, but—

Saoirse made the decision for him and pulled Rion toward the food stand. He stood on his tiptoes, trying to get a better look through the crowd before his sister grabbed him under his arms and lifted his small body onto her shoulders.

Rion didn't bother telling her he wasn't a little kid anymore. Not when he had a clear view above the crowd. He could let it slide this once.

Saoirse purchased the sweet but paused before handing it to him. "If you drip any of this in my hair, I'll never buy you another one."

He knew it was an idle threat, but Rion still nodded in reassurance. "I promise to be careful."

Rion's gaze was captured by a forest sprite as it floated above their heads, riding the wind on the back of a large oak leaf. It seemed to smile at him before speeding off again, propelled by whatever mysterious magic surrounded the tiny beings.

He carefully tore a bite from the cinnamon pastry, the crumbs falling into the paper tray. It melted in his mouth and he savored the thick flavor.

Saoirse walked at a leisurely pace, navigating through the throng of Fae. They always parted for her and bowed their heads in reverence. They used to do that to their mother, too—Rion shook his head. Saoirse had instructed him to have fun today for her sake. Because their mother would want him to. He swallowed the lump in his throat. Fought the tears that raced to the surface. His mother used to put him up on her shoulders all the time, too. They'd watch the performers and—

"What are you thinking about up there?"

Rion tried to force a smile and was glad his sister couldn't see his face.

Instead of answering her question, Rion quickly pointed to a stall full of stuffed animals. "I want one of those." Thankfully, his voice didn't crack. He was getting better at hiding it.

She paused, considering, and his heart raced. Rion didn't want to ruin the night for her. She'd been through a lot, too. Rion saw the red around her eyes even when she tried to hide it.

After a moment, Saoirse walked toward the vendor and Rion loosed a sigh of relief. One night. Just for one night, Rion would try to forget about the sadness that blanketed the palace halls and the way their father hadn't been the same since their mother's disappearance. For one night, Rion would pretend they were still a family. A real family.

Rion drew in a slow breath, just as Saoirse had taught him to do whenever he was upset. He focused on the stuffed creatures instead. Some resembled the Fairy Folk while others took on the likeness of regular animals. There were even a few shaped like the creatures in the ocean, some beautiful, others scary. Rion shivered at the sight of one with a long colorful tail and menacing teeth. He couldn't remember its name.

Rion looked through them carefully while they waited their turn and pointed to a stuffed red fox. "That one."

The male at the stall smiled up at Rion, then fixed his gaze on Saoirse. "Care for a game, My Lady?"

His sister studied the rings in the male's hand, then reached into her pocket. The male quickly waved his hands. "Oh, no, I couldn't charge a Lady of Brónach."

"And I can't cheat a merchant, especially one who brings such life to the festival."

The male's face turned red and he cleared his throat before taking the offered coins. "Okay, but two tries for the price of one. I insist."

She smirked. "It'll only take one."

It most certainly didn't take one. It was Rion's turn to laugh at his sister as she tried time and time again to get the small ring on the neck of the green bottles laid out before her. The game looked simple, yet the ring bounced off the glasses and hit the ground no matter what his sister tried. Rion threw a few, but quickly gave the rings back to Saoirse. Even the merchant laughed, clearly amused by her level of dedication.

It seemed like the millionth toss before the ring bounced from one glass to another and finally settled around the neck of a bottle. Saoirse jumped and shouted her victory. Several who'd paused to watch clapped their hands. Rion smiled at her and the merchant congratulated her on a job well done, his purse far heavier than it'd been before their arrival.

The merchant reached for the small fox. "This was the one, wasn't it?"

Rion nodded and took the stuffed creature. He buried his face in the soft fur, then looked up at Saoirse who was smiling down at him.

"Would you like anything else?" the male asked. "I'd feel terribly guilty if that's all you took."

His sister eyed the rack, eyes scanning, and finally pointed to a small pink creature that resembled a forest sprite save for the bright color. "I'll take that one."

"Done." The male packed it up and Saoirse handed the stuffed creature to one of the female slaves following them. The slave pulled a small black wagon full of little bags and trinkets Saoirse had purchased earlier. The slave looked at Rion's fox, but Rion held it tighter and stepped away from the slave's reach.

Another of the Fairy Folk whizzed by his head, rising higher and higher until it perched on one of the ropes above that served as a hand rail for any who strolled through the canopy. Many Fae sat up there now, watching the festivities from a long bridge above. He imagined the view resembled a fairy tale from one of his children's books.

Another of the Fairy Folk joined the forest sprite, balancing on the ropes before it pulled out a tiny instrument. With spindly fingers it lifted the flute-like contraption to its lips and began playing. Several others joined it.

The tune was pleasant and light and pulled at fond memories he'd nearly forgotten. Many paused to stare, marveling at the strange beings who kept balance in their world.

"Do you think I could play music like that?"

Saoirse followed his gaze, a soft smile on her face. "I think you could do anything you set your mind to."

Maybe he'd start reading books on it now and by the winter solstice, he could join the Fairy Folk in their ethereal melodies.

They continued walking. Saoirse didn't mention the performers again. In fact, she almost seemed to avoid them, and Rion wondered if she understood exactly how he'd been feeling earlier.

She purchased him far more treats than their father would have normally allowed, and played games throughout the night. Saoirse always won or kept going until she achieved victory. Rion played a few as well and proved he could be just as persistent.

He wondered if the Fairy Folk would visit his room that night. They always appeared at his window during the solstices, though no one ever believed him, Saoirse included. He'd been told no one could touch the small creatures. They were sacred. But when he was alone, they always found him. They would land on his shoulders and play at his feet before disappearing in the trees.

His mother had believed him.

Saoirse took his hand and led her little brother to another stall and another and another. He smiled, listening to the music and wished every night could be as magical as this one.

HOURS LATER, Rion's feet ached and his stomach was near-ly to the point of bursting. He'd have been content to curl up on a bench and sleep until morning, but Saoirse scooped him into her arms. Voices echoed around him, but he ignored their whispering, content to sleep in the safety of his sister's embrace.

"Rion," Saoirse whispered. He buried his head against her shoul-der, but she shook him again. "Wake up sleepy head."

He didn't want to wake up. He just wanted his bed and to sleep until noon or past it. Reluctantly, he cracked one eye open. "What?"

"I need to talk to someone; do you think you could wait here for a minute?"

Rion blinked and glanced around only to find them in their fa-ther's study. He didn't like coming in here, not anymore. There were too many important documents. He'd been told it wasn't a room meant for younglings.

"I'm not allowed in here," Rion said, followed by a yawn.

She set him down anyway. "I'll only be a minute. Just curl up on the chair, then I'll take you to your room."

He nodded and staggered toward the large, plush armchair in the corner. Rion wondered if anyone ever sat in it or if it was only there for decoration. Saoirse disappeared without another word, leav-ing Rion in the room alone.

A fire didn't warm the hearth, to which he was grateful; it was too hot for a fire. He curled up on the chair and held his fox close. Rion turned and stretched out one leg. He rolled again and reposi-tioned his arm. He kicked off his shoes and loosened the top button of his shirt. He wished he had his pajamas.

Sweat made his clothes cling to him and Rion turned again before giving up. He rubbed the sleep from his eyes and extended the little fox out to stare at it. Wide orange eyes the same color as its fur stared back. Rion mirrored its smile. Not because of the stuffed animal, but due to the memory he'd always carry because of it. He cherished those now and had a row of items on his bookshelf that reminded him of the family they used to be.

Before—his lips trembled and Rion bit the inside of his cheek. He wasn't supposed to cry, especially in a place where his father might see. Not that he saw much of his father these days. It was Saoirse who looked after him. Saoirse who ensured he kept up with his studies and training. Saoirse who cried with him at night when they both missed their mother.

He wished she'd hurry.

Rion glanced toward the door and debated walking to his room himself. It wasn't far, just up a few flights of stairs and down a hall. But he was so tired and his feet ached.

He looked toward his father's bookshelves instead. They were lined with old leather volumes. Gold writing on the spines. Most were in perfect condition, though Rion noted a few that were worn at the corners. Either a favorite, or a valuable resource. Maybe one day he'd be allowed to find out.

His gaze traveled down and finally landed on the large potted plant that stood beside his father's desk. It was taller than he was and the broad leaves were wider than Rion's palm.

Rion inclined his ear to listen for voices in the hall or footsteps that might tell him Saoirse was on her way back.

Nothing.

He stared at the plant again, debated another moment, then jumped from the chair. Rion carefully placed the little fox in the seat before approaching the plant. He couldn't hurt it, not unless his magic revealed itself and made the plant do strange things, but even that wouldn't damage the foliage beyond repair. Saoirse could always fix it.

Rion glanced toward the door again, listening, but silence still filled the hall. He extended his palms, just as their teachers had them do during class and tried to feel for the plant's life energy.

He was the only one in his class who still hadn't summoned his magic yet. *A late bloomer*, his teacher said, just as his mother had been. He was told it would make his magic stronger, but Rion was tired of being made fun of. Tired of the teasing from his friends who could already identify seedlings simply by feeling them in the earth. His best friend had summoned a tree last week and it had grown five feet tall.

He wanted to impress his teacher. Maybe even his father, if he were lucky. Saoirse would certainly be happy to see it.

Rion focused harder. Tension filled his small body and he took a deep breath, willing that tension to fade. Everyone said it would come naturally and that trying to force it would only result in the magic sinking deeper into his core. He needed to coax it out gently. Let it know his body was ready.

Another deep breath. Rion let his eyes close. He let the words from his classmates fade away. He wouldn't be like the magicless half-breeds. He was the son of the two strongest Fae in all of Brónach. He'd be strong, too. Able to defend his sister and eventually help her find their mother.

A shiver ran through his body. He turned his attention inward, listening and pinpointing everything just like his mother had taught him to do. He could feel his heartbeat. His breath. The pulse throughout his body. He ignored the things that were painful.

Another shiver. No, not a shiver, something else. Like another pulse. Rion centered his focus on that pulse. He coaxed it out, pulling and willing it toward the surface until he could almost feel it crawling across his skin.

Rion opened his eyes slowly and blinked. He raised his hand up toward the light overhead and stared at the tiny particles that circled his arm.

He looked back at the plant. It hadn't moved at all. Rion followed the bits of dirt rising from the pot, drifting toward him as if he were a magnetic force. Rion reached for them and they connected with his skin, moving in a slow spiral pattern down his entire arm.

He marveled at it, mouth gaping. He'd never seen anyone bend the earth. Nor had he read anything about it. Maybe it was in the books reserved for the older students. There were a few that Saoirse wouldn't let him read yet, despite him insisting he'd be able to understand it.

He'd read them now, just to see.

Rion's heart beat just a little faster as realization dawned on him. He had magic. He finally had magic. It was different, sure, but still earth-based in a way. And maybe, in time, he'd be able to control the plants, too. His teacher would know, she'd be able to teach him how to do it.

His excitement caused the grains and chunks of dirt to move faster, spiraling around his arm and now his body. Rion tried to contain himself to no avail. He didn't want to risk getting anything in his father's office dirty, but he had magic. Surely his father would overlook a few clumps of dirt on the rug, especially since most couldn't control their magic for the first week or so.

He'd get to join a special after school class for the next few weeks.

Rion concentrated on the small grains, but they slipped past his mental prodding. Instead of individual grains, Rion tried shifting the particles as a whole. They responded then, moving more to the left then the right. He expanded them and raised them over his head. Not all of them—some wouldn't respond at all and remained near his body. But he was moving his magic.

A wide grin spread across his face. Voices sounded down the hall followed by heavy footsteps.

"I told you a hundred times not to let him play in here." Father's voice was harsh, which was normal these days, but Rion didn't flinch away from it. He beamed when the door opened.

"He's not—" Saoirse stopped mid-sentence and both her and his father froze in the doorway. Their gazes traveled first to the particles circling his body, then to the ones above his head. Their lips parted and Rion heard their heart rates spike.

"Look," he said as if they couldn't plainly see the dirt floating around him. Rion shifted the particles lower and to his front. His smile broadened. "Look what I can do."

Neither moved. They didn't exclaim in excitement. Didn't run forward to hug or congratulate him. They just . . . stared.

Rion's smile faltered. He glanced around. He was certain he hadn't broken anything and the dirt was still all in the air. He didn't see any spots on the floor or the chairs. Even their father's desk was clean.

"Saoirse?" She looked like she wanted to say something, but her mouth didn't form the words. Their father hadn't moved either. Had he done something wrong? Saoirse looked as if he'd just broken something precious on her bookcase. Which he'd only done once. A porcelain horse that a friend had given her when she was in grade school.

Their father's breathing accelerated and Rion watched his fists clench. A muscle worked in his jaw. He stepped forward, but Saoirse grabbed his arm. "It's fine," she said. "It's just Rion."

His father didn't pull away. He simply stared at Rion. Stared long enough that Rion's own heart began pounding. A warning bell echoed in his head, telling him he should leave. Run. But this was his father. And Saoirse. There wasn't any—the plant beside Rion came alive and grew taller, towering above Rion's small body. Rion glanced at his father again and stumbled back. His magic reacted to his confused distress, moving in a frenzied pattern he couldn't control.

His father's throat bobbed, then the plant lashed out. Rion tried to duck, but a stem grazed his cheek and blood trickled down the side of Rion's face. He fell to his knees and scrambled back toward the bookcase.

"Father!" Saoirse screamed.

"I—I didn't break anything," Rion promised. His father had been sterner lately, but he'd never lashed out. He'd never physically injured any of his children unless they were sparing. Rion was still too young to spar with the adults though. He—another plant behind Rion burst to life and shot toward him. Its green branches wrapped around his wrist, squeezing tight. Rion's magic lashed out, cutting the plant in half. Rion pushed away from it, cornering himself. Saoirse lunged for their father then. She grabbed the High Lord's arm and wrenched him around to face her.

"Stop it," she screamed. "What are you doing?"

Their father glared at her, but somehow it seemed more sad than angry. "You know what he is."

"He's my brother," she yelled, still holding their father's wrist. "He's your son." Rion thought he saw a flash of pain on their father's face. His gaze flickered toward Rion again, then to the dirt that looked as if it were shaking.

The High Lord of Brónach shook his head. "The gods demand it, Saoirse."

"Then damn the gods."

He growled at his daughter and tried to shake her off, but Saoirse's own magic sprang to life, pouring from the pockets around her waist before wrapping around his body.

The room exploded. The planks in the floor ripped apart and every plant in the office shot toward Saoirse so fast Rion could hardly see them strike. Their father freed himself, then sent his daughter flying into the bookcase across the room. Rion heard the breath leave her body before the vase behind her hit the floor and shattered.

Cold, dark eyes turned to him. Rion clambered to his feet and backed away until his spine collided with the shelf behind him. He had nowhere to go. No where he could run.

Saoirse groaned and slowly pushed herself up. Blood leaked from the corner of her mouth. Her temple. Her arms where thorns had bitten into her skin.

Fear spiked through him. The world spun. He was going to be

sick.

"I didn't touch anything," Rion tried repeating. "I—I—I—"

"I know," their father said. His throat bobbed, but his magic only rose higher. "I'm sorry."

Rion's eyes darted toward the plants dancing around their father like obedient serpents. They sat there for a time, the High Lord and his son staring at one another. Then the vines moved. Rion clenched his eyes shut and threw his arms up. A wet gasp. Heavy breathing.

Rion cracked an eye open to find a vine protruding from the middle of their father's throat. Saoirse stood behind him, breath heaving. Blood dripped and their father tried and failed to cough.

Rion screamed. His magic exploded with the sound spinning around him in a ferocious storm that Rion was certain would tear him apart.

Books flew off the shelves and shredded. Vases and trinkets shattered. Then he vomited all over the floor.

Their father hit his knees before his head collided with the broken floor. Vacant eyes stared back at Rion. He knew what that meant. Knew what all the blood meant, too.

Their father was—was—Rion heaved again then gasped for breath, clawing at his throat. It wouldn't come. He collapsed and his chest felt as if something were pressing down on him. He might as well have been submerged under water. His vision blurred at the edges and his heart pounded in his ears.

Not real, he told himself. This wasn't real. Any minute now, Saoirse would hear him screaming and come to his room. She'd wake him, hold him close, and whisper words of comfort. She'd take him back to her room and make him a mug of tea or chocolate. She'd— she'd—But Saoirse was right in front of him, staring at their father with a hollow look in her eyes. Her hands were on the floor before her. Tears streamed down her face.

Not real. Not real. Not real. Not real.

Their father's personal guard blasted through the door and stopped at the sight of their High Lord on the floor in a puddle of his own blood. Their gazes all lifted to Rion and the magic surrounding his body. Rion didn't want it anymore. He wished it would go away. Leave him alone.

"Demon," one whispered. Saoirse's head lifted at the word. Rion met the warrior's gaze and the male stepped back. As if he were afraid.

This was the same male who'd killed on Rion's behalf just under a year ago. Back when assassins had entered the study with the intent to murder him and his family.

Back when their mother had disappeared without a trace.

The male drew his sword. Aimed it at Rion's chest.

"Stop," Saoirse pleaded, her voice breaking. They didn't listen. Their magic rose. His sister stumbled to her feet, but another warrior grabbed her by the shoulders and forced her back. She fought, screaming and kicking as they tried to tear her away from the room. Four males had their hands on her and were doing everything in their power to contain her magic.

The remaining three rushed Rion at once and he watched the scene unfold in slow motion. Their father on the floor dead. His sister fighting, not for herself, but for him. The males who looked at him with malice when they'd once held him in high regard.

Then something in him snapped.

Rion's magic exploded through the room. He didn't know how to control it. Didn't know if it would help, but the vines—they vanished—no, they were shredded apart, left as nothing more than tiny bits of green that dropped to the floor.

The dirt spun impossibly faster. Rion threw his arms out and the magic responded, shooting toward them. But where Rion had meant to push them back, to give him and Saoirse time to escape, it . . . obliterated them instead.

Their skin peeled away from their bones. Their screams filled his ears and the males clawed at their bodies as if they could fight the particles ripping through them from within.

Rion didn't understand. He tried to stop it. He tried to reel the magic back, but it wouldn't listen. It just kept moving until the warriors were nothing more than heaps of flesh on the broken ground next to his father.

Rion's body shook. His head spun. Another male appeared in the doorway, took one look at the scene, then raced away from the room, leaving the acrid tang of fear in his wake.

Rion looked at his hands. They weren't covered in blood, but he felt dirty.

"Rion." His sister's voice cracked, but Rion couldn't tear his gaze away from his hands or the sand circling his fingers. She moved, standing. "Rion." He slowly looked up and met those familiar green eyes. Her cheeks were red and tear stained.

"I—I didn't mean—" A sob tore from his throat, then Saoirse held out her arms. Rion's magic fell, as if he'd let go of everything as he ran to her. His feet splattered through blood, but he didn't look at it and instead buried his face in the crook of his sister's neck as she scooped him into her arms.

Saoirse held him close, her own body trembling just as much as his.

Rion didn't know how she found the strength to stand again, but she took a steadying breath and did it anyway. One of her hands cradled the back of his head while the other held him close. Rion didn't watch as she inched from the room then raced down the hall. He didn't look as she exited the palace, nor when they passed through a crack in Nàdair's redwood trees.

Alarms began blaring through the city, but they were already beyond the border, sprinting uphill toward the mountain.

Saoirse only slowed long enough to catch her breath before she was trotting again. Rion tried not to listen to the sobs that echoed through his sister. Tried not to focus on the scent of blood that wafted off their clothes. *It never happened. It never happened. It never happened.*

Wake up, he kept telling himself.

The alarm bells echoed in the distance, fading more and more with every passing step.

Rion never looked up.

He hoped that by hiding in his sister's tunic the world would shift and everything would just disappear. Maybe they'd return to that morning when their father's stern voice had instructed Saoirse to not let Rion eat too many sweets. Or when he'd told them not to be out too late.

But the world remained the same.

Rion clutched his sister's sleeve tighter. She did the same, holding her little brother as if he were her lifeline. He should be walking. He was too big to be carried around like a little kid. But Rion didn't think his body would move even if he wanted it to.

Minutes passed that felt like hours. Days. The sirens were barely a whisper now. His body calmed, stopped shaking altogether, and an overwhelming exhaustion settled through him. He wondered if Saoirse felt the same. If she did, she didn't show it.

Rion finally lifted his head. Darkness surrounded them, save for a silver of moonlight that filtered through the trees. Movement from the corner of his eye had Rion's heart rate spiking all over again, wondering if more warriors from their father's personal guard had pursued them, but a second glance told Rion it was only the Fairy Folk.

The small creatures kept their distance, their beady eyes glinting in the moonlight.

Right. It was the solstice. Their father—he'd died on the solstice. It was a day that was supposed to be sacred to Fae and Fairy Folk alike, but now—Rion swallowed hard.

Saoirse rubbed his back in soothing strokes but didn't speak. She just kept pushing onward, determination replacing her earlier fear and uncertainty.

He couldn't see the city lights anymore. Not even the glow of them through the thick trees.

Rion laid his head back against Saoirse's shoulder, refusing to reach for the magic that continued to pulse beneath his skin. He never wanted to touch it again.

It seemed only moments later that his sister slowed. She was probably tired. Rion pushed up and said, "I can walk."

Saoirse didn't respond. She didn't put him down either. Her emerald eyes searched through the trees and paused when they stood on the outskirts of a clearing, right before a dirt path that led to a single story cabin.

Candles flickered in the main window.

Flat square stepping stones carved a path surrounded by low-growing plants that Rion couldn't identify in the dark. His sister's heart rate spiked again and she retreated a step, looking back where they'd come. She chewed her lip and returned her gaze to the cabin, as if she wasn't sure whether to move forward or go back.

The door swung open and a large, silhouetted figure stood in the doorway.

"Saoirse?" A male's voice called.

A noise escaped his sister that bordered on the edge of hysteria. He wondered if she'd break down right here, but despite her trembling lips, Saoirse held herself together.

The male stepped down from his porch and onto the path. Rion still couldn't see his face.

"Gods, what happened?"

His sister didn't move. She'd frozen in place, still glancing between the male and the city they'd left behind. She stepped back again, clutching Rion close.

The male stopped advancing, seemed to look them over. His voice softened. "You're safe here. You know that." He stepped to the side and extended one arm as an invitation. "Whatever you've done. You're safe."

Her shoulders fell, then she stepped forward. Rion shrank away from the male as his sister entered the cabin, still holding him tight. The male peered into the darkness beyond, scanning the wood line before he joined them.

He pulled a folded blanket from the cabinet and spread it over a short sofa before gesturing for her to sit. She did. His sister seemed to relax, but Rion kept his eyes on the male as he moved toward the kitchen and filled three mugs with steaming water before retrieving a jar of tea. The male returned moments later, placing the three mugs on the table between them.

The male settled into the chair across from them and an uneasy silence filled the space. It was dark, save for the candles and embers that glowed in the fire place. Too warm. Rion was too warm here. Too nervous with this new male after everything that had happened. He wanted to leave.

The male surveyed them, scented the blood that covered their bodies.

"You're hurt." Saoirse didn't respond. The silence was nearly palpable. "You know better than to let a wound like that go untreated." Again, silence.

The male sat back, studying Saoirse as if he was trying to piece together a puzzle. His sister's breathing changed. She slowed it, eased her heart rate down, too. "I shouldn't be here," she finally said.

"Yet here you are."

"I'll leave in the morning. I just need a night, then I'll go."

"Where to?"

She cupped her face with one hand. "I don't know yet. North, maybe. Across the sea."

He raised a brow. "With him?" The male eyed Rion now, and Rion refused to turn away or back down. He thought he saw the male's lips twitch into a smile. Saoirse only nodded. The male leaned forward again, all trace of humor gone. "Saoirse, tell me what's going on."

She stared at the fire again and her lips wobbled before parting to take another breath. "Father is . . . gone." The male went unnaturally still. Saoirse was shaking now. "I—I didn't think. I just . . . reacted." She buried her face in her hands again.

"You killed him?"

Rion flinched at the words. Saoirse didn't look up. Didn't confirm or deny.

More silence.

The fire cracked and Rion jumped.

The male uttered a single word that sounded more like a command than a question. "Why?"

Saoirse shook her head. "I can't tell you. You won't understand."

His jaw worked. "If my High Lord is dead, then I need to be in the city. I heard the alarms, but I didn't think—"

"You'll find out when you get there. We'll be gone before you come back. I promise."

"If the High Lord is dead, then Alec is going to need you."

Saoirse shook her head again. "I can't face him after—he won't understand, either. I have to leave." She looked at Rion. "We have to leave."

"Saoirse." That commanding voice again. "I live in isolation for a reason. My views often don't align with those of others. I am loyal to my High Lord, but I am also loyal to his children. So I'll ask you again. What happened?"

She clutched Rion a little tighter. "You'll hurt him."

"Hurt who?" His voice held an edge of impatience.

Her voice wavered. "Rion." His sister pulled him impossibly tighter and he had to push against her to breathe. Rion watched the male carefully now as he assessed the pair of them.

"Why would I—" The male stopped talking. His eyes widened and Rion followed his gaze to the magic stirring along the rug at their feet. The particles rose up, circling Rion's legs, then his torso, and finally his arms.

Rion tried to stop it, but it was just as slippery as it'd been before. He had no control. None, and Saoirse was sitting right next to him. Would it hurt her by accident like it had the guards?

A lump rose in Rion's throat.

The male's dark brown eyes locked with Rion's. He scented the air again, seeming to take in everything around the pair seated in his living room.

Saoirse started crying again, but her arms were still around him as if she could protect him from the world.

"Just one night," she promised again, "and you'll never see us again. Please." He'd never heard his sister beg for anything. Many described her as proud, sometimes arrogant in the way the Fae were known to be arrogant.

Rion's magic moved faster as his breathing increased, his heart rate with it.

The male's voice was a near whisper when he said, "Your father tried to kill him." It wasn't a question, but Saoirse nodded anyway.

"I thought he'd see it coming. I just wanted to stop him. I didn't mean—" She buried her head in Rion's chest and her shoulders shook with uncontrollable sobs.

Rion locked eyes with the male. "The others weren't her fault."

The male's eyes narrowed. "Others?"

"The ones always around Father."

"His personal guard?"

"His magic," Saoirse said, her voice weak. "It reacted when they attacked him. He was just defending himself."

The male eyed the grains still floating through the air. They jerked in agitation.

"I won't hurt either of you," he assured. "You can put your magic away."

Rion sniffed the air, searching for the lie. He knew how to identify them now. Saoirse's head lifted, her eyes wide as if surprised.

"I—I don't know how," he admitted.

"Start by taking a deep breath. Calm yourself." Rion hesitated and met Saoirse's gaze for reassurance. She nodded and Rion did as instructed. As his mother had taught him. The strange new pulse in his body slowed, the particles with it. He watched them drift back to the rug before settling into the fibers.

The male's eyes flickered with a hint of surprise before he could hide it. "Good." He sat back again, observing the pair before returning his gaze to the fire.

Rion's skin itched suddenly and he was so, so tired. He glanced at his hands. He'd . . . killed someone. Several someone's. How many had there been? Five? Six? And then Saoirse. Saoirse had killed their father.

Rion looked at his sister. Large bags had formed beneath her eyes and the darkness made her look like the painting in their father's study that had always made him sad. He didn't want Saoirse to be sad.

"Rion." He jumped at the male's voice. "I have a question for you." Rion waited. "How far are you willing to go to protect your sister?" Saoirse's sharp gaze turned toward the male. She looked him up and down.

"I'd do anything for her." He'd already killed, even if he hadn't meant to. How much worse could it get?

The male interlaced his fingers. "Then I need you to let the world believe a lie."

"No." Saoirse's voice was harsh and her grip tightened on Rion again.

"We have to tell the people—"

"No," she repeated.

"You'd rather take him to another continent? Risk crossing the sea and praying the sirens don't tip your boat? Do you know how many vessels successfully make that crossing?" He shifted in his seat. "Listen to me and listen well. Your little brother is cursed." She tried to interrupt, but the male held up a hand. "Whether you want to accept it or not, it's true and there's nothing we can do about it. If you want him to live, then you need to recognize there will be a target on his back for the rest of his life. People will blame him for atrocities he's never even committed. There's no reason for you to be branded an exile alongside him."

"Why?" Rion's voice shook. "What did I do wrong?"

The male's gaze softened. "Nothing. Had your magic held off until the end of this year, you'd understand what it means. We don't teach the course until most younglings have already acquired their magic. Fear can hinder its arrival, therefore we try to mitigate that fear." He looked to Saoirse again. "Your sister can fill you in on the details later. What you need to understand right now is that the magic you possess is a curse and the gods demand us," he hesitated, "to eliminate that curse."

"Why would they let me have it then?"

The male's gaze softened again. "Why indeed?"

"Rion isn't a monster. He's never hurt a soul." Not until tonight, Rion wanted to correct.

"I know. But others aren't going to care. They'll only be concerned about the demands from their gods." Rion wondered if the male believed in the same gods. Gods his mother had talked fondly about.

"But—"

"The High Lord is dead. His personal guard is dead. This is not something that will be forgiven easily, if ever." Saoirse didn't respond. "The people will blame Rion regardless of your claim. They'll merely see you as a sister trying to protect her little brother. They'll sympathize with you for a while, but that sympathy won't be enough to clear his name."

She shook her head. "I can get us into Pádraigín's lands and take a boat from there. The sirens don't claim that part of the ocean. I just need supplies. Food. Clothes."

"Saoirse." She looked up at him, her eyes lined in silver. "You can't leave. Alec is probably frantic with worry. If you disappear, he'll send search parties to find you. And they *will* succeed. Rion's fate . . . might not turn out so well if you're caught on the run."

"Alec won't understand. If we tell him Rion did it—"

"Young Alec mimics your father in many beliefs. I'm confident this will be one of them."

"What am I supposed to do?" Her body was trembling again.

"Let me look after him."

Her head shot up. "How can I trust—"

"Do not insult me in my own home."

She snapped her mouth shut before continuing. "Why would you do that?"

The male sighed. "I trained with your father. Then I trained you and your brother. And Lady Eimear." Rion flinched at his mother's name. "We were close. I'd like to think I'm honoring her memory by caring for her final youngling."

Saoirse looked Rion over and his heart sped when he realized she was considering the idea. He didn't know this male. He didn't want anything to do with him.

"I want to stay with you," Rion argued.

Saoirse rubbed his arm. "I know."

Rion looked at the male again, glared at him really. The male offered a hint of a smile in return.

"Promise me," Saoirse said.

"You know promises from Fae only reach so far."

"I don't care." She looked him in the eye and sat straighter. "I want your word as a Fae that you won't hurt him."

His lips parted slightly. Rion knew enough about Fae honor to know what Saoirse was asking.

The male placed a hand over his heart. "I swear, on pain of death, that so long as Rion remains in my care, no harm shall come to him."

Another long moment of silence passed, then Saoirse nodded.

"But I don't want—"

Saoirse pressed a finger to Rion's lips. "We'll talk about it. I promise."

The male stood. "Rest. You know where the supplies are. You're welcome to anything in the house or outside of it. I likely won't be back for a few days."

"You're leaving?"

"My presence will be expected. I'll let Alec know where you are, but I'll leave Rion's location undisclosed."

Saoirse only nodded, but Rion watched the male's every move as he gathered a belt full of weapons and strapped it across his torso. He pulled on his boots and slung a broadsword across his back.

The male paused with one hand on the handle. Tension filled the room. "Did he hesitate?" Rion knew what he meant but wasn't prepared for the answer to sink through him like a lead weight.

"Once."

The male nodded before gently closing the door in his wake. He trotted down the stairs and Rion listened to his receding footsteps until they blended into the night.

Silence engulfed the space. The steam from their mugs had stopped rising minutes ago.

Images of their father and his guards returned, flashing through Rion's mind. Then reality hit him like cold water. Their father was gone. Rion couldn't return home. Alec would hate him. And from what the male had said, it seemed the rest of the world would too.

He'd wanted his magic for years. He'd prayed for it. And now . . . now . . .

"Let's get you cleaned up." Saoirse finally released her hold on him as she stood.

Rion squeezed her hand, remembering her wounds. "You should first. You're hurt."

She gave him a sad smile. "I'll be all right. Just . . . let me get you cleaned up, okay?"

He wanted to argue, but the sadness in her gaze had Rion nodding instead. He followed her to a small bathroom with a clawfoot tub in the corner. Surprisingly, the male possessed running water. Saoirse turned the knob and seconds later steam filled the small space.

Saoirse gave him some privacy to strip down before returning to wash his hair. She hadn't done that since he was little, but Rion let her now. He finished washing himself, then dressed. Saoirse examined his wounds before climbing into the tub herself.

Rion sat just outside the door as he waited for her to finish, then he watched her stitch up the wound in her side. Their father had done that. He bristled at the thought. Tomorrow. He'd learn how to care for wounds tomorrow, that way Saoirse wouldn't ever have to do it by herself.

Neither spoke aside from asking if the other was all right or if they needed anything.

Saoirse dragged the towel through her hair. Rion watched before finally asking, "Who is he?"

"My teacher."

"In what?"

"Everything. Combatives. Magic. Strategy." She looked him over. "He'll teach you, too."

"You're not leaving, are you?" Saoirse sighed and returned to the sofa. She pulled Rion into her arms and cradled him close as they stared at the embers. "Saoirse?"

"Not for a while."

"How long is a while?"

"I'll make sure you get settled in." She rubbed his back. "You have to stay with him from now on."

Rion pursed his lips. "What if I don't want to?"

"We don't have a choice. If you go back to the city—" she didn't finish her sentence. "You'll be safe here."

"But what if someone tries to hurt *you*?"

Saoirse adjusted the pillow on the couch and coaxed him to lie down at her side. "No one is going to hurt me."

"Because they'll think you didn't hurt Father?"

She was silent for a long moment. "You don't have to do that. You don't have to take the blame."

Rion sat back up. "He said you'd be in danger if I don't."

She clutched his hand. "*You'll* be in danger if you do."

"But I have you to protect me."

She smiled at that. "Now and forever."

"I want to help," he said. "I don't want anyone else to know."

Her smile turned sad. "All right."

"Promise?" Her eyes misted over. "Promise you'll let me do it. I don't want Alec or anyone else to be mad at you."

"Okay." She didn't meet his gaze.

"Promise."

Saoirse studied the defiance in his gaze and her lips trembled. "You'll hate me for it, eventually."

"No, I won't. Let me help." Rion could feel his magic stirring again, rising to circle them. He wanted to protect her, no matter what that meant for him.

A tear slid down her face and she relented. "I promise. Now try to get some sleep."

He settled back down at her side and watched the red glow from the dying fire. Saoirse pulled him close, wrapping one arm around his middle. He began to drift but didn't miss it when his sister whispered, "I'll always protect you."

THE CURSED FAE AND BROKEN PROMISES

CHAPTER ONE

Vines raced across the ground like serpents, ripping up from the earth and lashing out as Rion dodged and ducked beneath their rapid strikes. The stones and loose particles answered his call easily, veering to block the greenery and shredding it on impact before darting to the next.

He raised his sword and went in for the strike, right where he'd seen her vulner—a tree burst from the ground and clipped him hard beneath the chin before he could backpedal. Blood pooled in his mouth, but Rion ignored the coppery taste and dashed to the right. If he could move fast enough . . . more vines wrapped around his foot and dragged him down; he sliced through them with his magic and caught his balance before launching at her again.

She smirked, already anticipating his movements. She shifted into a perfect stance, her weight evenly distributed, sword up, ready to counter when he closed in.

The ground crumbled beneath her back foot. She tilted and cursed, then Rion used his magic to propel him forward. She pulled at the vines once more, but the ground moved beneath her other foot. There was no way for her to regain her balance in time.

Now. It had to be now. He'd never get another chance.

Rion slammed his elbow against her sternum and she hit the ground hard. He leaped, blood racing through his veins as victory closed in—a flash to his left, but too late. The trunk slammed into Rion's side, sending him flying. He skidded across the ground. Rocks and thorny branches cut though his skin and Rion cursed before righting himself and clutching his ribs.

"The hell was that for?" Rion roared.

"You weren't paying attention to your surroundings."

"I almost had her."

"And if she'd had a partner, you'd be dead." Rion slammed his sword down and cursed again. The male *tsked.* "No need for the language."

Rion glared at Caol, then at Saoirse who was quietly laughing to herself. Caol, their teacher, helped her up and Saoirse dusted off her pants. "Almost only counts—"

"I know," Rion interrupted her. So close. He'd never been so close to beating her and Caol, gods—Rion kicked a branch, snapping it beneath the force.

"Are you done throwing a tantrum, boy?"

"Don't call me that," Rion seethed.

"Then stop acting like one."

"You did that on purpose."

"And I'll do it again until you realize there's always more than one enemy on the field. *Never* let your guard down."

Rion's blood slowed. He drew in a breath and let the tension fall from his shoulders. Caol was right, of course, which only made the situation more infuriating. If he was ever going to beat Saoirse, he'd have to earn it.

He crossed the space separating him and Saoirse, trying not to limp from the pain radiating through his hip where Caol had basically thrown a small tree at him. "I had you."

A bloody grin. "Maybe."

Caol called, "Here, if you're so confident," Rion turned and caught the three sectional staff before it smacked him in the head. "Let's see what you got."

Rion grimaced but his pride wouldn't let him back down, not as Caol dropped into his own stance, wooden staff in hand.

He'd only been working with the three sectional for a month. Long enough to know the basics, but not nearly long enough to perfect it. He still had bruises from last week and a tender knot on the back of his head to prove it.

Caol launched at him without warning. Rion stumbled back and raised the weapon, gritting his teeth from the force of impact. The chains linking the staff together rattled, and Rion swung the right section up aiming for Caol's chin. The male spun his staff, effectively blocking the move, then brought up the other end and cracked Rion in the jaw again.

His teacher danced away, spinning his weapon in a taunt that had Rion's blood racing all over again. Rion rubbed his jaw, fighting the pain and the rage that accompanied it. After six years as Rion's tutor Caol knew exactly how to push his buttons and seemed to delight in it.

Rion gripped the weapon between his hands and summoned his magic. Caol's eyes sparked with challenge and mischief.

Six years and Rion had excelled at everything Caol had thrown at him; an awkward weapon wasn't going to stop him now. Rion launched forward again, remembering those first few months. They hadn't had a smooth beginning. Not by a long shot.

The two wooden weapons collided and a loud crack rang through the air. The vibrations raced down his arms. Vines reached out to yank Rion's feet out from under him, but he was ready and smothered the greenery in an instant.

Rion had outright refused to listen to the male in the beginning and he'd often snuck away to find Saoirse. An act that Saoirse had reprimanded him for every single time. There'd been tears and no shortage of tantrums, but when Caol warned Rion his actions could result in Saoirse's death or imprisonment, he'd stopped.

Rion ducked, feeling the wind from the staff's swing, and swept his leg at Caol's feet. He knew the male would jump. Rion sent his magic racing upward, but as usual, Caol was ready. Caol's magic whipped out and wrapped around the male's wrist, yanking him away from Rion's path.

Caol. He was the only one Rion saw for months at a time. Their bond was . . . interesting. The male had saved him on a few occasions.

The male had killed for him and yet still kept his distance. Not that Caol was any warmer with Saoirse.

"Watch your feet," his sister called. Too late, the vines broke through his swirling sand and grabbed his legs, pulling them out from under him. Rion's head slammed against the ground and stars shot across his field of vision.

Adrenaline pulsed through him. He knew Caol was coming. The male never let up until he had a weapon, be it staff, sword, or knife, pressed against Rion's throat. Just to prove to Rion he needed more training.

Not today.

Rion waited, counting the seconds. He heard the male's feet sprinting through the grass. Scented the magic sneaking up on him. Rion tightened his grip on the end of the staff and just like he'd seen Caol do a hundred times, he whipped the weapon out like a viper.

It extended, aimed right for the male's torso. Caol's smirk told Rion it wouldn't hit, but Rion didn't expect it to. Rion's magic was already around the wood, crawling up the shaft, and right before Caol blocked, Rion shot that magic out in one swift movement.

Caol's eyes widened. The particles of sand merged together and slammed into Caol's chest hard enough to send him careening backward. Caol didn't land gracefully. He hit his backside and flipped over, grabbing his chest as he fought for breath.

Saoirse let out an audible gasp and stared wide eyed before bursting out laughing. "This is going down in history as my favorite sparing session. I don't think I've ever seen you on your ass, Caol."

A *whoosh* flew through the air and Rion didn't have time to dodge as the end of Caol's staff slammed into his stomach. Rion coughed and doubled over, letting the wooden staff clatter to the ground.

Caol was already back on his feet, one hand pressed against his chest. "You didn't finish the match," he said, eyes gleaming. "*Never* underestimate your opponent."

CHAPTER TWO

ion took the bag of ice from Saoirse and placed it on his bruised stomach. Wincing, he slowly leaned back against the tree.

"You're going to feel that for a week," she said, setting her bowl to the side. Caol had been nice enough to make them dinner, even if the male was nursing wounds of his own.

"It was worth it."

"Definitely. I knocked him down once. Made the same mistake you did."

"And?"

"He broke my wrist."

"Gods."

"He felt bad for that one. I moved the wrong way and, well, metal against bone doesn't mix so well."

Silence settled over the space as the pair basked in the setting sun. It painted the trees in hues of red and orange, reminding Rion of a painting that used to hang in a long hallway inside the palace. He wondered if it was still there. Maybe Alec had replaced it with something else.

"When do you go back?"

"In the morning. I'll be gone before you wake."

Rion adjusted the ice. In the beginning, Saoirse had visited every other day, but as the months passed, her duties had resumed. It was only through careful planning that they'd kept Rion's location a secret for so many years. Caol never allowed visitors and Rion was only ever permitted to leave under Saoirse's careful supervision. Usually when Alec was away.

The mountain was both a sanctuary and a prison.

"Will you be here for the festival?" The spring festival was two nights from now. Not as grand an event as the solstices, but he treasured every opportunity to sneak down to Nàdair. The city breathed fresh life into him, brought up old memories.

Saoirse shook her head and his heart sank. "Not this time. I have—well, I'll be gone for a few days."

Rion studied his sister. "Is everything okay?"

She didn't look at him. "Yeah, I just hate leaving you. It's not like you can get out without me."

She was right about that. He'd been looking forward to it. Alec didn't usually assign her during holidays unless it was something important.

Rion did his best to keep the disappointment out of his voice. "It's fine. There's always the summer solstice."

She leaned back on her hands. "We should visit the lake house soon. Get you away from Caol for a bit."

"That'd be nice."

She side eyed him. "It won't be like this forever, you know. Just until—"

"Just until I can defend myself, I know."

Her face fell. "If it weren't for the attacks . . ."

"I get it, you don't have to explain it to me again." Silence stretched between them. He'd only had three incidents in the past six years, but they'd all resulted in someone's death. One look at his magic and they attacked without reservation. Saoirse had put down two, Caol had taken out the other.

Sometimes Rion wondered if he'd be able to show his face at all. If he walked through the city gates, would everyone try to kill him all at once? Did he even have a home to go back to?

"Give it two more years."

His head lifted. "Caol said five."

"Well Caol's not your sister, is he?" She stood and studied the landscape. "We'll start with the small villages. Let you help them out, then move on to bigger ones. We'll force people to see you're not a threat, even if it takes us a century to do it."

"Alec isn't going to give you a century."

"You let me handle Alec."

He chuckled. She was probably the only one who could.

"I'm turning in early, you coming?" Rion took her outstretched hand and followed his sister back to Caol's cabin.

Two years. He could handle that. He hoped.

CHAPTER THREE

Two days later, Rion wiped the sweat from his brow and plopped into one of the wooden chairs outside. He propped his feet up on the stones surrounding the unlit fireplace and leaned back. He could hear Caol rustling around inside, likely prepping lunch. Rion knew better than to offer his help. Caol treated the small kitchen like a temple. No one else was allowed to touch his utensils.

It also didn't help that Rion had nearly burned the cabin down when he was a youngling. It was a poor attempt at making lunch. Apparently grease didn't mix well with fire.

White clouds passed by at a snail's pace. He had the day off today, aside from the chores he'd just finished. No training, though Caol hadn't made him do much after chucking a staff into his stomach. The bluish color that had spread across his ribs was just beginning to fade.

He let the tension fall from his shoulders and closed his eyes. The spring air washed through him, pleasant and welcoming.

Rion's body jolted. He sat straight up in the chair, heart thundering through his chest. The forest was quiet. Rion twisted in his seat, searching for the sound, but—nothing.

He gripped his head, trying to massage away the headache creeping on. What had he been dreaming about? He couldn't remember, but Rion could have sworn—impossible. No one came within a mile of this place without Caol's knowledge.

A mouthwatering scent drifted from the cabin's open window. Judging from the sun's position, he hadn't been out long.

Stretching, Rion started for the door with one thought in mind. The festival. He couldn't go with Saoirse, but maybe, just maybe Caol would say yes today. Rion could control his magic now, mostly, and so long as he kept his hood up, no one would recognize him. It had always worked when he traveled with Saoirse.

Caol had nearly finished his plate when Rion walked through the door. "If I'd known you'd sleep the day away, I would have assigned you more to do."

Rion shrugged. "You said I had down time." Not that he'd meant to fall asleep.

The male grunted and popped another forkful of chicken into his mouth.

Rion sat across from him, his own mouthwatering from the smell of herb-roasted chicken, rice, and vegetables. Caol's cooking never disappointed.

The male poured them both a glass of water and returned to his meal.

Rion took a bite, savoring the rich flavor. He stared at Caol, his heart quickening as the question danced on his tongue.

"Out with it already," Caol barked without looking up.

Rion pushed a pea across his plate. "The spring festival starts tonight."

Caol drank from his glass. "I didn't think Saoirse would be here for it."

"She isn't," Rion started. "I was wondering if you'd like to go."

"You know why we can't." Right. Because if they were caught, then Rion wouldn't have a place to call home anymore. But he was so tired of being cooped up. Of only having Saoirse and Caol to talk to.

"We could wait until it's dark," Rion tried. "It'd be fun. Maybe we could find a few new weapons. Plus the food is always—"

"I'm not your father."

The statement hit Rion hard. Harder than he thought it would. His face heated. "I know that. I just thought—"

"Don't think. We're not here for you to think or to attend festivals. I entertain the idea because of Saoirse's insistence. You're here to get stronger, nothing more."

"I know," Rion grumbled. "I just thought it might be nice to switch things up."

Caol stared at his plate. "The solstice isn't far off. Saoirse will accompany you then." Caol stood and Rion gripped his fork. "Finish your meal before you storm off."

Rion didn't want to eat, his stomach had soured, but he did so anyway, clearing the plate as fast as possible before standing. "Thank you for the meal."

With his face still warm, Rion exited the cabin, careful not to slam the door, and marched straight into the woods.

He knew Caol wasn't his father, but Rion had hoped, with all the years they'd spent together, they might at least totter the line between family and friends.

Then again, maybe he wouldn't have gone to the solstice with Saoirse either.

Rion tried to quell his rising anger. Caol had done far more for him than anyone else ever had. He should be grateful. He was grateful, he just wished—Rion slumped against a tree and slid to the ground. He didn't know what he wished for. A friend, that'd be a good start.

Rion tilted his head back. The afternoon sky was still clear. Open and inviting. Birds flew overhead and Rion found himself envying their freedom.

He felt like a prisoner.

The logical part of his brain knew it was only for his own safety, but his heart, the illogical thing, begged for more. He wanted to know what it might be like to enter a restaurant with a friend at his side. To sit and laugh the way he'd seen so many other teens do. He wanted to take a female's hand and watch her blush as they strolled through the streets. He just wanted something other than—Rion looked around—this isolation.

The solstice. He supposed he could wait, but even though the day brought joy, it was also tinged with sadness, especially for Saoirse. It was both a celebration and a painful reminder of when their lives had gone to hell. Rion had found her crying last year, seated at their father's grave. She still blamed herself, and Rion wondered if she ever regretted saving him.

Rion let his magic spread through the ground. All manner of stones, both large and small, rose to surround his body. He studied it, this cursed magic the world labeled as an abomination. At least it responded better than it had in those initial months. It was only intense emotions that made it act out now.

Sometimes Rion wondered if a creature lurked beneath his skin, just waiting for the day it could break through and wreak havoc on Nàdair and its citizens. He supposed the only way to find out was to wait.

Rion relaxed his shoulders and let the magic fall again. He watched the clouds, the bugs crawling through the pine needles, the birds as they jumped from branch to branch.

How much peace could one endure before they lost their mind?

Footsteps padded nearby and Rion tilted his head to find Caol strolling toward him.

"You shouldn't leave yourself so vulnerable."

Rion returned his attention to the sky. "It's called relaxing. You should try it sometime."

Caol snorted. "I'm heading into the city for supplies. Do us both a favor and stay out of trouble while I'm gone." To Nàdair. During the festival. Rion almost clenched his fists but stopped himself. He didn't understand why the male couldn't set aside thirty minutes to accompany Rion through the crowd. Not that Caol would attend without him. The male didn't like big events, or crowds, or others in general.

Rion gave the male a dramatic thumbs up and Caol rolled his eyes, muttering beneath his breath before heading back to the cabin.

Caol only went to Nàdair twice a month. Less, if he could help it. He claimed to despise venturing into the city. But he always returned with his spirits lifted. Maybe he had a friend or two there. Perhaps even a female.

Rion's jaw worked. A teacher. That's all Caol was to him. Not a father. Not a friend. Rion stared after the place where Caol had disappeared.

Enough. He'd had enough. He'd face the repercussions later.

Rion waited until the sun had started to set before he entered the cabin, changed into plain black clothes, pulled a cloak from the rack, and let the door close behind him.

One night. He just wanted one night to pretend he was someone else. He'd stroll down the streets he'd once called home. He'd purchase sweets and pretend he had someone who cared waiting on him, too. Pathetic maybe, but it was far better than the lonely truth.

CHAPTER FOUR

$\mathcal{I}$t was dark before the tall redwood trees came into view.
Rion entered through a small break in the trunks. A tunnel
of sorts through the massive beasts that protected the city.
Saoirse had shown it to him years ago. Rion was sure others knew about
it, but she kept it hidden with a row of thick vines. With his sister's magic, the vines moved out of her way on command. Without her—

Rion pulled another leaf from his hair before flipping his hood up.
Soft lights illuminated the main street where the vendors were gathered.
During the solstice, the entire city glowed and there were more merchants than he could count. But this festival had been contained to the
main road that led up to the palace. He'd be careful not to venture too
close.

Rion ambled through the dark streets, watching the rooftops and
alcoves as he went. His feet were silent against the cobblestones and Rion
ran his hands along the freshly blooming flowers and foliage.

Sudden images of blood and mangled bodies flashed to the fore-
front of his mind. Rion gritted his teeth. He'd never forgotten the night
of his father's death. It was a scene that regularly haunted his nightmares.
Before that moment, he'd never witnessed death. Nor had he known a
body could produce so much blood.

A female's laughter rang through the air, burying one memory for another. He wondered what his mother would make of his life now. Would she try to appease the gods and kill him as well, or would she have hidden him away like Saoirse? Perhaps she wouldn't have done either. She'd been their High Lady, still was as far as most were concerned. Perhaps his life would have unfolded differently were she still around.

Saoirse had never stopped searching. He'd accompanied her on a few missions, but the trail always ended in crippling disappointment.

Voices grew louder and Rion stepped into the soft light of the street. He was thankful for the brisk air; it made keeping his hood up comfortable and kept any onlookers from turning his way. He knew to be careful. He wouldn't put Caol at risk of treason, nor would Rion lead anyone back to the male's home.

With a pounding heart, Rion entered the crowd.

Streamers and hand-crafted ornaments hung from the rooftops and wrapped along the railings and ropes above. Magic sparked through the air and Rion saw more than one citizen manipulate the flowers into full bloom. The very air teamed with energy.

Rion slowed his breathing and let himself get lost in the clamoring sounds. The laughing children. The exclamations of surprise. The chimes shifting with the breeze.

Vendors smiled at him, holding out their wares for him to view. He even purchased a cinnamon sweet and found himself blushing furiously when the female preparing it brushed his hand with her own.

Rion quickly retreated and found a quiet corner where he could eat and watch the festivities. Several held hands. Others laughed with what Rion could only assume was their family.

No one looked twice at the male lingering on the outskirts. It almost made Rion want to remove his cloak and join them. Perhaps he could ask the female running the pastry stand if she'd like to take a stroll. Rion imagined the conversation. The way she'd throw her head back and laugh. But even if the citizens didn't recognize him, the officials would. Maybe. They hadn't seen him since his father's death.

The pastry turned to ash in his mouth and Rion chucked the last of it into the trash.

Who was he kidding? Even here, amongst hundreds of Fae, he was still alone.

Memories swam through him as he wandered the open street.

A petite female tended to a tree and Rion recalled a time when his mother had coaxed a tiny sapling into full bloom. A youngling pulled on his mother's pants and the female picked him up and balanced him on her shoulders. His mother used to do that, too.

Then Rion watched a couple pass by, the female clinging to the male's arm. The pair smiled at one another. She blushed and Rion turned away. His stomach soured and he fought a burning sensation in his throat as he turned from the festival altogether.

Maybe he shouldn't have come after all. He was just tormenting himself, pretending to have a life that was never meant to be. Removing his hood and joining them would only paint a target on his back.

Rion raced from the busy street. He kept well away from the palace, but instead of marching straight back to Caol's, Rion took a detour toward his old school.

The trees thinned before parting to reveal open fields where he'd learned to play ball, made new friends, and discovered what it meant to be a High Lord's son. He wasn't always a favorite among his peers.

He recalled his first lesson in combatives and smirked when Liam's young face came to mind. They hadn't been friends at first. Not until Rion punched another child in the stomach for making fun of Liam's mother.

They'd been inseparable afterward.

Crickets chirped as he moved along the perimeter. An owl hooted in the distance then laughter floated toward him as if carried on a phantom wind.

Rion tilted his head to listen. He'd expected the area to be deserted, especially with the festival in full swing, but seven Fae raced one another through the tall grass, all chasing a ball.

One landed a hard kick, sending the ball flying, and the others exclaimed in excitement. Rion drew closer without meaning to. Four males. Three females. He watched as one fell on his backside and the others laughed before pulling the male back to his feet.

Rion's lips parted. This—these young Fae—he was staring at everything he'd ever wanted. It was as though the gods were taunting him, dangling his dreams just out of reach.

He glanced toward the trees on the other side of the playing field then back to the laughing faces.

Too close. He'd drifted far too close.

He should leave. It would be better to turn and disappear before they ever saw him, but the tallest male in their group glanced his way and Rion's entire body went rigid.

He was taller now. Older. He'd transformed from a slightly chubby youngling into a lean soon-to-be warrior. His feet weren't too big for his body anymore and his ears weren't overly pointed like they'd been in childhood.

The male squinted, tossing the ball from one hand to another as he surveyed the newcomer. The other six closed in, curious.

Rion swallowed hard.

Liam.

His childhood friend. The one he'd been able to tell all his secrets to, whatever secrets they'd had at seven years old.

He'd been there when Rion's mother had disappeared. Liam had comforted him, pulled him out of his room on more than one occasion. And here he was, standing right in front of him.

Did he risk talking to him? Would Liam listen when no one else had? Would he understand?

Rion's hands trembled slightly as he pulled his hood back. The ball stopped moving. The two males stared at one another.

Rion waited for the smile to spread across Liam's face, a familiar sight he'd longed for. He waited for Liam to rush forward and throw his arms around his shoulders and clasp him on the back. To ask where he'd been all this time and what had happened.

But Liam went unnaturally still. His eyes widened in recognition and when Rion dared a step forward, Liam stepped back.

A jolt of pain flared through Rion's chest. The scent of magic sparked through the air, from both Liam and those behind him. One of the females clutched the arm of another. The acrid stench of fear drifted across the field.

Fine, it's fine, Rion told himself. They just didn't know yet.

Rion slowly lifted his palms up. "I'm not here to hurt anyone." His voice wavered. His throat had gone dry. He could only imagine the stories they'd been told. Tales about a monster child who had murdered the High Lord and an entire unit of warriors in a matter of seconds. A ruthless killer.

It had been a mistake to isolate. He saw that now. No one had seen him in six years. Not since that bloody night. He was a stranger to everyone and now that he was almost an adult, they'd perceive him as even more of a threat.

Magic crawled at their feet. One of the females glanced around Rion as if trying to gauge whether she could make a run for it.

"What do you want?" Liam demanded, his voice stern. Rion didn't miss the way the male had positioned himself in front of his friends. He was willing to protect them. Die for them.

"I just came to see the festival, then I heard you playing and—" And what? Did he think they'd just forget the stories and invite him over?

Liam's jaw worked, but it was a female behind him that said, "You should leave." Rion was pretty sure she'd meant it to sound like a threat.

Pain radiated through his chest when Liam didn't answer. Rion's magic stirred against his will and the seven scrambled back three paces, their fear exploding. Liam crouched, ready for a fight. Rion could hear his friend's rapid heartbeat. The way his breathing had turned ragged.

He tried to get the magic under control. He begged it to obey him just this once, but the grains pulsed with his heartbeat. He tried and failed to take a steading breath. "I just wanted to talk." They could still try, right? Liam might give him a chance to—"I have nothing to say to you." The bite behind the words hit harder than a punch to the gut.

"Please," Rion pleaded. "Just let me explain."

The same female spoke up again. "Explain? You killed the High

Lord!" Her voice shrieked and she visibly shook.

Liam didn't react to her outburst. "Did you know when we were kids?" he asked. "Did you hide it?"

"No. I didn't know until—" He trailed off, knowing confirming the events of that wretched night wouldn't do him any favors. "I didn't know."

Liam's lips parted as if he wanted to say more, but a new scent drifted across the field. Rion whipped his head around to find three males stalking toward them, their eyes fixated on Rion's unobscured face.

Shit. Had they caught his scent? Recognized him? They had to be from the palace then. Fear snaked down Rion's spine as he eyed their drawn weapons. Did Alec know he was here?

Rion backed away. He shouldn't have come. He shouldn't be trying to talk to his former friend, let alone be discovered by the palace guard. How many times had Caol scolded him for not paying attention?

His heart hammered in his chest. Three. He could handle three, right? Images of Caol putting him on his ass resurfaced and doubt pooled in his gut. Rion only had a small knife in his boot. He hadn't thought to bring weapons into Nàdair. An oversight he was thoroughly regretting.

Always be prepared, Saoirse had once told him. Well, he certainly wasn't prepared for this.

The tension fell from Liam's shoulders and another sharp sting of pain cut through Rion's chest. Liam wouldn't help him. None of the seven would. In fact, they looked ready to join the warriors in bringing him down. If they did that—Rion's breath came faster as panic rushed through him. His magic rose higher without his prompting and spun around his body as if readying to shield him from the oncoming attack.

Should he run? He might be faster, but one glance at the trees told Rion he'd be headed right toward a trap. The warriors would use the trees and overgrowth to their advantage. He wasn't sure he could handle running, deflecting their magic, and ensuring his own didn't kill the seven. He didn't care about the three; if they chose to attack, they had it coming to them.

The warriors closed in with vines crawling across their bodies.

No choice. He had to go. It was either that or face all ten of them at once. Rion stepped toward the tree line, but right before he took off, the male warriors lunged straight for the seven.

It took him too long to process their actions, the reason, the surprise, and chaos. In seconds, one of the females' severed heads hit the ground with a sickening thud.

Two in their group screamed. Another vomited. Liam and two others tore their magic from the earth and stepped closer to their comrades.

The males didn't stop. A blade whined as it was unsheathed and Rion watched in horror as it cut through the young male who'd just vomited. With tears in his eyes, the male extended his arm, trying to shield himself only for his severed limb to go sailing through the air. A swift flick of the wrist and a blade was in the young male's throat.

The male sank to his knees, eyes wide and pleading.

Two Fae who were hardly more than younglings dead in an instant.

They started for Liam next and Rion moved, his magic with him. Reason and doubt left him. If he didn't have a blade, then he'd just have to take one.

Rion charged one of the male assailants, fury spurring him forward. Rion shot his magic out, hoping to catch one in the chest and be done with him, but a thick tree trunk erupted from the ground. Bark exploded on impact and Rion ducked around the small branches reaching out, all aiming for vital points along his body.

Rion's magic slammed into the tree again, shattering it, and he closed in on the male fast. His fingers grazed the hilt of a blade along the male's belt, but the male spun away too quickly for Rion to grab it.

Sharp pain shot through his upper arm and he cursed under his breath. The male angled his weapon and struck out again, but Rion dove away, his eyes trying and failing to track the male's quick movements.

A vine wrapped around Rion's left wrist, wrenching him down so hard his head collided with the earth. Stars blinded him and he barely had enough time to roll away from the male's angled blade.

Rion let his magic rip from the ground, severing the tightly coiled vine from around his wrist before shoving everything toward the warrior in blind fury. The male tried to duck, but Rion summoned the earth from beneath the male's feet. The warrior tottered and before he could regain his balance, Rion crushed his body.

He heard the bones grind, felt the male's chest cave in.

Less than a second passed before the next male was upon him, snarling and seething with anger.

Rion tried to jump away, but the male threw a blade aimed right at Rion's thigh. Sand deflected it, but the shift in attention cost him.

A knife plunged straight into the top of Rion's shoulder and the force of the impact sent Rion back to his knees. The male's hand shot out for his throat, but Rion grabbed his wrist only to feel the sting of the male's fangs in his skin.

The male head-butted him, then did it again and again. Anger flared through Rion's body, pulsing with his magic. He bucked the male off, then rolled to his knees. Rion snapped his arms up, dragging his magic with him, and wrapped a tendril of particles around the male's throat before crushing his windpipe.

The male's body fell limp, and Rion let his arms fall, sucking down breath after breath. Specks raced across his vision, but another cry had Rion spinning to find one of the females kneeling in the dirt, her gaze vacant as she stared at two bodies. Liam was screaming her name, begging her to move.

It hit Rion then just how young they were. How much more training he'd received due to Caol's and Saoirse's insistence. Because it would be a necessary component to ensure his survival.

But not theirs. Rion stared at the bodies, their blood mixing with the dirt. Here, in the city of Nàdair, citizens were supposed to live in peace. The redwoods created an impenetrable defense. The Fae weren't supposed to *need* to fight for their lives.

And yet here they were. And Rion had the power and training to defend them. He was the only one who could.

Liam deflected a direct blow, but he was too slow to react to the knife heading straight for his gut. With a surge of adrenaline, Rion's magic propelled him forward.

Not Liam. He couldn't lose him, even if the young male wanted nothing more to do with him.

Liam howled in pain when the blade pierced his flesh, but it was dwarfed by the roar that escaped Rion. Sand shot out and locked the male's arm in place, stopping all movement before he could do irreparable damage. Rion crushed the limb with ease, then sent the male flying.

He didn't hesitate this time. He was on the male in less than a second, ready to deliver the finishing blow—the warrior pivoted on the ball of his foot and slashed at Rion's stomach with a hidden blade.

It sliced through the fabric of his shirt and Rion cursed at the red line that traveled up his torso. He ignored the pain. Ignored the desire for self-preservation. The male had left himself wide open. He knew it too, judging from the wide look of panic on his face. Rion gripped the hilt of his knife then plunged the blade straight into the assailant's throat. He twisted then shoved the male back.

He didn't rise again.

Blood pounded in Rion's ears as he struggled to catch his breath. It had only been a few minutes, yet it had felt like a lifetime. The events played out, seeming to move in slow motion. The dead Fae. The warriors. Their movements.

A wet cough had Rion spinning.

It wasn't Liam, thank the gods. Another male lay on the ground with a blade protruding from his chest. Rion grimaced. It was too close to the heart and that heart was slowing. Fluttering.

Thick tears rolled down Liam's face. Liam reached for the protruding weapon.

"Don't pull it out," Rion warned. Liam's sharp gaze snapped up and he snarled. Rion softened his voice. "He'll bleed out if you do."

Liam's face paled and his worried gaze returned to the knife. Liam rested a gentle hand on the young male's chest.

"Go get help," Rion instructed one of the others. "He needs—"

"You did this." Liam's voice. Trembling, yet cold and murderous. The heartbeat slowed.

"You need—"

"You did this," Liam roared then lunged to his feet. Two others grabbed him, wrapping their arms around their friend to hold him back. "If you'd never shown up," Liam's voice cracked. "If you'd just stayed away—" A sob, then Liam collapsed to his knees. The two didn't release his arms.

Rion's heart pounded. Ached.

"Get out of here," Liam seethed. Rion opened his mouth to speak, to defend himself, but his friend looked up and Rion saw undiluted rage reflected in his tear-filled eyes. "And don't ever come back."

He couldn't breathe, couldn't breathe, couldn't breathe. Rion stepped back, feeling as if he were the one with a knife in his chest. He surveyed the broken field, the bodies, the dying male, the cuts and bruises on those still alive.

He stepped again.

He'd done this. If he'd never come, they might all still be alive. If he'd just listened to Caol—pain overwhelmed him all at once. His shoulder burned, his torso with it. The cut across his arm pulsed, but those wounds were superficial. They'd heal over time.

His bleeding heart was another matter.

Rion met Liam's gaze one final time and bowed his head. "I'm sorry." It was barely more than a whisper, then Rion ran as fast as his legs would carry him. Tears of anger and grief and frustration slid down his face. Rion swiped them away, fighting to keep his vision clear.

He failed.

He couldn't return to Caol's, not with the risk that someone might pursue him. But he needed medical supplies.

Rion diverted down a winding path where he knew a hollow sycamore tree waited with an emergency pack stuffed inside its hollow trunk. Saoirse had done that for him. She'd littered the entire mountainside in supplies should they ever find themselves on the run.

He was running now, he just wasn't sure where to.

Dozens of questions flew through Rion's mind as he separated himself from Caol's land. Hell, Caol might not even want him back after this. Rion had disobeyed him and Fae had died.

What had he done in another life to warrant this kind of punishment? What kind of horrible male had he been? And why did innocents have to be dragged into the middle of it all?

CHAPTER FIVE

Rion didn't sleep, but the growing darkness didn't scare him anymore. He'd encountered enough real monsters that whatever shadows his mind tried to conjure paled in comparison.

He shivered from the brisk spring air but didn't dare risk a fire. He knew search parties were looking for him. The gods only knew how Alec was reacting to the whole situation.

Thankfully, his magic had finally settled enough that he didn't leave a trail. In his panic, it had stripped the bark from numerous trees and carved a clear path right to him. At least it had led his pursuers away from Caol.

Once he'd wrestled his emotions into submission, Rion had veered north. It had been hours and the sun had just begun cresting the tree tops.

Now, he sat at the edge of a river, attempting to force a thin piece of thread through the eye of a needle with shaking hands. His arm had gone numb and was so stiff he could barely move it. Rion grimaced when blood trickled from the wound.

Giving up, he reached inside the medicine bag and withdrew a salve to numb the tender skin. A half hour passed as he waited for it to kick in. Birds chirped in the trees overhead and the river moved at a steady pace, calming the still riled parts of his soul.

With a sigh, Rion glanced at the open wound again, grit his teeth, then pushed the needle through. He hissed when it looped through his skin and had to pause. So much for the numbing agent. He'd learned to stitch years ago, but he'd never had to patch a wound this severe. Not himself anyway.

Rion tied the thread off using his teeth, then inserted the needle again. His arm twitched and pain flared through his shoulder anew. Rion cursed, slammed his back against the nearest tree trunk, and took to observing the morning sky. Angry tears fought for escape, but Rion bit them back.

He'd killed three Fae warriors from Brónach, but that wasn't what bothered him. It was the others who'd died for absolutely no reason at all. It was the unprovoked anger and fear directed his way from a childhood friend. It was the insanity of the entire situation.

What the hell had those males wanted? They couldn't have been part of the royal guard. If they were, Liam and his friends never would have been targeted.

His body trembled and the magic Rion so desperately wanted to control sprang to life again. He glanced at it. Maybe the ancient texts were right after all. Maybe he *was* cursed. Maybe his existence drove Fae to the brink of insanity just from the mere sight of him. He didn't bother trying to rationalize Saoirse or Caol.

Rion looked at the wound on his arm again, then continued the agonizing task of closing it. He'd have to stitch the cut across his other arm, too. He sighed and worked on his body as the sun made its way across the brightening sky.

CHAPTER SIX

ion moved on, never sleeping in the same place twice, but keeping close to the river.

Three days passed in a blur as he tried and failed to come up with a plan.

Rion had just pulled the bandage away from his shoulder when a branch cracked nearby.

He whirled, nostrils flaring and magic answering his call. He'd been careful to ensure he covered his tracks, but the familiar sight of blonde hair had his shoulders and magic relaxing.

"I've been looking for you for days." Saoirse's breath was ragged and when her gaze dropped to his shoulder, she grimaced.

Rion bent and filled a small pot with water before returning to his pitiful fire. "It's not as bad as it looks." Lie and truth. The skin around the wound was swollen and tender and moving hurt like hell, but it wouldn't do any permanent damage. Maybe a scar at most.

Saoirse gestured for him to sit and opened her bag, rummaging through the contents for what Rion presumed was her medical kit.

"Here." She tossed him an apple and Rion caught it with his good hand. He eyed the tender flesh of the fruit before sinking his teeth into it.

She settled on the ground at his side and folded her legs to examine his shoulder. His sister cleaned it with a delicate hand, then opened a tin and spread a greenish salve over the cut before binding it with a clean bandage.

"Alec sent out multiple teams to hunt you down," she said. "I couldn't stop him."

"I never expected you to."

Silence.

"What happened?"

Rion loosed a breath and ran a hand through his hair. "Honestly? I don't know." Images came flashing back, but he still couldn't make sense of them.

"Try," she urged. Her tone wasn't accusatory. She was probably the only person on the continent willing to let him explain himself.

"Caol told me not to go."

"Naturally." She sat back. "So why did you?"

"Because I'm tired of being locked up in that damn cabin," he bit out.

"So you went to the festival?"

Rion nodded. "I took my cloak and stayed hidden. I was leaving when I saw a group of Fae playing in the field." Rion looked down at his hands and the bruises across knuckles. "Liam was there."

Saoirse's body stiffened. She rolled the dirty bandages up and placed them in her bag. "What did he say?"

Rion shook his head, his heart aching all over again. "Nothing worth repeating. I was about to leave when three warriors showed up. I thought they were part of the city guard. That maybe they'd spotted me in the city. I knew I needed to get out of there, but—" He paused and clenched his jaw.

"But what?"

"They killed them. Just like that." He looked at her. "They killed them, Saoirse, no warning. Why would they do that?"

Her eyes searched his. "I don't know." She fiddled with the strap of her bag. "We couldn't identify the bodies. They weren't from Nàdair."

Rion sat straighter. "Where are they from then?

Saoirse shrugged. "Could be any one of the major cities."

"But why attack *them*? What was the point?"

"I wish I knew."

More silence. Rion relished the warmth from the fire after days without one. "Did . . . did the other male make it?" He wasn't sure he wanted to know. If he hadn't . . .

"He was still in critical care when I left. The healers are doing everything they can." She'd probably left two days ago. Rion looked at his hands. He didn't want to imagine Liam pacing outside the healing quarters. Liam's mother was probably with him, trying to comfort her son after the ordeal.

Rion dropped his head into his hands, rubbing his eyes. "It was stupid to go." He could feel Saoirse's gaze on him. "I just thought I could, I don't know, talk to him. I thought maybe he of all people would hear me out but—" Emotion swelled in Rion's throat, cutting him off.

Saoirse stared at the river. "He won't talk about it. He's been questioned by multiple officials and refuses to say a word." Rion didn't respond. "The others claim you were with the three males. They said you were about to strike out with your magic."

"And I'm sure everyone believes them."

"The whole lot of them are traumatized. We're not even sure *they* know what happened."

"Yet Alec still has teams hunting me."

"To bring you in, not kill you. I wouldn't have stood for that."

"And I suppose he'll just let me return to my old room and live a nice cozy life in the palace."

"If that were the case, I'd escort you back myself." She kicked a rock near her shoe. "He's consulting the council, but I think he plans to lock you up until they decide what should be done."

"I'm assuming you had an opinion on the matter."

She shrugged. "I told him if that was the case, then no one would find you. He took it for the threat it was." Saoirse met his gaze. "You should know by now that I wouldn't turn you in."

"I know. I just . . . don't risk yourself for me. We've kept things a secret this long for a reason."

"I never planned to keep you in hiding forever, you know that."

"Do you have a plan for when Caol finally kicks me out?"

Her heart jolted. "Did he mention something?"

"No, but given the circumstances—"

Her shoulders relaxed. "I won't lie, he's furious and you'll probably be cleaning every square inch of the cabin with the smallest brush imaginable when you get back, but he's not going to kick you out." Rion wasn't so sure.

"He's thankful you didn't come back right away. Alec's patrols searched there first, thanks in part to how often I visit." Rion's eyes widened. If they found his scent . . . "Don't worry, as soon as word reached Caol, he raced back and erased any evidence of you. His reputation with our father helped, too. Most still admire him from his service in the previous war."

"Maybe I shouldn't go back at all."

Saoirse didn't reply at first. "Where would you go?"

Rion shrugged. "It's kind of nice out here."

"You won't think that when winter hits and your toes freeze off."

He laughed, the sound bitter. "You mentioned the northern continent once."

Silence. "I'd never see you again." Rion didn't reply. She wouldn't, not for a long while, at least. The trip itself would take him weeks and he'd be forced to live in secrecy all over again.

"Let's go to the lake house for a while, at least until things blow over."

"Won't Alec look for us there?"

Saoirse went quiet. "No. I've been given a leave."

Rion studied the way her shoulders slumped and the way she gripped her bag a little tighter. "What happened?"

"I had a mission that didn't go well."

"You found a lead." Their mother.

"It doesn't matter."

"Why didn't you tell me? I could have gone with you."

"Because it was sensitive and I couldn't risk—" Couldn't risk anyone recognizing him or seeing his magic. Saoirse had taken him on a high-risk mission once before and it had almost gotten him killed. "It doesn't matter," she repeated. "It was just another dead end."

She'd never stopped looking. Not once. Rion looked back at the river and watched a stick float down, carried by the rapid current. It spun in circles, reaching for a bank it would never find.

"Okay," Saoirse glanced up. "Let's visit the lake house and go from there."

CHAPTER SEVEN

They spent two weeks reliving their childhood memories. Neither stepped foot inside their parents' room, though Rion stared longingly at the door every morning, imagining his mother exiting with a smile on her face.

The pair swam in the lake, made breakfast every morning, and basked in the warm afternoon sun. It was the life he longed for and the life he could never have.

Reality forced Rion to shoulder his pack. Saoirse had left before him, claiming she needed to return to the palace. He, in turn, took his time, unwilling to leave the little sanctuary where his life had been nearly perfect.

He'd had everything a child could ever want.

Now—Rion didn't allow himself to finish that thought.

Three days later and Rion stood before Caol's cabin. He could hear the male moving around inside and knew full well that Caol had sensed his presence a quarter mile off.

Rion heard a piece of silverware clank against a plate followed by the sound of wood scraping across the floor. The boards creaked. Rion swallowed hard. He didn't realize how nervous he'd be. He'd lived with Caol for six years and the male was like a father to him, no matter how much Caol denied it.

The door swung open on silent hinges. Caol crossed his arms, leaned against the doorframe, and stared him down. "You didn't run."

"Do I have a reason to?"

"You tell me."

Tension filled Rion's body. "I didn't do anything wrong." Aside from being somewhere he shouldn't have been.

"That's debatable." Rion clenched his fists then relaxed again. His magic stirred around his feet; it didn't go unnoticed.

Caol's gaze lifted and Rion tried not to step back as the male surveyed him. "Where have you been?"

"Saoirse sent a letter."

Caol's jaw ticked and he pinned Rion with a chilling stare. "A letter," he scoffed. "I'll ask again. *Where* have you been?"

Realization dawned on him. Caol wanted to see if Saoirse had lied. "We were at the lake house." Caol raised a brow. "Just myself and Saoirse. She had a leave after her last mission."

Caol scented the air. "Why did you come back?"

"I—" Saoirse had been certain Caol wouldn't kick him out, but . . . maybe she'd been wrong. Maybe he didn't have a home anymore. "Would you prefer it if I left?" He wasn't prepared for the pain that radiated through his chest. A far deeper one than the wound left by Liam.

"Three Fae barely more than younglings are dead. Three unidentified warriors from Brónach are dead. And those who lived claim you're at fault." The muscles in his forearm flexed. "And you *leave*," he seethed, "while the rest of us cleaned up your mess."

Three younglings, not two. "The male didn't make it." The words were barely more than a whisper.

Caol remained still, showing no signs of emotion. "He didn't. The blade was too close to his heart. There was nothing to be done."

Rion stepped back and slumped against the nearest tree. Liam would never forgive him now. Rion had seen the way he'd looked at the young male. The love and pleading in his eyes.

Rion's voice softened. "Did you ever find out who they were?"

"No. Their bodies are still being identified."

Rion shook his head. "They just . . . attacked us."

"Unprovoked?"

Rion didn't miss the accusation. "Yes, unprovoked. All of them would probably have died if I hadn't intervened."

"If you'd done as you were told and never left the grounds, they might all still be alive." The familiar ache of blame and guilt washed through him. Caol tapped his boot. "The younglings have an interesting spin to the story. They claim you were allied with the three males. Care to explain?"

Rion shrugged, his heart aching, bleeding all over again. "I suppose for the same reason they label me an abomination."

Caol pinched the bridge of his nose. "You realize you could have blown our cover? That I could be in a dungeon right now trying to explain why I've harbored you for the past six years? Did you bother to stop and think about any of that?" He had, but Rion had also been confident in his ability to stay hidden. Caol didn't wait for a response. "This is why I tell you to stay up here."

Rion threw his bag to the ground, magic swelling in an angry frenzy. "Maybe I'm sick of being trapped here! Maybe I'm tired of hiding from the world when I haven't done anything wrong!"

Caol pushed off the wall, his own voice raising. "Because of you, your father's entire elite force is dead."

"I didn't kill my father."

"You might as well have." Caol's words struck true. There it was, after all these years. Caol didn't blame Saoirse for the events of that night. He blamed Rion.

If not for the magic, then his father, the High Lord, wouldn't have reacted the way he had. And Saoirse wouldn't have been put a position to make a life-altering decision.

Caol blew out a frustrated breath and ran a hand through his hair. "I shouldn't have said that."

Rion didn't respond. He couldn't because Caol was right. Caol and his father had been close friends. They'd grown up together and were allies during the battles of their time. Caol had been friends with his father's guards, too.

And Rion had killed them when he was only eight years old. A fluke probably due to surprise but still, Rion was responsible for more than one of Caol's loved ones' demise.

Thunder rolled overhead and Rion glanced toward the pack he'd tossed to the ground. He should go. Release Caol from the responsibility put on him by his sister. Let the male return to a peaceful life.

A drop of rain fell from the gray sky and landed beside Rion's leather boot. Another landed just a few feet ahead, heavy and with the promise of early spring's chill.

"Come inside." A half-hearted command.

Rion stepped back. He could stay at the lake house for a little while, maybe even a year if he were careful. He could formulate a plan with Saoirse. They'd come up with something.

But he'd be isolated again.

Alone again.

The wind picked up and Rion shivered against the brisk chill. He reached down for his pack.

"Whatever you're thinking, boy, stop thinking it."

"You don't want me here."

"Maybe so." The words stung. "But you don't have anywhere else to go and your sister will string me up alive if you disappear again." Rion's jaw worked. "So you're going to come inside and we're both going to cool off while we eat a warm meal." Caol opened the door behind him a bit wider.

The drops continued, pebbling the dry earth at Rion's feet. "Why did you agree to take me in?"

Caol loosed a long sigh. "Because your sister asked me to. And because you were a youngling with nowhere to go. Do you really think I'd just turn my back on a child?"

A shrug. "My father tried to kill one."

"So did I once."

Rion's gaze slowly lifted and Caol looked away. The male never looked away. He'd never shown shame for any of his actions. Even those during the war.

"I had a nephew that—well, he was like you. It was centuries ago, but—" his jaw worked. "The memory of that day still haunts my nightmares."

"You killed him."

It wasn't a question but Caol shook his head. "A guard did, I just . . . didn't do anything to stop it. That night . . . it changed everyone involved." Is that why he chose to live in isolation? Was Caol punishing himself?

"His parents, my sister, are long gone from this world. As are my other nieces and nephews. The war wasn't kind to our family."

Silence fell over the space again. The rain picked up. "Now, will you please come inside so we don't have to sit out here and let the rain add to our misery?"

Rion debated again with another long look through the trees. He should go, despite Caol's confession. He should turn away and never look back.

But Rion walked down that familiar stone path and followed his teacher inside.

The male made him a plate without asking and set it on the table. Rion hung his pack and cloak up, shoved out of his boots, then settled across from Caol in his usual seat.

Silence was a heavy blanket over the space. Suffocating, really.

They ate without speaking. Rion showered and changed into clean clothes, then curled up on his usual cot in the corner.

Caol sat before the fireplace, staring at the embers as if they contained the answer to a centuries-old question. He'd seen a youngling killed before his eyes and he'd done nothing to stop it.

Rion raised his hand and glanced at his palm. The movement drew Caol's gaze a moment.

He never thought he'd kill or be part of anyone's war. His mother had always shielded him from the harsh things in life. But she couldn't shield him now. His reality had turned into a battle. One that was just beginning. One he'd likely never escape.

Rion rolled over, turning his back to Caol and closed his eyes. He could feel the male's gaze. Caol had possessed a strange look on his face throughout the night that made Rion wonder if he'd be better off outside.

He took another breath and set his fears aside. Caol had made a promise to Saoirse, and breaking that promise would mean tainting his honor as a Fae male. He wouldn't throw away decades of trust. Not after he'd put in so much time.

Rion hoped.

CHAPTER EIGHT

hings with Caol didn't return to normal and after a month, the lack of normalcy was . . . grating.

Caol refused to train him. He always offered an excuse and was gone more often than Rion was accustomed. When Rion had questioned him on the matter, Caol had simply said he was dealing with a few personal matters. Rion had asked Saoirse about it, but she didn't know anything about Caol's personal life. Caol seemed to be avoiding her as well.

Saoirse was gone more often, too. She and the council were busy dealing with rogue factions that had risen up against their brother. According to the elders, it was normal to challenge a new High Lord's authority. To test him, whatever that meant.

Rion never left the mountain side. He cleaned, tended to the gardens, and trained almost every hour of the day.

It wasn't enough.

His mind was restless, and living alone was far more difficult than Rion had previously imagined. Saoirse brought him stacks of books once a week. He flew through them, learning an assortment of new things from building to chiseling characters from wood, an activity that quickly grew into a hobby.

Rion sighed and let his hands fall lax. Maybe this was part of his punishment from Caol. That and cleaning the cabin from top to bottom. Perhaps this was Caol's way of teaching him exactly what complete isolation would feel like.

Saoirse visited Liam for questioning a few more times, but the male never talked, whether from fear or some other motivation, none knew.

Using a knife, Rion chipped another small piece off the block of wood. He'd already fashioned the base of what he hoped would be a small body. The Fairy Folk. Caol would appreciate their likeness in his garden. Or maybe Rion would give it to the little creatures just to see how they'd react. A smile crept to his face at the thought.

He was sitting beneath one of the apple trees, listening to the bees buzzing between the rotted bits of fruit when Caol appeared. Rion lifted his gaze, then shot to his feet at the scent of Caol's magic. The male hadn't even bothered to go inside first. Had something happened? His mind immediately went to Saoirse. Caol drew his sword and Rion's throat went dry as he stepped back.

"You're unarmed?" Rion nodded slowly. Caol *tsked*. "Get your weapons and be quick about it."

Rion's heart jolted, but he didn't argue. The two hadn't had a sparring session since his return, but Caol seemed . . . different today. Agitated. Maybe something had happened in Nàdair.

He returned quickly and followed Caol deeper into the forest.

They never sparred next to the male's home, just in case their magic got out of hand. Rion would hate to have to rebuild the entire cabin from the ground up.

Caol stopped then spun. Rion stepped back again. Something in his face was . . . off. His heart beat too fast and Rion swore the male's eyes were rimmed with red. Surely he couldn't have been crying. Rion scented the air, searching for any signs of alcohol. The male rarely indulged. Perhaps he just hadn't slept well.

"Do you want to talk about it?" Rion hedged, feeling more than a little awkward at prying.

"No." Caol's face turned to stone then. Indifferent. He dropped into a stance and Rion mirrored the movement. "We haven't spared in a while. Show me you haven't gotten lazy."

Rion rolled his neck and grinned. He could still smell Caol's magic. If he used it, then Rion would do the same.

Caol moved. He was as fast as lightning and struck harder than a battering ram. Rion gritted his teeth and barely held his ground. All right then, no holding back.

He pivoted, but Caol was there to thwart the movement, knocking Rion off balance. Rion grunted and spun away before repositioning himself. Caol allowed it, then the two lunged for one another again.

Fast. Caol was so fast. Faster than the males Rion had killed a month ago. More skilled too, or maybe the adrenaline in the moment had just helped him focus. Instinct had kicked in and those very instincts were usually the thing that kept Fae alive on the battlefield.

He could do it again, let his instincts take over and finally beat the male that had taught him everything. Maybe then Caol would show some pride—a blade flashed and Rion faltered. He barely had time to register it as the knife's tip sliced across his right cheek.

Rion scrambled back and touched the stinging wound only for it to come away bloody. His eyes widened.

Never once in all their training sessions had Caol drawn blood. Not deliberately. Not like this.

Rion looked up at him. The male wasn't even sorry for it. "What's wrong?" Caol taunted. "I thought you were ready to be out in the real world?"

It clicked then. Rion had been right. He *was* being punished and this was an extension of that punishment. An extreme extension. Caol intended to show Rion exactly what he'd be up against if he tried to leave again. Caol was probably getting his anger out, too. Anger for the younglings who'd died and anger for whatever personal matters he'd faced recently.

This wasn't a sparring match. It was a test.

Rion swallowed and summoned his own magic, letting it rise up and around his body. He watched Caol's magic crawl from beneath the forest's underbrush, snaking across the ground as if alive.

Alive and furious.

Vines, small plants, bushes, and trees all answered Caol's call.

Uncertainty flooded Rion's body and warning bells kept echoing in his head. Something wasn't right. Caol was too angry. Too . . . something. They shouldn't be sparing. Saoirse should be here to monitor at the very least, just to ensure the male didn't push things too far.

But how many times had Rion resented them for treating him like a child? Isn't this what he'd been asking for? The chance to be treated like an adult? Like an equal?

Rion had witnessed the brutality of Saoirse and Alec's sparing sessions beneath their father's watchful gaze. They'd often left the ring with bruises, scrapes, and the occasional broken bone.

This was Brónach. They weren't a weak nation and it was time for Rion to stop acting like a youngling and begin the transition of becoming a full-fledged warrior.

"Finished day dreaming?" Caol asked, impatience in his tone.

Rion drew in a steadying breath and calmed the pulse in his veins. He let the magic flow through him like the current of a river. Strong and unyielding.

Rion locked eyes with Caol, then lunged.

The two males' weapons sang through the trees as metal bit against metal. Sand and dirt and greenery collided and exploded on impact, decorating the forest in bits of rock and debris.

Caol moved impossibly faster. Rion tried to pivot around another strike but found himself tumbling to the ground instead.

Caol didn't hesitate. Vines shot out of the soft earth and forced Rion to roll away as they struck the ground with lethal force.

He looked to his teacher, willing the male to afford him a moment of reprieve, but Caol struck out at him again.

And again.

And again.

Rion kept rolling out of the magic's path and had barely stumbled back to his feet when sharp pain pierced through his lower back. Rion gasped from the sudden heat and the impact propelled him forward. He grimaced and reached for his lower abdomen only to find four thin vines protruding from his flesh. The bloody leaves unfurled and reached for the high noon sun above.

Rion looked to Caol for . . . for . . .

Anguish covered the male's face. "I'm sorry." Rion's head swam. "It's for the best. I—I'll make sure your sister knows. I won't bury you to be forgotten."

Rion stumbled then fell to his knees, the jarring of the four vines eliciting another round of blinding pain.

His body trembled, then the vines withdrew and blood rushed from the wounds, soaking his tunic. He clenched his fists and ground his teeth so hard Rion was sure they'd crack. "You promised," he gasped.

"I know," Caol replied. "I'm sorry."

More vines rose, ready to finish what Caol had started.

"You're sorry," Rion mocked then snapped his head up to meet Caol's forlorn expression. "You're—" Rion gasped when another shock of pain rolled through his system.

Caol approached slowly. "I won't drag this out." Rion must have imagined the break in his voice. "I'll make it quick so you don't have to suffer. Is there anything you want me to tell Saoirse?"

Rion scoffed. Caol wanted him to say his final words? He wanted—the male kneeled at Rion's side. A hand reached for his shoulder.

Then Rion exploded.

No. His magic exploded.

He hadn't even realized he'd raised his hand to swat Caol's away before the male was on the ground across from him with a dozen jagged holes punched straight through his torso.

He only moved once before falling still. Red soaked through his cream-colored tunic. The vines fell limp.

No.

Another wave of blinding pain. Another strike to his already battered heart.

His mother.

His father.

Liam. And now . . . now . . . Rion doubled over and roared into the earth. It cracked beneath him and fissures spider-webbed their way across the ground, splitting the very rocks beneath his crumpled body.

His voice didn't stop. Couldn't. Not as his heart raced and bled out right there over the damp mossy ground. He'd told himself he didn't care. That Caol was just another male, but . . . but . . . gods, *why, why, why?*

Rion slammed his fist into the ground and it caved in from the force of the impact. Or maybe that was his cursed magic. He didn't care. Not as he did it over and over again, letting the physical pain radiate up his arm.

He didn't care. He didn't care. He didn't care.

Hot tears rolled down his face. Small rivers that would never cease.

Rion cursed the warm sun overhead, damning it for its brightness when color had faded from his life. He cursed the ground where Caol's vines lay unmoving. He cursed the particles rising up, circling as if they might protect him from the pain lancing through his heart.

Nothing could help him now.

Not with this.

His chest rose and fell and sobs tore through him until Rion's body shivered from the cold.

Not the cold, a rational part of him said. Something else. Something dangerous.

Reluctantly, Rion lifted his head from the earth and touched a hand to his abdomen.

It came away bloody. Soaked. A spike of adrenaline raced through his veins. *Too much. There was too much.* Rion forced himself to stand, then stumbled back until his body collided hard with the rough bark of a tree. He sucked in breath after breath, willing the dizziness to pass.

He'd waited too long. Rion clenched his teeth and glanced down at his abdomen again before looking away. Caol had struck true, but Rion had no way of knowing if the wounds were fatal.

He needed to get back to the cabin. Caol had supplies there, but . . . Rion doubled over again, the pain almost forcing him back to his knees.

No. It wouldn't be enough. He needed—gods, was he actually going to die?

Rion glanced down the path that led to Nàdair.

Saoirse would help him, but was she even at the palace or was she off on another mission? Could he make the journey?

Rion tried to breathe through the pain. It would be so much easier to succumb to it. To tilt his head back and enjoy the warm sun one last time before darkness pulled him under.

But—Rion clenched his jaw. He had to try. For Saoirse, he had to try.

Rion pushed off from the solid maple, still bracing with one hand for balance. The dizziness wasn't fading. What were his chances?

With gritted teeth, Rion stepped, then stepped again. One foot at a time.

His pace was slow as he made his way down the trail, leaving the male who'd promised to protect him behind to be swallowed by the forest.

Caol. Caol had tried to kill him. Might have succeeded.

Maybe he'd personally known one of the younglings that had died. Maybe he'd been consoling the family all this time and that's why he'd returned angry. Caol blamed him, just like he blamed Rion for the High Lord's death.

Maybe he really was a curse.

He wished he'd been born normal. He wished he had friends. That his mother was still around to give him advice. He wished he'd never gotten magic at all.

As a child, he'd often feared being left magicless. He'd thought it the worst fate imaginable.

He couldn't have been more wrong.

Rion stumbled and his knees barked when they hit the ground. Blood trickled down his thighs now. He was going to die right here in this forest and be forgotten by the world. Maybe Saoirse would find his rotted corpse, if the animals left anything behind. Fear jolted through him. Or maybe she'd only find a trace of his scent and his sister would be left searching for another member of their family.

Rion balled his fists. He couldn't let that happen. Even if it took his last breath to get there, Rion would make it to the edge of Nàdair. For Saoirse.

He fought to rise. Fought against the pain and numbness settling over his body. Time warped around him. Speeding and slowing all at once. The forest faded in and out. Shadows crept through the trees.

Rion slipped through the hole in the giant redwoods. Night had fallen, or maybe he just couldn't see anymore.

He found the marble steps of the palace. Or what looked like steps? Was this home or just another residence? An illusion? He trudged down white halls. The pain was receding. Not a good sign, but a pleasant one. His mind was clearing, too. Saoirse. He just needed to find Saoirse.

Faint voices echoed when he rounded another corner, his feet carrying him to places unknown. Then a figure emerged. And maybe it was just wishful thinking, but he could have sworn their mother's eyes greeted him.

Rion tried to smile, just so it would be the last thing she saw.

Then he gave in. His body fell.

Darkness caught him in its warm embrace.

Darkness whispered his name, begging him to hold on.

CHAPTER NINE

The shadows stirred again. Rion fluttered his eyes open to stare at a familiar ceiling. He scented the room and recoiled from harsh antiseptics and blood.

The lights were off, thank the gods.

He tilted his head. Sunlight filtered through the drawn curtains on the other side of the room. His room, he realized. He tried to swallow and failed, his throat raw.

His body felt like a husk of its former self but—alive. He was alive.

Rion turned his head again and found Saoirse sleeping in the armchair next to his bed. Her feet were propped on the mattress and her head hung at an awkward angle. Bandages were piled off to one side of the chair. A bowl of clean water sat on the desk with a plate of uneaten food beside it.

Moving slowly, Rion lifted the edge of the sheet to examine his stomach. Someone had wrapped him in a bandage and judging from the stinging pain, they'd stitched him, too. Emotion swelled through him. He'd made it.

Saoirse's eyes fluttered open and immediately shot to him. She froze. The siblings stared at one another for a long moment, then Saoirse swung her legs down and reached for the water pitcher on the end table.

Ice still floated on the surface, telling Rion the slaves were likely tending to her needs.

She withdrew a small vial from her pocket and put a few drops in the glass before carefully sitting at his side.

Rion fought to sit up and she set the cup aside to assist before handing it back to him. Rion's hands shook and Saoirse helped to steady the glass as he lifted it to his lips. He downed every drop, not bothering to ask what she'd put inside. It wasn't like his sister would poison him.

Saoirse set the glass aside but didn't stand. Her eyes were blood-shot and heavy bags hung beneath them. She clasped and unclasped her hands. "How are you feeling?"

"Like hell." His voice croaked and he winced.

Saoirse looked him over. "I need to change your bandages again, but we can wait until after you eat something." Silence lingered like a thick fog. She fiddled with the edge of the sheet, folding and unfolding a small corner. "What happened?" she whispered.

It all came rushing back. Caol. The betrayal. The anger and hurt in the male's gaze. Rion wasn't even sure where to begin. "They found Caol's body," she continued. "Or what was left of it. The wolves got there first."

He wondered if Saoirse had come clean about where he'd been staying. Beyond that, he wondered how she'd convinced Alec to let him in the palace at all. After the situation with Liam, Rion wasn't sure he'd ever see this room again.

"Caol," Rion choked, "I don't think he believed me about the attack."

She chewed her lip. "You mentioned him acting strange, but I never thought—"

"He said he wanted to spar," Rion continued. He felt as if he were reliving the moment all over again. He glanced back down at his abdomen.

"I'm glad you came."

"I didn't think I'd make it."

"Neither did the healers. The slaves came for me when you barged through the front doors. They said you were calling my name."

Fear burst through him and Rion felt himself pale. "I didn't—"

She shook her head. "They knew not to approach. You didn't hurt them, but, gods, Rion, you almost bled out." Saoirse refilled the water cup and offered it to him again. "You're going to stay with me from now on," she said in a serious tone.

"I'm sure Alec will love hearing that."

"Alec and I already had it out. You'll be at my side during every mission."

"Saoirse, you can't—"

"I can," she bit out, but Rion could see the way her jaw trembled. Her eyes shone in the dim light. "I'm not going to let anyone else hurt you."

Rion didn't respond; if he tried to argue, she'd only cry. He glanced toward the window instead.

Home. He was finally home.

His jaw worked as images of Caol flashed through his mind. Images of the male teaching him how to hold a sword. Reminders of a male who'd been patient with a heartbroken child. He'd taught Rion how to control his magic. Caol had taught him about Nàdair's history. He'd walked him through the strategies of elite generals before their time. He'd taught Rion how to survive.

Rion couldn't stop the emotion rising through him. "I killed him."

"You were just defending yourself." Again. It felt like the same repeated excuse. How many times could one defend themselves before the world turned on them? How long before his sister stopped believing his side of the story?

"I wasn't trying to," Rion whispered. "He was—" Rion shook his head, not wanting to relive Caol's final words or the pain in the male's voice. "I was just trying to push him away."

"It's okay," she said, her voice soft.

"I don't have enough control. I need to learn how to keep it in check, no matter what it takes."

Saoirse nodded again. "We'll figure it out."

Rion tried to sit up more but hissed from the pain. "I'm serious.

Whatever you know, whatever books you can find. I need to learn. What if it happens again with someone who isn't trying to hurt me? What if I accidentally hurt you or Alec or—"

"Rion," she took his hand, "calm down, we'll work through it, but you have to heal first. I'll hire private tutors, we'll get the books, but you almost—" Her voice broke and a tear rolled down her face before she could turn away.

Rion settled again, forcing his heart and spinning magic to do the same. Saoirse never reacted to the particles. She never watched it with a wary eye. She was the only one who'd never been afraid.

She'd be the only one he trusted from here on out. Not Alec. Not the slaves or servants and certainly not the Fae nobles and warriors who wandered the palace.

She'd brought him home. Rion looked around his room again. Home.

Heaviness still hung in the air and it would for a while, but eventually, the familiar halls would feel the way they used to. And maybe, just maybe, he'd get to live a halfway normal life.

He knew it would be hard and come with its own trials.

Rion watched his sister wipe her eyes, still hiding her face from his view. "Is there anything to eat?" he asked, trying anything to distract her.

A half-hearted laugh. "I'll go see what I can find."

CHAPTER TEN

$\mathcal{S}$aoirse went above and beyond, hiring every tutor she could find. Some lived in Nàdair, while others traveled from cities in the south. Of course, it was all under the guise that they'd be training her.

Many balked when they walked into the room and found Rion waiting, but Saoirse always assured them their lives weren't in danger. Some had outright refused, while others only agreed after being offered three times their normal salary.

Rion drilled them with questions and implemented their advice with lethal efficiency. Saoirse spared him often and hired others to do the same. She'd had to reprimand a few who made attempts on his life, but Rion never retaliated. If anything, it made the training more valuable.

And just as she'd promised, Rion accompanied Saoirse on every mission. Alec hated it, if his raised voice was anything to go by, but Saoirse always told her elder brother the same thing: Either Rion went or she didn't.

He enjoyed traveling at Saoirse's side. It allowed him to experience the world, but he couldn't help but notice how some started to resent his elder sister. They whispered behind her back and often avoided her altogether.

Saoirse noticed it too, but whenever Rion mentioned it, she'd just shrug it off.

His presence was hurting her, just like Caol always promised it would.

Even Alec was growing tired of his presence in the throne room. His brother glared relentlessly. He was their High Lord. He bent and bowed to no one. Except Saoirse. His only remaining family. The only one that counted, anyway.

Months flew by. While they were out on missions, Rion learned from Saoirse. Learned from others, too, and was often at the receiving end of disdain when he offered better strategies. Their missions were always successful, much to the council's chagrin. They hoped he'd fail, if only to get rid of him once and for all.

When he turned sixteen, Saoirse made him a cinnamon dessert for his birthday. It was a poor attempt, but they both ate the doughy pastry and laughed endlessly at her failure. She'd also purchased him a new set of throwing knives.

Roaming the palace halls was . . . strange. Alec tried to keep Rion locked in his room, but he hadn't listened and no one dared to force him. He found himself fortunate that there'd only been one attempt on his life, aside from the tutors. He'd been in a side garden and his magic had blocked a rogue arrow. He'd never found the one responsible.

Rion knew he should be happy. He was thankful, really. He was back home, no longer in isolation, but he couldn't keep relying on Saoirse to protect him. He was old enough now and it was time for a change.

Rion gathered himself. He'd been preparing his speech for a week. Steadying his magic, Rion pushed open the double doors that led to the throne room. He'd waited until Alec's morning meeting had adjourned.

A tall, lanky male lingered, whispering to Alec in hushed tones. A noble who didn't care for Rion in the slightest. Not that he was alone. The male looked up and his face paled. He bowed to his High Lord, gathered a stack of papers, then rushed from the room.

Alec glared at Rion, then shifted that glare to the magic swirling at Rion's feet. Rion was doing his best not to appear threatening, but he couldn't risk putting his magic away completely. First, because almost everyone in the palace wanted him dead. And second, because he needed a constant flow of it to take the edge off.

One of the teachers Saoirse had hired hypothesized that Rion had too much magic coursing through his body, which led to it seeking an escape beyond his control. They'd advised him to keep it in constant use which, theoretically, would diminish the strain.

To his surprise, it had worked. The teacher had also mentioned that time would help. As he aged, his body's ability to harness magic would grow with him. She was probably the only one who'd given his predicament any honest thought.

"What do you want?" Alec barked. Rion's hands clenched and unclenched. Alec stared him down, impatiently tapping his fingers on the arm of his throne. Short brown hair hung over light brown eyes. Gods, he looked so much like their father it was ridiculous.

Rion paused before the first step, just like he was supposed to, but unlike others, he didn't bow. He couldn't risk exposing himself like that lest Alec decide to damn the consequences of Saoirse's wrath and be rid of him for good.

"I request permission to take a solo mission."

"Denied."

Rion hadn't expected him to accept right off. "I'm sixteen and I've passed every required test." Most didn't take solo missions until their animal shifts appeared, but a shift was just one thing on a long list that the gods denied him. "I'm just as capable as any other warrior, I don't see any reason why—"

"You know damn well *why*," Alec growled.

Rion clenched his fists and his sand responded by jerking in an agitated pattern. One guard drew his sword.

"You can't keep me locked up here."

"You're only here because of Saoirse. You're a walking abomination that should have been killed the moment your cursed magic appeared. If things had happened the way they were supposed to, then Caol and Father would—"

"Alec," Saoirse's harsh voice echoed through the main hall. Alec's angry gaze shifted to her. His jaw flexed. "That's enough." Saoirse turned to him, her eyes full of worry. "I told you I'd discuss it with him."

"I'm done waiting. I'm not a child anymore." He didn't need his sister fighting his battles. He'd already waited two weeks.

"She did," Alec confirmed. "And I'm telling you the same thing I told her: No."

"He's just as capable as any other warrior."

"It's not about his strength," Alec shot back. "What happens when the Fae in distant territories refuse to listen to him? Who's to say he won't just kill them like he seems to do everyone else?"

Rion bit back the bitterness rising in his throat. "I'll follow whatever protocol you set forth."

"And I'm just supposed to believe you?"

"You'd know if I was lying."

"We're having an issue in the south," Saoirse interrupted. "Send him to deal with it."

"That," Alec emphasized, "is a sensitive topic not to be discussed outside our war meetings."

"He's family," she declared. "Whether you want to accept it or not. He's not going to do anything to jeopardize our family name."

"He already did."

Saoirse's lips parted and she quickly glanced at Rion before looking away. Rion didn't balk at Alec's accusation. If Caol had been right about anything, it was in accusing Rion of shouldering the responsibility for their father's death.

"Caol was my teacher, too," Rion said. He could have sworn pain flashed across Alec's face. "He taught me everything from strategy to negotiations. I'm just as well-versed as you and Saoirse." Probably more so, given all the years spent with Caol one on one.

Alec pinched the bridge of his nose and stared at the arm of the throne for a long minute. He heaved a defeated sigh and rubbed his eyes. "You can go," he finally said. "But Saoirse is going with you and I'm sending a team to evaluate. Once their report returns, I'll make a decision."

"But—"

Alec cut her off. "He's young. Regardless of tests, I'm evaluating and I'll make my decision afterward." Saoirse closed her mouth and nodded. "Gather your team and meet me in the war room in two hours. We have a lot to discuss."

The Cursed Fae and a Shattered Heart

CHAPTER ONE

Rain rolled down the side of Rion's face as he peered around the stack of piled wood. The fabric wrapping his knee soaked up the muddy water surrounding him. Thunder rumbled through the sky above and lightning snaked across the darkness.

Two Fae warriors screamed over the downpour, instructing five others who promptly raced across the muddy field in the wrong direction.

He smirked.

They knew he was here. Knew The Demon was in their midst and they weren't taking any chances. He had watched them round up their warriors. Had seen the traps on the ground and redirected their attention on purpose.

It would have been easier to just kill them all. The act of killing didn't bother him anymore, but there were at least a hundred Fae in this camp, and he didn't feel like taking them all on at once. Instead, Rion had dispersed his magic across multiple entry points, forcing the warriors to chase after him.

The rain had been a blessing, even if it made his clothes cling annoyingly to his body.

Another group of ten sprinted past with their weapons drawn. He loosed a breath, studied the darkness, then darted from his hiding place. Rion moved across the earth like a wraith. He wasn't a child anymore, nor a teen. He'd honed his skills to near perfection.

Rion paused beside the window to a small warehouse and peered inside. Empty. Good. They were scrambling.

He couldn't rely on his sense of smell tonight. A disadvantage due to the water pouring down in droves. But in his current situation, he'd take the advantages over the disadvantages.

He carefully cracked the door and slipped inside.

Crates were piled to the ceiling and lined every wall. Rion found a bar leaning against the nearest one and used it to pry the box open. He saw the straw first and carefully moved it aside before grimacing at the contents.

A dozen glass vials full of a greenish liquid sat in two neat rows, each evenly spaced.

Poison. Just as Saoirse expected. It was an ongoing issue they'd been fighting for a few years. A rebel faction was responsible for using the deadly substance on more than one village that had refused to conform to their delusional ideology.

Rion carefully placed the vials on the floor then scattered the straw. He'd suffered the effects of poisoning before. He would have killed the one responsible had Saoirse not gotten to them first. But this—this was said to drop a Fae in less than five minutes. He'd seen the agonizing effects. Body convulsions. Profusive vomiting. Uncontrolled fever.

Thankfully, someone with a brilliant mind had crafted an antidote and Nàdair's warriors were now required to carry it on their person at all times. He was no exception, at least where Saoirse was concerned.

Rion opened another lid, carefully set the vials aside, then spread more straw across the floor.

At least it was flammable.

He pulled a match from his pack, threw it into the scattered straw, then sprinted through the open door.

A group of ten warriors waited for him on the other side.

They paused. Their mouths fell open, but Rion didn't have time to stop. He charged and they stumbled back. Rion shoved the nearest two out of his path, then the building exploded.

Muddy earth rose up behind him to block the shrapnel that flew in all directions. His ears rang, but Rion pivoted in time to see a male racing toward him with six following in his wake.

Rion drew his sword—one hundred on one. Not the best of odds, but there was only one way to see who'd emerge victorious.

Rion raised one arm and a wall of squelching mud rose with him. Those nearest to it tried to dive out of its path, but Rion shoved the dripping magic straight for them. The force of the impact knocked the breath from their lungs. They hit the ground and the mud washed over their bodies, dragging them under.

When facing warriors from Brónach, Rion always ensured he maintained control of everything beneath his feet. He'd learned far too many hard lessons. Seedlings wriggled in the mud, reminding Rion of an angry swarm of insects, but he squashed each, refusing to be caught off guard. There were too many warriors in this camp to allow any mistakes.

The male to Rion's left lunged, blade drawn, a dozen vines in his wake. Rion smirked at him. Another followed, but his fear already coated the vicinity. Rion crinkled his nose. Someone had wet themselves.

He usually let those who fled escape, but these Fae were part of an organization hell-bent on bringing down their family line. And he couldn't allow that. For Saoirse and for his pride.

A tree trunk erupted from the ground and spurred toward him. Rion jumped away from it, losing his grip on the ground around his feet. A bush burst from the mud, but Rion used his magic to propel himself into the air, avoiding the snake-like strike from the thorny branches.

More trees emerged and Rion raced along the branches, ducking and dodging everything that came at him. It was often a game. To see how long they could last while he outran their maneuvers. He was always faster. Always stronger. He'd almost grown bored over the last few years, but when he encountered large groups like this one—

Freedom. That's what fighting was. A chance for him to use his skills and implement the new ones he'd picked up along the way.

A trunk bent at a ninety-degree angle and slammed into Rion's side. Breath left him and Rion grimaced before using his magic to grab his own arm and yank himself away from the magic trying to close in.

Rion rolled across the ground, blocked a knife aimed for his throat, then spun in a circle. The surrounding ground lifted all at once. It morphed into hundreds of pieces of rock the size of his palm, then shot out at a high velocity in all directions.

The warriors covered their faces, but Rion was already running for the nearest of them. He drew a knife from his belt and flicked his wrist. It buried itself in the male's throat. He pulled another out and let it fly. It sank into a male's chest, stopping his heart on impact.

The next one had recovered enough to block Rion's sword, but Rion spun and smashed his elbow into the male's face. The satisfying crunch of bone told Rion he'd broken the male's nose. Another lunged and Rion grabbed his arm, twisting it back at an unnatural angle.

One strike for each opponent. That's how he fought groups. Incapacitate each individual until he was left with a pile of injured warriors who would rather crawl away than fight.

Not that he'd let them. He'd seen too many children dead to forgive these monsters.

Rion planted his fist in another male's face and shoved him away when a sound echoing from the other side of the field drew his attention.

Fae were screaming. Battling. Rion couldn't afford to stop, but he tried to glance through the pouring rain. Friend or foe? Had Alec sent someone as backup? Unlikely, and Saoirse was busy with a mission of her own.

A knife cut through Rion's sleeve. He ripped the blade away from the warrior and plunged it through the male's arm arm.

Rion shifted positions. He summoned his magic again, this time using it to shove his enemies back. Then he took off toward the new sounds. He still had warehouses to destroy. If his enemies had sent a back-up unit to retrieve the vials, then he needed to put a stop to them first.

Rion stopped short. Three Fae fought side by side, each guarding the other's backs from the onslaught of warriors rushing toward them. One female, two males.

Not his enemy, then. Were they from Nàdair?

A blade whizzed through the air and he spun, catching it before launching it right back at its owner. He didn't bother to see if it had landed.

The female's piercing gaze swung toward him. She made a hand sign and, perplexed, Rion glanced behind. No one else, aside from his enemies struggling to regain their balance.

She was already fighting again by the time he looked back, but— she wasn't struggling. No, she was dancing around her opponents with grace. A blade swiped toward her and her companion, a male with dark hair, blocked it, sending her attacker flying back.

Rion ducked beneath another swing and broke the arm of the male who had attacked. He let his magic soar, shoving earth and rock through his opponents before turning to look at her again.

She was watching him from the corner of her eye. So were her companions.

She gestured again. More aggressively this time, as if she were aggravated that he hadn't listened. The thought was almost comical. Rion closed the distance, dispatching warrior after warrior in his wake.

Adrenaline rushed through his veins. His breath was ragged. Alive. This was what being alive felt like.

The earth was always more difficult to move when it was wet and it had been raining on and off for days.

The female closed the remaining distance, but Rion kept his guard up in the event she was present for more sinister reasons. He was no stranger to assassins.

But the female wasn't looking at him. She was too busy focusing on the Fae advancing on them all. Two large groups, one from either side. He wasn't worried.

"Can you handle the ones on the left?" She was breathless, and her clothes were covered in blood and dirt. She hadn't just arrived. She'd been on the other side of the field, for how long, he didn't know.

Rion looked her over. She was covered in cuts and bruises. Her left eye had nearly swollen shut. One of her companions had a thin stretch of fabric hastily tied around a bleeding wound in his upper arm.

"Yeah, I can handle them."

"There are two other warehouses to destroy," she said. "One north, the other west. They also have one just on the outskirts. Some have already fled there to—" Her sentence was cut short when magic burst from the ground at their feet.

She jerked her own up and wrestled with the plants, fighting for control. Rion upended the ground, knocking the female and her companions momentarily off balance. He righted them as a courtesy, then proceeded to focus on his own group.

His blade cut through them one at a time. It could have been minutes or hours. The blood pumped through his body, fed by adrenaline as he relished in the sight and sound and smell of battle.

The trio never strayed far from his side and as a group, they brought down Fae after Fae, rendering their magic useless. The three kept a sharp eye out for him and he did the same in turn, always watching for that extra knife that might be thrown his way.

Only when he was afforded a gap did Rion race toward the nearest storehouse. The northern one. He kicked the door in, ripped open one of the crates, and threw a match inside before sprinting away.

Rion made it a few feet before the box exploded, then the ones next to it followed suit. He yanked the ground up to protect his body once again.

Fae were screaming on the outskirts of the storehouse, some swiping at flames, while others grabbed for their throats.

No wonder Alec wanted it destroyed.

Another explosion echoed from the west and two dark silhouettes raced toward the trio.

No one stopped. No one asked for help.

The battle ebbed, slowly quieting. Rion hunted the few who'd attempted to hide, but their rapid heartbeats gave them away. He didn't give them time to beg for mercy.

Rion wiped the blood from his sword and eyed the female from earlier. The rain had shifted to a light drizzle. She stood in the center of the chaos, whispering to two of her companions while two others shifted through the dead. He didn't want to know what they might be looking for.

He stared at the five, wondering whether to approach and thank them or get to the last building, destroy everything inside, and make his way home. He'd kill for a hot meal.

The female's gaze shifted his way. She eyed him for a long moment before approaching, sheathing her sword as she closed in. "Well," she started, still a bit breathless. "I suppose you don't need an introduction."

"You're from Nàdair?"

She nodded. "We've been tailing a small group of them for about a week. They led us here." She eyed Rion, then their surroundings. "There's one more storehouse. Do you want the honors?"

Rion looked her up and down, then turned away. "Have at it."

"We could travel back together if you wanted."

He raised one hand in farewell and kept walking. He knew better than to trust anyone. He'd learned far too many lessons the hard way.

CHAPTER TWO

"I do not need a team," Rion said for the third time. It was the same argument before every assignment. Nàdair's rules were strict when it came to missions. Warriors were to be sent in a group of three or more. Two to carry it out and one to report if anything went awry.

He was the only exception to that rule. Mostly because half the time his team members tried to take matters into their own hands where his life was concerned. It never ended well. "You and I both know they'll just get in my way."

Alec quirked a brow at him as if to accuse Rion of enjoying it. He'd done that more than once, too.

"They've already been assigned." Rion tapped his foot on the marble floor and glared at his brother. A look that sent others running in fear. It certainly made the male standing beside the throne uncomfortable enough to inch back a step.

Rion bared his teeth. He'd never cared for the male or the way he often looked at Saoirse. But Alec had chosen him as an advisor. Short of killing him, he was here to stay. Rion's gaze traveled down to the ring around his finger depicting a crow. Such a gaudy thing.

Alec propped his face up with one hand, watching Rion carefully. He let the ring on his other finger tap against the arm of the throne. At least Alec had more taste where jewelry was concerned. The guards stood pensive, as they always were in Rion's presence.

Rion ground his teeth. A team of gods-only-knew how many. All with blades poised to strike him down as soon as Rion turned his back.

When Rion didn't reply, Alec waved his hand toward a slave. The female jumped to attention and ran for the side door, opening it with her head bowed.

Her chains rattled, and Rion cringed at the grating sound. He hated the iron and wondered how many might possess magic if they were ever set free. Probably a lot more than the Fae wanted to give them credit for.

A female prowled into the room with a predator's gait. She held her chin high. Sharp features surrounded analytical eyes and—he recognized her.

Rion's mouth gaped as he stared at the very female who'd stumbled upon him less than a month ago.

He looked her up and down. Her wounds had healed and her face was far more pleasant to look at without the swollen eye. Too pleasant.

She wore casual clothes today instead of the black fighting leathers he'd seen her in before. Her sandy bronze hair was swept up into a braid that circled the top of her head and she'd gone as far as weaving pale blue flowers between the strands.

She'd tucked her tan tunic into her black pants and wore a belt with a pouch on one side. No knives. No weapons.

Her gaze locked with his and Rion sucked in a breath. She surveyed him too, raking her amber gaze up and down his form. Rion didn't move, but he couldn't stop the magic that rose up to surround his body in response.

She smiled, actually smiled, before turning to Alec. Rion gaped.

The female gracefully dropped to one knee and bowed her head, something Rion had never done. "My Lord." Her voice. It was definitely the same female.

Alec offered her a warm smile. A true smile. "Selina," he nearly purred. "Rise." She did, the movement just as graceful.

"You summoned me, My Lord."

Alec's gaze shifted to Rion momentarily, but Selina's didn't follow it. She was solely focused on her High Lord, as a good warrior should be.

Alec gestured to Rion. "I'm told you've already met. Rion, this is Selina. She'll serve as your commander for this mission. She's been briefed on the sensitive details."

Rion glanced between them, then crossed his arms. "You expect me to walk into this blind?"

"I expect you to follow orders," Alec bit out. Gods, Rion would love to pummel him just once.

Instead, he took a calming breath. Surely, he could rationally talk his way through this. "I've never failed a mission. I don't need anyone's help."

"Glad to know you won't ruin my reputation, then." His gaze slid to hers. His blood sparked at the challenge in her eyes. "But even I can't infiltrate multiple locations at once without the risk of an information leak."

"Is that what we're doing?"

She tilted her head. A cat studying its prey. "Perhaps if you decide to tag along, you'll find out." She looked him over again. "That is, unless you're not up for it. Or is it because I'm a female? Surely you don't share the attitude of those who refuse to follow a female's lead? It would be very . . . human of you."

Rion glared at her. She was baiting him already. Great. She'd likely try to kill him before the mission even began. "It has nothing to do with your gender." He'd followed Saoirse's lead on plenty of missions.

She turned to face him fully, and Rion was keenly aware of Alec's watchful gaze. "The targets are very high profile. It requires absolute secrecy. You won't be the only one going in blind."

"And what happens if you die?"

She smirked. "Well, don't you just inspire confidence?"

"I'm being practical. If you're the only one who knows the details, then—"

"In the event of your commander's death, you'll return here to await further instructions," Alec cut in.

"You might be powerful, Rion of Brónach, but I assure you, my team is one of the best. You're simply a requested asset."

"Requested?"

She gave him a sideways smile. "I've heard great things about you." He doubted it.

"And?"

"And I have an appreciation for Fae with your . . . tendencies."

She'd discover those tendencies soon enough when she tried to put a knife in his back. "I think you're relying on too many rumors." Most were exaggerated to near child-like levels. Some whispered about him as if he were death incarnate. Others feared he'd kill them for simply being in his way on the street. He'd even heard things about cannibalism that had his stomach turning.

If Fae believed those things, it was no wonder they wanted to usurp Alec for tolerating his existence.

Alec's authoritative voice cut in. "You have three days to prepare."

Selina turned back to Alec and bowed deeply at the waist. "Consider it already done. I promise a swift return." Without looking at him, Selina pivoted on her heel and disappeared through the side door from where she'd emerged.

Rion stared after her, then turned back to his brother. "Is the mission time sensitive?"

Alec didn't look at him, as if he couldn't be bothered. "You'll receive all your information from your commander." A dismissal. Rion balled his hands into fists, debated arguing further, then decided it wasn't worth his energy. Fine, let Alec send him with this female and her team. When he returned with their blood on his hands, his brother would have no one to blame but himself.

Rion marched from the throne room, opting for the main door. He ignored the way the guards tightened their hold on their weapons and even smiled at one in passing just to antagonize the male. Saoirse often told him to leave them be. It wasn't his fault they were afraid of a bedtime story. Ancient texts indeed. More like how to scare your children into behaving in the best way that benefited society.

Selina. An asset, she'd called him. Just a tool to be used and discarded. But the way she'd smirked at him. The way she'd challenged him knowing full well who he was.

He smiled despite the irritation of the whole situation.

Maybe this mission wouldn't be so bad after all.

Chapter Three

"Rion." He turned at the sound of his sister's voice, the old wooden chair creaking beneath his weight.

He'd returned to the study after grabbing lunch. The tray still sat on the floor at the foot of the dresser. He'd chosen to fill his time by reading a new book on advanced chess strategies.

The glass chess board sat before him with pieces scattered across the tiled squares.

The study separated their two rooms. His sister had once played other games with him in this very room. They'd make up imaginary villains and pretend the bookshelves were castles they had to climb and defend, much to their father's chagrin. But their villains had become quite real over the years.

He smirked at the memory and moved the glass chess pieces before she could pick apart his new strategy.

Saoirse sat across from him, her hair still damp from her shower. She wore a casual set of green silk pajamas that were patterned with tiny smiling cacti waving their arms.

A smile pulled at his lips.

"Really? Every time?"

"I didn't say a word."

"I could get you a pair," she offered, pushing her hair back from her face. "Maybe it would change a few minds."

"Ah, yes, why didn't I consider that before?" He sarcastically waved a hand. "Tiny cacti to the rescue."

She reached for the white pieces on the board and began setting them up. "I heard Alec assigned you."

Rion reached for the black ones. "Apparently, I need a team." He still hated the idea and didn't try to hide it.

"Selina." She practically spit the name. "I told him to choose someone else."

Rion studied her, but she kept her gaze on the board. She'd walked in relaxed, but now her shoulders were pensive.

"Anything I should know?"

Saoirse met his gaze, hers full of warning. "Keep your guard up around her."

He smirked. "Worried about me?"

She kicked his shin under the table. "You know damn well I worry about you." Saoirse leaned back and crossed her arms. "She's taken special classes and knows how to weave her words. Some claim she can even outright lie."

Rion moved his first piece. "She knows how to manipulate, so what? It's nothing I haven't encountered before."

"She's never failed a mission."

"Neither have I."

Saoirse sighed. "I know, but . . . most of her missions aren't . . . normal. She goes undercover and is a master at gaining the trust of her target. She's set a record for getting things done faster than anyone we've ever seen."

Rion indicated for her to move. "Is that what this mission entails?" He wasn't sure how he'd assist a covert operation if they were supposed to blend in. Everyone knew him by name.

Saoirse finally moved, a mistake on her part. Rion moved again. "I don't know. Alec wouldn't give me the details."

"I thought you were in charge of assigning missions."

"Not this one, apparently."

"Why?"

She moved her knight. "He just said the information was sensitive and he didn't want to risk telling any more people than necessary."

"That's sketchy."

"Maybe you shouldn't go. I'm sure they can handle it on their own."

"I'll be fine."

"You'll be outnumbered and somewhere remote."

He shrugged. "Again, nothing I haven't encountered before."

She lowered her voice. "I wish you wouldn't insist on taking missions at all."

He snatched one of her pieces. "Why, so I could be attached to your hip forever? I'm nineteen, not nine."

She took one of his in turn. "At least I'd be able to keep an eye on you."

"I don't need you to anymore."

"I know." Silence passed as they both studied the board. "Just—promise you'll be safe, okay?"

He moved once more and cornered her king. "I always am."

She tipped the piece over, then began resetting. "Another game?"

"A glutton for punishment tonight?"

"Don't get cocky. I'm still older than you."

"Doesn't do much for your skills."

She set her queen back in place. "Would you care to play a different game? I'm sure the sparring rings are open."

He clenched his jaw. He might be faster than her now but beating her in the ring was still a challenge. He'd only succeeded twice.

"That's what I thought." She moved first. Rion responded and the pair stayed up well into the night playing game after game as if they didn't have a care in the world.

A MESSAGE arrived at his door two days later. The slight knock was jarring enough, but when Rion opened his door and found a male slave standing with his head lowered and arms extended, Rion almost did a double take. No one ever knocked on his door, aside from Saoirse, and she'd left early that morning.

Rion broke the heavy seal on the envelope and read one word.

Midnight

He turned it over, searching for details, then looked at the half-breed who was visibly shaking. Rion eyed the chains around his wrists and the scars underneath where the iron had bitten into the male's flesh. The slight scent of blood drifted up from the wounds.

"You're dismissed." The male bowed even lower, then rushed from his sight, limping on his left foot. Half-breeds, bound in shackles just because of how they'd been born. Rion let the thought slip from his mind. He had the day to himself. He wasn't going to waste it thinking about things outside his control.

Rion gathered his satchel and slipped it around his shoulders before closing the door behind him. Alec hadn't been wrong about others listening in. Someone had been tailing him for two days and Rion had yet to force them out. They were slippery. A shadow. He planned to corner them today and demand answers.

Rion jogged down the stairs then walked down the crisply maintained halls. The windows were open, letting in the summer breeze. It billowed through the top of the tied-off curtains and brushed against the leaves of the various plants lining the halls. A floral aroma had tension falling from his shoulders. He'd always admired the decor, mostly because it was his mother who had put it all together.

Alec hadn't changed a thing.

Thin rectangular tables lined the walls, and elegant round ones occupied the corners. Lightly colored vases sat atop lattice table runners with robust flowers reaching toward the sun. Pictures of nature lined the halls. All bright and airy and welcoming.

Rion exited through a side door and marched across the immaculate lawn toward the rear training rings.

Sometimes, he wished he could remember how his mother had treated the slaves. They'd spent a lot of time at the lake house, but the slaves had never been present. And he didn't have the heart to ask Saoirse, not when she crumbled at every mention of their mother. For all he knew, his mother held similar views to their neighboring country Móirín. She and the High Lady there were said to be close allies, perhaps even friends. He prayed he'd get the chance to ask her himself someday.

Rion passed the first few occupied rings and made his way to the back. Those nearest to him stopped to stare at the abomination in their midst before packing up and moving away. He tried his best to ignore them.

Rion threw his satchel next to one of the wooden benches, then began his normal morning routine. He reached for the ground, flattening his palms in the dirt, then rolled back up, feeling each taunt muscle lengthen with the movement.

He stretched his arms over head, pulling on his elbows, then bent again to grab his ankles. Rion breathed long and deep, letting his mind drift to somewhere far away.

"Just the male I was hoping to see." Her voice was light and welcoming, like the sunrise after a long, cold night, but something in the undertone had Rion expecting a storm to follow.

Annoyance and curiosity flared through him in equal measure. He slowly rose to his full height, then his throat went dry.

He hadn't intended to gape.

Her hair was down today, falling just past her shoulders. She wore a casual blouse with the top strings undone. He couldn't resist following the curve of her neck, but his gaze stopped at the simple tear-drop pendant hanging over her chest.

The female flashed him a mischievous smile. Manipulative, Saoirse had warned. He wondered if everything she did, from her clothes to her scent, was all part of the game. Rion tried to ignore the way she smelled, but gods—her scent reminded him of the wildflowers bending with the breeze. Of long summer nights, doing all the things he'd dreamed of doing with a female.

He shook the thoughts away, wondering how many had fallen for her ruse. Too many, according to Saoirse.

Selina tied her hair back in a low ponytail, then sauntered over and plucked a blunt training sword from the rack. The female tested the weight by rolling her wrist with the blade in hand then executed a series of swift movements.

She smiled at him again. "Have time for a sparring match?"

Rion quirked a brow. "You're kidding." No one volunteered to spar him. Ever.

Another smile. His stomach fluttered. "Not in the slightest."

His gaze roamed across her body, searching for weapons. He found four. "Plotting to kill me before the mission even begins?"

A spark of mischief flashed through her eyes and she tilted her head toward the sword. "Not sure a blunt blade would get the job done."

"Your other weapons might." If she could hit him.

She smirked. "Keen eye." Then reached for the knives. Two hidden in her boots and two along her belt beneath her shirt. She held them up, then dramatically deposited them next to his satchel at the edge of the ring. "Happy?"

Rion only walked to the weapons rack and drew a blunt sword himself, staring back at her incredulously. She'd just disarmed herself in his presence. Others were watching their exchange carefully, as if unsure whether to intervene.

"What's to stop you from using your magic?"

She shrugged. "What's to stop you from using yours?" Her eyes darted to the grains circling at his feet. "I do believe only one of us has a bloodthirsty reputation."

"Is that what made you recruit me?"

"A female's allowed to be curious. Rumors and all."

He scoffed. "Right, because they're believable."

"I guess we'll see."

She shot toward him, her body low, balanced. She angled her sword across the front of her body, ready to cut him in two.

Caol had taught him to dodge such attacks. Blocking only expended unnecessary energy.

But he'd never completely listened to Caol. And he wanted to test this female. Meet the challenge in her gaze. Break the façade.

He still hadn't scented any fear.

The pair clashed, metal ringing out and Rion's forearms vibrated from the impact. Selina went sprawling backward. Her eyes widened, but she caught herself, then greenery split through the earth at their feet.

Rion was ready for it.

He allowed the first few bits of young trees to unfold. Let the vines grow until they were taller than him. Then his magic roared to life. His body ignited and the secondary pulse quickened. Warmth spread through his veins and into the ground at his feet.

The vines and bushes bent toward him, rushing to strike, but Rion's magic spun in a vicious storm that shredded the leaves and branches in one stroke.

Selina snarled and lunged again, her weapon raised. Rion parried it and she—let it go. His eyes widened when she reached for his throat with her bare hands. Rion grabbed one wrist and spun them. They tumbled to the ground, their magic and bodies both wrestling for dominance.

Selina twisted his wrist and bucked her hips, but he rolled with the movement and slammed her back on the ground. One hand pinned her wrists above her head and he trapped her arms with his magic.

She kneed him in the gut, but Rion didn't break his hold. He pinned her legs with his own, then braced his free hand beside her head while the other closed around her throat. She wasn't breaking the hold his magic had on her arms.

Her vines still grappled with his magic three feet below the surface. One tendril escaped his hold and emerged, but he crushed it with half a thought. Another almost broke the surface and he suffocated the attempt.

Their chests were heaving, the pair pressed tightly against one another, then her body fell slack, her magic with it. And she . . . laughed.

His eyes widened again as a singsong voice echoed from beneath him. "Fine, fine, I yield."

Rion didn't move. He kept one hand on her throat, the earth locked around her body. He studied her, then her magic.

Manipulative, Saoirse's voice reminded him. He wouldn't be lured into a false sense of security only for her to stab him in the back. Those watching took half a step forward. If he killed her, he'd likely have to fight them as well.

Selina held his gaze without flinching. Hers seemed to soften, as if realizing the thoughts running rampant in his mind. That gaze drifted to his arm. "Are you going to let me up?"

"Are you going to stab me in the back?"

She chuckled. "Not today. I mean, we can stay like this if you want, but if I'm going to be on my back, I prefer not to have so many layers between us."

Rion's face heated and he ripped away from her as if he'd been burned. He watched the earth and her movements, waiting for the strike. A hint of magic. Another hidden blade.

Nothing came.

Selina dusted the dirt from her pants and straightened. "Well, I guess at least some of the rumors are true." She reached to undo her hair tie and smooth out the wild strands.

"And the rest?"

She shrugged. "We'll see as we go. Come on, I'll introduce you to the others."

She was so . . . casual about it. She'd been pinned beneath him and still hadn't shown an ounce of fear. And what she'd said . . . Rion shook the thoughts away and followed her.

"I thought the team was classified."

"The mission is classified. The rest was just your brother trying to irk you, I think." She spoke of Alec casually, too. Perhaps they were friends then.

"Your reputation doesn't precede you, I'm afraid."

She smiled over her shoulder before spinning to walk backward with her hands clasped behind her back. The motion reminded him of a youngling. "Being covert is part of my job. If you'd heard about me, I wouldn't be very good at it, would I?"

"Are they all assassination assignments?"

She spun forward again. "Most."

"And the bystanders who see your face?"

"I'm sure you can use your imagination." He could, but if she eliminated everyone who'd seen her, then that made her more ruthless than he'd previously given her credit. He tucked the information away.

Rion eyed the rooftops, searching for the tail that'd been monitoring him. If they were meeting her team— "I have something I should probably deal with first."

She didn't stop walking. "Anything interesting?"

He wondered if he should mention it at all and decided his commander should probably know their enemies were on to them. "I've had a tail the last few days. I'll deal with it."

She didn't pause. "How do you know you haven't already been dealing with it?"

He stopped at that, staring at her back. Rion reassessed the female, took in her scent and the faint hints of vanilla. The very scent that had lingered whenever he'd tried to corner the one tracking him.

"You."

"I'm surprised you caught on. Not many do."

Rion erased every preconceived notion about the female and tried to focus on her skills instead.

Selina gave off an air of innocence. One that was strong enough to lure others into believing she was a novice. Young. But her skills said otherwise. It had Rion wondering if she'd thrown their sparing match as part of an act.

Two could play that game. He'd participate for a while. Feel her out. "I couldn't pin down your exact location, if that makes you feel any better."

"You were close a few times." Rion could hear the smile in her voice. "I honestly thought you'd found me yesterday on the roof."

Rion recalled the moment. He'd been more than frustrated by the unknown presence, her presence, and had said to hell with all his train-ing. He'd used his magic to propel himself to the rooftop, intending to confront her directly. But she'd vanished before his feet landed. He'd scoured every inch of the place to no avail. "Where were you hiding?"

She spun again, a child-like grin on her face. "I can't go sharing my secrets now, can I?"

Right. Well, he'd get to the point then. "If your team is so good, why do you need me?"

She turned and Rion wished she'd just stop walking so he could study her face. "I'm always on the lookout for new recruits. Who better than the strongest Fae in Brónach?"

"That's a bit overstated." There were many warriors who had cen-turies on him. He wasn't delusional enough to think he could take them on and come out unscathed.

"Not as much as you might think. I've read the reports. Not to mention the fact that you took out an entire elite unit when you were just a child."

Rion suppressed the growl forming in his throat. "I'd rather not talk about that."

She peered at him from over her shoulder. "Why not, it's—"

"Because it's not a day I'm proud of."

She paused again, meeting his gaze and the fire he knew simmered behind his eyes.

"Sorry," she stammered. "I just thought—"

"You thought wrong. Are we going?" He didn't want to give her room to question him on the matter. He'd worked too hard to keep the truth about their father's death a secret. He wouldn't slip up here.

She studied him for a long moment, assessing his body language and the dismissal of the topic. Perhaps she'd presumed he would be proud of that night. That The Demon would relish in the blood of his enemies no matter how young he might have been.

But Rion wasn't proud of it. He'd lost his father, his friends, and the only home he'd ever known. He still had nightmares about torn flesh and pools of blood. Sometimes Rion wondered if his subconscious delighted in tormenting itself.

Selina was silent as they walked through the rest of the training grounds. Rion noted those who stared after the pair, some gaping at the exchange they'd just witnessed. Several tightened their grip on their weapons and Rion scented their magic in the air. He knew they wanted to strike him down, but fear won out it seemed.

Selina waved at a few and they awkwardly waved back, their gazes darting between her and Rion in confusion. Well, he supposed he could count them out as being part of any assassination attempts.

Rion watched her back and noted the skip in her step. Selina certainly wasn't dressed properly if she intended to catch him in an ambush. Not with her hair down and the small weapons she'd brought. But that could be part of the ruse, too. Perhaps she was just the lure and her companions were lying in wait.

No, doing it now would be too predictable. They'd likely wait until they were far away from Nàdair. Maybe even a few days after so he'd let his guard down. He'd been attacked once in his sleep, he was sure it would happen again.

They walked through the barracks next. Fae roamed the open yard, many either returning from or preparing to head out on assignments. Once again, the female before him waved at Fae she knew.

They ambled through the main stretch of the city, then beyond it. Impatience rose through him at her slow pace, but he didn't comment on it. She marched off the beaten path, then through the trees to emerge on the other side. Five small single-room cabins stood in a row next to the giant redwoods that circled Nàdair.

A light flickered in the window of the one on the far left. Shadows moved within and Rion braced himself for the impending fight.

Selina turned to give him a reassuring smile as if she knew the thoughts racing through his mind. She trotted up the two steps and walked inside.

Rion paused on the threshold.

Twelve warriors stood within. Seven male, five female. All carried a small arsenal of weapons across their bodies. All were dressed in black.

Their heads snapped up and, as a unit, they drew their blades.

Fine, they weren't waiting. Neither would he.

His magic snapped free and Rion dropped into a stance, but as his fingertips grazed the hilt of his sword, Selina's voice cut through the tension. "That's enough. He's with us."

They paused, gazes darting toward their leader. None relaxed and Rion saw the first bits of greenery sneaking up through the floorboards.

One snarled. Another snapped their teeth.

"I said *enough*," Selina's voice echoed through the space. Not the soft voice he'd heard minutes ago. Not the singsong laugh that had him questioning whether she could truly be manipulative. This was the voice of a commander, and as Rion raised his head to look in her eyes, he saw it. A dangerous warrior. One who'd fought her way through the ranks and earned the respect of each Fae in this room.

They straightened one at a time. Two exchanged uneasy glances but put their weapons away. The others followed. Their magic remained visible, just slightly.

Rion let the dirt particles glide back to the floor, but he did nothing to clear it from the room. It was thirteen on one. Not that he hadn't faced worse odds.

Selina stood at the head of the room, a small table separating her from Rion. She pulled a few pieces of folded parchment from within her tunic and tapped them on the side of her face, meeting each of her warrior's gazes one at a time.

"Our upcoming assignment won't be a fast one. Recent intel suggests the problem is escalating. Scouts have confirmed the issue is wider spread than the High Lord previously hoped. We are to obtain intel first, then eliminate the problem."

"Eliminate what, exactly?" A male to her right asked. Rion looked him up and down. He stood closer than the others. Short brown hair hung just over dark eyes as if the male were due for a haircut. The male stared back at Rion. Glared really.

Rion smirked, showing his fangs and the male growled in response. He was of medium build, had a bit more muscle on his frame than Rion did, but one look at his stance told Rion he'd knock the male on his ass in seconds. Best team indeed.

Selina eyed the two. "I'm unable to provide further details until we're in a secure location."

"We've already secured it," a slender female with a silken voice said from his right. Her hair was braided in five sections against her scalp, each connecting in the back to form a short ponytail. Rion studied her and the pair of females who stood just behind her. Sisters. Triplets. The females were almost identical save for the difference in hair styles.

Selina studied the female, then a smile broke across her face. "I should have known better than to doubt my best trackers." The female stood straighter. Prouder. He had to remind himself that Selina was their commander.

Her face turned serious again. "There is a large, organized faction that is working to overthrow the High Lord."

No one looked surprised. Alec, despite holding his position for eleven years, was still largely untested. Nàdair was a flourishing city and it would take a truly neglectful High Lord to mess that up. He had the council and elders to guide him.

But no one knew how he'd react if war suddenly showed up on his doorstep. Nor how he'd handle it if their neighboring countries turned against them.

And then there was Rion to consider and the fact that Alec hadn't done away with The Demon like the gods commanded.

The male beside Selina shrugged. "That's nothing new. We've dealt with plenty of rebels before, what makes this one different?"

"Their size," she said simply. "The council has kept an eye on them for years, but they've begun to amass, and their tactics are . . . concerning."

"The poison," a female confirmed.

Selina nodded. "They're openly executing those who refuse to join their cause." She unfolded the parchment in her hands to reveal a map of Brónach with several circled cities and villages.

"With their recent bout of activities, we've narrowed down the location of their headquarters to seven possible areas. The problem is that once we infiltrate one, the others will know we're on to them." She met their gazes again. "With the recent uptick in violence, we can't afford to let them go underground again. Our primary objective is locating their leaders and production warehouses."

One of the sisters, this one with her head half shaved and the remaining hair braided across the side of her head, scoffed. "Find me a hostage and give me an hour with them. I'll have them spilling every secret they know."

A half smile from Selina. "I have no doubt, but unless we find someone in their inner circle, I'm afraid it's a lost cause. We've already interrogated a number of their followers and no one appears to have any information on the individuals pulling the strings." Her voice lowered. "They've been careful and have likely learned from the mistakes of those who came before them."

"How long have they been organizing?" the final sister asked. This one had her hair braided back in a single strand that stretched to her waist.

Selina sighed. "Too long. They've recruited known criminals from past organizations as well. All are more than eager to assist."

"Explains how their numbers grew so fast," the male beside Selina commented.

She nodded. "And they're recruiting more. We've found evidence of slanderous propaganda in the underbellies of all our major cities. Nàdair included."

A male at the back of the room hissed through his teeth. "The summer solstice is in six weeks. You said this will be a long mission."

"I'm hoping to use the festivities as a distraction and a reason for our travel. We'll be better able to slip in and out without attracting too much attention."

The solstice. It was normally a time for celebration, but after what had happened to Rion's father, the citizens also mourned the loss of their High Lord. The Fairy Folk were always quick to comfort those who were upset with their songs and dances. He was no exception.

Rion usually visited their father's grave with Saoirse the week before to pay their respects. But from the sound of it, his sister would be alone this year. The thought didn't sit well. His heart ached at the thought of her sitting before that cold stone without anyone to comfort her. He was the only one who knew the truth.

He clenched his fists. A mission was a mission. He couldn't decline it over sentimentality. Saoirse could certainly pull rank for him to stay, but he wouldn't ask that of her either. Not when she and Alec already fought over him endlessly. He'd make it up to her when he returned.

"Before we proceed," Selina continued, "I need to ask each of you a very serious question." They stood straighter. "You will not be jailed or tried for treason for your answer, but I need to know if anyone harbors ill feelings toward their High Lord." Everyone stared at her unblinking. "We can use your feelings to speak plainly to the masses in hopes of drawing someone out from their inner circle." She scanned their faces until her gaze stopped on Rion. "What about you? Do you despise your brother enough that you'd kill him?"

Every pair of eyes studied him now and Rion met their intensity with his own. Despise. That was a strong word. Did he despise his older brother? They'd never been close, especially after what'd happened to their father, but did he hate Alec enough to want to kill him? "No." The word fell easily from his lips. He didn't even need to factor Saoirse into the equation.

More than one pair of eyes widened at the truth in his voice.

If they'd asked him whether he fought for his brother's sake, he would have also said no. He fought for his sister, his home, his mother, and the innocents that couldn't defend themselves.

Selina shrugged as if she'd expected the answer. "It was a far-fetched plan anyway." Rion arched a brow, wondering what sort of plan she'd concocted in that manipulative head of hers.

"Remember: Intel first. I'll disclose further information once we reach our first check point." Selina looked toward the sisters. "Even with your caution and expertise, I won't divulge everything here." The sisters nodded in unison and without complaint. "Let's pray we're able to complete the mission swiftly and return home victorious."

"Forgive the forwardness," a female, short of stature, said from Selina's other side. Her hair was cropped into a bob that reached to her chin. "But this sounds just like missions we've handled before. So why is he here?" She jerked her chin toward Rion.

"Fear," Selina said simply. "We'll be making the leaders' executions quite public. It will let the world know that The Demon will punish anyone who tries to rise up against the High Lord."

Understanding swept through him. "And simultaneously tell the world that Alec didn't make a mistake in keeping me around."

Selina didn't back down. "Precisely. It's no secret that many have had reservations about his decision."

The male beside her crossed his arms. "And we're just supposed to pretend he's actually loyal?"

Selina loosed a long sigh and lowered her voice. "I'm only going to say this once." Every eye in the room zeroed in on her and the promised threat in her tone. "I personally requested *Rion*," she emphasized his name, "for this mission. If *any* of you puts a single boot out of line, then you're done. Not just with this mission, but every assignment from here on out."

No one spoke. "This is too important. If we fail, we could be facing a civil war that will last generations."

"You'd choose him over us?"

"I'd chose my country over you." Something like pain flashed across the male's face. "You'd be removed for failing to follow a direct order. We are strong because we trust one another when it matters."

The male glared at Rion. "If you expect me to trust him—"

"Enough," Selina barked again. "If you can't work with him, then save yourself the shame of returning home with your tail between your legs and opt out now."

The male stared at Rion for another long moment, then turned back to Selina. She lifted her brows, clearly waiting for an answer. He swallowed hard, then lowered his head in shame.

"That's what I thought. Now, if no one else has any objections, you're all dismissed. Gather whatever provisions you need, but pack light. You already received instructions for when we're to set out."

No one moved for a long moment, their gazes drifting from her to Rion and back. The sister with the braids in her hair stepped first, followed closely by her siblings. Two males stationed near the back wall exited next, then the rest followed suit.

Rion remained, along with the male at Selina's side. Selina was studying the map and the points she'd marked across it. "You're dismissed," she repeated without looking up. The male looked her over, glared at Rion, then pulled a long knife from his belt. Selina smiled slightly when he placed it on the table before leaving.

Rion didn't care that a few lingered outside. "So I'm here to instill fear?"

Selina folded the map. "I didn't think that would be a problem for you. Neither did Alec."

Rion flexed his fingers. "I never set out with that goal."

She glanced up and raked her eyes down his form. "Goal or not, the fear is there and we can use it to our advantage. You're known as one of the strongest Fae in Brónach. You already have a reputation. I only plan to utilize it."

"Alec just wants to paint me as the enemy."

"Are you?"

He frowned. "No."

She leaned back against the wall. "So you claim."

Rion flexed his jaw. "Is this a test?" She shrugged, but kept her eyes locked with his. "I didn't ask to be born this way." The particles at his feet rose, jerking in agitated spirals. "I didn't ask to be branded an outcast."

"And yet you killed the former High Lord. Your own father."

Rion looked away. "You wouldn't understand even if I explained it."

Silence stretched between them. "It's difficult for the world, for anyone, to believe you wouldn't resort to killing another member of your family. Many worry for Saoirse and say her days are numbered."

"I would *never* hurt Saoirse."

She circled the table, prowling like a cat. "Is she the one who steadies your hand then?"

Steadied him, as if he were an animal who required monitoring. "I won't kill Alec because he is my brother. He's family."

"And that circles us back around to your father." Rion sighed and turned away. "I'm simply trying to understand. You can't blame a country for resenting the male responsible for murdering their leader."

"I can blame a country who slaughters innocent children for nothing more than being born different."

Selina's mouth gaped as if she'd never considered the act anything more than duty. She cleared her throat. "If you resent it so much, why stay? Why fight to defend it?"

"Where else would I go?"

She shrugged. "The world is vast with plenty of unexplored territory. I'm certain there are continents out there that know nothing of our history. You'd live a blameless life in their midst."

Another continent. He'd considered the idea before. A place where he'd be forced to hide his heritage and race. A place without Saoirse or Alec or even his mother when they finally found her. Rion shook his head. "This is my home."

"I didn't take you for the sentimental type. I get it though. It's hard to pull a tree's roots from rich soil. Of course, there's always the possibility of your mother—"

"Do *not*," Rion interrupted, his voice laced with venom, "speak about my mother."

Her eyes widened and Selina stepped back. There it was. The trace of fear. Just slight, but it was there. She dipped her head. "I didn't mean to offend. The High Lady was, is," she corrected, "held in very high regard. I only wish to see her safely returned."

Silence filled the space but Selina's apology did nothing to ease the heartache pulsing through him. He turned on his heel and stormed out without another word.

CHAPTER FOUR

"Weeks?" Saoirse exclaimed as they sat across from one another in the study, their usual chessboard between them. Rion waved a hand. "Could be months, but—"

"What do you mean *months*?" She could hardly keep the growl from her voice.

"Don't make it a big deal, you go out on long missions all the time."

"With warriors I *trust*," she emphasized. "With comrades I've trained beside for *years*. You don't just go on a mission like this with a group of strangers. You haven't even sparred with them. You don't know their formations or how they function within the unit."

"I sparred one." Saoirse made a face. She hadn't approved of that, either. His sister was certain Selina had been baiting him, holding herself back to make him perceive her as less of a threat. But he'd already figured that much out on his own.

"It'll be fine."

"Withdraw."

"No."

"Rion, you can't seriously be considering this. It's unethical and unheard of. I don't know what's going through Alec's head, but—"

"The citizens are rallying against him because of me."

"That's no—"

"It is," he leveled her with a stare. "And threatening him is the same as threatening you." Which he most certainly wouldn't tolerate. "They plan to use this mission not only to eliminate the rising faction but to prove my loyalty to the High Lord."

"You don't need to *prove* anything."

"Don't I? The world perceives me as a monster. Perhaps painting a different picture will change a few things."

She went silent and placed a finger on her bishop, rocking the piece back and forth before saying, "I never should have let you take the blame." He didn't respond. They'd had this conversation a million times. He never budged on the matter.

"I've been thinking—"

"No."

"You didn't even let me finish. It's not right for everyone to keep blaming you for something you didn't do."

"It wouldn't change anything and you know it."

"It might."

"Saoirse," he sighed. "Their opinions of me won't change no matter what you say. There's no point in dragging your name down, too. They'll probably just think you're trying to protect me anyway."

"Alec would know the truth. The council would know the truth. Then maybe you could join in on the meetings and—"

She stopped talking when he shook his head. "The only thing the truth will accomplish is tainting your reputation. You might even lose your position at Alec's side. If you lose their trust, then any move you make in the future will be met with doubt. Alec might even be forced to imprison you and have you tried."

She shrugged. "He wouldn't let it escalate that far. Besides, I've sat in a cell before. It's not that bad."

His voice turned icy. "I'd tear the whole damn palace apart before you spent ten minutes in a cell."

"It's not—"

"I couldn't handle it," Rion finished. "Besides, you still have to find our mother."

Saoirse looked away at that and finally sighed. "Fine, after Mom, then. When I bring her home, will you finally let me tell Alec the truth?"

Rion stared at his sister and the silver lining her eyes. His mouth had gone dry all over again. "Do you think she'll—"

"She won't think anything of it. You're her son." A smile spread across Saoirse's face. "And arguably her favorite."

Rion smirked at that. "I was just a kid."

"A very cute kid that she hid away from all the cruel things in life."

"It always irked Father." His smile faded. "Do you think she knew?"

Saoirse finally moved a piece on the board. "It's hard to say."

Silence again.

"I miss her," Rion admitted.

"Me, too."

Rion moved his piece and the siblings played in silence for a time. Saoirse had entered the room dressed for a mission. He didn't know how long they had.

"I could request to go with you," she said.

"Ever the overprotective sister."

"That's a little hypocritical coming from you."

Rion moved his rook, capturing her bishop. "I wouldn't dream of pulling you away from your friends. I've heard how excited you are."

A guilty smile. "Have I been too loud?"

"Only on the nights you stumble back drunk."

"I don't get *that* drunk," she challenged.

Rion looked up from the board. "I literally heard you tell your closest friend that if he wasn't a male—"

She threw up her hands. "All right, all right, I was drunk." She grimaced. "And I did not intend for you to hear that."

"The entire palace heard it."

Color tinted her cheeks. "Well, at least I keep things interesting around here. If it were up to Alec, the entire place would be as cheery as a graveyard."

Rion chuckled. "He should get out more." And he meant it.

Saoirse's smile faltered. "I can't even remember the last time I heard him laugh." She claimed his rook.

"The lake house," Rion said. "With Mother. He was swimming and we were jumping from the rope swing."

"You almost didn't let go."

"Mother was furious the two of you talked me into it."

A smile graced her features. "I remember." She moved another piece, forcing Rion's king into submission. He made a face. He hated losing. "When I come back, I'm forcing him to take a holiday. He's never going to meet a female locked in that throne room all day."

"Gods help the female that has to deal with him."

Saoirse kicked Rion under the table. "Gods help the female that has to deal with *you*." He playfully kicked her back before resetting the board.

"You can still decline, you know. There's no rule that—"

"I'm going," he interrupted. "If there's someone hell-bent against Alec, then you're on their list, too."

"You don't have to protect me. I am the older sibling."

Rion shrugged. "You've always done it for me."

Her voice lowered. "It was a promise to our mother."

Rion lips parted. "You've never told me that."

"It never came up. I would have protected you anyway, you're my little brother. You and Alec mean more to me than anyone else in this world."

"Now you're getting sentimental."

She puffed out a breath and glanced at the clock. "I'm allowed to get sentimental when I won't see my little brother for a few months."

"Afraid you won't be able to find a good enough chess partner?"

"That's bold coming from someone who just lost."

"Only to you." Her smile faded, so Rion added, "I can handle myself. It'll be fine."

She stood, still staring at the game board longingly. Too much time had passed and he hadn't even asked her about her upcoming mission.

"Just watch your back. And her," Saoirse warned.

"I've traveled with groups before. I know how to be cautious."

"Good. See you soon."

With a final embrace, Rion watched Saoirse walk out the door, then sat back down to stare at the game set.

He wouldn't fall prey to Selina. He'd beat her at her own game just like he'd beat Saoirse the next time they saw one another.

Chapter Five

Rion settled himself into the dark alcove of a nearby building and waited. He watched Nàdair's main gate. The sentries stationed there had no idea The Demon was so close, evidenced by the one who snuck off and returned with a pair of steaming mugs. Rion hoped for their sake there was only coffee or tea inside. Stronger substances would result in them losing their positions. It was a law his father had implemented after their mother's disappearance.

Rion's gaze drifted to the pack he'd placed on the ground. There wasn't much inside. A pair of clothes, a small medical kit, a vial of tea from Saoirse. The latter probably wasn't what most would consider important, but it was small and wouldn't do anything to weigh him down.

Rion returned his attention to the gate. He'd arrived an hour early just to see who would get there first. He wanted to study them. Saoirse had been right about one thing. He'd have to constantly watch his back, otherwise he'd end up having a very bad day.

He was nothing to them. An expendable asset. He should have refused. It would have been the smart thing to do, yet Rion couldn't convince himself to do it. He reasoned it had nothing to do with a pair of amber eyes that had looked at him as if he were a normal Fae instead of a monster.

Thirty minutes later, the triplet sisters arrived. He watched the one with short braids. She appeared to lead the other two. Perhaps she was the eldest. The most dangerous, for certain. She was a walking storm just waiting to be unleashed.

All wore black and possessed a small arsenal across their bodies, both weapons seen and unseen. The sentries stood straighter in their presence. None spoke and they positioned themselves among the shadows, blending in so well that if Rion hadn't arrived first, he might not have seen them at all.

The male with brown hair arrived next with the shorter female following close behind. The others trickled in, but again, no one talked. Probably for the best since they wanted their departure kept quiet.

Surprisingly, Selina arrived last, right on time. Rion emerged from the shadows then, letting his magic rise up to surround his body as he strode forward. Their cautious eyes flew to him. Selina offered a quick nod, did a head count, then gave the signal, and they were off.

She'd promised more information at their first checkpoint, wherever that was. Likely not too far off, given how lightly they'd packed.

Rion trailed just behind, keeping a steady eye on each should they choose to turn on him. The importance of the assignment hadn't hit him until last night after his sister's departure. Selina was right: If they failed, they could very well see a power shift among the nobles, and Rion ventured a guess that it wouldn't be in Brónach's favor.

The Fae warriors began shifting. Two grew wings, one brown and large, the other black and small. They shot into the open sky, soaring among the canopies and stars above. The three sisters shifted into wolves. One black, one gray, one white.

Another shifted into a panther, its fur black as the night itself. Selina's body bent and Rion watched as her fingers retracted and morphed into wide paws. A tan fur coat replaced her clothing and a tail grew out from the base of her spine. Her muscles rippled with each stride.

A lioness. A huntress. A predator.

Saoirse's words returned to him. *Be careful.* Rion steeled himself. He would be. Selina wasn't the only predator capable of hunting.

The final few remained in their Fae forms, leaving Rion to assume their animals shifts weren't suited for traveling long distances. He was silently grateful. At least he wouldn't have to explain that he lacked the ability, even if most of Nàdair already knew he'd never get one.

Demons with desolate magic weren't permitted such a thing. They weren't given a mate, either.

He knew Saoirse hadn't meant to sting him with her words, but they floated back anyway. About a female dealing with him. The unbearable truth was that none likely would. He'd be utterly alone where that part of his life was concerned. Unless, of course, he ever chose to flee and conceal his identity. He grimaced in the dark. Tricking a female didn't exactly sound like the healthiest way to start a relationship.

Rion shook the thoughts away and kept running, following the lead of the others as they weaved between the trees they'd all known since birth. Southeast, then.

He glanced up through the canopy overhead and caught glimpses of the night sky through the boughs. Bright and clear and full of stars, the moon nothing but a sliver in the darkness.

He'd return before it was full.

It was just another mission. Another task to complete. He'd be successful just as he'd been successful with others, and avoid any pitfalls along the way.

THEY RAN through the night at a steady pace, only stopping once to catch their breath. The trees disappeared as they crossed the terrain. They waded through waist-high water, trudged through an area covered in ash, then found themselves back under the trees again.

It wasn't until they closed in on a large cabin in the middle of the woods that Selina slowed her pace. The others fanned out and Rion hung back to watch their movements. Selina hadn't given him orders, so he stayed close and kept his magic low.

She prowled forward on silent feet. Rion steadied his breathing, willing his heart to slow. Sweat rolled down his neck and he pressed himself against a tree when Selina stopped.

He listened. Waited.

No lights flickered to life inside. No heartbeats, either.

He scented the air, then eyed the lioness and those who awaited her command. Why were they waiting? Surely they could hear the same things he did. No one occupied the space.

Rion focused his magic, searching the grounds for any signs of vibrations. He only felt the slight footfalls of the thirteen currently present.

Selina moved closer, still cautious.

Who had Alec sent him out with? Novices?

Rion clicked his tongue, earning what he thought might have been a glare from Selina. He walked forward anyway, no longer caring how much noise he made.

He could have taken the opportunity to learn their formations but he was tired, and hungry, and couldn't wait to get his boots off.

Rion's magic rose from the ground and surrounded his body as he strode through the wooden door. The hinges creaked from misuse, piercing the silence. Rion wiped away a spider web just inside and flooded the space with his magic. It raced toward the back, up the walls, into the corners, over the dusty furniture, and beneath the tables.

Still no one.

It took rummaging through a few drawers before Rion found a candle. He pulled a match from his pack and lit it, blinking against the offending brightness.

A thick layer of dust covered everything, along with cobwebs in every corner. No one had occupied the space for a very, very long time.

He lit another half-burned candle seated in a dusty brass holder. Then another and another before he placed the candle in a stand of its own in the center of the half-rotted wooden table. He wouldn't dare sit on the furniture for fear of falling through or disturbing some unpleasant creature.

Selina stormed in, no longer in her lioness form. She bared her teeth at Rion, her mask of innocence gone. "This mission is meant to be covert."

"No one's here," he said, his tone a bit bored and borderline irritated.

"You didn't know that."

"I did, actually." And they should have, too. "There weren't any heartbeats."

"Believe it or not, Rion of Brónach, there are Fae in the world who are able to conceal such things."

"Not in Brónach there aren't."

"And did you just automatically assume everyone we're after is from Brónach?"

"Who else would want to overthrow the High Lord?"

"Those who might benefit politically. We still don't know how far this faction's reach has spread. If Pádraigín, for instance, was involved, we'd need to report such things back to the council. So unless you want to explain to your brother how you blew our cover on day one, then I suggest you follow my lead from here on out."

He blanched and the fury in Selina's gaze somehow made him feel smaller despite her chin barely reaching his shoulder. He opened his mouth to retort, but nothing came to mind. He'd assumed the issue was a civil matter, but she was right. If other countries had gotten involved, then he could have just given them away.

She huffed. "We are meant to function as a team. Even without the possibility of other countries working against us, this was a good training exercise and—"

Rion interrupted with a soft snarl. "If your warriors still require training, then perhaps they shouldn't be here."

Tension filled the air. "For *you*," Selina snapped. "I was hoping to give you the chance to see how we work together so that I could implement you into our regiment."

The male, who was beginning to somehow remind Rion of a loyal dog despite his animal shift, growled as he said, "Selina is our commander. You would do well to show her some respect."

Selina held up her hand to silence him, then returned her cold glare to Rion. "How am I supposed to know you'll follow more complicated orders later if you can't follow simple ones now?"

His face burned and Rion was suddenly glad he hadn't lit more candles. Saoirse and Caol had been the only ones to ever reprimand him. And this female with her hands on her hips and stern gaze made him feel like a youngling all over again.

He should have apologized. Should have just stayed behind her instead of marching up the stairs. Instead, Rion bit out, "You're not. And don't pretend I'm your underling. We both know the entire lot of you would rather see me dead." She opened her mouth to reply, but Rion beat her to it. "Let's make it simple for both of us. I'll play the little role you and Alec have planned and you can stop pretending I'm anything more than another target for you and your team."

Selina sighed and rubbed her temples. "Aila, Orla, light the oil lamps. Alana, see if it's safe to get a fire going." The three sisters obeyed. No one else moved. "Listen," Selina said, stepping forward despite the particles of earth moving at her feet. "I know you don't like working with others. You're the solo type, I get it, but we can't have anyone jeopardizing this assignment."

"You get *nothing*," he seethed. "You and everyone else in Brónach can pretend I'm the *solo type*," he emphasized, "because I chose to be." He closed the space between them and those behind her drew their weapons. She held up a hand to steady them. "But what everyone fails to realize is that I wasn't given another choice." Something in her gaze softened at that. Rion hated it. Hated seeing sympathy where he expected resentment. Resentment was easier. Resentment he knew.

"I'll complete the mission with or without you for Alec's sake, but if I feel like you or anyone on your team is luring me into a trap, rest assured I won't hesitate to confront it."

Her brows rose. "You think we're setting you up?"

He finally looked at the shadowed faces standing behind her. The sisters hadn't taken their eyes off him. "Don't try to deny that any one of you would kill me without a second thought."

"I won't," she said. "But maybe you should consider that the reason everyone feels that way is because of what you put off. You're not exactly friendly."

He scoffed. "You expect me to be friendly?"

"I expect you not to judge our team based on experiences from your past. Give them a chance. You might be surprised at the outcome." Rion opened his mouth and closed it again. Selina sighed "Look, we're all tired and hungry. Let's call it a night and we'll pick things up in the morning." Never mind that morning was only about an hour off.

She turned her back to him, but the others didn't do the same. They didn't sheath their weapons either. He saw the truth in their eyes, even if hers had been different. Even if hers had seemed to . . . understand.

Rion stormed from the room, his magic following in his wake.

He didn't want to try. There was no creating allies where you weren't wanted.

CHAPTER SIX

The sun had illuminated the sky with the beginnings of dawn before he'd finally fallen asleep. Now it blared overhead. Still midmorning. He listened, expecting to hear Selina's team gearing up, but it seemed only one of them was awake below.

Rion sat up slowly, his back stiff and sore from sleeping on the roof. With his magic, it was as safe a place as any.

Rion cracked his neck and let the rest of the earth that had been encircling him fall to ground as if it were large clumps of snow melting away with the spring sun.

Shame flew through him. Shame and that same feeling that made Rion feel like he was an adolescent again. He chewed the inside of his cheek. Maybe he shouldn't be so quick to judge, but it was a hard habit to break when so many had tried to shove a knife through his back.

He wanted to believe Selina was sincere. That perhaps she really had been searching for new talent. But the alternatives seemed more likely. Either she planned to kill him, or she just flat out felt sorry for him. Selina had seen him fight before, so maybe there was a small chance.

Maybe for once he was wrong about someone. Rion shook his head. He wasn't holding his breath. Not after Caol.

Rion stood, stretching stiff muscles. He slid his boots back on and jumped from the rooftop. He followed the steady heartbeat and found

Selina staring at a kettle hanging over a small fire.

Rion watched her for a long moment. She'd once again braided her hair into a crown at the top of her head. He wondered if she expected them to encounter trouble today.

"Do you need something?" she snapped. He cringed at the tone. He deserved it after last night.

"When are we heading out?" She hadn't given any instructions last night.

"I don't know."

He opened his mouth once, closed it. "What do you mean, you—"

"I prefer to keep my mornings quiet until I've had tea." He could have taken the dismissal right there. Could have pivoted and stormed back to his place on the roof or found the nearest river to wash his face and refill his water skin. But something in the way her shoulders drooped had Rion wanting to stay. To . . . comfort her somehow.

He opted to sit on the log opposite the fire. She watched him but said nothing, then returned to staring at the kettle.

"Tea?" Rion inquired. He stared at the small glass vial in her hand, not unlike the one stowed away in his pack. His obsession with the warm drink was one him and Saoirse had developed to commemorate their mother. It was far better than the bitter aftertaste of coffee, though a warm drink was a warm drink if he had no other choice.

She didn't respond so he continued. It was as if something in him demanded he get an answer out of her. "We're on an important mission that could alter the course of the entire country and you're worried about tea?"

She looked up at him. Glared more like. He'd overstepped last night. Maybe too far, but he wouldn't back down from the challenge in her eyes. Couldn't.

"I am allowed to keep a bit of normalcy to my life, mission or no."

Rion couldn't help the smile tugging at the corner of his mouth. Here she was, a fierce commander and she was grumpy because she hadn't had tea.

"What?" she snapped. "Don't you have routine things you do during your day?"

"Not while I'm out on an assignment."

She scoffed. "Then I guess you're nothing more than a boring brute like the rest of the males I know."

Boring brute? He couldn't help it as he said, "Oh yes, I'm just a normal male who can idly do whatever he pleases."

That earned him a smile, even if she didn't look at him. "Normal. My, how my father would react to hearing that."

"Not a fan I take it. I get that a lot."

She added a few more sticks to the fire and scooted the embers with her boot. "He harbors the same beliefs as many in Nàdair."

"You don't sound like you agree."

Selina eyed him. "Giving me a chance to speak today?"

He grimaced. "Maybe your words rang a little too true last night."

She didn't respond for a long moment. The kettle whistled and she grabbed for it like a youngling reaching for chocolate. It wasn't until she'd placed a tea ball in the mug that she said, "Maybe the texts are outdated." She didn't look up. "I'd venture to say no one knows who you really are when you're not fighting for your life." Rion wasn't even sure *he* knew who he was without the constant stress.

He shrugged. "Their loss."

Another smirk as she swirled her tea, gripping the mug with both hands. "You know, I thought you'd be a bit more . . . scary."

He heard those inside moving. Someone stood at the window. "How so?"

Selina gave a half-hearted wave of her hand. "You know how rumors go. You're supposed to drink the blood of your enemies, bathe in it if there's anything left. Everything that walks is supposed to fall at your feet or you'll turn them into dust. You know, the crazy things."

Rion smirked again and felt some of the tension release from his shoulders. He picked up a stick and poked the fire, stirring some of the embers to life. "I must be the epitome of disappointments."

"The absolute worst." She laughed and the sound drew his gaze to her face, down the curve of her neck. "I'm actually relieved."

"Why recruit me then?"

Another shrug. "Maybe I was curious. Maybe I wanted the challenge." She smiled. "Restraining you would have been exhausting."

"You could have certainly tried."

Her eyes slid up to his, sparking with a glimmer he was already beginning to crave. "You think just because you bested me in one sparring match that I couldn't take you on?"

Rion met that challenge with a spark of his own. "Oh, I know you couldn't take me on."

"That has to be the most arrogant thing I've ever heard."

"Then I guess the humans have one thing about us right."

She shifted the coals again. "Were you holding back that much?"

"Only a lot." Never mind the fact that her magic had been easy to subdue as well.

She shook her head. "Well, there goes my bragging rights."

They sat in silence, letting the sun warm their bodies as Selina sipped her tea. He'd be working with them for a while. With all of them. He supposed he could make some sort of effort. If it backfired, well, it wasn't like he hadn't faced that before.

"You lean too far forward when you strike. It makes your movements predictable."

She stopped and stared at him, her mouth slightly agape. "You didn't have to tell me that."

No, he didn't, especially when he could have kept the information to himself and used it against her. "Call it my attempt at being friendly."

A smirk played on her lips. "The Demon of Alastríona, being friendly with a Fae he barely knows. Life the way we know it must be coming to an end."

"Let's hope not."

She poured herself another cup. "Can I expect your friendliness to extend to my comrades?"

Rion tilted his head toward the cabin and caught more than one face staring at them, hands no doubt gripping their weapons.

He sighed. "Don't push your luck." But Rion couldn't hide the smile on his face.

CHAPTER SEVEN

reakfast was short, awkward, and unsatisfactory as the warriors each served themselves from the dried reserves in their packs. Rion's stomach grumbled even after he finished off the jerky.

They stared at him as he sat in the far corner nearest to the door. Selina offered an easy smile, but the rest—he wasn't sure friendly would extend to him let alone the other way around.

Selina. Their short conversation had been . . . interesting. He'd never imagined there would be Fae who didn't believe in the ancient texts. Everyone he'd ever countered followed them.

It gave Rion some hope for the future. Maybe he could have friends after all. Maybe not every female would run at the mere sight of him.

Once they'd finished, Selina unfolded her map and spread it out in the center of the floor. No one bothered with the furniture.

They drew closer to watch as she studied her hand-marked dots.

"We're here," she pointed, then slid her finger down the map. "And our first target is here."

"Fernsworth?" the short female asked, her brow arched. "Weren't they the first to volunteer warriors two years ago for," she paused and looked at Rion.

"He lives in the palace," Selina said. "He knows." The humans had threatened an invasion that hadn't gone over well when they tried to cross through the Sirens' territory. They'd carried all manner of iron weapons, but only one boat had successfully made the crossing. Brónach hadn't shown them an ounce of mercy.

"A lot can change in two years. According to the logs, several merchants are set to arrive tomorrow and begin preparing for the solstice. We'll use the foot traffic to hide ourselves among the citizens."

"We're all going?" another asked.

Selina shook her head. "Three will accompany me. The other nine of you will be infiltrating the smaller villages to gather information."

"And the city farther south?" the eldest female asked.

"We'll hit it last. Their involvement is merely suspected."

"They could be the central hub. They'd have the funds," the male said.

"We'll see; remember, intel first."

Selina assigned their teams. It was easy. Gathering intel was short and to the point. They'd each spend two weeks at their given locations, then meet back at the cabin to exchange information.

Rion's assignment was the only one that differed. He'd expected as much. What he hadn't expected was her outlandish plan.

"EXPLAIN TO me again why this is necessary?" They strolled down the dirt road leading to Fernsworth with Selina's arm in his. Grassy plains surrounded them on all sides and a cool summer breeze kept lifting Selina's hair, hitting him with her intoxicating wildflower scent. It was bad enough that she was on his arm, her body pressed close to his. He swore the gods were testing every ounce of his self-restraint.

They'd left the safe house two days ago. Selina had ordered the male and the short-haired female to accompany them separately. Rion wasn't sure if they lingered behind or had already entered the city. His guess was that they'd gone ahead, just to be sure Selina wouldn't run into any trouble.

"Because you need to learn to relax before we walk through those gates. You're as high-strung as a Fae at their first sparring match. Keep that up and you'll blow our cover before we even begin." She wasn't wrong. His entire body had locked up as soon as she'd looped her arm with his.

Rion swallowed hard, trying not to look at her. "I meant," he cleared his throat. "Why do we have to go through with it at all?"

He caught her smirk from the corner of his eye. "Because seeing you with a female will throw them off and make them think you have a heart beneath that cold shell of yours." He wasn't inclined to agree.

His face burned when she leaned closer, her body brushing against his. "I want them to underestimate you. You're here as a distraction. With you drawing their focus, the others will be free to look around. Plus, being who you are, the governor will be forced to invite you to his estate."

"And you plan to snoop around?"

"With you distracting him, yes." Right, because they were just going to let her wander the halls without an escort.

Rion tried to slow his breathing, but only ended up inhaling more of her scent. It felt like every nerve in his body had ignited all at once. *A tool*, he reminded himself. He was nothing more than a tool to her.

Rion glanced down at their linked arms and the way Selina's slender frame moved next to his. She was so *close*. Closer than any female had ever dared. And she still wasn't afraid.

Don't let her manipulate you, Saoirse's warning rang through him.

He was failing. This female's entire essence was far worse than any alcohol he'd ever consumed. He was in such deep shit already.

Rion felt her eyes on him, but he kept his head forward, staring at the city gates in the distance. "Does this make you uncomfortable?"

His face burned hotter. "Saoirse warned me about you."

He saw her brows rise from the corner of his eye. "Your sister? How so?"

"She said you were good at manipulating people."

Selina laughed, that same singsong sound he'd heard after they'd spared. And damn it if it didn't do something to his already addled mind. He needed to step away from her. Get some air.

"Well, she wasn't wrong." Selina was silent for a long moment. "Is that what you think I'm doing to you?"

"Aren't you?"

She smirked and shifted her focus back to the city ahead. "Maybe a little."

He stiffened all over again. "Why?"

She shrugged. "I have the chance to make the most powerful Fae in Brónach uncomfortable and you think I wouldn't take it?"

Rion clenched his jaw. The guards came into view. Four of them, all standing where they should be. He glanced down at her again. Noted the small smile on her face. He didn't know why he opened his mouth, why he bothered to say anything at all, but the words tumbled out, making him feel inferior in a way he hadn't felt since his father had scolded him for dripping paint on a new rug.

"I've never had a female . . ." he trailed off, internally kicking himself. He should have just kept his mouth shut.

Selina tilted her head up again, exposing her slender neck. A neck he hadn't been able to stop staring at since their sparring session. A smile played on her lips despite her effort to keep it hidden. "You're, what, nineteen, right?" He nodded. "And you've never had a girlfriend?"

He couldn't look at her long. Not with her this close. Rion rolled his eyes instead and waved a hand out to encompass the grass shifting with the breeze. "I'm sure there's a line of females waiting outside my door back home. I'll be sure to pick one."

She jabbed him with her finger and for a moment, Rion's heart jolted. He half pulled away, expecting to see a knife protruding from his ribs, but—

"Relax, geez." His heart wouldn't stop thundering. "Maybe you need to do more group missions, forget that solo life for a while. Get out in the field and you'll bed a female or two."

Rion was certain his face had turned another color entirely. He cursed the way his heart skipped and damned the thing for pounding so hard. Rion tried clearing his throat and prayed his voice wouldn't betray him. "I suppose you've bedded your share of males?" A flash of anger rose in him and she laughed, that beautiful voice carrying over the vast open field.

Rion was certain it wasn't part of her façade as she said, "Males are always so territorial." He bit the inside of his cheek. Selina continued. "Males, a female or two just to experiment. I've had my share of lovers, but none worth introducing to my family."

"Why not?"

She scoffed. "Because my uncle has certain . . . expectations." Not father. She wrinkled her nose. "He's too protective, as most males are, and won't approve of a match that is anything below his standards."

"I'll be sure to be on my best behavior then."

Selina smirked. "If we succeed and you make a good show of it, perhaps I'll put in a good word to some females back home." She playfully nudged him with her shoulder. "Maybe land you a real date."

A date. With a female. The thought was absurd. Anyone with him would just be another target for assassins. He was sure that would be a good conversation starter.

But no matter how ridiculous it sounded, the image of him walking the streets of Nàdair with a beautiful female at his side sounded . . . nice. To take her to dinner. Talk to her about plant life and possibly even chess if she was interested. To open doors for her. Treat her. Please her.

A fantasy. But a nice one nonetheless.

He glanced down at Selina and found her smiling back. She had her arm looped through his, her hand resting lightly against his bare forearm. The feel of her calloused palm had his heart racing all over again. Maybe, just maybe, he would be permitted something good for a change.

The only problem was that he didn't want another female. He was happy with this. With her. "I'll make sure my acting is sublime."

The white pillars of the city gates reflected the sun. Intricately carved vines raced up the marble columns, a structure made to resemble the palace halls in Nàdair.

The sentries stationed at the gate appeared bored as they leaned against those very pillars, passing cards between one another. Their swords were sheathed and a few bottles rested against the marble.

It took far too long for one of them to look up, but when the male at the far end cared to glance their way, he scrambled to his feet, knocking over the bottle that had been resting against his knee. The contents spilled onto his companion's boot and the male cursed at his friend before following his gaze.

At Selina's request, Rion already had his sand up, billowing around them both in a display of power. He kept the grains from touching her though, just in case she didn't welcome the feel of his magic.

The first guard kicked a third who was still kneeling in the dirt with a pair of dice in his hand. The male gave his companion a vulgar gesture, then followed his eyes and jerked upright. He swayed a bit on his feet and Rion noted the bottle he tried to scoot out of sight with one foot.

"M-my Lord," the first said, his voice shaking. The male swallowed hard as Rion surveyed them, then their game, and finally the liquor that littered the ground. Far too many bottles for a single day. No wonder this place was on Selina's list. It would be easy for a rebel faction to infiltrate it. They probably let anyone through the gates without question, or were paid to look the other way.

If he'd been here for any other reason, Rion would have reprimanded them, likely fired them, and assigned new guards. But he wasn't here for that today.

"At ease," Rion said, keeping his voice as calm as he could manage. Something in him demanded he protect the female at his side, even if he knew she could protect herself. "I'm here on pleasure." None of them relaxed. Rion eyed the bottles again and they shifted nervously. "I trust I'll not be disrupted by," he searched for the word, "unnecessary disturbances during my visit?"

The first male nodded again. He seemed to be the only one capable of doing anything. "You have our word." He bowed at the waist and after a moment of hesitation—or perhaps a delay in their ability to think clearly—the others did the same.

Rion forced a smile. "Good." He made a show of looking Selina over and she offered him a smile in return. It wasn't entirely for show when Rion's gaze traveled to her lips, then the alluring curve of her throat before he said, "Enjoy the rest of your day then."

Rion forced himself to walk through the gates at a leisurely pace. Selina rested her head against his shoulder and he tried to keep his heart steady. The guards said nothing, but he could feel their stares burning into his back until they were out of earshot.

"I think you've undersold yourself," she whispered. "You're quite the actor." He didn't mention that some things weren't entirely an act.

They ambled down the busy street and Rion watched as Fae scrambled from his presence. Word of his arrival would spread quickly, which was what Selina hoped for. She wanted the governor to call on them. The male was first on her long list of suspects.

Fingers pointed and a few couples walked down side streets to avoid him. He clenched his jaw when they stared at Selina then whispered about the way she held him.

A warrior reached for his weapon on their left. Rion pinned him with a stare and the male froze, confusion written all over his face.

Selina patted Rion's arm. "Now, now, we're here for a bit of fun, remember?" She said it loud enough for those in the immediate vicinity to hear. As if she were the only one in the world who could quell the monster in their midst.

Another male reached for a weapon. Two more flinched. Rion braced himself, ready to protect Selina at any cost, but then the female was in front of him, staring into his eyes with a sweet, disarming smile. Rion's breath hitched. He was paralyzed. Frozen in time and space as she reached up and wrapped her arms around his neck.

His heart didn't know how to function anymore as she stared at him as if he were the only one who existed. Her amber eyes took him prisoner and he gladly let her hold the chains.

Then she kissed him.

Her lips were softer than he ever imagined. He didn't know what to do with his hands. His mouth. His breath. His body.

Her lips moved against his and he moved with her, wrapping his arms tentatively around her waist. He had no idea what she'd permit, where she drew the line.

She tasted like vanilla and sin and horrible decisions. All things he'd gladly live with for the rest of eternity.

She pulled away too soon, leaving him reeling. She offered a gentle smile and the way her face lit up was enough to challenge the sun in its glory.

Her arms slid down his chest, then she took his hand and laced her fingers between his. His body was on fire, cheeks just as flushed as hers. He knew he should turn his attention back to the Fae in the vicinity. He should access them for danger, but he couldn't drag his gaze away from her.

Selina ducked her head, as if suddenly bashful and all but dragged the abomination of Brónach through the streets like a love-sick teenager.

A breeze swept between the buildings, clearing his senses enough to take in the shocked faces surrounding them. The Fae who'd been reaching for their weapons now stood gaping at the pair. Those who'd been ready to flee had frozen in place, too stunned to move.

What she'd done—he knew the ruse. Knew what it could mean. But to have her touch him physically. To do so without revulsion . . .

He still tasted her on his tongue, still felt the slight gasp she'd loosed when he'd kissed her back. The shadow of her touch still caressed his neck and his heart wouldn't stop pounding.

An act, his mind kept repeating, but his heart wasn't listening. It was drugged, beyond reason or rational thought.

They continued down the street, Selina guiding his every step. Rion wanted to say something, but his tongue was too heavy, his thoughts jumbled. He didn't even realize where they were going until Selina pushed open the door to an inn.

Another smile and she released his hand and headed for the counter. Rion took the time to collect himself. He let the scents of alcohol and polished tables distract him from the female.

Only a handful of patrons occupied the space but they were too focused on their drinks to bother looking up.

Rion wondered if Selina had visited the city before and already planned to use this particular inn. With its low lighting and assorted tables, it was a perfect meeting place to exchange information with her comrades. Rion imagined her sneaking down in the dead of night when the other guests were too drunk to notice.

He heard his name and turned in time to see Selina pointing. The owner fumbled his cup at the sight of Rion's magic. Magic that was still dancing to the frantic beat of his heart.

Rion swore he heard Selina whisper something about Rion waking up grumpy if he slept on a poor bed. He rolled his eyes.

She exchanged coins for a key and minutes later, Selina was half skipping toward him, twirling the set on one finger. "All set," she declared, as if her mind weren't reeling whatsoever from what had occurred minutes ago.

"Glad my reputation could be useful." He couldn't look her in the eye.

She shrugged. "Can't blame a female for wanting a decent bed to sleep in."

Fear burned his nose and Rion looked behind Selina to find two males staring at them with wide eyes. He'd probably just ruined their buzz.

He followed her up the creaking stairs to the second floor like a creature on a leash. Only, instead of a tether, she controlled him with the sway of her hips and the way she batted her lashes.

She could control him with a lot less if she wished. He was willing to bet she knew it, too.

Doors stretched down a short hallway. Selina turned to one on their right and placed the heavy key into the lock. The wooden door swung open to reveal a mid-size room that was likely considered luxurious by the inn's standards.

A cold fireplace stood off to the left. The caretakers had already piled wood off to the side. More than enough to get through a few nights if they needed. Judging from the heat in the room, the flames wouldn't be necessary for anything other than boiling water.

Light sheets were neatly tucked along the bed and thick furs rugs surrounded the bedframe. Rion had marked the bathroom at the end of the hall but was glad to find one within the room.

"Take off your shoes," Selina demanded. "I don't want the furs ruined." Rion closed the door behind him, then eyed a stain already marring the rugs. They weren't new by any means. He could have argued, but decided against it and tugged off his boots.

Selina did the same, then marched straight for the bathroom.

"What are you doing?"

She already had her socks off and in hand before turning to him. Selina eyed the bathroom door as if to state the obvious. "Just because we're posing as travelers doesn't mean I have to smell like one. I'm taking a shower, dressing in something presentable, then going to the market."

Rion crossed his arms. "And what am I supposed to do in the meantime?"

A feline smile spread across her face. "You could always join me." His heart stopped then she laughed and his face heated. "Do whatever you like, but meet me in the market in two hours." She shut the door before he could reply. The water switched on and Rion tried not to imagine her removing her clothes. He definitely wasn't thinking about how her body had felt pressed against his own.

Rion stormed from the room. He need air. She hadn't even brought up the kiss, which meant it was just part of the ruse. Of course it was. She'd told him the whole thing was just an act. He inwardly kicked himself. They were on a mission and despite the awkward things this particular mission entailed, he needed to maintain an air of professionalism.

Rion bit the inside of his cheek so hard he tasted blood. Gods, why was she so . . . he'd never had a female . . . play with him the way she did. Hell, he'd never had anyone play with him or toy with his emotions as if he were anyone else in the world.

It was . . . refreshing. And despite the feelings coursing through his body, Rion wasn't sure he ever wanted it to stop.

He breathed in the fresh air of the bustling street and let his thoughts clear. He'd talk to her later. Or maybe they'd pretend it never happened. He could do that, he supposed.

Rion observed the Fae and half-breeds walking the streets. They regarded him oddly now, as if they didn't quite know what to do with him after Selina's very public display. A few had bags in their hands. He wondered if they were traveling for the solstice or fleeing the city due to his presence.

Rion marched straight for the governor's estate. He'd visited a time or two with Saoirse while on the hunt for their mother. The male who ran the city wasn't exactly what Rion would call a warrior. Not anymore, at least. All children with heightened magical talent were required to undergo rigorous training, but once a Fae graduated from the academy, it was up to them to keep up on that training.

The governor worried more about his social standing and political image than his swordplay. Rion briefly wondered how Selina planned to handle the male. Certainly not with physical threats if she wanted to keep their mission a secret. Hopefully she didn't plan to deal with him in another physical manner.

A growl escaped his throat at the thought of another's male's hands anywhere near her. Two civilians jumped and fled down a side alley.

Rion took a breath and made a sad attempt at burying his instincts. A mission, he reminded himself. Selina wasn't his and she might never want to be. If she needed to do certain things to ensure their success, then he couldn't let himself interfere. It wasn't his business.

But he wanted it to be. Rion wondered, not for the first time, if he'd ever shake the teachings of the ancient text. If a female might one day look at him the way Selina pretended to.

The buildings grew larger, some towering to a third story with long flowering vines draping from the balconies to create a blanket of mixed colors and pleasant aromas.

It was always jarring to visit another city. While Nàdair had plenty of regular buildings and storefronts, the citizens mostly lived within the trees, opting to warp them as they saw fit to accommodate their families. The elders claimed it kept them close to their heritage. According to them, living apart from nature and the Fairy Folk risked the Fae forgetting where they came from. Some older Fae even sneered at those who lived in handmade structures rather than utilizing the trees.

The road widened then split, circling around the governor's estate and the large expanse of land surrounding it. The manor itself was only two stories, thank the gods for that, but it stretched wide. Rion counted the windows, grimacing at the number of rooms they might have to search.

A pair of guards stood at the front gate, looking ready to doze in the warm sun. At least they'd be easy enough to subdue. The entire yard was surrounded by a metal fence with easily climbable vines weaving between the posts. Fountains and red brick led up to the front door and wrapped around the perimeter. A pristine cobblestone walkway stretched into a garden that smelled of roses and peonies.

He snorted at the immaculate lawn. He doubted anyone was even allowed to walk on it. Such a waste. They could have at least planted a few trees to add some shade and color.

Rion prowled the perimeter. Some noticed his presence, mostly those working in the garden, but they wisely avoided his stare and busied themselves elsewhere. One retreated inside the manor, no doubt to report his presence to appointed officials. Rion estimated he had about ten minutes before someone came out to greet him.

He found two more guards at the rear entrance, but none prowled the yard. If they held secrets about a rebel faction, they weren't doing much to protect them.

Rion heard the familiar clank of chains and glanced toward the garden only to find a slave staring at him. She quickly looked away. He surveyed her clean clothes and full figure. At least they seemed to be treating them fairly here, which was more than he could say of some nobles.

Most deemed the half-breeds so below their station, they weren't worthy of new clothes or even daily meals, but there were those among the higher circles who frowned upon having a dirty creature touching their things. Let alone having to stare at them day in and day out. Their care was purely a selfish motivation. One he could hardly stomach.

Rion clenched his jaw. Saoirse had offered him a slave once. Just someone to sort and tend to his personal things. He'd never been angry with his sister before, but he'd come close to snapping that day. Saoirse had taken the slave for herself and never offered another.

He didn't need someone following him around. Those who worked in the palace were bad enough.

Footsteps had Rion turning to find a well-dressed Fae male approaching from behind. The male paused several feet away, almost too far to warrant a normal conversation, and promptly bowed at the waist. "My Lord." He rose and struggled to hold Rion's gaze. "We didn't expect your arrival." The male's voice trembled and the fear radiating from him had Rion's stomach turning. "Please allow us to accommodate—"

"That's not necessary," Rion interrupted before the male could list a dozen inns that might suit him. The male wrung his hands together. Sweat beaded on his forehead.

Rion let his gaze drift toward the pair of slaves waiting before the gate. A cart, just large enough to accommodate a single person, stood behind them. No horses, of course; that was what the slaves were for.

He clenched his jaw. He didn't care about their histories. Seeing the half-breeds treated as little more than animals boiled the blood in his veins.

"I didn't realize I was required to announce my arrival." His voice came out rougher than he'd intended. The male flinched.

"No, of course you don't, My Lord. I only meant that we could have prepared—"

"At ease. I'm not here on business."

The male didn't seem to know what to do with that. He opened his mouth, closed it, then said, "Oh." It took him a moment to collect himself, likely to think through why Rion, The Demon, would be standing in front of the governor's manor if he wasn't here to address their ledgers. "Would you like me to arrange a meeting?"

A smile tugged at Rion's lips. Selina would be thrilled. "If it doesn't cause too much trouble."

"Of course not," the male beamed, his demeanor relaxing by the second. Maybe he hoped to be rewarded in some way for the arrangement. Or maybe he was just happy to avoid Rion's wrath. What had Selina claimed again? That others believed he drank the blood of his enemies? He shivered at the thought. He didn't even like his meat rare.

"We actually have a banquet tomorrow evening to celebrate a new trading partnership with Whiteridge." Rion blinked at the mention of the southern city. "Of course, if you prefer a more private meeting, then I can arrange that as well. The governor would be more than happy to accommodate whatever—"

"The banquet will suffice," he interrupted again. Selina had dismissed Whiteridge's involvement, but if the two cities were connected in a trade agreement, then perhaps they were more involved than previously assumed. Were both cities plotting against Nàdair?

Relations with Whiteridge had always been strained. Just a few years ago, he'd accompanied Saoirse on an assignment there. It had been one of the most intense missions he'd ever been on. It was also where they'd first discovered the poison or a variation of it. Despite Selina dismissing them, it wouldn't surprise Rion in the slightest if they were at the center of everything.

"I'll be bringing a guest," Rion said.

The male's eyes widened. "Is our Lady Saoirse with you?" He glanced behind Rion as if he might spot her wandering around.

"No, she's a . . . personal friend of mine." Rion wondered for a moment if the words would come out as a lie. They didn't.

The male bowed. "Any guest of yours is a guest of ours."

"Good. What time shall we arrive?"

"We're serving appetizers and wine at five. Dinner is scheduled for six."

Rion nodded and the male bowed again. "Is there anything else I can do for you, My Lord?"

Rion's gaze returned to the manor. He noted the faces peering through the curtains. They ducked away when he caught them staring.

"You're dismissed."

Another bow. A lingering stare, then the male was gone, rushing away as fast as he could without running.

Rion smirked. Selina would be pleased. He hoped. Everything was already lining up and it was only day one.

After circling the property a final time just to rile them up a bit, Rion turned toward the market. The hot sun had risen high and was beating down on his already tanned skin.

He'd spent the beginning of summer outside every day, learning to perfect the magic that still tried to slip from his control. He had a far better grasp on it than he had five years ago, but if someone provoked him too much, it would roar to life of its own volition.

He still practiced day in and day out, willing the magic to yield to him completely. He didn't need to unintentionally kill someone again.

Caol's death still . . . bothered him. It didn't matter that Caol had tried to kill him first, Rion hadn't wanted the male dead. It was an unfortunate incident that would haunt him for the rest of his life.

"You shouldn't look so serious," a familiar voice drawled. "You'll scare everyone off." Rion turned to find Selina, a much different Selina, staring at him with a hand braced on her hip.

In place of the black clothes, she'd changed into a pale blue shirt that dipped in the front, revealing far too much skin. A dark pair of loose shorts showed off the muscles of her tanned legs.

The memory of the kiss returned two-fold. He imagined running his hands up and down her thighs. Wondered what it might feel like to have them wrapped around his waist.

She'd left her hair down, the strands still slightly damp from her shower. Her eyes were alight with amusement as his gaze tracked up and down her form.

Selina cocked a teasing smile and tapped the side of her face. "You have a bit of drool."

Rion snapped his mouth shut and turned away, suddenly interested in a very plain loose stone jutting out of the path. They should fix it. He should tell the governor when they visited. Someone could trip.

"You aren't armed," he said, trying anything to distract himself.

Selina sauntered closer and Rion had to resist stepping away as she wrapped her hands around his arm and pulled him close. Gods, she smelled like heaven.

"Why would I bring weapons when we're simply going for a stroll through this beautiful city? Besides," she nudged him. "I have a big bad Fae male to fight all my battles for me."

Right, their mask. The mask that felt all too real because his stupid instincts wouldn't stop roaring at him.

At least two dozen eyes watched the couple as they wandered into the main hub of the market. Patrons and shopkeepers alike paused mid conversation, many trying to decide whether to finish their transactions or outright flee.

Selina approached the first vendor that caught her eye and the male running it twisted his hands nervously, glancing between her and Rion as Selina scanned the jewelry laid across his table.

He watched Selina run her fingers over various pieces. Beautiful pieces. Many were items his mother would have likely worn.

"Is there something the miss finds to her liking?" The vendor's voice shook and the fear leaking from him burned Rion's nose. He'd always hated the smell.

Rion turned his attention to the shadowed corners and the lowlifes waiting to take advantage of unsuspecting guests. If it weren't for his presence, Selina would have been a prime target. Her casual dress made her look like a tourist and the lack of weapons only amplified the ruse of her innocent nature.

For the first time, Rion was seeing a picture of exactly how she worked. And how well she wore her disguise.

Too well.

She picked up a golden necklace with red jewels inlaid throughout and lifted it toward the sun. Rion scanned her again. Surely she wouldn't seriously leave herself vulnerable. Not when Alec and Saoirse claimed she was one of the best commanders in Nàdair.

A shift of her hip had Rion looking lower. She stood with her legs just a little wider than usual. Against her inner thigh then but given how short her shorts were meant the blade would be high.

He stopped thinking about it. Tried to stop thinking about her altogether and failed miserably.

Selina carefully set the beautiful necklace back on the small cushion. "What do you have that would match his eyes?"

The shopkeeper's mouth gaped, mirroring Rion's own expression. But reluctantly, as if it might cost the merchant his life, the male shifted his gaze to Rion and met his eyes. Something not many dared to do. Fear shone there and amplified when Selina sauntered over to Rion, her hips purposefully swaying.

She linked her arm with his, leaned close, and Rion forced himself to look at her. "I love his eyes. They carry so much depth, wouldn't you agree?" She turned back to the shop owner and the male nodded, his expression changing from a fearful Fae to an artist inspecting his canvas. Rion refused to move, no matter how much his body demanded it. He didn't like being the center of attention. Not like this. He'd never had another survey him so . . . intently.

The male glanced at the items laid out on his table, then moved behind it and pulled out a chest full of tiny drawers. He surveyed them, opened a few, then his eyes lit up in triumph.

The male presented Selina with a pair of small gemstones barely as big as the tip of Rion's smallest finger. "Will these do?"

Selina stepped closer to inspect the stones and Rion sagged with relief. He couldn't look away, however, when her eyes lit up, truly lit up in a way that he was sure had nothing to do with their assignment.

"These are—" Words seemed to fail her.

"You won't find another pair like them. I traded with a male on the northern continent. He claimed the gemstone is rare, even in their mountain ranges."

"You went to the human lands?" Rion said, a bit of skepticism in his voice. Fae couldn't lie, but setting foot on the northern continent was largely unheard of. Especially with their history.

The male nodded, his fear sparking anew. "I just returned a few months ago. It was . . . quite a journey." Rion would say so, considering a Fae had to travel to the port city of Pádraigín, then cross the sea, which, he'd been told, was a two-week journey in itself.

"What can you make them into?" Selina asked, not at all interested in the male's story about how he'd acquired them.

The male studied Selina and Rion had to resist the urge to growl to indicate the female was taken. A perfect part of their ruse, sure, but far too real. He was certain Selina would notice.

"Would you like a pair of earrings?"

She beamed. "That would be lovely."

It occurred to Rion that he hadn't informed Selina about the invite to the governor's party. He asked, "Could you have them finished before tomorrow night?" Selina cast him a questioning glance. "We've been invited to a banquet," he said by way of explanation.

Selina clasped her hands, but the surprise on her face was real. "Oh, you didn't tell me." She turned back to the merchant. "You'll have to forgive him, my companion doesn't seem to understand that artistry takes time. I understand if—"

"They'll be done before sunrise." The male puffed out his chest as if he'd just been challenged. "You shall wear your gems at the event even if I have to be up all night."

Selina gave him an easy smile. "I look forward to it."

The male bowed. "Of course, My Lady." Silence stretched for a long moment, then Selina seemed to catch on to the male glancing at her purse.

"Oh, right, I'm sorry." She leaned close to the male, an action that had Rion wanting to protest, but whatever she whispered to him had the male's mouth gaping.

"Truly?"

Selina held a finger up to her lips and winked. "It'll be our little secret."

He bowed again. "Of course, My Lady." She took Rion's arm once again and pulled him away from the stall, moving toward the next.

Rion didn't wait for them to be out of earshot before he asked, "What was that about?" Surely the male wouldn't give her something so expensive in exchange for her . . . attention, but—

Selina lowered her voice to a whisper. "Just using a family name to my advantage."

"Mine?"

She balked. "*Mine*. You're not the only one with money, you know."

Right. He glanced back at the male who was already bent over his table. "You probably just promised him an entire month's wages."

"More like six. Hopefully he spends it well."

"And your . . . uncle," he'd almost said father, "is okay with spending that kind of money on jewelry?"

She shrugged. "He likes to dote on his niece."

Rion smirked, placing a hand over hers when a pair of males looked too close. They turned away. "So you're protected and spoiled."

"I am not spoiled. I'm immaculately cared for. He likes it when I pick out my own gifts. Says it saves him the trouble."

They moved on to another stall and Rion watched Selina purchase a gold necklace. At the next she picked out a matching bracelet.

The female before him was supposed to be a warrior and he was supposed to be the cursed Lord of Brónach, yet in this square, walking arm in arm, he felt . . . normal. He wondered how it would feel to have her walking with him in Nàdair. Would everyone glare forever or would they eventually accept his presence?

Selina disappeared into a clothing tent, claiming she needed to try on a few things. He waited outside, still watching the shadows. Thankfully, Rion wasn't forced to carry her trinkets. She paid someone to carry them back to the inn.

If her intention was to draw attention, she'd certainly done a fine job of it. Every merchant in the square now eyed her as if she could pay an entire year's wages with one purchase. She probably could, given what he'd already seen. Or her uncle could, at least.

Rion wondered if Saoirse knew more about her family. Likely so. It would be yet another question he'd have for his sister, once she calmed down, of course. He was sure Saoirse would have a thing or two to say about him showing interest in the female.

Selina emerged from the tent and they continued through the marketplace. She purchased a few items he deemed useful, like a new set of throwing knives. And went unnecessarily extravagant for other items, like fancy soaps and shampoos. Apparently the inn's weren't good enough.

After what seemed like hours, the pair made their way back to the inn. The owner greeted Selina by the door and claimed all her belongings had been placed just inside the room. Selina deposited a few extra coins into the male's hand.

He bowed and asked Selina to let him know if she needed anything else. Rion wasn't even sure he existed anymore. He arched a brow. Maybe he should have just resorted to buying people's favor from the beginning. He wondered if extra coins might have earned him a few less attempts on his life.

The Fae were surprisingly . . . kind with Selina around. Maybe they thought she held him in check. He wasn't sure he minded. Sure, they were still cautious, but with their attention on her—or rather, her purse—he was nothing more than a dark shadow. He was . . . free.

Selina turned on him as soon as the room door shut. "Spill it. What banquet?"

Rion gave her a knowing smirk. "There's an event at the governor's house to celebrate a trade deal they made between themselves and Whiteridge."

She raised a brow. "That's—I left you alone for less than an hour. How did you secure an invite?"

Rion shrugged. "Family name and all."

She pursed her lips. "Tomorrow?"

"Dinner is served at six." He kicked off his boots by the door. "Don't worry, I didn't do anything to draw attention. I was just scouting the perimeter and one of the staff saw me."

"And he just . . . invited you?"

"You sound skeptical."

"Don't people generally try to, you know," she pulled a finger across her throat.

"Thanks for the reminder."

She braced her hands on her hips. "Well, how do we know they don't plan to kill us?"

Rion shrugged. "We don't."

"Great." She blew out a breath. "I guess I'll have to hide a few more weapons on me. I might have to revisit the tailor to see what she can do." She huffed again. "Do you know how difficult it is to carry weapons in a dress?"

"So don't wear one."

Selina balked. "You need to work on your expectations if I'm going to introduce you to females."

"We're on a mission. It's an entirely different situation." He had a sister. He knew how much some females liked to dress up.

"Yes, a mission where I'm supposed to be enjoying a summer retreat with my new boyfriend." She said it so casually, but Rion's face heated all over again. "If I walk in there dressed like a warrior, they'll get suspicious."

"Maybe they'd assume I prefer a warrior over a noble."

"Do you?"

The question jarred him enough that he stopped counting his knives and looked at her. Her face was wholly serious.

"I—I don't know. Maybe."

A smirk. "I'm just teasing. Regardless of your personal preferences, they need to see me as a noble woman who needs a Fae male protecting her. It will give me certain . . . privileges."

"Such as?"

She pulled one of the boxes toward herself and opened the lid. "The chance to sneak off and search a room or two. If I present myself as having a fraction of intelligence, they won't let me out of their sight."

"If you're gathering information, what will the others be doing?" He hadn't forgotten about her comrades. He'd been searching for them in the marketplace, but they'd kept their distance.

"They have their orders. We'll exchange basic information tonight and go from there."

Rion watched her pull out the new knife set. She loosened the belts and fitted them to her thighs. The way her fingers glided over the buckles distracted him long enough that Selina asked, "Anything else?"

He made to turn. *Leave it alone*, he chided himself. "Earlier," he started. She let the buckles fall loose. "Never mind."

"Don't *never mind* me, what?"

"When we first entered the city . . ." Gods, why was it so hard to form words?

She stared at her weapons now. "The kiss?" He was silent as she fiddled with the straps again. "Sorry. They looked as if they were going to maw you right there in the middle of the street. It was the only thing I could think of that might distract them."

"Right." He should have just let it go.

She peered up and Rion turned away. "It was your first, wasn't it?"

"It doesn't matter."

"I—"

"I need to shower." He entered the small bathroom and quickly locked the door behind him. Rion leaned back against it and steadied himself. Gods, what the hell was wrong with him? What was this female doing to him?

Pitiful.

They were on an assignment and everything she did was just part of an act.

But gods, she did it so damn well. That was the whole problem. He was clinging to every word, every brush of her body and hands.

Rion shoved his feelings down and pushed off from the wall before stripping out of his dirty clothes. At least his reactions added to their ruse. He'd let those stay genuine. Selina was right. Having her at his side was the perfect distraction.

He could play along, perhaps even let himself believe it. Just a bit.

Rion turned on the water and let it reach near scalding temperatures. He could do this. He could pretend just as well as she did.

CHAPTER EIGHT

ion dried off, dressed quickly, and reentered their shared room to find Selina sitting cross-legged on the floor with a map and an assortment of documents spread out before her. She clutched a mug in one hand, an enticing earthy aroma curling up from the rising steam.

She glanced up once, then returned to her documents without a word. He wondered if she'd already met with her comrades downstairs. He'd heard her leave while he was in the shower.

She wore a new set of pale pink pajamas with a large floral pattern stretching across the middle that reminded Rion of Nàdair's spring gardens. Thank the gods she'd buttoned the shirt all the way to the top of her throat. Maybe now he could focus.

"Seàn secured the layout of the area this afternoon." She tapped a finger on the blueprint. "But it looks like there's a single-floor basement that isn't listed."

"Do you plan on searching the basement?"

"I plan to search everything, but it's not a priority. They'll likely have their secrets stashed somewhere obvious. A safe hidden behind a picture frame or inside of a hollowed-out book." She shook her head. "They think themselves clever, but it's all been done before."

Rion leaned against the bathroom doorframe. "And how do you

plan on getting in?"

"You did that part with the invite."

"Right, but it's not like they're going to just let you wander the place."

She waved a hand. "Once they're all drunk, I'll sneak off to the bathroom. A female has to check her makeup and all."

"That has to be the oldest trick in the book."

"Yet it works every time." She batted her eyelashes and clasped her hands. "No one bothers to look twice at a pretty female who feels the powder on her nose is misplaced."

"And if you're caught?"

She dropped her hands and picked up her mug again. "I'm drunk myself, of course. And lost because the manor is just *so* big and there are so many rooms. Oh, and an interesting painting caught my eye."

"You'll be alone and they'll be drunk, as you pointed out, what happens when a male decides to take advantage?"

She scoffed as if he were being ridiculous. "Do I look defenseless to you?"

"They could have iron."

She crinkled her nose. "Doubtful, but if that happens then it's a good thing my big bad boyfriend will come to the rescue."

He raised a brow. "And you just . . . trust me to have your back?"

She leveled him with a look. "Are you planning to abandon me?"

He ran a hand through his hair. "Of course not, I'm just trying to figure out why you'd trust me with this instead of one of the others."

"They're not the ones with an invite, for one. And two, it's your job and last I checked, you have a flawless record. I doubt your pride would allow you to fail on my account."

Rion stared at her. Her relaxed posture. The lack of weapons or magic. Night had fallen and shadows danced along the wall as the candle flames flickered. Voices trickled up from downstairs, but the second floor was silent. They were alone.

"Why aren't you afraid of me?"

She eyed him, then the fire. "So many questions. You probably should have asked them before we left Nàdair."

"As I recall, the details of this mission weren't exactly disclosed. Otherwise, I might have."

"You knew you'd be working with us. Last I checked, putting one's life in the hands of their comrades is fairly normal."

"Not for me it isn't."

A shrug. "Maybe you don't give people enough credit."

"Oh, I have." His voice was a near whisper. "And I've regretted it every single time." Not just Caol. No, he'd worked with plenty of groups that had wound up dead by his hand. "Three days was the longest any of them waited."

She stretched out her legs. "Then I guess we're setting a new record, aren't we?"

"I want to know," he pushed and she looked at him from beneath lowered lashes. His breath caught from the way the firelight illuminated her eyes. "Why aren't you afraid of me?"

She huffed. "Maybe I'm just good at hiding it."

"Exceptional."

Her jaw worked. "Maybe you're not who I thought you'd be."

"Is that good or bad?"

She smirked. "Take it however you want." She stood and Rion followed her every move as she poured hot water into another cup, refilled her own, then returned to her place on the floor. She set the mug before her and placed a fresh tea ball inside before gesturing to it. "I made you some."

She'd already had the tea ball ready. His eyes traced her face, her pulse, the gentle rise and fall of her chest. "Is it poisoned?"

At that, she chuckled. "I take great offense to that." She lifted his cup to her lips and sipped the hot liquid before meeting his gaze again. "Rest assured, Rion of Brónach. When I try to kill you, it won't be with a cup of tea."

He couldn't draw breath and wasn't entirely sure his voice was steady. "*Do* you plan to kill me?"

Another smirk. "I haven't decided yet."

CHAPTER NINE

He drank the tea, mulled over plans, slept on the floor with his magic laid out around him, and had far too many inappropriate dreams about a certain bronze haired female.

Rion woke before sunrise and raced from the room, desperate to separate himself from her. He just needed fresh air, a moment or two to collect himself.

His mind refused to settle. Rion ran the perimeter of the city twice before he could think clearly. He moved through a series of training exercises until his muscles shook, then marched back through the city gates.

The guards were the same as before, with the exception of an added female. All nodded and this time none appeared glassy-eyed or inebriated.

Familiar scents of eggs, steak, and bagels wafted through the air and Rion found himself drifting to a storefront. He swore the poor female inside would die on the spot. She greeted him with a smile on her face but couldn't stop her hands from shaking as he purchased a few pastries from the window shelf.

Mimicking Selina's actions, Rion left a generous tip. Even so, he'd choose a different shop tomorrow. Saoirse had been poisoned once before and she'd taught him all the ways to avoid it.

Her first tip: avoid routine.

It was still early by the time he returned to the inn. A few patrons remained, some still dozing at various tables with their mugs in hand. They'd have a raging headache when they woke.

The male who owned the inn gave Rion a subtle nod in greeting and appeared to relax when Rion headed straight for the stairs.

Selina was in the bathroom when he entered.

"I'm back," he announced, just so she wouldn't exit in anything indecent, though, from what he'd already learned about the female, she might do it anyway just to get a rise out of him. He sighed. Perhaps he wouldn't survive this mission after all. Not if she had any say in the matter.

Moments later, Selina emerged, her hair damp and, thankfully, clothes on. A casual outfit similar to yesterday's. One look at him and she wrinkled her nose. "I hope you plan on showering."

He smirked. "Maybe the governor would be less inclined to follow us through the manor if I didn't."

"You will shower, or I'll find someone else to go in your place and make up a grand excuse about him representing you." Rion chuckled, then she eyed the bag. "What's that?"

"Breakfast."

Her eyes lit up. "You brought me breakfast?"

"I thought it would be impolite to eat in front of you."

"Gods bless whoever taught you manners."

"Best behavior, remember? I have an uncle to impress."

She strode over and snatched the bag from his hand. "Which ones are mine?"

"All of them." Her eyes widened again and Rion scratched the back of his head, suddenly feeling like he'd gone overboard by purchasing six pastries. "I wasn't sure what you liked and I ate mine on the way here."

"Probably stuffed it down your throat like a heathen. Typical male."

He ignored the jab. "You have errands, right?"

She nodded, having already taken a bite of a jelly-filled roll. Powder covered her lips and he had to look away again as he tried not to imagine wiping it off with more than just his finger. Gods save him.

"I'll see you this afternoon then."

THE MORNING passed without incident. Rion went to another shop for lunch, paying special attention to those who prepared his food. He wasn't sure the male cooking had ever moved so fast in his life.

Rion missed having Saoirse at his side. She'd always put people at ease with her quick charm, a quality he didn't seem to possess, even with extra coins.

He circled the manor again, then toured the city, marking abandoned buildings and the dark streets that civilians seemed to avoid. People stared and whispered, but none confronted him. He ventured back to the market where those working the stalls were a bit more . . . inviting. He was certain their uneasy smiles were due to Selina and the hope that she'd visit again.

Rion searched for her companions but they'd vanished entirely. He wondered if they'd try to ambush him at some point. He supposed it would wait until Selina made up her mind about killing him.

She was so . . . casual about it. He'd thwarted several assassination attempts. She knew it, everyone knew it, and yet she found it appropriate to joke about such things as if they didn't matter. Maybe to her they didn't.

Rion found a spot in the shade and opened a book he'd purchased from a vendor that morning.

Hours flew by with the breeze rustling his hair. Birds and small animals played in the tall grasses and he stretched out his legs, shifting positions until it was time to meet Selina. Just because they were on a mission together didn't mean he was required to spend every waking moment with her.

The inn was far busier when he reentered and the sharp scent of alcohol assaulted his delicate senses as he pushed through the heavy doors. Rion ignored the lot of them and marched up the stairs.

Selina stood beside the bed when he entered.

He blinked. His throat went dry.

She was bent at the waist, one leg hiked up on the edge of the bed as she fought with the buckles of her shoe. No, her heel. Gods, she was actually wearing heels.

Unable to tear his gaze away, Rion traced the exposed muscle of her calf. Higher. Her thigh flexed and the long dress fell around her legs, the fabric moving like water.

A gold belt wrapped around her midsection. She smiled at him and it took every ounce of Rion's self-control to remain where he was. To not step closer and move the strand of hair that had fallen over her eyes. Her beautiful eyes, emphasized by the kohl he'd often seen other females wear.

"What do you think?" She spun in a circle, looking herself over.

He swallowed once. Twice. She'd softly curled the ends of her hair and she wore gold cuffs around her wrists. A matching necklace dipped toward her chest, resting perfectly in the V formed by her dress. He didn't allow himself to look lower.

And the earrings. The merchant had indeed finished them.

Her smile faded. "Is it too much?"

"No," he said a little too fast. "It's . . . perfect." And gods, he meant it.

That smile returned and Rion never wanted it to fade.

She hadn't needed to ask. She knew exactly what she looked like and the response she'd get from him and other males.

Selina pointed to a jacket laid out across the bed. "I purchased you a few things too, since everyone is pretty much terrified of you. I think I got the sizes right."

He hadn't even thought—he needed to get himself together. They had a job to do. Rion tore his gaze from her and gave Selina a wide berth as he circled the bed.

"We can't have you looking like, well . . . that," she gestured to him, "when you're supposed to be on vacation with your new girlfriend." The term made his heart leap into his throat. *A mission. A mission. A mission,* he kept repeating.

Rion picked up the black button-up shirt and matching pants. The opposite to her white. A balance in the universe. Maybe when they returned to Nàdair, Rion would ask to court her. She'd promised to introduce him to other females, but standing in this room, with her dressed like that, Rion decided he didn't want other females. He wanted her. If she'd have him.

He draped the garments over his arm and turned toward the bathroom. "I'll be out in a second."

"Your hair."

He half-turned. "What about it?"

Selina did nothing to hide her grimace. "When was the last time you cut it?" He shrugged and she sighed. "I thought so." She pulled a pair of scissors from the drawer beside the bed.

Rion stepped back, all thoughts of courting gone in an instant. "You are *not* cutting my hair."

"Relax, I've cut lots of hair. I won't mess it up." She stepped forward and Rion retreated, his lips curling back before he loosed a soft snarl. She paused and stared at the sand rising between them.

Selina sighed again. "Killing you with a pair of scissors wouldn't be a very epic story, you know."

"I don't care."

"Fine." She tossed the sharp object and Rion caught them by the handle. "Cut your own hair." She turned away and he relaxed a fraction. "I'm in an expensive dress, you know; staining it with blood isn't exactly high on my priority list."

He didn't respond. Instead, Rion closed the door to the bathroom and breathed deep. Images of Caol flashed through his mind. Images of his father. He beat the ghosts into submission and leaned against the counter.

His reflection stared back. Judgment filled those green eyes. Judgment and the stain of everything he'd ever done, his fault or no.

Rion looked away.

It took him thirty minutes to finish his hair. He dusted the strands off his arms and neck, then dressed in the clothes Selina had purchased for him. He'd pay her back later. Or Alec would. He was certain Selina was the type to count every penny spent on anyone other than herself.

When he exited, Selina was seated on the bed, her ankles crossed as she flipped through the book he'd been reading earlier. She held it up. "What is this atrocity?"

"A book on strategy and the way—"

She held up a hand. "A nonfiction reader. Enough said." She stood and moved closer to examine him. "Not bad. The back is a little uneven though."

"It's fine." He seriously doubted anyone would be paying much attention to his hair.

Selina shrugged and picked up a tiny white and gold trimmed bag, the strap a thin piece of leather, before draping it over her shoulder. "Shall we?"

He relaxed his facial features and donned the mask of the male he was to play tonight. Not that it was much of a mask. Selina earned more than a few glances as they descended the stairs that had Rion snarling softly in warning. She patted his shoulder and when they exited, Rion extended his arm like a gentleman.

Selina gave a warm smile, a show for those currently gaping on the streets, and slid her arm through his.

The sun was still high overhead, the heat a bit unpleasant with his long sleeves.

Selina kept her voice low. "How do you normally greet officials?"

"I don't. Saoirse usually handles all the talking."

"Well, this ought to be a pleasant evening. Watching them feel you out will be the highlight of entertainment."

He grimaced. "You said you wanted a distraction. You brought one."

"That was my plan."

"Just don't take too long in the *bathroom* later."

"I'm a lady, I can take as much time as I please." He wasn't sure she qualified for the title. "And if they grow antsy about my absence, you can just come get me."

"What happens if we're both caught?"

She huffed. "You paint too many scenarios."

"I like to be prepared."

"What happened to spontaneity?"

"We are on a critical mission, in case you forgot."

"You're no fun," she huffed. "If we're caught, then you better get busy with your hands and make it look good."

He blanched. "You want me to—"

"It's *critical*," she said in a mocking tone. "If the situation calls for it, you best treat me as if I'm your newly found mate and you can't resist my alluring charms." He wasn't sure if he could resist now. If he got another taste of her . . .

Something in her body language shifted. He met her gaze and found . . . sorrow. "I'm sorry," she said, quickly looking away, "I didn't mean to imply—I only meant I won't throttle you for it."

Pain flared through his chest. A new kind of pain he'd never needed to process. He was the only Fae on the continent that wasn't allowed the deepest connection their species could experience. A mating bond. An individual who would know him on the deepest of levels. Someone who wouldn't need to be afraid of him because they would *know* how he felt.

Even if he and Selina's companionship developed into something more, he wouldn't be her mate. And if that male ever came along . . .

"Props to me for ruining the evening."

"It's fine," he said a bit too quickly.

"If it's any consolation, most never find their mates anyway." It wasn't, but he nodded. "I, for one, hope I never find a mate."

"Why?"

"Because I don't want someone pining after me just because some bond tells them to. It just seems . . . I don't know, forced, I guess. If a male wants to be with me, then they better be willing to put forth some effort."

He smiled. "I'll be sure to keep it in mind."

She playfully nudged him, then the pair found themselves before the estate's gates.

A pair of guards, both dressed in black, bowed low. Their gazes lingered on Selina and one's face flushed when she flashed him a bright smile.

He'd learned how good Selina was at manipulating people by watching her in the market. She knew exactly when to smile, when to bat her lashes, when to expose a bit more flesh. She was doing all of that and more now.

The pair walked down the short path that led into the manor and voices echoed from within. The servants bowed and offered a flute of bubbling liquid. Both took them. Neither drank.

They were twenty minutes late, a deliberate delay on Selina's part so they would be the center of attention upon arriving. There was already a small crowd present.

Selina wanted the governor to see Rion with a female on his arm. To have a conversation in front of all the guests so they would let down their guard.

Conversation halted in a wave.

The first couple saw him, then his magic. The female stepped behind her companion, though he looked ready to bolt and leave her behind. The second couple stared, frozen with fear at the sight of his sand. It was subdued, at Selina's request, but not entirely gone. Just to be sure everyone knew who was in their midst.

Rion spotted the governor before Selina did. Her gaze was preoccupied with the food lined along the rear table. Tonight, she was a female who cared little for politics, especially when there was food and art to enjoy.

The governor spread his hands and smiled wide. "Welcome, Lord Rion, to my humble home." He sketched a bow, probably the only time this male ever bowed to anyone. If he held any resentment for the gesture, he didn't show it.

He too wore a long sleeve button-up shirt, though his was sage green. The male had enough gold across his person between rings and necklaces that Rion was certain he never went anywhere without an escort.

Rion nodded in greeting, playing his normal role of disinterest. As he'd told Selina, Saoirse had done most of the talking when they'd last visited.

"It's been an absolute delight already," Selina replied, her eyes alight as if she'd never visited a foreign city before. The male's gaze slid to her, his cobalt eyes gliding down her form and lingering on the curves of her body. The precise ones that had caught Rion's eye.

She pretended not to notice as she beamed at the male and took in her surroundings. Only Rion knew what she was really doing.

The male's gaze traveled lower and as his lips parted, Rion couldn't hold himself back. He loosed a low growl that had the governor's attention jolting back to him. Those in the vicinity retreated a step. A tray of glasses shattered, two females screamed, and fear blasted through the room.

Everyone froze, the governor included, as they stared at The Demon and the sand circling Selina.

But Selina, in all her grace, looped her arm in his. She patted it before turning back to meet the wide-eyed governor's stare.

"Forgive him, he can be a bit possessive."

The male blinked in surprise. "I—" He cleared his throat. "Forgive me, My Lord. I didn't realize you were together."

Rion's tone was colder than he meant. "Why else would I have a female with me?"

"Right." The governor glanced around as if someone might rescue him from the awkward position he'd put himself in, but whoever usually bothered to do so didn't step forward. "Rest assured, I meant no offense."

The room waited. Waited to move. Waited to die. Waited for the abomination of Brónach to do all the heinous things he was known for.

Instead, Rion met Selina's gaze and forced a wicked smile to his lips. He pulled her close. "So long as your hands don't wander, I won't ruin the evening over a lingering gaze. She is quite lovely to look at."

"Impeccable taste. I would expect no less from a Lord of Nàdair." Selina stiffened slightly against him. Not from his hand around her waist, he realized, but at the male's comment. As if she were a prize to be won.

The governor gestured for a wine bottle and a servant strode forward reluctantly. The male topped off Rion's glass, not seeming to realize he hadn't drunk anything, then lifted his flute of bubbling liquid and raised his voice. "To good fortune and many years. May the gods rain blessing down on us all."

The crowd murmured and lifted their glasses. Rion waited until the male had nearly drained his flute before taking a sip himself.

Selina did the same.

An awkward silence fell over the space, then soft music started from another room. A few began whispering amongst themselves. One male downed an entire flute of alcohol before pouring another. Good, just what they wanted.

The governor cleared his throat once again and gestured them toward the table of food. "I hear you've come on pleasure rather than business."

"A little of both." Not a lie, but he had to be careful with his words. "Selina," he angled his head toward her, "wanted to visit a few of the southern cities."

The male waited for Rion to continue. When he didn't, he took it upon himself to push the conversation along. "There are many great things in the south, as I'm certain Lord Rion knows. The coastline is especially beautiful this time of year. Do you plan on traveling that far?"

"We might," he said. Selina was too busy stuffing her face with a lemon cake.

"What is the business part of your trip, if I might ask?"

Rion could have ignored the question altogether. Instead, he used a bit of information he'd discussed with Saoirse before coming. Just in case he needed a cover. "My sister tells me some of the cities are behind on their ledgers and that our treasurer is throwing a fit about not being able to balance them."

The male blinked. Then blinked again. "The ledgers?" His eyes widened in surprise, then his shoulders dipped with relief.

Rion made a show of sipping his drink. "I'm not sure which cities in particular, I was simply told to pass the word along."

"I'll be sure to have my staff send updates, just in case they didn't arrive and we're on her radar."

"Saoirse will appreciate it. Alec can be a pain when affairs aren't in order."

The male stared at him again, as if astounded someone would dare to speak about the High Lord in such a manner. "I imagine our High Lord has the best of intentions for our great nation."

Selina snuck another chocolate tart onto her plate, content to let the males converse as she looked around. Even so, she didn't wander far.

Rion glanced at those still eyeing him. "There's something else."

The male lowered his glass. "Oh?"

"There are rumors circling about a rebel faction on the rise." Selina stiffened ever so slightly and tilted her head toward him. If he'd bothered to meet her gaze, he knew she'd be glaring.

The male's face paled. "Rebels. Against the crown?" Rion nodded. "I've heard a few things, but I haven't seen any official statements released."

Rion eyed the male. His heart had quickened a fraction. He was definitely involved. Or feared being accused of involvement. Rion kept his voice casual. "Alec didn't want to instill panic, especially over a rumor." He shrugged as if it weren't a big deal. "I'm sure they'll figure it out."

"I see." The governor swirled his drink. "I suppose even Nàdair's elite don't get a full vacation."

Rion loosed an exasperated sigh, as if the whole ordeal was beneath him. "You have no idea." He needed to visit the lake house with Saoirse.

Silence stretched between them, but before the governor could open his mouth, Selina waltzed over and complained in a whiny voice, "Must you males always talk about such things? We're supposed to be on vacation. Can we not simply drink and pretend the problems of the world don't exist?"

The governor sketched another bow. "My apologies, My Lady." He glanced to Rion again. "It appears I haven't been a good host. Your guest is already bored with me."

"She bores easily. It's exhausting."

Both the governor and Selina stared at him, their lips parted. A scowl appeared on Selina's face and Rion gave her a playful smirk.

She turned from him as if he hadn't spoken and pointed to one of the paintings along the wall. "This piece is exquisite, would you care to tell me about it?"

"Allow me to give you a tour." He extended one arm and glanced to Rion for permission. Selina waited as well, such was her role. Rion nodded and the pair were off. "That piece is from the first—"

Rion turned away, uninterested in the history of anything in the room. He eyed those who weren't drinking. Their hands still lingered too close to their weapons. Those unarmed avoided his gaze and he laughed under his breath at how much they feared a simple conversation with him.

Not that he wanted one. In fact, he didn't want to be here any longer than was necessary. But Selina had to wait until they were drunk. Beyond drunk. Which meant they had a few hours to kill.

Rion took up residence beside a pillar and stared out the window. He watched the governor from the corner of his eye and found the male watching him in turn. His hands never strayed from Selina's arms.

Three guards stood next to the stairs. Even if the guests were too drunk to notice her absence, the guards wouldn't be. They'd clock her every move. He estimated she'd have less than five minutes to search through whatever room she chose. Her comrades would have to take the others.

Rion clicked his tongue. They should have just broken in from the start instead of wasting time socializing. It would have taken him seconds to knock out the guards. They'd have been in and out before the staff even knew they were there.

But if this wasn't the central hub, then whoever led the rebel operation would know they were onto them.

Patience wasn't his strength.

Dinner came quickly. Selina sipped her drink and dug in. The roast chicken was delicious. He'd served himself from the main table, despite the servants offering.

Selina brushed her hand across his often and made a show of leaning against him as the governor and others talked about everything ranging from the weather, to food, to politics.

It was the world Rion had lived in as a child and a world he hated now just as much as he had then.

Selina's voice grew louder as the night wound on. Her movements more sloppy. She was an excellent actress. If he hadn't seen her sneaking half empty flutes back onto trays or outright dumping them into potted plants, he might have bought her ruse.

She waited until the sun had disappeared before inquiring for the bathroom. A servant pointed to the one downstairs, but Selina whispered an urgent need and made a show of dancing on her toes.

They glanced to the governor who nodded his permission, then the servant led her toward the stairs. Selina stumbled once and Rion caught her arm, inquiring if she were all right like the dutiful boyfriend he was. The guards watched, their gazes wary.

Five minutes. That's all he'd be able to give her.

She made a good show of tripping up the stairs before disappearing into a dimly lit hall. Rion shook his head as if annoyed with the state of his companion.

The governor busied himself with another couple and Rion leaned against the wall nearest the stairs to wait for her, doing his best to appear indifferent. A servant offered him a glass from the tray they carried. Rion took it, then watched to be sure the other patrons were drinking from the same tray before he dared a sip. He figured they were probably too drunk to plan his assassination without risking the health of others, but one couldn't be too careful.

Three minutes passed.

Then four.

The guard at the top of the stairs peered down the hall. Rion made a show of meeting his gaze and glancing toward the same hall as if impatient.

Another minute.

The guard exchanged a concerned look with one of his companions.

Rion sighed, set his flute down on the edge of the railing, then proceeded upstairs. The male at the top stiffened before he pointed down the hall. Rion followed her scent, but it didn't lead to the bathroom. It led around the corner and three doors down. She'd left the door slightly ajar.

He pushed it open with the tip of his boot and found her leaned over a cherry wood desk, silently rummaging through a drawer. There were papers scattered across the surface and more littered the floor.

Rion glanced down the hall again before closing the door in his wake. "Find anything?" he whispered.

"No," she hissed, closing one drawer before moving onto the next. "There's a safe behind the large picture frame downstairs though."

Rion arched a brow. "How do you know?"

"Because the paint on the lower corner is rubbed off. Someone moves it often."

"That's probably where you'll find what you need then." He wasn't sure why she'd even bothered with the room.

Selina placed her hands on her hips and huffed. "I know, but getting—" She was in front of him before Rion could blink. Fast. So much faster than he'd seen her move before. He stepped back, but then her lips were on his, her hands trailing down his chest to his belt. Then somehow, those hands were on his skin, running up his back, tugging him close.

He thought he'd prepared himself, thought he could control the urges, but then her tongue glided into his mouth and he was hers. Totally. Irrevocably.

He pushed her against the desk, knocking whatever sat there to the floor. He didn't care, not as he lifted one hand to cup her face then knotted his fingers through her soft hair. Rion angled her back, just the way he wanted.

Desire flooded his body. He wanted to rip the dress to shreds and claim her right there on the desk.

Her legs wrapped around his waist and Rion leaned in, grinding his hips against hers, moving on instinct and nothing more.

She sighed into his mouth and his hand traveled down her body to the slit in her dress. His fingers grazed her thigh—a throat cleared by the door.

Slowly, ever so slowly, Rion pulled himself away from Selina and turned to the guard standing there, his hand resting lightly on the knife in his belt.

Undiluted rage blinded him. Rion's sand rose and his lips pulled back to reveal razor sharp fangs. Then he moved. In less than a second, he had one hand around the male's throat, lifted him from the floor, and slammed his body so hard into the rear wall that the plaster cracked. It spider-webbed outward and toward the ceiling. Pictures fell from their hooks and Rion's magic crawled across the male's body, pinning his arms and legs in place.

The male's mouth gaped, his eyes wide. Stunned.

A singular thought pulsed through Rion's entire being.

Mine.

This male wouldn't touch her, wouldn't look at her, wouldn't desire her.

A pair of hands grabbed the back of his arm, tugging, and Rion spun to find Selina staring, bewilderment written across her face and . . . there it was.

He'd scented it from her once before, but she couldn't hide it now. The familiar coppery tang invaded his nose, addled his senses. Fear poured from her, even as she stood in his magic.

Rion's eyes slid to those down the hall, more guards, a few guests, and the governor himself. Half were shaking, too afraid to speak or move. The other half were ready to fight. He growled again. Let them. If a fight was what it took—

"Enough." Rion blinked. Looked at Selina. Her tone sounded as though she'd ordered him to stop several times already. He surveyed her form. Her swollen lips. The disheveled dress. No blood. He hadn't hurt her. "Let's just go." It was almost a plea and Rion wasn't sure if it were real or not.

What she'd just done—that had felt real. So real his mind couldn't think around the taste of her.

A mission. He didn't want it to be a mission. Not anymore. And that was the whole problem. In a matter of days, she'd broken through the defenses he'd put in place after Caol. It had been so easy for her. He'd let her get close; one more step and she'd be able to put that knife in his back and he'd never see it coming.

It needed to end now. All of it. Her. Him. The mission. Everything. Let them try to find the rebels their way. He'd take on the task himself. Separate. Work in a different city. He'd already memorized the map.

Rion met Selina's gaze again, then let the male fall to the floor. He scrambled away from Rion's magic. Judging from the smell, the male had wet himself.

His jaw clenched, then Rion pushed past Selina and stormed down the hall. He didn't care what she did from here. He just needed to escape.

The guards reached for their weapons.

"Move," he growled, his own power rising in answer.

They scrambled back, pressing themselves against the wall. Wisely, the governor said nothing as Rion stormed past and raced down the stairs.

Selina paused behind him. "Thank you for having us," her voice shook. He still didn't know if it was fake. "I apologize for the . . . interruption."

Part of Rion wanted to turn around and show them just how much of an interruption he could be, but he kept walking.

He needed to leave. He'd allowed himself to get too involved. Maybe he'd head straight back to Nàdair and tell Alec to shove working with others up his pompous ass. Let Selina feed him her own story.

Maybe she could use her manipulative skills on the governor after his episode. Play the role of poor abandoned girlfriend. He was beginning to think bedding a male for information wasn't beyond her. She'd likely done it before.

Rion shoved the thought from his mind. He breathed in the cool night air, letting it quell his all-consuming rage. He didn't expect to hear Selina's heels clicking behind him seconds later.

He turned slightly, watching her hold up the edge of her dress as she ran for him. The outside lights cast a soft glow on the street, bathing her in an ethereal light. Guilt washed through him. Guilt and shame.

She scowled when she finally caught up to him. "What the hell was that?" she waved her arms. "You just alerted every single one of them about why we're here."

Her voice echoed far too loud. Rion looked up and down the empty street. "Congratulations, you've just alerted the rest."

He tried to turn, but she ran to his front, that earlier fear gone. Surely she couldn't have faked it. "What part of this do you not understand?" she hissed. "We had a perfect opportunity and you go and ruin it by getting all pissy?"

Rion swallowed his anger and the shame that came with it. "They're involved, what more is there to know?"

Selina placed her hands on her hips. "Information," she emphasized. "We need information. We need to figure out who's leading them, and now they're probably scrambling to burn everything they possess thanks to your stupid questions."

Rion shrugged. "Take them out. Make it look like an accident. Problem solved."

"It's not that simple and you know it. This group has been growing for years. They're bigger than anything Nàdair has ever faced and they're attacking Brónach's citizens. We're one tiny step short of an entire revolt. Killing them is just going to create martyrs and rally more to their cause."

Rion crossed his arms. "That's not my problem."

"Not your—what do you mean not your problem? I thought you were here to protect the crown. To protect your sister at the very least. What do you think will happen when they overthrow the city? You think they'll just let her live?"

"If anyone touches Saoirse—"

"Yeah, yeah," she waved her hand. "You'll kill them. But even you can't take on the entire continent."

"I have so far."

She rubbed her temples. "You're being petty." He shrugged and made to walk away. "Where are you going?"

"Leaving."

"Why?" He clenched his jaw, unwilling to answer. Childish. He was being so childish and stupid and—

"Because I can."

"This is ridiculous. You can't just abandon a mission for no reason."

"I thought your team was one of the best in Nàdair," he challenged. "Surely you can handle a few rebel forces on your own. Or are you as incapable as you seem?"

She bared her teeth at him. "The whole reason Alec send you on this mission was to see whether you're capable of following orders if he's going to keep—" She stopped. Her eyes widened. Lips parted.

"Care to finish that sentence?" She swallowed once. "Keep me alive? Is that what you meant to say? To see if I'm worthy of the trouble? To see if facing Saoirse's wrath might be preferable to dealing with me?"

Anger rose in him anew. Perhaps his other teams hadn't been trying to kill him on a whim. "Nothing's been an accident, has it? Every step was planned by him. My own brother."

He scoffed. Selina's team was different for a reason. She was different because the other attempts had failed. Alec was trying to lure him in. To play dirty in order to be rid of him. "Glad to know where he and I stand."

Selina cupped one of her elbows, looking for all purposes ashamed. Rion didn't give a damn. "I wasn't supposed to say that. I drank too much at the party."

"He ordered you to do it, didn't he?"

She didn't answer at first, but her refusal to meet his gaze said enough. "He mentioned if the opportunity arose."

Rion let a mirthless chuckle escape, then ran his hand through his hair. And he'd fallen for it. Hard. He'd learned nothing.

"So that's what this whole thing has been about, huh? The teasing, the flirting and kissing?" He shook his head. "All bait to lure me in." He looked at her again. "You're quite good at it, you know. You just about had me."

"No, Rion, I—"

"No?" He raised his brows. "Which part is wrong exactly? The teasing? The kiss?"

"I tease everyone."

"Before or after you kill them?"

"Look, I—"

He growled again and she stepped back. "I don't want to hear it. I've seen the way you act around other males."

"Because they're comrades."

"And I'm a target."

"That's not what I meant."

A breathless laugh. "Are you going to try and say I'm special? That it's different with me? Yeah, try again." He stepped away and she seemed to notice the way his sand had worked itself into a frenzy. She didn't try to approach again. "I'm going back to Nàdair. Finish the mission or don't, it's not my concern anymore."

"You can't just go." Her voice was so soft. Another lure.

"I suggest, for your own safety, you stay the hell out of my way."

CHAPTER TEN

Half-truths. Rion was tired of listening to them. She'd been given more than an "if the opportunity arose" command. He'd seen it all over her face. But Selina hadn't been lying when she'd said she hadn't decided whether to kill him. Maybe the command had been more subtle.

Gods, he'd fallen for it. Fallen for her. To think that his brother, the High Lord of Brónach, had stooped so low. Rion clenched his fists. Alec was willing to pay someone to seduce his younger brother. And they called *him* the abomination.

Even with the truth revealed, Rion still faced a pressing matter. There really was a rebel faction trying to overthrow the crown. She hadn't been lying about that part. He'd do his own research. Push them back underground and hunt them one by one, even if it took a decade to finish the job.

But first, he needed to leave this city.

Rion shoved through the door to the inn and bolted up to their shared room without greeting the male at the counter. Said male was gone when he descended a minute later.

He'd worry about changing and finding a meal later. He wanted to put as much distance between him and Selina as possible.

Clouds hid the sliver of moon from view as Rion marched down the empty street toward the city gates. It was quiet.

Too quiet.

Rion paused at the stillness and calmed his breathing to listen.

No animals.

No insects.

The hairs on the back of his neck rose.

Rion continued walking. Great. Well, he had his answer then. If she couldn't lure him in, then he supposed killing him outright was her next move. Maybe the others in her group hadn't been assigned to other villages after all. Maybe they'd been lying in wait this whole time.

Thirteen.

He could handle thirteen.

A lump formed in his throat. He could handle twelve. The thirteenth. The thought of seeing the light dim from her amber gaze . . .

Brónach's magic sparked through the air. He could taste it. Feel the earth pulsing with their energy.

No one peeked from the windows or moved behind the drapes. No shadows shifted in the dark corners.

She'd claimed to be one of the best. Perhaps now he'd get to see her skills.

The city itself seemed to hold its breath as he continued through the streets at a leisurely pace. He gripped a knife in his belt. Perhaps they were waiting until—footsteps hit the cobblestones.

Rion counted.

One.

Their magic broke through the stones, cracking the seams, and shot toward him with blinding speed. Earth rose to form an impenetrable wall at his back. He tore the road to shreds, ripping up chunks of rock and breaking them into tiny pieces. Those pieces launched toward the greenery.

Two.

Bodies dropped from the rooftops, more emerged from the shadows. Not just thirteen. Three dozen. More. The knife left his hand, sinking into a shoulder. More blades were drawn. A storm of earth surrounded his body, circling in a dizzying field of deadly rock.

Three.

The first lunged with a second and third following close behind. Bodies dressed in midnight black circled from different angles, all in paired groups of two or three. Normally, he might have smirked at their creativeness, but he wasn't in the mood today. Not with who was likely responsible.

Rion ducked around the first male's body. He grabbed the second's extended arm and twisted it behind the male's back, positioning his body so that it shielded Rion from the blades flying through the air.

The male grunted in pain.

Four.

Rion shoved the male away and ducked again. He drew two more knives from his belt and let them fly. One landed in someone's throat. Another sank deep into a thigh.

Five.

Vines raced for his feet, but he didn't jump back in time. One caught his ankle and yanked hard. Rion only lost his balance for a split second before righting himself again.

Six.

He dodged a sword then broke the male's arm at the elbow.

Seven.

Rion concentrated on the ground at his feet and all the wriggling things beneath. He crushed them, then his magic found the arms of two warriors closing in.

He crushed them, too.

Eight.

Residents began flicking on their lights. Blinds moved in the windows and a door cracked open.

Most were horror-stricken when they saw bodies littering the street. Warriors writhed in pain, clutching limbs they'd never use again.

But others were angry, so angry they did something Rion never expected. Clad in nothing but their night clothes, battle cries fell from their lips as they rushed toward him. Some carried makeshift weapons, an umbrella, a candlestick, the leg of a chair. Others drew traditional blades.

He stopped counting.

Rion ducked around their magic and untrained movements, reining in his sand to prevent it from lashing out.

He ducked around a broom handle and didn't even bother moving when someone threw a book at him.

Rion backed away, ready to flee, but then the warriors were back. Not Selina's. He didn't recognize a single one of them. Which meant the governor himself had set this up. Or perhaps the attack was from the rebel faction.

He cursed when a knife sliced across his left arm. Not deep and certainly not enough to incapacitate. But they were getting too close.

Civilians. Fae who'd likely never held a weapon in their lives were willing to risk everything to rid the world of his existence.

He swallowed the pain building in his chest as he danced and dodged around their movements.

Maybe this was why Alec was trying to eliminate him. If this many people wanted him dead, if this many joined the rebels—

Rion couldn't bring himself to hurt them. They were mothers and fathers with children and families of their own. They were just doing what they thought was right for the world.

At his expense.

Using his magic, Rion shoved them away. They'd suffer with a few bruises come morning, but nothing life-changing. Not like the assassins who'd be lucky if they woke up at all.

Rion ducked around a sharp piece of wood and punched the male in the stomach. The last of Rion's blades flew from his hand when two assassins followed up.

He broke another male's arm, then heard a female's ankle shatter when she hit the ground at an awkward angle. Rion grimaced and prayed she wouldn't have a limp for the rest of her long life.

Sharp pain pierced though the back of Rion's arm and he spun to find a knife embedded in the skin. He ripped it out and let it fly.

Blood trickled down his fingers, but four more were upon him, charging while wielding both magic and weapons.

Two villagers cried out as they rushed from his other side. Rion ducked away from flying knives and heard the civilians cry out when the blades sank into them instead. He didn't have time to check if the wounds were fatal.

Rion blocked another kick to his face, gripped the male's ankle, then sent him flying sidelong into three of his companions.

Vines raced across the ground from all directions and caught his legs. They crawled up his body in a frenzy, securing his limbs and binding him enough that he toppled to the ground.

Feet rushed forward and for a split second, Rion wondered if it would be easier to just let it happen. But Saoirse—he'd witnessed her grief first hand with their mother's disappearance and again after their father's death.

If she lost him, if she lost Alec—

Rion screamed, letting the roar echo through the night as his magic spun. He shot it out in a violent wave that knocked everyone, civilians included, to the ground. The particles attacked the vines binding him, freeing his hands and legs in seconds. Those on the ground scrambled back to their feet.

Hatred shone in their eyes. Such deep hatred for a complete stranger.

Anger rose in him, too. He was sick of their judgement.

Rion slammed his magic into the next two so hard he heard their noses break, something else too, likely a jaw or eye socket. They writhed on the ground, screaming in pain as blood gushed from their faces.

He spun when slender fingers wrapped around his wrist. She'd been so silent that—fury poured from her. So much fury that it made him step back.

Too slow.

He'd been too slow as a sharp pain shot through his wrist and up into his arm. His skin bulged, then ruptured in half a dozen places where stems pushed out from beneath his flesh. Bloody leaves unfurled.

His magic reacted quicker than he could think and pierced through her torso in several places. All vital.

Her fingers slackened and Rion recoiled, gripping his arm, unable to bend or move it without blinding pain.

No time. There was no time to process it as another figure lunged. His heart was racing, beating through his chest like a violent drum. And his magic reacted again, tearing the flesh from a male's outstretched arm.

A knife sank into Rion's right shoulder, then Rion let his magic explode. It surged beneath and around him, tearing through the rest of the cobblestone, swirling in a storm that prevented any from getting close. It peeled away their skin and muscles, leaving large hunks of flesh dangling from bone.

Screams echoed from somewhere in his mind. A voice that begged him to use restraint, but something else was there too, egging him on, claiming they deserved it.

Maybe they did. After all, they'd attacked him first. Everyone always did. He'd been born into a world that'd deemed him cruel so perhaps cruel is what he should be.

Let them suffer for a change.

"Monster," a female sneered, blood dripping from between her teeth.

Monster. He'd been called that before. He saw the surrounding carnage. Knew exactly what it would look like to those who cleaned up the streets tomorrow. It was so easy to blame the creature they all feared.

Rion exposed his fangs and growled back.

He was done with mercy.

They fell one at a time. Died in vain as they sacrificed their lives for a false belief.

It was only after he was covered with their blood, only after the street had been bathed in gore that the civilians began to retreat.

Rion stepped and they stepped back.

He growled and they ran.

But when he turned his back, heading straight for the governor's manor, they lunged at him again.

And Rion bathed the streets with their blood.

CHAPTER ELEVEN

Rion slammed his hand down on the sink's edge and let the tweezers clatter to the drain, splattering droplets of blood along the white marble in their wake. He gritted his teeth then grabbed the bottle to his left and took another swig. The amber liquid burned his throat, but it paled in comparison to the inferno pulsing down his arm.

Everything ached. Or it had before he'd downed a quarter bottle of liquor. He'd taken it directly from the governor's personal reserves. The male wouldn't be needing it anymore anyway.

Another breath, then Rion grabbed the tweezers again and angled himself in the mirror. He grimaced. It looked as bad as it felt.

Starting at his wrist and extending all the way to his bicep, the skin along his arm was raised and bulging. It had turned various shades of purple and red and blue, and small openings had formed along the skin where the vine had broken through.

A civilian. He cursed and stared at the place he'd been working on for over an hour. He'd hoped the alcohol would dull the pain, but it hadn't helped nearly enough.

A puddle of his own blood sat by his feet and the lower part of his arm had gone numb. On the outside, at least.

Rion drank from the bottle again. He just needed to get it out. Fast.

Then he could move on from this nightmare of an evening.

"You left quite the mess downstairs." He closed his eyes in frustration at the familiar voice, trying to pretend he didn't hear it. Maybe if he stood in silence long enough, she'd just disappear.

Rion opened his eyes to find Selina leaning against the bathroom door frame, her arms crossed. She grimaced at his wound.

"Feel free to leave." His words slurred. Rion examined his arm again.

Selina clicked her tongue. "And here I was thinking you were done being an ass." He leveled her with a glare. She didn't flinch away.

She sighed. "As much fun as it is watching you torture yourself, I could help." She pushed off from the wall but Rion spun away before she got close. His bare chest heaved and her lips parted slightly at the sight of the sand rising, ready to protect in ways she couldn't imagine.

Or perhaps she could if she'd been watching his fight and the hell he'd unleashed upon this place afterward.

His voice was low as he said, "I've had enough close calls for one night." An hour ago, he'd contemplated whether he could kill her. But now, staring at the concern on her face, at the way her eyes darted across his injuries, cataloging each in turn. He wasn't sure he could go through with it.

His magic was a raging mess and he'd drank far too much. One wrong move, one misjudgment, and she'd wind up just like Caol.

Selina's gaze drifted to his arm again. "You think I'd do that?"

"It's the perfect opportunity, isn't it?"

Selina put her hands on her hips and glowered. "I do have my pride to consider. I'm not going to jump a male who's already down."

"Down?" He gestured to the doorway and the bodies he knew lay bleeding out on the first floor below. "I'm sure they thought I was down, too."

"Are you planning to clean that up?"

He turned back to the mirror, watching her in the reflection. "Why? Let the damn civilians worry about it."

She inclined her head. "Did a civilian do that to you?"

He gritted his teeth. "Does it matter?"

"No," she studied the wound again. "I was just curious if she was trained."

"She was sloppy."

"Thank the gods, otherwise it'd be in your heart."

"Are you finished?"

"I will be when you give me those tweezers and let me help."

"You're not touching me. Leave."

Selina sighed and lifted her hands in mock surrender. "I promise on my life that I will not try to kill you tonight or at any point in the coming week. There, satisfied?" She held out her hand. "Now will you hand me those damned things?"

He scented the air. Processed her words. No lie, but could he trust his addled brain to pick it up?

He looked at his arm again and sighed in defeat. He was never going to get it all out alone.

Rion leaned over the sink again. "Give me a second." He needed to get his magic under control first. If he couldn't do that, then he'd have to wait until he was sober again. Not the most pleasant option. She watched him, waiting, and he finally said, "I can't always control it."

Selina eyed the grains swirling at his feet. "Really? I didn't know."

"No one does."

She nodded at his tone and approached slowly. Rion handed her the tweezers and watched her through the mirror as she assessed the damage. Her fingers prodded the tender skin around the top of his bicep and he hissed in pain.

Selina winced and nodded toward the bottle of whiskey. "You're going to need a few more drinks of that."

Rion tilted the bottle to his lips and drank until his throat couldn't bear it. He set the bottle down and leaned against the sink again.

She prodded another area. "It would be easier if I used my magic—"

"No." Hell no, he was done with Brónach's magic for a lifetime.

She clicked her tongue, then placed the tip of the tweezers against one of the many holes in his arm. Rion ground his teeth when the metal prodded his flesh and searing pain shot all the way down his arm. She dug deeper and he felt a section of the offending greenery shift. Rion squeezed the lip of the sink and couldn't hold back a grunt when she pulled a piece free.

He took several deep breaths and she held it up to the mirror for him to see. It was barely longer than his finger.

"This is stupid. You're going to die of blood loss before we're done."

He reached for the bottle again. "No magic."

She huffed and placed the tweezers into another hole; this time Rion growled against the pain. He was panting by the time she pulled it out. It was even smaller than the first.

"I'm not doing this." She let the tweezers fall back into the sink. "Either you let me use my magic and get this done in a few seconds, or you do the rest yourself."

"Then get out."

"Gods, does alcohol make you stupid? How do you expect to get every single piece out? It's embedded deep, and the small roots will be impossible for you to find." She looked him over. "You look ready to hit the floor as it is."

Rion gritted his teeth. She was right and he hated it. He could handle the pain, that part wasn't what bothered him. But even if he managed to get the largest sections out, the smaller would remain. They'd cause infection, which would only complicate matters further.

He squeezed the edge of the sink. "Swear it again."

Selina sighed. "I swear I will not try to kill you with my hand, magic, command, or any weapons at any point tonight, tomorrow, or even into the coming week."

Rion studied her again, searching for the lie. Nothing burned his nose. He'd never allowed himself to be vulnerable with anyone aside from Saoirse. To put his life in Selina's hands, despite her words—

She'd been sent to kill him. She was a manipulator. Maybe her words weren't true at all.

He saw the concern in her gaze as she stared at his arm. But maybe—maybe this one time she was sincere. Maybe, despite her orders—

"Do you always think this much or is that the alcohol, too?"

Rion gritted his teeth. "Get it over with." He'd see if he woke up tomorrow.

She pointed to the bottle of alcohol. "Finish that first."

He did. Rion downed the contents, then slammed the bottle in the sink so hard it shattered. Glass flew everywhere, scattering across the tiled floor. "Happy?"

"Almost. Sit." She pointed to the wall.

His vision blurred. "Why?"

"So I don't have to catch you when you inevitably pass out, that's why."

Rion turned, stumbled, caught himself, then slumped against the wall and sank to the floor. The coolness from the tile seeped through his back and he leaned into it.

No one moved for a long minute. His mind tottered on the edge of fading, but her voice broke through. "You mentioned you couldn't always control it. Do I need to be worried?"

Rion studied the grains at his feet. They were just as sluggish as he felt. He didn't have the strength to open his eyes. "It's fine."

She must have been surveying him because it took a while for her to approach. Adrenaline spiked through him anew when he scented her magic. He cracked his heavy eyes open and watched her place her hands over his skin. This was stupid. After all the training he'd done, after all the things he'd endured, he was going to die thanks to someone who'd likely never trained a day in their life.

Her hands kept moving over his skin, poking and prodding as she went. "I think I can get it all in one go." Her voice was distant, floating through his mind. He tried to piece together her meaning then white hot pain erupted through his body.

Rion screamed, unable to contain it and tried to pull away from the source of the pain. It lanced through his arm, tearing at the muscles themselves. They were being ripped away, pulled out through his very skin.

No, that was the vines. They moved like giant worms, tearing him from the inside out.

Stupid. Idiotic. Foolish. He'd made himself an easy target.

The pain vanished, leaving a burning sensation in its wake that grew to unbearable levels. He tried to reach for it, to wipe it away, but gentle hands stopped him.

A warm cloth met the tender skin. His body trembled, then Rion embraced oblivion.

CHAPTER TWELVE

ion woke with a splitting headache. His mouth was dry, eyes strained, and it felt as though someone had poured molten lava through his veins.

He shivered from the cold floor and risked opening his eyes. The room was dark, save for a sliver of sunlight trickling through the cracked door.

He forced himself upright and pain shot through his arm. A different sort of pain.

Rion's stomach churned and he barely had enough time to scramble for the toilet before it emptied itself into the porcelain bowl. He expected no less after drinking an entire bottle of liquor the night before.

He stayed there, hovering before sinking back on his knees. Rion peered down at his arm only to find it wrapped in a tight bandage.

It took his mind too long to recall the events of last night and how—Rion glanced back toward the blanket that had been draped over him. His heart beat just a little faster. Selina. She'd kept her word. More than that, she'd bandaged his arm and ensured he was cared for.

Her words floated back to him again. *I haven't decided yet.*

Did she plan to disobey Alec? Was that too much to hope for?

Rion rubbed his temples, nursing the splitting headache before he carefully stood. He flipped on the light and blinked against the offending brightness. She'd left another roll of clean bandages on the edge of the sink, along with a container of salve. Things she didn't have to do.

Rion peered into the hall, searching it up and down before seating himself on the cushioned bench in the bathroom.

Slowly, he peeled away the bandage along his arm. It stuck to the dried blood and he winced at the discoloration and swollen skin. He should probably clean it first. Rion eyed the glass in the sink, then opted for the shower.

Afterward, Rion raided the governor's room for clothes. At least the male had decent taste. He collected weapons and avoided the cold bodies still littering the floor.

Rion hadn't intended to kill everyone, but when he'd accused them of working with the rebels, they hadn't denied it. They'd attacked him instead and after the governor's comment about his sister, the male had found himself without a hand, then a head.

Rion tore a strip of sheet in half, then fashioned it into a sling before making his way downstairs. He paused at the picture frame Selina had mentioned last night. She'd torn it from the wall and emptied the safe behind.

Had she left? Perhaps she'd taken her companions and already traveled south. Maybe she'd found a list of names and had gone out to wrap things up.

Selina—he was alive because of her. Despite his childish actions, she'd come back. He just needed to figure out if she'd come back for him or to watch how he handled himself in a fight. He still wasn't sure whether he should continue the mission or head back to Nàdair.

Rion walked past the last of the bodies and crinkled his nose at the mess. The blood.

He stepped over broken glass and the splintered wood of the door, then exited to find several dozen Fae standing just outside, all whispering and pointing.

Officials were dressed in their uniforms and quietly tried to usher onlookers away.

He stepped beyond the threshold and all eyes snapped to him. Several stepped back while others drew their weapons. He eyed them and his magic rose in answer. He really didn't feel like fighting again. Not with his head near splitting from the bright sun.

Rion stepped again and they retreated. Two in the back outright fled. Their gazes were wary, fearful, disgusted.

Several whispered prayers to the gods, and the crowd parted to give him a wide birth as he followed the broken path.

Rion paused to address the nearest official. "The governor is dead." The male sucked in a breath. "He and his staff were responsible for illegal activities against the crown and paid for it with their lives. See to it that such mistakes aren't repeated."

Rion didn't wait for the male to respond before he left them all behind.

He ignored the citizens who fled from his presence. Ignored the inn where he and Selina had slept beneath the same roof, and ignored the street still stained with blood.

No one tried to stop him.

No one spoke to him.

And best of all, no one lunged for him again.

Gods he needed a hot cup of coffee.

Outside the gates, Rion caught Selina's floral scent and followed it toward the wood line. He wasn't sure if she even wanted to see him. If not, he'd begin the long trek back to Nàdair where he'd heal and collect his own information.

The afternoon sun beat down upon him and Rion had a sheen of sweat covering his face by the time he entered the trees. He could smell the alcohol dripping from his pores. He already needed another shower.

A small cabin hidden by the trees entered his view but raised voices had him slowing. He caught another's scent. A male's. What was his name again? Seán? Rion edged toward the side of the cabin, keeping his footsteps quiet.

"I cannot believe you," Seán sneered. "He's the entire reason we're out here. He's why the people are rebelling in the first place. You're telling me you had the perfect opportunity and you didn't take it?"

Rion clenched his good fist. Seán was too close, towering over Selina with his hands raised. She shrugged, refusing to back down. "I still need him."

The male looked ready to argue further, then his lips parted. "You care about him." It didn't come out as a question. Selina looked away and disgust crawled over the male's face. "I don't even know what to say to you right now."

Selina squared her shoulders, but Rion couldn't see her face. "Then don't say anything. Your job is to follow orders."

"Given your abhorrent fascination, maybe someone else should be giving them."

Her fists curled, but Rion emerged from the shadows. Seán visibly responded to his presence. His lips pulled back from his teeth and one hand went for the hilt of the long knife at his hip. His eyes darted to the sling holding Rion's arm in place.

Selina lifted her brows in surprise.

Seán growled, "If you won't do it—"

Everything happened all at once.

Vines broke from the earth's surface and shot toward Rion's torso. His own magic answered in kind, rising to greet a partner in a deadly dance. Rion drew his blade at the same moment Seán did. He let the sling fall away and ignored the pain radiating from the recent wounds.

Selina's scream roared above it all.

The two clashed. Steel sang against steel.

Seán pivoted. Rion ducked around snaking vines. Chunks of earth ripped the greenery to shreds.

Rion studied Seán's movements, slowing enough to keep pace. The male was sloppy, almost a novice compared to Selina. How he'd managed to earn a place on her team, Rion couldn't fathom. This weak male wasn't worthy of her. He couldn't protect her, and he certainly didn't deserve to stand at her side.

Rion wrenched the blade from Seán's grasp, planted an elbow in the male's sternum, then gripped his throat with one hand and squeezed the delicate muscles.

The male's magic whipped out in desperation, trying to fight Rion off, but Rion strangled the life from it. The male's nails raked down Rion's good arm, but he only squeezed tighter, watching the male's face turn purple as he struggled for breath. Sand wrapped around the male's wrists and pinned them down at his sides.

"Rion."

He froze.

His name from her lips yanked Rion from his bloodlust. He was powerless against the pull. Completely at her mercy.

Reluctantly, he shifted his eyes away from the male and his stomach knotted when he met her gaze.

"Don't hurt him." Her wide amber eyes darted between Rion and the male. Frantic. Desperate.

Rion turned back to the male and growled low as he said, "If you ever speak to her like that again, I'll rip you apart."

Seán nodded slowly, then Rion released him and stepped back. The male fell to his knees, coughing and spluttering as he gasped for air.

And Rion might have relished standing over him. Just to show Selina he was the more dominant of the two. More qualified to protect her.

Seán caught his breath and sat up to glare at him with bloodshot eyes.

"Go."

The male stumbled to his feet, glanced at Selina once, then disappeared through the trees. The two stood in silence for a long while. He cast her a quick glance, but she was looking at the place where Seán had disappeared.

Rion clenched his jaw. She stepped, gave him an apologetic smile, then followed the male.

He loosed an uneasy breath. Her comrades would always come first. And he couldn't really fault her for it. He was still mostly a stranger, after all.

Rion pivoted on his heel and followed the scent of the nearby river. He relished the sound of the water. The crisp scent that filled and cleared his lungs.

He found a tree and collapsed near the bank, letting his back rest against the trunk. Water was the only thing that ever seemed to calm the raging storm in his soul.

Rion scattered loose dirt around his body then let his eyes drift shut. It wasn't long after that he heard her faint footsteps, then scented the wildflowers.

She sat at the edge of the bank without speaking, far enough away that she couldn't touch him, but close enough that Rion kept an eye on her.

She'd helped him. Saved him hours of agony. Yet she'd been commanded to kill him by her High Lord. Where would that leave them in the end?

Would she try to kill him later? Use him then kill him? Decide to defy his brother altogether and not kill him at all? Was it pity that steadied her hand or something else?

"Thank you," she finally said. He cracked one eye open to see her wrap her arms around her knees. "I know he can seem harsh, but we've been friends since we were younglings."

Rion perked up at that. "You grew up together?"

She nodded. "He was my first rival of sorts. We didn't like each other much back then."

What about now? He wanted to ask. Were they more than comrades?

Silence stretched between them again.

"How are you holding up?" she asked.

"It won't hinder my abilities." He flexed his hand and winced.

"I meant, how are *you?*" she emphasized. He raised a brow. "You know, your well-being?"

"What about it?"

She gave him an incredulous look. "You were just attacked. I thought that maybe—"

"I'm used to it."

She turned away. "I'm sorry."

"For what?"

"That you have to live with that. It's not . . . well, I certainly wouldn't want to live that way."

He ventured to guess that most wouldn't. "It's the hand I've been dealt."

"Fate's a cruel mistress."

"She can be."

Selina pushed a strand of hair from her face and clasped her hands around her knees again. "Seán and Niamh intercepted two birds carrying orders south. Both were informing unnamed parties about the governor's death." She waited to see if he'd respond before continuing. "Both carried the depiction of a flying crow in the corner. We've seen the mark a few times before."

"So what are we waiting for?" Selina looked at him. "Your cover isn't blown, we can continue the mission. Most will just assume I was acting out."

"That happens often, doesn't it?"

His jaw worked. "Again, I'm used to it."

"What about your injuries?"

"They're nothing I can't handle."

"Good, because our bags are packed."

He blinked, then smirked. "Please tell me you didn't pack all the junk you accumulated over the last few days."

"It's not junk," she feigned offense. "And since you're hurt, I can't expect you to carry it, now can I?" She waved a hand. "I've already arranged shipment back to Nàdair. There was a very enthusiastic merchant happy to accept a month's wages and free lodging."

"Be careful that your bags aren't tampered with when you get back."

"Worried for me?"

He scoffed. "You've been seen with me. A lot of Fae are dead. If you sent anything edible, I certainly wouldn't risk it. Poisoning doesn't seem like a glorious way to go."

"Oh, you don't have to worry about that. I have full intentions to die on the battlefield with a small army at my command."

"That's . . . dramatic."

She waved a hand. "What can I say, I've always had a flare for theatrics."

The river filled the silence again. A fish jumped, breaking the water's surface momentarily before disappearing again.

"South, then?" he inquired.

"Northeast."

"We're splitting from the other two?"

"Naturally."

"You found something in the vault."

"Maybe. It could be nothing, but I won't know for sure until we arrive."

Rion tried to conjure an image of Brónach's map in his mind. "What's Northeast?"

"A small village off the beaten path. A great hiding place, don't you think?"

"Just you and me?"

"Is that a problem?

"Didn't anyone ever warn you not to trust strangers?"

"You're only a little bit of a stranger, and you didn't kill me last night so—"

"That's my line."

She shrugged. "You could have easily added me to the body count. You didn't."

"It's called common courtesy." He thought back to her argument with Seán. "Is that why Captain Asshole was so pissed? Because you'll be alone with me?"

She laughed at that. "Yeah. But he doesn't like the thought of me being alone with any male."

"He . . . desires you?"

She shrugged. "He's not been subtle about it, but I think I need alcohol to travel down that road."

Rion's stomach rolled. "I think I've had enough of that to last a lifetime." He stared at her sidelong. "Thank you, by the way, for—well—last night."

"You're welcome." She stood and dusted off her shorts before approaching and offering her hand. "Come on, let's get moving and see if we can't find a decent inn before nightfall."

CHAPTER THIRTEEN

Their pace was slow, almost annoyingly so. If he'd been with anyone else, Rion would have blown them off and pressed forward.

But he was with Selina. And she was caring for him in ways only Saoirse had ever done.

Selina insisted they stop every few miles to check and clean his wounds. He kept telling her he was fine and that the bandages could wait, but the female refused to listen. He wasn't exactly pushing her away, either.

Rion watched the way her face scrunched, the way she tilted his arm to inspect the wounds, and how carefully she spread cooling salve across the still open holes along his arm. She wouldn't let him carry anything, no matter how much he insisted.

Did she really care or was that part of her act, too? She'd already admitted to being sent to kill him. Was it too much to hope that she might disobey her High Lord? Had Alec commanded her or was it merely a suggestion?

She hadn't struck out at him while he'd slept. She hadn't tried to poison him. And she hadn't finished him off the other night when she'd had the perfect opportunity.

He'd been watching her for days, trying to figure her out. He'd wait before pursuing anything, just to solidify her intentions. Get to know her better as a comrade and see the female behind the mask.

They'd been on the road for three days and had only discussed the mission, the weather, and their next destination. Selina pointed out all her marked locations. Some were manufacturing warehouses while others were small villages that'd been targeted by the rebel forces. Their presumption was that the villages had refused to join the rebel cause.

The dots along her map were heavy in the north around Nàdair and outlying villages. They hypothesized that the rebels intended to hit those very places before they'd been discovered.

Caravans had been caught in transit further south, some by accident, others by warriors scouting the land.

But two things were perfectly clear.

First, Alec wasn't bluffing. The rebel operation was just as large and concerning as he'd made it out to be.

Second, it was painfully obvious their main operation centered in the south. Likely in Whiteridge, despite Selina dismissing their involvement.

But the female had found something else that had caught her attention, which was why they were trekking north instead of south. It was too far for his liking. He wanted to get this mission over with, but as reluctant as he was to admit it, he needed time to heal, too. Whiteridge would likely end in bloodshed, and he needed to be in top form before the confrontation.

Rion sat on the edge of the bed, watching Selina carefully as she re-wrapped his bandages. His blood ignited with every brush of her fingertips and his heart betrayed him, beating too fast. He knew she could hear it and was thankful she never commented.

"I doubt news of what happened in Fernsworth has reached the village, so we shouldn't have to worry. There's an elder there in charge of things who should have probably faded decades ago."

"And you think they're the ones involved?"

Selina shook her head. "Another name was mentioned in a coded letter. From what I gathered, he's the one in charge of their financials.

He's been smuggling funds and materials through their underground tunnels."

"What do you want to do if we encounter them?"

"Nothing. We need to lie low after Fernsworth. If we hit them again in a main network, they'll know we're on to them and might go underground."

"What about the civilians who'll suffer if we do nothing?" Because that poison wasn't headed for Nàdair. Not yet.

Aching sadness swept across her features. He hated that look. He'd do almost anything to never see it again. "Sometimes sacrifices are necessary."

Rion's jaw clenched. He wanted to argue, but reality was cruel. She was right: If they hit the rebels again before discovering the leaders, they might disappear and it could be years before they resurfaced. With how the poison had already progressed, Rion didn't want to imagine them getting more time to perfect the formula.

"When we find the one responsible for all this," Rion said. "I'm going to rip him apart."

"Not if I get to him first." Rion smirked at that. Selina glanced at her hands and Rion waited for her to continue. She sat close. So close her floral scent was affecting his reason. His plan. "About what happened at the manor—"

Rion came back to himself as if she'd dumped cold water over his head. After days of travel, he was hoping she wouldn't bring it up. His face burned. "I was out of line." He stood. "It won't happen again."

Rion crossed the room, separating himself from her, and stood before the small fire. He watched the flames trying to flicker to life beneath the embers.

"I apologize." He heard her stand as well. "It wasn't my intention to push your boundaries." Her voice was soft and sensual. Alluring.

"It's fine." He couldn't turn to look at her. Didn't want to.

"Instincts can be . . . volatile. If you'd rather us use a different ruse, I'm sure I can . . ."

"It's fine," he repeated.

"If we have to . . . repeat what happened in the office," she paused and his face burned at the thought, "are you going to be okay with it?" No. No, he certainly wouldn't be. It was too real for him. Everything he wanted and might not be able to have. It's what he wanted to do to her now. To turn and run his hands through her hair, to pull her in for another kiss. To press his body against hers and listen to the sound of her breath in his mouth.

"I'll deal."

"Okay." Silence again.

"When we get there, they'll see that I'm hurt. They might attack before we have a chance to search anything." There was no hiding the soft scent of blood on him. The wounds were almost closed, but he needed another day, maybe two before his Fae blood completely sealed them shut.

"Not with me around." He glanced back and found her seated once again, leaning back on her hands. "I can play protective lover. Pull on their guilt and pity." That didn't hurt his pride at all. He swallowed it down.

"You won't be doing much shopping there." They'd be lucky to find an open inn given how small it was.

"Oh, I don't plan to. I'm saving that for Whiteridge. I've only visited once and the shoes were to die for." Rion groaned. "What? I didn't make you carry *that* much last time."

"It was the most boring experience of my life."

Selina tilted her head back and laughed. His blood sang in answer. "It's the best way to get the layout of the streets and see who wanders them."

"I can easily get that without carrying a dozen bags on each arm."

"Yes, but then you wouldn't be able to communicate. Not that you do anyway. I've got it covered for both of us. Besides, you'll still be injured before we get there."

"I will?"

"Of course. We're going to play it up and make them underestimate you for as long as possible." He wasn't sure that was the best of ideas.

Her eyes flickered down to his arm and her gaze softened. "How's it feeling?"

Rion flexed his fingers. "Better. It won't hinder my movement."

"Does it still hurt?" Concern laced her tone.

"I wouldn't want to block with it yet, but that doesn't mean I couldn't."

She nodded and studied the worn rug on the floor. "It'll take us at least a week to get to the city down south. I was wondering . . ." she chewed her lip. "Would you—would you be willing to train me?"

His brows lifted. "Train you?" She nodded and he scrunched his forehead in confusion. "You seem like you know enough already."

"I do," she said a bit defensively. "But the way you move is just . . . different. And you're impossibly fast, even by Fae standards. I just thought—" she huffed. "Never mind."

Rion noted the hint of red on her cheeks. "Sure. Why not?"

She turned. "Really? It's not some family secret?"

He chuckled. "No. It was something developed by my great grand-father. He passed when my father was just a child, so I never knew him."

She moved closer, joining him beside the fire. "Was it your father who trained you?"

An old pain blossomed in his chest. "No."

She waited. "Who did?"

The pain spread and Rion gripped the area as if he could stop his heart from bleeding. He wondered if it would ever heal. "A—" Rion stopped himself. "It doesn't matter. He's been dead for years."

Selina sat in the small chair. "I'm sorry to hear it." More silence. "I lost my father when I was young. It was stupid. He went on an assignment to confront a group of humans attempting to settle in Brónach territory. They caught him with iron, a weapon I think. It stopped his magic long enough for them to put a blade through his heart." She clenched her fists. "I've never forgiven him for being so careless. Who lets themselves get killed by humans?"

"A lot of Fae, apparently." Their history with the humans was a bloody one. He imagined her uncle was likely the one responsible for seeking retribution. Human settlements never lasted long.

She looked at him, as if waiting for Rion to share his own story. But Caol wasn't someone he wanted to talk about. Not tonight. Perhaps not ever. The remembrance of that night made his soul bleed. If he ripped open the wound now, he might not be able to close it again.

Selina glanced toward the bed. "I suppose we should try to get some rest. We'll be there in the morning."

"It's that close?" She nodded. "Then we should wait until it's dark."

"You don't want to make another grand entrance?"

Rion shook his head. "It's a small village." He glanced out the window to the rain peppering the glass. "And if the rain keeps up, they won't be able to pick up my scent."

She shrugged. "They probably wouldn't recognize it anyway. Not many from these small villages get to travel all the way to Nàdair." She leaned forward. "What's your plan?"

"You're letting me decide?"

She shrugged. "I'm interested enough to hear it."

"We find one of the unused tunnels and move in while it's dark. Get what we need and get out."

"That's no fun."

"We can save the *fun* for Whiteridge."

"Fine." She eyed the bed, then grimaced. "I'm not laying on that."

Rion followed her gaze. "I'm sure it's clean."

"It looks like someone died there."

"They probably did."

She gaped at him. "Would you sleep on it?"

He inclined his head. "I'm taking the floor, so it doesn't matter."

"I'm requesting a different room."

"Don't, it'll just draw unwanted attention. If you want new sheets, go down to the closet and take some. No one will ask questions."

Selina placed her hands on her hips, glared at the bed, then disappeared into the hall. Rion sank into the chair and let his shoulders relax. His arm ached, but whatever salve Selina put on his wounds eased some of the discomfort. The bruising had shifted to a yellowish color, but it still hurt more than he thought it should. Not that he'd ever experienced vines shooting straight through his arm before.

When Selina opened the door again, her arms were full with an entire stack of sheets, two fluffy blankets, a pair of new pillows, and two steaming tarts. Lemon, from the smell of them. "The caretaker said I could take whatever I wanted."

"I'm sure you didn't give him any incentive."

She waved a hand. "The key to a pleasant life is making others love you."

Rion rolled his eyes. "You can't buy everything."

"Sure I can. What's the point of money if I can't spend it?"

"Do all these extras come from your personal funds or the crown's?"

"Does it matter?"

He shrugged. "Just trying to figure out how to write up the reports when we get back. I can't imagine the treasurer being happy with you listing bribery for fresh blankets as a necessary expense." In fact, Rion was pretty sure the male would blow his top.

"Not that it's any of your business, but my family is very well off. I'm more than capable of paying for my own things."

"I thought the earrings were a gift from your uncle?"

"They are. He manages the family funds. My father owned a bunch of land before his passing and my mother didn't want the headache of it all. We sold several properties and have enough finances for the next few generations to live in luxury."

"Why sign up to be a warrior then?"

She gave him an incredulous look. "Can you imagine me playing the piano and attending fancy brunches with the other ladies of the court?" No, he couldn't. Not unless she carried a hidden knife in her belt meant for sinister things.

"I imagine they'd have quite the time with you."

She popped a piece of the tart into her mouth. "Don't act as if you don't enjoy the finery Mr. I'm-the-son-of-a-High-Lord."

"Fair point." Alec hadn't banned him from using the family vault. He supposed he should be grateful for that at least.

Selina tore the sheets from the bed, doing her best to avoid the stains, remade it, then plopped down on the rickety mattress. She fluffed the pillows and sighed in relief. "So much better than the ground."

Rion snorted, then fanned out his set of blankets close to the fireplace. She tilted her head to watch him. He tried to ignore her but caught her gaze and stilled.

She was reclined back on the bed, her legs dangling over the side. Her bronze hair had fallen so that part of it covered her throat while the rest splayed out above her head.

Selina's throat bobbed and he thought he heard her heart skip when his heated gaze traveled down her body. Rion imagined touching her again. Imagined the feel of her soft curves against his hard body as he coaxed sensual sounds from her perfect mouth.

She cleared her throat and sat up. "You should probably rest first, with the injury and all." He didn't look away. Rion waited instead. For the invitation. For her to make a move. He just needed one indication. Just one and he'd be across the room faster than she could blink. "You can have the bed."

His voice was husky as he said, "I'll sleep on the floor."

"There's no reason for you to. We won't be sleeping at the same time anyway." She stood, made a show of brushing off her clothes even though there wasn't anything on them, then walked around the bed toward the fire. "Best to take advantage while you can."

Look at me.

She didn't and after another moment, Rion crossed the room and fell onto the mattress, trying his best to wrestle his instincts into submission.

He failed miserably.

Sleep came faster than he expected, but he was plagued with shadows from his past. Demons that hunted in the recesses of his mind. Creatures and beasts and beings that prowled through the darkness, tugging at every vulnerable corner in his subconscious.

A presence hovered nearby. Too close. Too real. The monsters . . . A hand pressed against his chest and he gripped the slender wrist before twisting and flipping the individual over and pinning them with his hips.

His magic whipped out and danced around the Fae beneath him, grazing against their skin, daring them to move. His hand gripped their throat, but he didn't remember putting it there. He held, but didn't squeeze, as if he knew—

Wide amber eyes stared back. She didn't move. Didn't fight. His panicked gaze scanned her hands, searching for the weapon—

Nothing. He looked over the mattress. Nothing there either. No blade. No poison.

Rion met her gaze again then sat back on his knees and ran one hand over his face, trying to steady his ragged breathing. "I'm sorry."

She didn't sit up right away, as if afraid the movement might set him off again. "You were having a nightmare."

Rion didn't meet her gaze. He blew out a breath instead. He'd almost snapped her neck. "It was nothing. I'm fine." But his voice shook.

"You didn't sound . . . fine."

He scooted from the bed and walked to the fire, staring at the glowing embers, willing them to chase the remnants of his own monsters back into the shadows. "Get some sleep."

Silence for a breath. Two. "You weren't out long." Was that pity in her voice?

"I won't be able to go back to sleep anyway." Not after seeing Caol's body again. His father's. The guards'.

"All right. Do you need—"

"I'm fine," he repeated. It was a mantra he'd repeated his entire life. Because he had to be fine. There was no alternative. Not without Saoirse. But maybe . . . maybe if Selina let him in—no, not tonight.

She waited another moment before curling up on the mattress. Rion glanced back to see her drag the heavy blanket over her shoulders. He might have imagined her burying her face into the very pillow he'd used. Might have sworn he saw her inhale his scent.

But those were likely just dreams too, waiting for the opportunity to shift into nightmares.

CHAPTER FOURTEEN

With morning, Selina fetched them breakfast. He'd wondered out loud whether it might have been tampered with but she'd rolled her eyes before cramming a muffin down her throat. Rion resisted the impulse to comment about how she ate like a male. He dug into his potatoes instead. Selina snatched his pastry despite complaining hers was too dry.

She watched him, but thankfully didn't comment about the nightmare. Rion subtly searched for any signs of bruising around her neck and was thankful to find none.

"Any ideas about what we should do until nightfall?"

He shrugged. "Relax, I suppose."

She feigned shock. "Does Rion of Brónach know the meaning of the word?"

"You caught me reading."

"That wasn't reading, that was torture."

"It's a small village. It'll take you ten minutes to see the entire thing."

She huffed. "Well, I'm going to take a look anyway. It beats being crammed in here all day."

The rain had stopped, much to Rion's dismay. He kept his magic reined in and quiet, but just as Selina predicted, no one seemed to recognize him.

A pair of males stumbling from the only tavern didn't look at them twice. A beggar seated against the wall of a small shop even reached out his hand. Selina handed him a coin. The male didn't even have the curtsy to wait until they were down the street before he ran into the tavern, waving the coin above his head. He'd be drunk within the hour.

"He's going to hound you when we get back."

She shrugged. "If he can drink an entire gold coin's worth of ale in one sitting, I might pay him double just so I can watch."

Rion would pay him triple to bathe first.

They explored everything in less than thirty minutes. From a mediocre bakery with, according to Selina, less than average pastries, to a tiny building they called a library. Rion would have thought the librarian dead were it not for his faint snoring.

Not a single soul recognized him. It was a small village, completely cut off from the outside world. A sanctuary where no one called him a demon.

Selina didn't like it. She complained endlessly, but Rion found himself surveying the area, wondering what it might be like to settle in such a place. Sure, Saoirse would never be able to visit; he'd be found out if she did. But to have people look at him as if he weren't a monster. To be treated as any normal traveler or Fae was . . . refreshing.

"Why are you smiling?" Selina inquired with a puzzled look on her face.

"No reason."

"It's creepy." She furrowed her brow. "You can't seriously like this place."

He shrugged. "It's quiet."

"Too quiet. I miss the city."

He wasn't sure he agreed. He'd always loved the lake house, even if Saoirse complained about the lack of room service. She never brought slaves. He'd always thought it was because of him, but Rion was fairly certain their mother had never allowed slaves on the grounds either. Maybe it was some unspoken rule he'd never learned.

A light breeze carried a revolting scent that had Rion recoiling. Selina crinkled her nose. "Well, whoever that is isn't having a pleasant day."

With nothing better to do, the pair followed the scent. It led them outside the village and toward a narrow river bend.

Four Fae males stood beside a dead horse, all whispering in hushed tones. Their gazes looked the approaching pair up and down but none reached for their weapons, fear didn't sting Rion's nostrils, and one even waved in greeting.

He definitely preferred this over the city.

"If you've come for water, best to head back. The innkeeper should have a reserve." He was short with a stocky build. The calluses on his hands spoke of hard labor. Rion doubted the male had ever wielded a sword in his life, but he still noted the hunting knives in their belts.

"What happened?" Selina asked, staring at the poor creature with its tongue rolled out. Rion grimaced. He could deal with bodies, but for some reason horses always got to him. He might have even called them a favorite animal if he were given the time to think about such things.

"The water," another said, his voice even gruffer than the first. "It's been killing our livestock for weeks. We try to keep them fenced off, but occasionally they're too smart for their own good and work around the latch." The male shook his head. "A shame he wasn't smart enough to avoid the water."

Selina exchanged a glance with him. "Has anyone else been . . . hurt by it?"

"We had a few younglings fall ill, but they recovered. The nearby wells are tainted, too."

"How do you get water then?" Rion asked.

The four males looked him over, sizing him up, he realized. They made eye contact, puffed out their chests . . . then relaxed.

"There's a small lake on the edge of the mountains." The male pointed north. "We take a wagon full of barrels every few days to restock. Works well enough."

"That sounds . . . miserable."

"It's starting to affect the crops, too. Dain's entire field shriveled up last week. And Imogen's is beginning to do the same."

"Have you gone upriver to see what's contaminating it?" Selina asked.

They nodded. "We went as far as we could travel in a day, but didn't see anything unusual. Just more dead animals along the way."

"The wolves forced us to turn back," another chimed in. "Unlike you lot, we're not exactly equipped to fend them off. Especially not a pack that size."

"I keep telling you, those weren't wolves. Wolves don't leave footprints that size."

"Don't go scaring off travelers with your theories."

"I'd love to hear them, actually," Selina inquired.

One of the males rolled his eyes as the other continued, his voice dropping to a whisper. "There's Dark Fae about."

"There are not," his friend chided.

"There are," he argued. "They've come down from the mountain."

"Why?" Selina asked and Rion thought she might honestly be interested.

The male shrugged. "Who can say? Maybe they're tired of being confined."

Vines snaked up from the ground and Rion stiffened, anticipating a fight, but they simply wrapped around the horse's back hooves. "We ought to bury the poor fellow. Lest those wolves—"

"Dark Fae," his companion interrupted.

"Lest they catch the scent and decide we're their next meal." He glared at his companion.

"The inn should have a vacant room if you two need a place to sleep tonight."

"We found it," Selina said. "Thank you."

He nodded and the other three followed as they dragged the carcass away from the village. Rion watched them for a time, somewhat marveling at the casual exchange.

"I guess it's safe to say they don't recognize you."

He didn't comment. Instead, Rion turned toward the water. "What are the chances?"

She shrugged. "We are up here for a reason."

He continued staring. "If I don't use my magic, the rebels won't know anyone from Nàdair was involved."

"Can you fight without your magic?"

He glared at her. "I *am* a trained warrior, remember?"

She shrugged. "I've never seen you fight without it. What about you losing control? Do we need to worry about that?"

"If the situation calls for that, there won't be anyone left to spread the word anyway."

"Are you saying you want to take the time to help these people?"

"Are you saying you don't?"

She chewed her lip. "Well, if it turns out to be another manufacturer, it would still be within the parameters of the mission."

"And if it doesn't?"

She shrugged. "Then I'll tell Alec you went rogue and demanded we save a village of innocents."

"He won't believe that."

"I can't lie."

"He still won't believe it. He'll likely think you're delusional and send you off for an evaluation."

"Then I guess you'll just have to butter up your sister for me."

He smirked. "Need lunch before we set off?"

"Lunch and to pay the innkeeper. Can't have someone stealing my clean sheets while we're out."

CHAPTER FIFTEEN

The innkeeper acted as though she'd met a celebrity when Selina deposited five gold coins in her hand. Always gold with her, never silver or copper.

The female even went so far as to pack a lunch for their travels and warn them to be careful on the road.

They'd just left the village when Selina dug through the pack to examine the contents. "My word, she gave us everything." She fished out a small leather satchel tied with a cord. "Medical kit." She tossed it up to feel the weight. "A nice one, too."

"I imagine she probably sells them."

Selina pulled out a wrapped bag of jerky, examined it for all of two seconds, then tore off a piece before speaking with her mouth full. "Well, they might not know how to bake, but the dried meat is divine." She definitely wouldn't fit in with the court ladies.

"I'll take your word for it if you're still standing in thirty minutes."

Selina patted her bag. "Not to worry. I have extra antidote should we accidentally ingest anything foul." He did too, but Rion didn't tell her that just in case she tried to poison him herself. It wouldn't take much to drop a full grown Fae male.

Less than an hour later, the pair stumbled upon the first dead animal. A deer, the carcass half ripped apart while the other half was left to rot. Selina crept closer to observe the animal and prodded it with a stick. "No wolves here. Just birds who must have decided they didn't like the taste."

"It must be bad if even the scavengers are turning away from it."

She crinkled her nose, then shifted her attention to the ground at his feet. "Are you really not going to use your magic?"

"I thought you wanted this to be covert?"

"I do, but your arm—"

"I can manage."

"Oh, so you're so high and mighty now that not only do you not need your magic, but you don't need an arm either?"

"You're the one who wants to train with me. I figured the confidence in my skills would only impress."

She snorted. "We'll see."

"Shall we make a bet on it?"

"On what?"

"My abilities."

"Someone thinks very highly of himself."

"I do, in fact."

"Fine," she placed her hands on her hips and began walking again. He followed. "If you can make it back to the village without a single scratch, be it from animal or Fae, then I'll give you whatever you want."

"That's a dangerous offer."

She stared at him. "Fine, whatever you want *within reason*."

His throat suddenly went dry, but somehow Rion kept his voice steady as he said, "A date."

"I already promised you that. You have to give me some time to talk to them though. Once this mission is over—"

"With *you*." She stopped walking. Turned to stare. Her mouth fell open as if she intended to speak but words didn't come out.

Shit. Too forward. Too soon.

He needed to divert. Give her an out.

"Only if I come out unscathed, of course. Unless you already—"

"Fine. One date." She held up a finger. "But I warn you, I've very high end."

He tried to keep his excitement at bay. He forgot what to do with his hands, his eyes, and nodded as casually as he could.

"And if you lose, then you owe me a favor."

"What kind of favor?" he asked.

"Whatever I want, to be disclosed at a later date."

"Done."

They continued at a steady pace and only paused when the sun began sinking toward the horizon. Selina didn't dare use the river to clean his wounds.

"I haven't seen any signs of wolves."

"Or Dark Fae," Selina added with a hint of sarcasm.

"You don't believe?"

She shrugged. "No one has seen them in years."

"Those who venture to the mountains claim differently."

She scoffed. "Convenient that their stories always happen after sundown."

"What about the bodies?"

"Predators, obviously."

"The Fairy Folk are real."

"And mysterious little things. That doesn't mean big bad monsters are lurking in the shadows waiting to snatch us up. Those are just children's stories told to keep us all in line."

"My mother talked about the harpies a lot. And the sirens."

She stopped rummaging through her pack and seemed to dive into her own memories before saying, "Mine, too. She claimed she'd seen one once."

"A harpy?"

Selina nodded. "She said it looked like a half-naked woman with winged arms and feathers that ran down her torso. She also said she was one of the most beautiful creatures she'd ever seen. Until she showed her pointed teeth."

"What else did she say about them?"

Selina continued digging until she found the jerky. "Nothing. She ran."

"Probably smart. Was she lying?"

"No, but my mother was . . . eccentric. She said a lot of things that we . . . well, she thought they were true enough. She was never . . . right, after my father's passing."

Rion took the offered food. "I'm sorry to hear it."

They ate in silence for a time. The sun set behind the treetops. The shadows lengthened and a small fire crackled at their feet.

"I know it's a tender subject for you but," she glanced at him. "Do you think you'll ever find her? The High Lady?"

He stopped chewing. Rion stared at the flames. His stomach became a pit and soured out.

His mother. It had already been eleven years and they hadn't found a single trace of her. "Saoirse still looks. I go with her when I can. I don't think she'll ever stop."

"And your brother?"

"He sends out units every month. Alec is . . . cold, at least toward me, but I remember him with our mother. I don't think he's properly laughed since then." No need to mention the grief they'd all suffered at their father's loss.

Selina rubbed her hands on her legs, then repacked their bags. "I'm going to try to get some sleep. Wake me if anything happens."

RION LET her sleep through the night. He watched the shadows, listened to the movements in the trees. He stared at the moon and questioned the gods' plans as memories of his mother resurfaced.

She'd done so much for Brónach, and now she was gone. Forgotten in some small recess of the world.

There was always the possibility of a fade. There'd be no trace, according to the ancient texts and scholars. But his mother wasn't old enough for that. Nor would she have willingly left her mate or her children.

Rion watched the inky blackness above and imagined her staring into the same star-flecked sky.

One day he'd find her.

One day he'd bring her home.

CHAPTER SIXTEEN

Two more days passed and the dead animals lining the bank increased in number. The scent of the river burned his nose. Selina's face was pale, almost greenish as she tried to cover her face and block the rotting stench of carcasses.

Neither dared to speak. Not as they spotted fresh footprints in the dirt and scented several males and females that had recently passed through.

They moved slower now, opting to trek along the tree line and use the trunks for cover. It wasn't until he heard a collection of voices that Rion raised a hand. Selina stopped and strained to listen, but only shook her head. He pointed and they crept forward, moving like wraiths in the woods.

The voices grew louder until the pair happened upon a small cottage. Rion eyed the smoking fire before the front door, then the vials piled off to one side.

A glass jug of liquid sat next to a log, filled with a purplish brew.

A female emerged from the only door and warmed her hands by the fire before proceeding to pick up an empty vial. She glared at it, sighed, then slumped onto a log.

The female, a half-breed slave, tied a cloth over her mouth and nose before carefully picking up the jug.

Rion grimaced. Of course they'd have slaves filling the vials. It prevented any of the rebels from risking their own health. He imagined the female had to ingest the antidote regularly.

A male emerged next. Neither had chains connecting their wrists, but the shackles were still present. He carried another crate full of small vials, each one vertically balanced in a grid, and set them down beside the female.

She coughed, and the action caused her to spill some of the mixture onto her hand. The half-breed hissed and the male was before her in an instant, pouring water over her already blistered skin.

Her eyes watered, but she didn't cry. Instead, she retrieved the vial and started again.

Rion surveyed the area, searching for the Fae who owned the two slaves.

The female suddenly shot to her feet, bottle and vial in hand, staring at the liquid as if it were a plague.

"Don't," the male warned.

Her hands shook. "Why not?"

He glanced around, as if waiting for someone to emerge from the trees. "You know why."

The female swallowed hard, clenched her teeth, wiped her nose on the back of her sleeve, then collapsed back down in defeat.

Rion stepped beyond the tree line.

The male jumped to his feet at the sight of Rion and placed his body between Rion and the female. The female froze, her face full of terror.

"Are you the only two here?" Rion asked. His magic beat against the cage he'd put it in. It wanted to surround him, protect him, cover him so that no enemy could ever pierce his heart.

The male nodded. "You're not . . . with them."

"No." He wasn't exactly sure who "them" referred to, but Rion wagered a guess. "How long have they been gone?"

"A few hours."

"How many?"

"Two dozen."

Rion glanced at the cottage, then back to the half-breeds. Burn marks lined both their arms. "You're making it?" Rion inclined his head toward the bottle.

The female stood. "They force us. We don't want to. We—I've dumped as many bottles as I could into the river." The male turned on her, his eyebrows raised. "I don't want to hurt anyone anymore."

"Lex." The name was a plea. The male's gaze flicked between her and Rion. Over and over, as if he wouldn't know what to do if Rion decided to punish her for it.

"You won't have to." Rion pulled a set of matches from his pack, then set the place on fire.

"WELL THAT was anticlimactic." Selina complained as they settled far enough away from the fire that the smoke didn't cloud their lungs. No one returned to check on the half-breeds or the smoke billowing through the sky. Maybe whoever had been in charge of them had met their demise on the road. It would certainly make his life easier.

"We'll need to veer toward the mountain before we head back." They'd run out of water.

"What about them?" Selina sneered as she looked at the half-breeds.

"They're coming with us."

"Why?"

"We can't just leave them in the middle of the woods."

She scoffed, but then her eyes widened. "I didn't realize you were a sympathizer."

That's not exactly what he'd call himself, but—was he a sympathizer? He'd always loathed the entire concept of slavery. He'd even contemplated ways to release them, though he'd never acted on it.

Rion studied the two half-breeds. They sat on the ground, clinging to one another, watching and waiting for his answer. "We'll drop them off at the village. I'm sure the innkeeper could use a few extra hands."

The male relaxed at that and something in his eyes almost seemed to thank Rion for the mercy. There were a million worse things a slave could endure.

Selina pinched the bridge of her nose. "Fine, but they're your responsibility, not mine." She glanced up to study the billowing clouds. "It doesn't look like anyone is coming."

Rion shrugged. "Fine by me." He pushed off from the tree. "Let's move. I want to reach the mountainside before sundown."

Selina sighed again. "Just so we're clear, our bet doesn't count if we don't get to actually fight anyone."

He smirked. "Those weren't in the terms."

Selina grimaced. "I'm going to throw a rock at you when you're not looking."

"It won't hit."

"Fine, a stick then." She turned to the half-breeds and they visibly shrank away. "Don't fall behind. I won't wait."

They trudged through the trees until nightfall, the trip mercifully uneventful. Rion listened to the half-breeds whisper words of comfort between themselves. Promises that told Rion they were lovers. Even they had found some happiness in their wretched lives.

Rion watched Selina's back as the female walked ahead, surveying the canopy. Maybe he could find some in his, too.

They found water, fresh and clean compared to the foul liquid they'd left behind. The female half-breed hadn't apologized or made excuses for her actions. She'd likely dumped the poison thinking it would dilute enough that it wouldn't cause further harm. He doubted she'd be happy to learn the truth.

The half-breeds didn't question their route. Didn't ask for food. Didn't do much of anything but sit and wait, as if they didn't know what to do without orders.

"It was a lot more fun when it was just you and me," Selina remarked.

The half-breed's heartbeats quickened. Strange that they were more scared of Selina than him.

"What's wrong, can't perform with an audience?"

She puffed out her cheeks like a child. "It's just . . . weird."

"You don't have slaves in Nàdair?"

"Of course I do, I just don't have to look at them."

"Poor pampered princess."

"Don't call me that," she snapped.

If it weren't for the fury behind her eyes, Rion might have taunted her. Called her by the name for the rest of their trip. But something about her body language had an apology balancing on the tip of his tongue instead. "Which part?"

Selina's fists clenched. "Princess."

"Why not?"

"Because I don't like it." She was . . . serious. Angry about a nickname. Then sorrow flashed across her face and guilt tugged him to relent. Maybe she didn't elaborate because of the half-breeds present.

"All right."

Selina calmed herself. "So what's the plan, we drop them off, tell the villagers what we found, then set off?"

"Essentially."

"In that case, why not just head straight for the other village?"

"I thought you already paid for your room?"

She shrugged. "Doesn't matter. I have more where that came from." She patted her coin purse, then eyed the half-breeds. "Besides, what's one innkeeper over another?"

He supposed she had a point. Either village would take the half-breeds in if it meant free labor. If Rion found the next innkeeper unpleasant, he'd just take the half-breeds back himself and let Selina whine all she wanted.

"Okay."

Night descended and Selina instructed him to sleep first. He didn't argue, he needed the rest anyway.

He eyed the half-breeds, watching the pair curl up against the trunk of a tree, the female's head resting in the male's lap. He stroked her hair, far too preoccupied with his companion to pay Rion any attention.

Carefully, Rion shifted the grains beneath him, inching them close to his body. The male's head jerked up, as if he'd sensed something, but after a quick observation, he dismissed it and settled again. It seemed he was more Fae than human then.

"Careful," Selina whispered from his side. "You'll lose the bet if your cover is blown."

A stick flew at him and Rion caught it with one hand. "And you'll lose if you cheat."

She shrugged. "It was worth a try."

Rion folded his hands over his chest and let himself drift. It seemed only seconds later that leaves rustled nearby. He strained to listen and might have chalked it up to the wind if it weren't for a crunch of loose bark from the opposite end.

He cracked his eyes open and tilted his head to survey the woods. The shadows stretched and loomed in the distance. None moved. Slowly, he turned his head to look at Selina. She already had one hand on the hilt of her dagger.

Their fire had faded to little more than embers. The half-breeds were sound asleep. Faint moonlight trickled through the trees.

Another shuffle of feet. Too soft to be Fae.

A jaw snapped, then Rion rolled, pulled his sword from its sheath, and cleaved the jaw of a very large four-legged creature in two.

Half its head hit the ground while the other half of its body twitched in the dirt.

The half-breeds jolted and the male shoved the barely awake female up the nearest tree.

Rion faced the beasts. A pack, like wolves but not. Standing on all fours, they stood taller than his waist. Long canines extended past their jaws. Brown and black coats allowed them to blend with the shadows.

One of them lunged for the half-breeds and sank its fangs into the male's ankle. He let out an ear-piercing scream, as did the female as she watched her companion be dragged into the woods.

Rion leaped for him, but another of the creatures grabbed the male's arm and shook its massive head. Rion heard the bone crunch, then flesh separated with a squelching sound that had a shiver running down Rion spine.

Selina danced between three, twisting and turning with her magic in tow. It briefly had him wondering why she felt she needed more training at all.

A third closed in on the screaming male. To hell with their bet.

The ground beneath the male came alive and rock slammed into the three beasts tearing at the half-breed. They yelped on impact, then Rion used the same particles to snap their necks. He did the same with the creatures surrounding Selina, then twisted toward six more hiding within the trees.

They were dead in seconds.

The female leaped from the tree and ran toward her companion. He writhed on the ground, clutching his shoulder where his arm used to be attached. Blood gushed from the wound and the female tried to stop it with her hands.

That was panic on her face. Panic and terror at the thought of losing the only one she likely loved.

Rion removed one of his knife belts and tossed it to the female. "Tighten it above the wound." She scrambled for it, hands shaking. Footsteps sounded in the forest again. Those were definitely Fae.

Two males walked ahead of the others. All were dressed in black, all had their weapons and magic at the ready. Rion counted. Six just behind. Four to his left, still hidden. Five to his right, also hidden. He heard more footsteps behind but didn't dare take his eyes away from the males to his front.

One smirked, the action pulling at a deep scar at the corner of his mouth. "The fabled Demon Lord of Brónach." Rion raised a brow. "I've been looking forward to this."

Rion felt the male's magic pulse through the air, sensed it crackle and dance. The male threw his sword sheath to the ground and cracked his neck.

"What are you waiting for then?"

Tree roots shot from the ground and wrapped around Rion's ankle faster than he could anticipate. He cursed as they yanked his feet out from under him. Rion used his elbows to brace against the impact, then rolled to the side, using his magic to slice the roots in half. The male was over him less than a second later, his blade stabbed through the dirt a hair's breadth away from Rion's face.

"Rion!"

He ignored Selina's voice and slammed his palm into the male's solar plexus, hitting him with both his body and magic. The male didn't balk from the pain; he almost seemed to welcome it.

The male laughed, then positioned himself into a low crouch, a movement that reminded Rion of someone else. Someone he didn't want to think about. Rion's heart pounded.

The others moved in, but the male's voice roared above the silence. "He's mine." He snapped his teeth for emphasis and his companions backed away.

Rion could sense Selina's anxiety. He could feel her magic too, sneaking toward him beneath the ground, but he couldn't afford to let her distract him.

Rion ripped the ground apart, splitting rock and stone until they were nothing more than fine particles. They swirled above him like a swarm of insects awaiting command.

The male only watched, his eyes calculating, cold, stern.

"I never could quite figure out why Caol took you in." Rion's heart stopped. "But seeing you now, I think I understand. To train someone like you, to be the one to claim they'd tamed the monster. I can see the appeal."

"You knew Caol?" It explained why his movements were familiar.

Another smirk. He was enjoying the taunt. "Some called us brothers. After years of rolling through shit and blood, I suppose it was a fitting title. At least until the wretch went and found himself a mate. He grew soft and went even softer after she died."

The male shook his head, disappointment in his tone. "The late High Lord allowed him to wallow in the grief too long. Honestly, it's probably best that you put him down." He looked Rion over again. "My father once spoke of a time when the High Lords were ruthless and no one dared to challenge our country. It's probably best that you put your father down, too. How long until that brother of yours follows? Or your sister?" He sighed. "She's the worst of the lot. Going against the gods themselves to hide you when they demand your sacrifice." He shook his head. "If it's up to me, I'll have her body—"

Fury split the ground at their feet and Rion raced forward. His sword slammed into the male's blade and the male barked in protest, his feet sliding backward across the ground. Vines and greenery rose to defend him, but they couldn't penetrate Rion's magic.

His heart thundered in his chest. They were part of the rebel forces. A unit ready to eradicate his entire family. He wouldn't let them touch Saoirse. Not so long as he drew breath.

Sand crawled up Rion's arms and lashed out, wrapping around the male's throat. The male gritted his teeth, fighting for breath, then he yanked one of Rion's knives out and plunged it into Rion's side.

He refused to buckle from the pain. Rion didn't let up, didn't jump back. He only pushed harder, squeezing until the male's eyes bulged from his head. "You will not touch her."

His warriors rushed forward then, ready to intervene, but one final squeeze and the male's windpipe collapsed. Selina moved behind him, joining the fray, and Rion let the male's body drop to the ground. He spun and let a wave roll beneath the ground, knocking the warriors off balance long enough for Selina to incapacitate them.

Rion stole the killing blows, relishing in each stopped heartbeat.

Swords clashed and he caught the smile on Selina's face as she engaged the enemy, uncaring that they were outnumbered. But he couldn't smile, not when each and every one of the Fae before him would gladly eliminate his family without a second thought.

"You traitorous bitch," a female yelled.

Selina shrugged. "That's a foul name to call someone."

"You—" Selina's magic tore from the ground and impaled the female, stopping her heart on impact. The two males beside her roared in anger, but Selina moved through them with ease.

Rion danced around their weapons, moving with the fluid grace Caol had drilled into him. He listened the way his mother had instructed. He was patient the way Saoirse demanded he be.

A blade flew through the air. Rion blocked it with his sword, then ripped the last of his knives from his belt and sent it flying right back.

Two tried to run, but it was Selina who grabbed them by the ankles and dragged them back. Rion finished another with a quick slash to the throat, then turned to find Selina strangling the life out of the remaining two. She stood over them, staring them down as if she were enjoying their final moments.

Then she snapped their necks.

Silence engulfed the forest once again. Rion stood still, letting the bloodlust roll through him and slowly dissipate. Selina seemed to be doing the same.

He took a calming breath and remembered the half-breeds. Rion grimaced. The female lay face down beside the male, blood pooling around her body. He clenched his jaw and cursed. He'd forgotten about them after the male mentioned Caol's name. He hadn't paid enough attention to his surroundings . . . again.

Rion glanced down at the knife protruding from his side, took a breath, then yanked it free. He pressed a hand to the wound and turned to find Selina studying him.

His previously injured arm throbbed, but it had held up.

Selina seemed to be waiting for something, then he caught her gaze drifting to his feet.

"I'm in control," he assured.

"Just thought I'd hang back in case." She surveyed the area and her eyes paused on the half-breeds. "Well, that's a shame." He wasn't sure she meant it. Her gaze kept roaming through the trees. "You think that was all of them?"

Rion shrugged. "Most likely." They probably had a few scouts in the distance. Unfortunately for them, they'd be burying their comrades instead of greeting them.

"Good, let's get out of here." Rion raised a brow. "To the village.

No sense in delaying." She looked him over. "Did you pack a change of clothes?"

He only nodded. "I guess I lost our bet."

She smirked. "All for two half-breeds that," she glanced at them again. "Well, I think it was fast for the female, at least."

Rion grimaced again and words from Caol came floating back to haunt him. Selina only watched as he hollowed out the earth and slowly lowered their bodies inside, placing them side by side before covering them up.

He idly wondered what kind of life they might have had if freedom had been an option. He wondered if they would have lived for eternity at one another's side.

Maybe he was destined to experience the same fate. To find a partner only to have them ripped away the way everything else had been torn from him.

CHAPTER SEVENTEEN

A light rain had started by the time they made it to the village. Both opted to walk around the outskirts and keep out of sight. One light glowed in the window of a tiny shack beside the main gate. Rion was fairly certain the rickety old structure would collapse if the wind picked up.

Gods help them if an invasion swept across the land. The northern villages were poorly manned and to say that they weren't prepared for an attack would be an understatement.

He'd mention it to Saoirse when he returned and see what might be done.

Rion funneled his magic into the ground and searched for one of the tunnels cited in Selina's document. There were several and from the surface, Rion had no way of differentiating which were used more often than others.

He picked one and traced its entrance all the way to the coastline. Vines covered the wooden doors that were half sunken into the earth. A clever hiding place. Selina coaxed the greenery away with her magic and Rion pulled the heavy doors open. He covered his nose against the musty smell and walked down the four narrow stairs to gaze into the darkness.

No heartbeats. No torches or lights inside, either.

Rion gestured for her to follow. He pulled a torch from the pack Selina had picked up in town, then struck a match to light it. Rion blinked a few times against the offending light and held it high to view the space within.

Water pooled at his feet and the dirt walls were about six inches taller than he was. There were more unlit torches lining the walls, but Rion wasn't certain they'd catch with all the moisture in the air.

He turned to find Selina pulling her cloak up as she peered inside. He swore she'd turned a shade paler.

"Absolutely not," she said.

"Do you have a better idea?"

She scowled at the webs hanging overhead, her gaze searching through the nearly translucent strands. "The window."

"How original."

"I'm not walking through this. It's disgusting, and it looks like the entire spider population of Brónach is living along the walls."

"Don't be so uptight. I'm sure you've had to crawl through worse."

"Not willingly."

He rolled his eyes. "Come on." Rion stepped inside, moving thick webs as he crept through the dank space.

He turned slightly to find Selina holding her cloak close as she watched the ceiling.

"You're not seriously afraid of spiders."

"We're not going to talk about it," she snapped.

Rion held the torch higher. "Would you like to take point?"

She glared and Rion laughed before venturing further inside. He might have even pulled a few webs down, just as a courtesy.

Selina followed at a slow pace, carefully watching her surroundings.

"If the rebels are using the tunnels to smuggle things in and out, they're certainly not using this one."

"Or the information you found is dated."

She grimaced. "Let's hope not."

A slight gasp, then fear flooded the tunnel in an overwhelming wave. He whirled, magic out, ready to silence whoever had snuck up behind them.

Selina had her head ducked and shoulders scrunched in tight, cursing under her breath. "Get it off me." She inched closer, her body curling in on itself. She kept her eyes shut. "Get it, get it," she begged, putting her back to him.

Rion smirked and moved fast, plucking the tiny offending creature from her shoulder. It dangled from its web, legs fanned out, then twisted to climb back up the single strand.

Rion simply placed it on a root that jutted out from the dirt wall and let it climb to safety.

Selina shuddered. "Did you kill it?"

He laughed. "No."

She looked around as if she'd spot it coming for her again. "You should have killed it."

"I'm not going to kill something just because you and others find it wretched."

"Do not," she said, "make this about you. I am allowed to find little creatures with far too many legs creepy, and I'm allowed to be disgusted by the thought of them crawling over my body."

He tried not to laugh. "Should we include said little creatures as part of your training? One only learns to conquer fears by confronting them."

"If you do, then I quit. I draw the line at spiders."

"Glad to know your limits."

Her body shuddered again. "Can we please move on and stop talking about them?"

"Are you sure you won't scream if another one drops down from the ceiling?"

She glared upward. "I didn't scream."

"You almost did."

She stuck out her tongue, then he turned and continued down the tunnel. A spider. He couldn't help but laugh to himself. Here she was, trapped underground with someone who could quite literally bury her alive and she was more afraid of a tiny eight-legged creature.

The tunnel ended at a wooden door. Rion listened for any signs of movement before he cracked it open and peered inside.

A damp, musty basement full of rotted crates greeted them.

Rion pushed the door open and Selina raced from the tunnel, searching her clothes for any more tiny creatures. Beasts, she called them. Finally satisfied, she spun to search the small space.

"No chance they'd stack a bunch of important documents down here, huh?"

"Not likely."

She huffed, then proceeded up the narrow staircase. Selina pressed her ear to the door before pushing it open. Rion followed behind her, trying to ignore the way the rain clung to her scent, making it impossibly more alluring than before.

Control, he chided himself. He needed absolute control. He doubted she'd repeat events after what had happened last time. Shame still burned through him at the thought.

Damn his ridiculous Fae instincts.

They crept up and down the halls, searching for any who might have lingered after hours, but Rion only found one guard dozing by the front door.

Judging from the half empty bottle in his lap, he wouldn't be doing a perimeter check anytime soon.

"Well, I guess that gives us the run of the place."

It was tiny really, a two-story building with seven rooms in total.

"Lucky us."

She placed her hands on her hips. "Upstairs or down first?"

"Up. I doubt there are any hidden safes behind picture frames here."

"You'd be surprised."

They ventured to the next level. "I assume you speak from experience?"

"I found an entire room behind a bookshelf once. It was the most luxurious part of the house. Stupid, really, considering its size. It wouldn't take a genius to realize there was a hidden room if they paid attention to the layout."

"Did you find anything interesting?"

"Oh yes, lots of records, not to mention ancient relics and jewels. I confiscated it all, of course."

"Of course. I'm certain you handed it over to the proper authorities."

She tilted her head. "I might have kept a piece or two as a souvenir. It's not like the crown needs an extra tiara."

Rion couldn't hide his smile. "Your secret is safe with me."

They paused by the first door. "I can't believe this place isn't better guarded."

She pulled a pair of picks from her pocket, then kneeled and set to work on the lock. "I'm sure to someone like you, the thought is absolutely abhorrent."

"Do you realize what could happen if our enemies discovered how vulnerable these villages are?"

"Who's going to notice? It's a tiny village on the seaside, and last I checked, there isn't a continent anywhere nearby."

"That we know of. This place was built to stand watch. Growing lax is exactly how empires fall."

She shrugged. "Nothing lasts forever."

"The Fae do."

"We fade, but to live even that long would probably be miserable." The latch clicked and Selina stood.

"I thought every Fae intended to fade."

She shrugged again. "Maybe. We'll see. When eternity starts to bore me, maybe I'll rile up a few of those enemies you think we have."

Gods help Alec if he was still around.

The first room was simple, with a large wooden desk near the far window, a rich green rug covering old wooden floorboards, and matching dusty drapes hiding the midnight sky. Bookshelves lined both walls, filled with texts and trinkets alike.

He took a moment to observe the space before approaching the first shelf. Selina took the desk.

Rion ran his fingertips along the spines, flipping them and tugging on a few large tomes just in case they revealed a secret room like the one Selina had mentioned. His assignments usually involved killing; leafing through documents and literature was a new one for him.

Selina knocked along the outside of the desk in search of hidden compartments and he did the same to the shelf. No hollow points.

Fifteen minutes later, Selina made a sound of triumph. She held up a thick leather-bound book with loose papers sticking out of the pages.

"Was that in the desk?"

"A false wall within the drawer."

"Could they be more obvious?"

She shrugged. "I told you, they think themselves clever when they're not."

Rion moved closer and peered over her shoulder to read a list of names scribbled in a single column. Dates and abbreviations were separated by a large space. He squinted, trying to make sense of the letters, then Selina shifted her weight to her back leg.

It put her close. Close enough that her wildflower scent drifted off her damp hair.

Rion tried not to move. He didn't want to pull away or involuntarily lean closer. His heart skipped, the treacherous thing.

Selina had opted to braid her hair to one side today. It left the pulse in her neck exposed. He traced the delicate curve with his eyes and briefly wondered what her warm skin might feel like beneath his lips.

"What do you make of it?" Selina asked without turning.

He swallowed hard, but couldn't focus. "I'm not sure."

Get it together, he chided himself. She looked up at him and furrowed her brow. Close. She was too close. "I'm sure there's more in a journal somewhere." She flipped through the book. "Or in this book. Do you think it's worth searching the other rooms?"

Rion tried to clear his throat and finally stepped back. "We're already here. It couldn't hurt." He eyed the desk, remembering how it felt to have her pressed against one.

Not his, not his, not his.

They proceeded down the hall to the next room, then the next and the next. Some held other potentially promising documents, but they all needed a key for decoding. A key they hadn't found yet.

Selina took everything, stashing it in the bag at her side. Some items were probably personal, but since they didn't intend to return, it didn't hurt to confiscate them.

Downstairs, Selina sauntered over to a glass case filled with an assortment of expensive alcohols. She opened one, sniffed, and recoiled. "It wouldn't take much of this to get the job done."

"Surprised the guard outside didn't take that with him, too."

"I'm sure he sneaks a drink or two." Selina turned the bottle in her hand and whistled. "This one is a few decades old." She stuffed that into her bag as well.

Rion just rolled his eyes, running his hands along another desk when the front door opened.

Their eyes met across the room, and Selina ran for the nearest door. He followed close behind and found himself in a closet. How amateur. He wasn't even sure why he'd followed Selina inside.

Rion wondered what someone would think if he found The Demon of Alastríona hiding in a closet with a female. A female who was standing very close to him.

Thick coats lined the space, their scent of old oak, likely from the chest at their feet. The heavy materials pushed against their bodies and forced the pair to remain close to the door and to one another.

Rion tried to step back, to give her room and separate himself from her scent, but he tripped and Selina grabbed his tunic to hold him steady.

Their breaths were too loud as they listened to the footsteps marching down the hall.

This was ridiculous. He was a Lord of Brónach. He should just step out and announce his arrival, tell them he was searching for—his mind froze when the male cursed from the hallway and slammed a door shut.

Selina's body heat was seeping through his clothes. His heart began racing and he was drunk on her all over again. He knew she could hear every breath, feel every movement.

Whoever had entered didn't linger. They grabbed something upstairs, then exited the door again without even waking the guard.

Another burglar? Or perhaps someone who'd forgotten something in their hurry home.

At least whatever they'd come looking for hadn't been something Selina had stashed in her bag.

Rion shoved the closet door open and sucked down fresh air. He raced straight for the basement, refusing to let Selina see the heat that had crept up his neck.

Once again, Selina wrapped her cloak tightly around herself, but they exited without Rion having to rescue another eight-legged creature.

It had stopped raining by the time they emerged.

"Well, that was a close call."

He nodded, still unable to speak. Close. She'd been too close.

Rion started toward the village, but Selina lingered, her gaze drifting toward the coastline. "Care for a detour?"

Rion raised a brow. "To where?"

"How often do you get to experience an ocean view?"

Rion eyed her pack. "Don't we have documents to review?" And decode.

She shrugged. "Sometimes you have to live a little. We only do it once."

"We live forever," he reminded her.

"Not out in the field."

Rion paused at the sudden grimness in her gaze and something in him faltered. "Lead the way."

Her steps lightened again and she practically skipped toward the raging ocean in the distance. Rion could hear the waves crashing against a rocky shore. It didn't take long for a cliffside to appear. Thankfully, Selina didn't go anywhere near it. He didn't trust that she wouldn't try to dive off. Instead, she settled on the damp ground and withdrew a bottle of the stolen liquor.

Selina gave him a feline smile. "Are you going to make me drink alone?"

Rion sat beside her. "You're a bad influence, you know that?"

She placed one hand over her chest. "I'll take that as a compliment." Selina took a long drink from the bottle, then hissed and smacked her lips. "Now *that* is good."

She passed him the bottle and Rion tried to ignore the fact that her lips had just been on the rim. He tried to ignore that it tasted like her, too. The amber liquid glided down his throat, leaving a pleasant burn in its wake. It reminded Rion of the bottle Saoirse had stolen for his sixteenth birthday. "I thought you said it was horrible?"

"The other one was horrible," she corrected. "This," she gestured to the bottle, "is liquid gold."

He shrugged. "They all accomplish the same goal."

"I'm going to pretend you did not just say that."

Rion passed the bottle back to her. She took another long drink, then shifted her gaze to the heavens. They passed it back and forth, and Rion watched the clouds roll by overhead. No stars tonight.

The ocean roared from beneath the cliff and the salty air brushed his face. It was all a lullaby he didn't want to resist.

He lost count of the drinks. Stopped thinking entirely as he laid back and tucked one hand behind his head. It had been too long since he'd allowed himself to relax. He ought to carve out more time to appreciate the world. Once again, moving to the countryside didn't sound like such a bad idea.

A shadow passed over him, then Rion was looking up into Selina's hooded gaze. Her eyes darted to his mouth. Once. Twice. His lips parted and he scarcely risked a breath as he reached a hand toward a loose tendril of her hair.

She stared at that hand and Rion froze entirely when she reached out and ran her fingertips through his hair. She did it again and let her hand linger there, playing with the short strands before her gaze dropped back to his face.

Her eyes darted to his lips. The curve of his jaw. His throat. She could have it. She could have him.

"Is this okay?" she whispered.

Rion nodded, unwilling to trust his voice. She was touching him. Selina was touching him and it didn't have anything to do with the mission or façades.

The way she was looking at him. Leaning closer. He hadn't instigated.

Would she allow him to sit up and capture her lips in a gentle kiss? Would she balk if his arms slid around her slender frame?

Rion slowly pushed up onto his elbows, watching the rapid rise and fall of her chest. He listened to the flutter of her heartbeat, tasted the slight nervousness in the air.

It's just the liquor, a voice in his head whispered.

But her hand lingered, drifted to his neck until those fingers rested just over his racing pulse. She leaned closer and the scent of wildflower dipped in whisky threatened to be his undoing. Gods, he wanted her. He wanted this female like he'd never wanted anything in his life.

Her lips parted, eyes wild and wary—a twig snapped to their left. He whirled, grabbing Selina and shoving her behind his body as his magic lifted to surround them on all sides. Rion palmed a knife, ready to launch it through the dark. Antlers emerged from within the trees ahead and a deer paused to stare at the pair. It lazily chewed on a piece of bark.

Rion exhaled through his teeth and fell back to the damp earth. He draped an arm over his eyes, dropped the knife in the grass, and struggled to calm his racing heart.

"Gods above," Selina whispered.

"I know," he groaned and peered around his arm. He contemplated putting the dagger through its hide just for ruining the moment.

"No. You. Gods, I didn't even see you *move*."

He smirked at that. "I told you I was fast."

"That's not fast. That's god-like reflexes."

"And I'm inebriated, so imagine me at my best." His smile faltered when she didn't return it.

"Right. The alcohol." Her face pinched and he wondered if it had all been a mistake. Maybe he shouldn't—Selina suddenly grabbed her stomach and, to his absolute horror, hurled all over the ground near his feet. Well, if the deer hadn't ruined the moment, that certainly did.

Rion stumbled to his feet and turned away to give her some privacy.

She heaved again and Rion walked over to the edge of the cliff, peering down at the sheer fifty-foot drop. Rion tilted his head into the breeze, letting it ruffle his hair. The sea felt so powerful. It sang to him in a way nothing else ever had. He wondered if it always would.

After collecting herself, at least somewhat, they started back. Her face was still pale and a light sheen of sweat covered her brow. The pair slipped inside an inn under the cover of darkness. No one asked questions. Dawn wasn't far off, but a few hours of sleep was better than nothing. *If* they were able to sleep.

Selina cleaned herself up in the bathroom. He busied himself by the fire. A cup of tea would help to calm her stomach.

Upon exiting, Selina went straight for her satchel and pushed the half empty bottle far away. She pulled out the documents and books and began spreading everything out in neat piles.

Right. They had information to go over but—

The room was silent as she combed through the documents, her brows furrowing as she tried to piece things together. Rion waited until the kettle was warm, pulled the tea from his own bag, and made them both a cup.

She took it without comment and kept reading.

Rion didn't know how she could focus on the words. His mind was still reeling. Fantasizing what else they might be able to do in a room alone together.

He studied her. Was she waiting for him to break the silence? She'd initiated first, so perhaps she was waiting to see if he reciprocated.

Then again, maybe Rion shouldn't allow himself to become distracted until after the mission was over. Maybe rifling through documents *was* the perfect distraction.

He downed his tea, letting it burn his throat, then refilled both their cups.

Rion sat in the small chair and waited. The fire crackled and shifted to embers. They emptied three more cups a piece. His head began to clear, the pleasant fog shifting to a pounding headache.

Selina finally clicked her tongue and let the papers fall from her hands.

"Good news?" Rion questioned.

"Yes."

"Then why do you look so frustrated?"

"Because I was hoping we wouldn't have to travel south again."

"Whiteridge?" She nodded. "We suspected they were involved from the beginning. What now? Do we inform the others?"

Selina shook her head. "It would take too long to find them." She tapped her chin. "It'll just be you and me again. We can scope the place out and move on the solstice."

Rion raised a brow. "Why the solstice?"

"For the same reasons as before. That's when everyone lets their guard down. There will be Fae from all over the countryside coming to participate in the festivities. It'll be the perfect cover."

Rion tilted his mug, watching the remnants of leaves at the bottom. "Is there any clue as to *where* they gather?"

"The palace. Where else would you expect?"

"You realize it's almost as large as the one in Nàdair, right?"

She pursed her lips. "I've seen it from the outside once."

"It's guarded just as well, too."

"Yes, but you're a Lord. Surely that entitles you to certain exceptions."

"They still won't let us go anywhere without an escort."

"You're kidding."

"Not in the slightest. However," he studied the fire. "They're always throwing parties in the main ballroom, especially around the solstice. I think there's one every night."

Selina perked up at that. "You mean I get to dress up, dance, eat good food, *and* infiltrate one of the most well-guarded places in Brónach? You might as well call this the best day of my life."

Rion rolled his eyes. "I met their governor a few summers ago when

I was out on an assignment with Saoirse. We didn't think much of it at the time, but poison was being distributed back then."

"The same stuff?"

"It wasn't as strong, but I'm willing to bet it was a precursor to what they're putting out now."

"And where did the ones responsible go?"

"To prison, on Saoirse's order."

"You think they're out?"

"Could be, or they've found a way to still pull the strings. Their governor wanted to overthrow my father. The two never got along. He even tried to break off from Nàdair and start his own country. Only threats of war have kept them in line."

"War." She tasted the word. "Brónach hasn't experienced one of those in a long time."

"Let's hope we keep it that way."

"All right, so the governor is suspect number one, noted."

"That city has eyes and ears everywhere. We won't be able to breathe a word about the mission, even if we think we're safe."

"Afraid I can't keep it together?"

"You can be a bit . . . eccentric."

"I resent that." She crossed her arms and stared into her steaming mug. "Are you ready to take them all on?"

Rion flexed his fingers. "I've been itching for a good fight."

Selina held up a finger. "No fighting until we have the information."

"And food, I presume."

She laughed. "I do think you're getting to know me a little too well, Lord Rion."

CHAPTER EIGHTEEN

The two decided to sleep for a few hours before grabbing a quick lunch and heading out. She never mentioned the almost kiss. Maybe it was a mistake on her part, or maybe it was too much of a distraction with the conclusion of their mission fast approaching. He wouldn't pressure her on the matter.

Days passed as they continued their trek south. The temperatures rose to peak levels that had sweat rolling down the back of his neck. He was glad he'd cut his hair. The event seemed like both yesterday and a lifetime ago.

Rion cracked his eyes open just as dawn began illuminating the clear sky. Their fire had shifted to ashy embers and Selina was—gone. He shot up, throwing out his magic in all directions.

Her pack still sat on the ground, just out of reach. Her water skin, too. Which meant she couldn't have gone far.

Rion stood and scented the air. Close. He grabbed his sword belt and fastened it on before jogging slightly uphill through the thin trees.

He didn't have to go far.

There, just at the top of the hillside, the sunlight creating a halo around her braid, Selina stood with her body lowered in a perfect stance. She moved her foot in an ark and lowered further, her chest expanding and contracting with deep, controlled breaths.

Sweat dripped from her hairline and rolled down her exposed collarbones. She wore the same shorts from yesterday but had opted to shed her top shirt, leaving her clad in nothing but a tight wrap around her chest that left her stomach and arms exposed.

Rion swallowed hard, trying to keep his gaze from drifting. Selina pulled her blade from its sheath, then exploded in a series of movements. She jumped and dodged and rolled, her magic following every movement with lethal grace.

Rion sank back into the shadows to watch. Her foot shifted, but instead of pushing forward in the manner that had previously given her body away, she lunged without a tell.

Fast learner. A dark voice in the back of his mind whispered that it had been an act. Maybe it had been. Maybe at the time she'd intended to follow through with Alec's orders. He studied her. She'd saved him and nearly kissed him again. Perhaps she'd damned those orders.

He let her go through her routine without interruption. He waited until she stood and wiped the sweat from her brow before emerging from the trees.

Breathless, she waved him over. "You slept in late."

"I've been up for a while." He threw the water skin.

She caught it and popped the top to take a long swig. "Watching, I presume?"

"For a bit."

"Creep."

Rion chuckled. "You said you wanted me to train you, remember? What better way to see what I'm working with?" He drew his sword.

Selina arched a brow. "Now?"

"Now." He lunged without warning and Selina barely had enough time to lift her blade. They clashed and she gritted her teeth, her feet scooting back slightly as she tried to maintain her balance.

Rion didn't relent. He kept battering her with strike after strike, moving in different patterns to see how she'd adjust. She was fast herself, though the exhaustion slowed her down.

His magic danced around the pair, eager and excited. Selina ignored it. She ducked beneath Rion's next strike and came up at his side with her sword aimed for his thigh.

Rion already had a knife in his other hand and shifted his forearm to block the movement, bracing his arm against the steel with magic.

Selina retreated a step, briefly scanned his body for any weakness, then lunged at him again. Rion simply stepped out of the way, but she dropped to a crouch and swept his legs out from under him.

His body hit the ground hard, then she was over him, a knife aimed at his throat. Rion's heart jolted and his magic sped to wrap around her wrist, stopping the blade just before it met his skin.

"How was that?" she breathed, a hint of triumph flashing in her eyes.

Rion's mouth had gone dry, an exhilarating mixture of trepidation and awe coursing through him. Selina's legs were on either side of his hips, her body hovering just above.

Rational thought disappeared entirely as he studied the swirling amber depths of her eyes. He knew he should say something, or at the very least remove the sharp object from her hand. Instead, Rion's hands drifted to her thighs. He wouldn't move further without her permission.

Her eyes tracked the movement, then she met his gaze. For a brief moment, Rion thought she might try to kiss him again. In fact, he hoped for it. Just to feel her close. Wanting the way he wanted.

But Selina stood instead and Rion didn't stop her. He tried to remember her question and cleared his throat. "You don't lean forward anymore."

"I've been working on it." She didn't meet his gaze.

Perhaps he shouldn't have touched her at all. "About before."

"We were drunk," Selina interrupted, her voice cold.

It hit him like a blow. "Right."

"It's best not to linger on anything that could complicate the mission."

"Right," he said again and turned to stare at the rising sun. Palpable silence filled the morning air.

Selina sighed and threw her hands up. "Look, I know it was my fault. I'll own up to that. I wasn't trying to lead you on or anything, I just—"

"It's fine."

"No, it's not. We have a job to do and I don't need you out of sorts because I did something stupid."

A smirk played on his lips. "Worried for me again?" He pressed a mocking hand to his chest. "I'm touched."

He turned that smile toward her and could have sworn color tinted her cheeks. Selina cleared her throat. "I'm going to the river to rinse off. Don't you dare peek."

"I wouldn't dream of it."

Rion watched her go and despite the temptation, he returned to their camp. He wouldn't push her into anything she didn't want. That wouldn't be fair for either of them.

Once she'd cleaned herself up and Rion had washed, they ventured the rest of the way to Whiteridge in silence. He caught her staring several times, but she always looked away. *After the mission*, he told himself. It wouldn't take much longer. Once they were back in Nàdair, he'd ask her on a real date and see exactly how far she was willing to go.

They found the city before sunset and Selina whistled at the size.

"I take it you've never been?" he asked.

"I have, it's just been a long time." Her eyes traced over the three-story buildings and bustling streets. "Please tell me the food is still good."

"Delicious," he confirmed and meant it. Saoirse had brought him a few years ago, back when no one this far south knew him as The Demon. He'd been blissfully unrecognizable. Most probably still wouldn't recognize him if he kept his magic to himself, which wasn't in the plans.

"You know," he started. "We could try to sneak in, blend with the crowd for a bit before they figure out who I am."

"You think they won't recognize you?"

He shrugged. "It's worth a shot."

She looked at his arm. "I don't suppose I can play overprotective girlfriend, seeing as you're almost healed."

"Sure you could. I'll roll my eyes and everything."

She shook her head. "We'll see how they react at the gates and go from there." Selina batted her eyelashes. "I could always grab your arm and feign the utmost concern for your safety."

"They'd run just to get away from you." She slapped his arm and they laughed.

The pair ventured closer. Unlike Fernsworth and the smaller villages, the gate to Whiteridge was closely guarded by sentinels on full alert. Their hands rested on their weapons and tightened upon seeing the two.

Rion let his sand billow up and around their bodies. Selina tried to slow, likely to talk, but Rion kept walking, tugging her along, her arm once again in his.

Recognition flashed across their faces and the guards drew their swords. Not exactly the greeting he'd hoped for.

"My Lord," one male said, his voice strained. He didn't bow or incline his head. "We were instructed to escort you to the governor's estate upon your arrival."

Rion lifted a brow. "Am I expected?"

"No, My Lord, it's simply a courtesy. Special rooms have been prepared for any who visit from the capital city." As if he'd ever sleep in those. It had assassination written all over it.

"I'll make my own arrangements."

The guard stepped into Rion's path. "The governor insists."

Rion raised a brow. "Am I to be denied entry into the city if I refuse?"

"O-of course not," he fumbled. "I—"

"Then *move*." The male stepped back, opened and closed his mouth, then decided against whatever he'd been about to say. Rion stalked past, but stopped just inside the gate. He eyed the male, barely suppressing a snarl. "If the governor wishes to see me, he can request my presence. Otherwise, I'm afraid I'm busy." Rion wrapped one arm around Selina's shoulders. "I'd appreciate not being disturbed. It's almost the solstice, after all."

All six guards took Selina in at once. The way she leaned into Rion.

Her hand delicately draped around his arm. The shy smile she offered to the male she claimed to love.

Their eyes widened in surprise and Rion turned, giving them his back. He counted his steps, waiting for the battle cries and hurried footsteps.

They never came. Maybe those in the south valued their lives more than the Fae up north.

A pleasant floral aroma greeted him as he paraded down the main road. The cobblestones were perfectly placed and those ambling up and down the sidewalks didn't look at them twice. He'd already let his magic fall. It would be nice, pleasant even, to experience the city from a tourist's point of view before the world recognized him as the monster from their nightmares.

Vendors were already set up, selling their wares despite the festival being a while off. He knew more would arrive over the course of the next week. Then the streets would be crowded as bodies pressed into one another, seeking stall after stall of finery and goods.

As they passed through the streets, Rion watched some Fae position ladders before carrying large streamers up to the second-story balconies. They fashioned them with vines and plant life, coaxing the flowers into full bloom.

"It really does rival the one in Nàdair," Selina said.

"Do you think the Fairy Folk come to this one, too?"

"I don't see why they wouldn't."

"I always thought they only visited Nàdair, you know, because of the trees and all."

"Who's to say they don't attend both?"

Rion looked at her. "It's across the continent; it wouldn't be possible to attend both."

"Not for us."

"You think they just, what, magically disappear?"

She shrugged. "Why not? They vanish in the forests. How do we know they don't go somewhere else entirely?"

"And here I was thinking you were the reasonable one."

"I am, I'm just speculating based upon what I've seen."

"And you've seen them disappear?"

She made a motion with her hand. "Into thin air." He didn't want to mention how much time he'd spent around the Fairy Folk. It would only lead to questions he wasn't ready to answer, not until he knew he could trust her completely. Maybe not even then.

"I'll take your word for it."

"Liar."

He smirked and spotted a small bench with tiny trinkets and boats and leaves all shaped for the Fairy Folk's use. Nàdair did something similar. The small creatures always seemed delighted by the offerings. Most were made by children, and they too were often just as delighted to see the sacred beings playing with their creations.

They were such strange and enchanting little creatures. Powerful, most claimed, yet none had ever seen the extent of that power. Mostly because the Fae didn't challenge them. They were sacred on a level that rivaled the gods.

He remembered watching the Fairy Folk play tricks on a few younglings after their failed attempts to capture the tiny beings. They were kind, but clearly possessed a sense of humor. Two of the children had ended the night covered in honey and feathers.

"Well," Selina said, looking out over the sea of people. "I'm willing to bet at least half the inns are already full."

"Don't worry, a vacancy always appears when I walk in."

She rolled her eyes. "Of course it does."

"You haven't complained before."

"Well, maybe I don't want to piss anyone off today. I would like to enjoy *some* of the festivities."

He rolled his eyes and they kept walking. Selina looped her arm in his and he glanced down at the female.

Her eyes were practically beaming. She paused at a few stalls, admiring the wares, and proceeded to tell him every detail about some unimpressive jewelry. The shop owners were more than happy to let her try things on. She purchased a few trinkets, but promised others she'd return once she had a room to store her possessions.

Rion had to resist rolling his eyes a number of times. But when hers lit up and she acted as though his opinion meant the world, he didn't have to feign interest. He wanted to know how to earn her favor and he wanted to know how to keep that smile on her face.

A shop owner declared himself partial owner of an inn that resided closer to the city's center. After seeing the gold in Selina's hand, he'd practically barreled over other patrons to tell her they had ample space.

The shop owner had a young male escort them.

It was charming, immaculately clean, and intricately decorated, as were most structures toward the inner part of the city.

Selina, of course, requested their finest room. The young male was only too happy to oblige and led them to the third floor. He announced breakfast and lunch schedules and excitedly told Selina about a restaurant around the corner that served the best cheese she'd ever taste. She promised to visit.

The male bowed low, first to her, then to Rion before he raced back down the stairs and disappeared.

"Well, he was lively."

"I'm sure it had nothing to do with the gold coins you threw at those shoes." He eyed the box in her hand.

"Did you see them? How could I possibly resist? I'll have to find a—" she pushed open the door and paused to gape, "—dress," she finished.

Rion followed her inside. Sand-colored curtains fluttered elegantly as a cool breeze flowed in through the open window. Matching sheets covered the large canopy bed off to their right and enough pillows were piled next to the thick oak headboard that he'd have no trouble using them to make a bed of his own.

An unlit fireplace sat in the opposite corner and Selina all but raced to inspect the connected bathroom. He heard her gasp when the lights switched on.

"Now this is what I call a room. Maybe we should drag this mission out until the winter solstice."

"Somehow I don't think Alec would tolerate that."

"He wouldn't believe his little brother?"

"Not a chance, and Saoirse would be down here in less than a month if we didn't show progress."

Selina grimaced. "She's never been my biggest fan."

"Did you disagree with one another while on an assignment?"

"She didn't tell you anything?"

"Not really. What happened?"

Selina ran her fingertips along the wooden desk positioned before the window. "It's not worth repeating. I was—I made a few calls that some deemed . . . unethical."

There were a million possibilities, but if Saoirse had disagreed, he was willing to bet it pertained to the treatment of innocents. She'd never believed in sacrificing them for the greater good.

Which left him to wonder just how far Selina was willing to go in order to achieve success.

"I see." He'd ask Saoirse when he returned. Hopefully, it had been over nothing more than a petty squabble.

"Anyway, if I'm to find a decent dress, then I should probably get to it. Gods know the good ones will get taken if we wait."

"Now?" He glanced out the window and noted the darkening sky.

"No, in the morning. And don't worry, I'll find you something worthy of a Lord to match."

"I'm not going with you?"

She lifted a brow. "Do you *want* to come with me?"

"Not shopping."

"That's what I thought. I figured you could get a head start on scouting the palace. Get a count of the guards and see if we might be able to break in around the parties."

"Not likely. Breaking in should be reserved as a last ditch effort. Things will take a bloody turn if we're caught."

She made a face. "Well, at least this won't be boring."

Selina looked over her documents again before tucking them away in her bag and curling up on the large bed. Rion took the floor. They slept in intervals.

At dawn, Selina showered, then headed off to the market. There were a few vendors about to have a very good day. At least she was generous where her coin was concerned.

Rion left twenty minutes later and kept his magic in check as he wove through the crowds. More decorations littered the street.

Garlands and streamers and flowers all along the railings, up the gutters, dangling from overhanging balconies. The chief designer had definitely spent some time in Nàdair, though nothing could ever compare to the capital city.

A few blocks later, Rion stood before the massive palace. Its towering four stories promised an abundance of wealth inside.

Wealth and greed.

He circled the outer perimeter. No fence separated the street from the lawn, only thick five-foot-tall hedges that were immaculately maintained. Morning glories and wisteria grew in between, and the flowers were spread evenly as far as Rion's eye could see.

He glanced up, counting the windows. Guards were stationed at regular intervals.

He peered over the hedges and into the yard only to find more guards, their hands lightly resting on their weapons as they watched civilians excitedly pointing from the street.

Rion rounded the back and lifted a brow at the large fountain spraying water into the air. That was new, as was the rear addition. It might actually be bigger than the one in Nàdair now. Saoirse would demand an expansion once she found out.

Rion thought back to the mission at hand. If they failed, this place could very well be the new capital of Brónach. The new Nàdair. The other would likely be destroyed, just so no one could claim it in the future.

Neither Alec nor Saoirse had children yet. If the rebels succeeded, the family line would end with them.

Perhaps one of his siblings should do something about that soon, Alec at the very least. Rion wasn't certain Saoirse even wanted children.

"The young Lord of Brónach has deigned to grace us with his presence? I shall have to make a grand statement welcoming you to the city."

Rion turned slowly toward the familiar voice, his sand rising to surround his body as he did. He stared at the male's shoulder-length brown hair, at the matching eyes, then the sharp angular jaw his sister had broken the last time they'd met.

"No statement needed, unless it's to explain why you're not behind bars."

The male waved one hand and Rion watched it intently. He didn't need Selina digging any more vines out of his flesh. "Simple," the male purred. "There wasn't enough evidence and the governor dismissed the case."

"Last I remember, there was plenty of evidence."

The male shrugged and slid his hands into his pockets. A sly smile broke across his face. "I suppose the lawmakers were careless then."

Rion surveyed him again, then turned to observe the palace. He kept a close watch on the male through his peripherals. Rion didn't need to look much further to determine who sat in the inner circle. This male, Foley, had been involved last time. He'd crafted the first batch of poison that had led to the death of dozens.

Foley could be at the very center of it all. But if Rion arrested him now and he turned out to be wrong—

"Perhaps they should resign if they can't be trusted to do their jobs."

Foley's smirk didn't vanish. "So like your sister. Not an ounce of tolerance for the occasional error."

Rion eyed him again. He didn't let his magic fall. "I hope you're spending your newfound freedom being productive."

"I am, as a matter of fact. I've made my way onto the city council. They've invited me in as a key speaker at the upcoming ball. One of many, as I'm sure you're already aware. We have elaborate plans to house those displaced by all the recent attacks." His brow furrowed. "Nàdair's lack of concern for the issue has raised questions."

"It's being addressed."

"But not publicly." The male sighed. "I tried to convince Saoirse to allow me to take the brunt of the public eye. The offer still stands." He looked around. "Did our esteemed Lady not accompany you?"

"She's on her own assignments."

The male's brows lifted. "I thought you'd still be attached at the hip. Good on you for finally breaking the chain."

Rion kept his temper in check. "It's been a few years. It was time."

Silence engulfed them and a small crowd had started to form at the other end of the street. Whispers floated close. Rion grimaced. So much for remaining anonymous.

"Why are you here, Rion of Brónach?"

Rion forced a smile. "Am I not allowed to take a holiday?"

A small disbelieving smile. "I didn't realize your lot knew the term. Do be sure to visit the spa. It has excellent skin healing properties."

"I'll do that."

Foley's hand left his pocket and went for the inside of his dress tunic. Rion's eyes darted toward the movement, but the male held his other hand up in mock surrender. "Just a private invitation," the male assured before holding out an envelope with a thick wax seal depicting a crow.

Rion met his gaze, wondering if it were a taunt. Foley gave nothing away.

After a moment's hesitation, Rion took the envelope and the male continued. "All those of significance will be there, the governor included. Can I assure him he need not worry about a repeat of the things that happened in Fernsworth?"

Rion opened his mouth, but a light voice interrupted. "There you are." Both males turned toward Selina as she half jogged toward them dressed in a pair of light tan shorts and a white top. She wore a necklace depicting a starfish and dangling earrings with sea turtles at the ends. "How are we supposed to get dinner if you're out sightseeing?"

Selina slipped her arm through his and pressed herself close, no doubt sensing the distressing nature of the conversation. She'd likely seen the crowd and had come running.

Foley's shock wasn't feigned. His lips parted and his gaze wandered down her form and back up before taking careful note of the way her arm was looped through Rion's.

Rion offered her a disarming smile. "My apologies, I ran into an old," he paused and made a show of looking the male up and down, "acquaintance."

"Oh." She looked Foley over as if she were just seeing him for the first time. "Do you mind if I steal him back?"

The male sketched a bow and smiled. An evil wicked thing full of dark promises. Rion had seen the same look on Foley's face after the male had successfully poisoned an entire village of innocents. They hadn't gone peacefully.

"Not at all." He stepped back. "Perhaps we'll meet you and your . . . friend?" Selina tilted her head into Rion, but didn't speak. "After the event."

"We'll see," Rion replied.

The male inclined his head to Selina. "It was a pleasure," he waited.

"Selina," she offered.

"Selina." The male tasted her name, savoring it as though it were a fine wine. "I was just inviting the young lord to an exclusive after party. I hope you'll both attend. Things tend to take a more . . . pleasantly heated turn after hours." He made another show of looking her up and down. Rion clenched his fists. Selina pinched his arm.

They most certainly wouldn't be joining anything of the sort. The thought of anything heated with Foley in the same room was enough to make Rion's stomach churn.

Foley turned away first, then Selina tugged on Rion's sleeve and guided him back toward the inn in silence. Both glanced over their shoulders and into the shadowed alcoves.

"You should have waited for me," he said.

"I did, then I got bored and when I saw the crowd, I thought you might need a little help."

"You just painted a target on your back."

She shrugged. "I did that the moment I recruited you." She glanced back again. "Who was that anyway?"

"Someone who should be behind bars."

"Your doing?"

"Saoirse's, though I was there. He's the original creator of the poison."

Selina cringed. "Well, I guess we know we're in the right place then."

"He'll be keeping a close eye on me. If I'd known he was involved—"

"There's no way you could have, especially if you thought he was locked up."

"He talked as if Saoirse already knew . . ."

"Maybe she does."

"She wouldn't allow him to walk free. Not after what he did."

Selina shrugged. "Politics are complicated. If there's no proof to keep him behind bars, then there's not much she can do."

"She could tear his head off."

"She could, but then she'd probably just alienate the governor and his council even more. It's no secret that Whiteridge and Nàdair have their issues." Rion's jaw clenched and she patted his arm. "Don't worry, once we get the information we need and weed out the ones involved, I'll help you raze the whole damn place."

"Feeling destructive?"

"Vengeful." Her voice darkened. "I've seen what that poison does, and if he's the one responsible for its creation, then he should have it shoved down his own throat."

"That'd be too quick for the amount of pain he's caused."

"Maybe so, but at least he wouldn't be able to sneak out again and hurt anyone else."

Rion stared at the invite. "I'm willing to bet this secret meeting is exactly what we're looking for."

She crinkled her nose. "Please tell me we're not going."

"I don't know. We'd get a clear view of their faces and it might be fun to see you squirm for a change."

"That's cruel. I wouldn't send my worst enemy into that place. Just his eyes gave me the creeps."

"It's a good thing you aren't my enemy then." She didn't respond to that; in fact, she turned away and studied the civilians filing by. Rion swallowed hard and decided to press his luck. "You mentioned dinner."

"Because I'm starving."

"Would you like to go?"

She turned to him and a wide smile broke across her face. "Why, Rion of Brónach, are you asking me out on a date?"

"I'd like to."

Seriousness suddenly returned to her face. Her lips parted. "I don't know—"

"One date," he clarified.

"We need to find the blueprints—"

"After then. Tonight."

"Rion, we have a job to do and I don't want—"

"Who said we weren't going to talk about the job?" She peered up at him. "We can even take the blueprints with us if that makes you feel better."

He allowed her to think another moment before she finally nodded. "Fine. But I warn you, I'm expensive."

"I'll be sure to empty the family vault."

CHAPTER NINETEEN

They ambled toward the library, stopping along the way to study different trinkets as various stalls. Apparently, Selina didn't have enough in their room already. Nothing ever seemed to satisfy her.

Rion studied the shadows, watching for anyone who might be under Foley's employ. His involvement complicated things.

Rion kept his magic in check for Selina's sake, just so he wouldn't scare off the vendors, but even with some knowing he was present in the city, not everyone recognized him. A relief, especially when he could engage in normal conversation.

Once again, Selina paid to have her items delivered to their room.

"How's your aim?"

She stopped pulling him along and twisted to stare at him in confusion. "What?"

"Your aim. With weapons."

Selina snorted. "Such grand conversation to have before dinner."

"I thought you wanted it to stay professional."

She scrunched her face. "My aim is just fine, thank you. I'm not a novice."

"You're the one who asked me to train you, remember? I was just thinking it might be wise to carry a few daggers instead of walking around unarmed."

Her playful smile returned. "What makes you think I'm unarmed?"

At that, he reassessed her gait. The way her hands moved.

"Where are they?"

She smirked. "That's for me to know and everyone else to find out."

Selina spun back around with a little skip in her step. Rion studied her form, then decided he didn't want to linger on the areas where she might have hidden her weapons. Instead, he simply said, "Well done."

She snorted at his compliment. "As if I need your approval."

He tried not to smirk. "Isn't that what all students seek?"

"I'm interested in your unique hand-to-hand, not weapon skills."

"Maybe those are unique, too."

"I've seen them. They're not."

"You've seen Saoirse fight." It wasn't a question, but he wanted to know more about the female's confrontation.

"In the field, but we never fought against one another, in case that's what you're wondering."

"I was."

She tsked. "You're a nosy one, aren't you?"

"I'd call myself curious."

"Haven't you ever heard what curiosity did to the cat?"

"I'm not a cat, now am I?"

She rolled her eyes and they continued on, walking three blocks until they reached the library. It was a rather impressive building with two small cafes flanking either side. Both had lines stretching out the door, much to Selina's disappointment.

She pushed open the heavy double doors and gestured him inside the library. The scent of old books greeted Rion like an old friend. His gaze automatically scanned the shelves, searching for the historical section. He wondered if Whiteridge contained old tomes he'd never set eyes on or if they taught their youth a history that differed from Nàdair. Maybe they even possessed parts of history Nàdair wasn't privy to.

Patrons sat at various tables, some with small stacks of books while others leafed through a single text. They sipped from steaming mugs and none looked up when the door closed behind the newcomers. Rion had the distinct impression that if he spoke, they'd all jump out of their skins before scolding him for making noise, demon lord or no.

Reluctantly, Rion turned away from the shelves and proceeded to the main desk. They waited a full ten minutes for someone to show up. Rion scowled at the male's slow pace. Selina busied herself by flipping through a nearby book. Her hand covered the title.

"Can I help you?" the librarian whispered. His voice was rough, calloused, as if he were offended that anyone stood before his desk at all.

Rion lowered his voice a fraction, if only to be polite to the other guests. "I need blueprints to the palace."

The librarian didn't look up or hesitate before saying, "Those documents are classified."

Rion raised a brow and waited for the librarian to meet his gaze. He did. The male scowled and widened his eyes as if to say, *anything else?*

It was both difficult and pleasant to be in a place where not everyone recognized him.

"I think a Lord of Brónach would meet the necessary qualifications."

"He certainly would, but—" The male stopped talking when Rion's magic inched from beneath his sleeves, twisting up and around his arms in a lazy pattern.

Fear filled the foyer and the male retreated a step, his look of annoyance shifting to one of absolute terror.

Selina peered over her book. "I'd suggest hurrying. We're hungry and you've already kept us waiting." Rion glared at her, but the librarian rushed off after a quick bow and muttered apologies.

Rion faced her. "They're afraid enough without you pushing the issue."

She slammed the book shut and three Fae jolted, then pinned her with a glare. "You really don't like it, do you?"

Rion opened his mouth to reply, but the librarian returned, out of breath, and directed them to a secluded table upstairs. "You won't be disturbed here. Is there anything else you require?"

"No, we're fine, thank you."

The male bowed again before scrambling back down the stairs, his heart beating faster than a hummingbird's wings.

"Well, he's a jumpy fellow."

"Comes with the reputation, unfortunately."

Selina eyed him again, but Rion shifted his attention to the blueprints. Every room was outlined in stark detail aside from the basement, which led Selina and Rion to the same conclusion.

"Well, that answers that. When's the ball again?"

"According to the invitation, in a few days."

Selina stretched her arms overhead. "I heard the spa is divine. We could always pay it a visit."

"I thought you just wanted the food."

"There's no reason I can't have food and a spa day." Her stomach grumbled. "Speaking of food . . ."

Rion carefully rolled the prints back up. "Did any of the restaurants catch your attention on the way in?"

"Nope. I figured we'd walk the streets until we found something that smelled good."

Well, that could certainly add to their ruse. It would also give him a few minutes to see where the business districts ended and the residential ones began. He'd mark the storefronts and who ran them. Then he'd watched the governor's palace over the next few days to see which vendors he chose to visit. Maybe Rion could figure out how they were shipping the poison and put a stop to it before the ball.

"If you're done thinking, can we get a move on?"

He smirked. "Lead the way."

CHAPTER TWENTY

When Selina had claimed her tastes were expensive, she'd meant it. Either that or she was just testing him, trying to see if he'd live up to his offer to spend the entirety of his family's money.

He probably wouldn't succeed even if he tried.

Rion cast a glance toward the line of waiting patrons. The females all wore fancy dresses and were adorned with expensive necklaces, rings, and earrings. The males were dressed in finely pressed tunics with their hair combed back and shoes polished.

He and Selina looked like beggars in comparison. "I'm not sure we're properly dressed."

A wicked grin. "Should we see if they try to throw us out?"

"You're going to use me to your advantage again, aren't you?"

"Isn't that the whole reason you're here?"

Rion rolled his eyes and held out his arm, leading a practically bouncing Selina to the hostess stand the restaurant had stationed outside. The hostess, a female dressed in a short black dress with flowing blonde hair, looked them over and crinkled her nose.

"We'd like a table," Selina said in her sweetest voice.

The hostess gave an apologetic smile to those waiting in line. "It's formal attire only, I'm afraid."

Selina made a show of looking down at herself, then to Rion. "I wasn't aware those rules applied to a Lord of Brónach."

The hostess's eyes lit up, but upon inspection, her excitement shifted to disappointment. "I'm afraid you'll have to come up with a better—"

Rion didn't wait for her to finish her sentence as his magic came alive and swirled up his body. He'd never liked being the center of attention, but Selina seemed to delight in it. She even offered him a hint of a smile. He didn't return it.

Her smile faded.

Rion thought the hostess might faint on the spot and leave them to either venture inside unannounced or seek another establishment. She collected herself and pivoted instead, gesturing them inside with her hands as though she no longer possessed the ability to speak.

They followed the female through the dimly lit space, all the way to the back where a single round booth sat on the left-hand side. A table reserved for high-paying patrons, especially those who didn't wish to be disturbed.

The hostess set a pair of menus before them, her fingers trembling, then offered a house wine. Rion didn't listen to her description of the flavors, he only nodded and waited for her to pour each of them a glass before rushing away.

Selina swirled the drink, staring at the contents before saying, "It really bothers you, doesn't it?"

"What?"

"Their fear."

Rion flipped open his menu. "It's certainly made making friends a breeze."

He glanced up when she didn't respond and found something like sadness written across her face. She set her glass down. "I'm sorry. I should let you enjoy your times of anonymity."

"You put yourself in danger too, you know?"

"Worried about me for a change?"

He smirked and read through the short list of dinner options.

"Maybe."

"Well don't. I have a big bad Fae boyfriend to keep me safe." She tapped her chin. "Although, I wonder if that male from earlier could take you on?"

He lifted a brow. "Foley? You're not serious."

She leaned forward. "How old were you when you first fought?"

"Fifteen."

"It's been a few years for both of you, then."

"A few years that he spent in prison."

"Supposedly. For all you know, they might have released him the very next day."

Rion clenched his jaw at that. To think they might have been curating the poison for that long. Experimenting on unwilling subjects.

A new female arrived to refill their drinks and take their orders. Rion downed the wine, savoring the hints of a floral aftertaste.

Selina sipped from her own glass. "And you say I have an alcohol problem."

He set the glass down. "You do, and clearly you're a bad influence. I shall have to tell my sister."

"That'll really get us in a brawl. She's always been protective of you."

Rion lifted a brow. "Does she talk about me often?"

"No, just prevents anyone from slandering your name. Gods help them if they do."

"Ah, so that's what happened."

She sat back. "I was just curious. It was the others who called you a monster."

"I take it that didn't go over well for them?"

"Saoirse knocked their teeth out, so no, it didn't."

He chuckled, "They're lucky that's all she did."

"You've seen her do worse, I take it?"

"There were a few tutors that . . . well, they took their shot. She saw it and snapped their arms before exiling them from the city."

"Gods above."

"Don't worry, I'll keep you on her good side."

Selina swirled her drink again and sipped on it. "Isn't fifteen kind of young to be going out on missions? Weren't you supposed to be in school?"

"Saoirse schooled me herself. When she had assignments, she took me along. She didn't believe I'd be safe otherwise. That's how I got involved."

"What about when you were a kid?"

Rion ran a finger through the condensation on his glass and downed another drink. His voice was low as he said, "I had someone who looked out for me then." Selina watched him, waiting. "Caol was . . . like a second father."

"Caol." She considered the name. "The Fae we encountered before mentioned his name."

"He was our teacher. My father's ally. The two of them fought together on the field and he trained my siblings and I."

"But?"

Rion shrugged. "There was an . . . accident. He didn't believe me, or maybe he thought I'd become too much of a liability."

"So you killed him?"

Rion kept his gaze on the glass, running his fingers around the rim. "I didn't mean to. My magic was more volatile back then. It reacted to his killing blow. I barely made it back to Saoirse in time."

She was silent. "It's funny how the truth of some stories never sees the light of day." Selina lifted her arm and the waitress returned, refilled their drinks, then took their orders.

"Back to the mission when you were fifteen," she said. "I'm guessing Saoirse didn't plan your involvement?"

He smirked "No."

"Details, that's how dates work."

Rion's heart jolted at the word. Date.

"It wasn't anything spectacular, if that's what you're hoping to hear. I just wanted to see the city." She waited. "I went for a stroll and after a while, I realized not a single soul recognized me. It was . . . refreshing. I jumped from stall to stall and purchased so many things I could hardly carry them."

"So you do like to shop."

"I was fifteen and had an endless supply of money. I think most just assumed I was some rich merchant's son." He drank again. "I even had a female smile at me for the first time."

Selina leaned forward with a mischievous look on her face. "Was she pretty?"

"Beautiful. If Saoirse hadn't found me, I might have even gotten the chance to talk to her."

"Wait, wait, wait, you're telling me you haven't even *talked* to a female before? No wonder you're so charming."

"Didn't we already cover that when I mentioned how many are lined outside my door?"

"Yeah, but you have the whole alone type, bad boy persona going for you. I figured that would give you at least *some* advantage. Females usually go for that sort of thing."

"Do you?" The question was out before he could stop it.

He shifted in his seat, but rather than letting her smile falter, Selina seemed to delight in his discomfort. She lifted her glass again. "My uncle seems to think so. He claims all my suitors have been . . . how did he phrase it? Disappointments."

Rion smiled and took another long drink, emptying the glass. Their entrees arrived and Selina dug in, mercifully splitting the bread and cheese rather than snatching them for herself. She'd ordered a steak smothered in onions and gravy that made his mouth water. His own plate held steaming herbal chicken on a bed of rice.

It smelled divine, too

Selina stuffed the bread in her mouth. "So," she said around the food. "What's our plan?"

He bit into his food, content to make her wait for an answer, and froze. A tingling sensation crawled over his tongue, numbing it, and he promptly spit the food out. He snatched Selina's wrist and she almost jumped out of her seat in protest.

"Don't." Rion kept his voice low, even as his heart rate sped. His vision was already blurring.

It was impossible, he hadn't even ingested anything. But Foley was lurking in the city. Had he developed something worse than the poison spreading across their country? Rion's gaze swept over everything on the table. The bread, the flowers, the cups of—wine. The wine.

Shit. How many glasses had he downed? He looked up at Selina's half-empty glass. She'd only had a bit, which meant she wouldn't be as incapacitated. He hoped.

"What?" She questioned, her gaze darting across the food on the table.

"We have to go. Now."

"What do you mean, we just go—"

Rion spun and shoved his hand down his throat, forcing himself to vomit. Selina's chair scooted against the wooden floor.

"The wine," he breathed. "There's something in it."

He turned to watch her face go pale before she grabbed their glasses and sniffed each in turn. Selina sipped the liquid, then spit it out again, cursing herself. "I have the antidote," she reached into her pocket, but the surrounding shadows were already moving.

Rion stood to his full height, wiping the edges of his mouth. He heard the slow whine of blades and let his magic crack the ground at his feet. It rose up, surrounding his body in a slow spiral.

"Friends of yours?" Selina asked from the other side of the table.

His voice was a low growl. "Hardly."

They charged and Rion drew the knives at his belt and let them fly, his magic in their wake. They parried his blades and lunged. Rion drew his sword and met them blow for blow.

Chairs throughout the restaurant scooted across the floor and screams filled the air when Rion tossed one of his assailants down the long hall, a blade protruding from his heart.

Tables tumbled over and another blade slashed out, forcing Rion to tilt backward, barely moving in time before he lost his balance and tumbled backward over the table. It fell with him and Rion's back hit the ground hard. The male lunged, but Rion pulled his knees in and kicked the table. It hit the male's shins followed by a resounding crack. The male screamed, then Rion's magic engulfed him.

Rion rolled back to his feet, the world tilting as he did. He ducked under another blade, then lunged and buried his knife up to the hilt in the male's torso.

He fell and didn't move again.

Another lunged from his left, roots reaching out from the floorboards. The tendrils wrapped around Rion's ankles, yanking him from his feet. Rion caught himself and twisted away, using the earth to strangle the roots and vines before it dove for his attacker's airways.

His vision blurred further.

The antidote. He had the antidote. Rion reached inside his satchel, but a boot planted itself in the side of his face, knocking him to the floor again. Vines latched onto his wrists and arms and torso, all squeezing. Thorns tore through his flesh, sawing back and forth as they stretched and tightened.

Rion roared. The planks of the floorboards splintered and shattered beneath the pressure of the earth tearing up from beneath. He shoved tendrils and grains in all directions and relished in the sound of the whimpers that followed.

Rion rose and a fist landed across his jaw, knocking him back to his knees. Another tried to follow, but Rion grabbed the male's closed hand. He met the frightened warrior's gaze and slowly stood, squeezing that hand until the bones cracked beneath the pressure of his magic.

The male cried out. A chair flew at him from his right, but Rion's magic shattered it in the air. The splinters fell away and Rion turned his hateful gaze on his enemy. They stepped back, their chests heaving.

He snapped his teeth and used his magic to prevent them from escaping. A hand severed. Then an ankle. He slammed his magic into the nearest male's torso and punctured the ribcage of another.

His world tilted. Spun.

Selina.

Rion whirled, looking for her, fear suddenly snaking down his spine. He hadn't been aware enough. If he'd—she still stood beside their table, an empty vial already in hand. But she was . . . frozen, as if in shock. Warriors didn't go into shock.

"The hell are you doing?" he slurred, then reached inside his satchel, withdrew a vial, and downed the contents. He was only supposed to take half, but he couldn't afford to take too little. Not with Selina here and his body on the verge of giving out. If they went after her next—

Footsteps sounded behind and Rion twisted, but Selina was faster, her blades hitting fatal points along their bodies.

The world fell silent. Mostly. Those who'd taken cover were whimpering and praying to the gods for their own survival. Many were hidden behind overturned tables and chairs, doing their best to protect their heads and vital points.

Rion observed them, looking for any who might be ready to join his now-dead assailants before turning toward Selina. His breath came labored and ragged. His pulse was sluggish.

He should have known better. He shouldn't have been so distracted by the idea of having dinner with a pretty female.

A female who'd suggested they come here in the first place.

She wouldn't—panic seeped through him. Had his first instinct been right? Had she been stringing him along all this time just waiting for an opportunity to—

Selina ran at him, but he reacted too slow. She ducked under his arm and—draped it across her shoulder. His gaze flickered to hers, uncertain. She studied the bodies on the floor, then the patrons rising to assess the damage. She sniffed the air, then tugged him along.

His magic rose up and surrounded her. She froze, her own breath labored. "Are you in control?" she whispered. That was fear stinging his nose now. Fear of the sand wrapping around her body, snaking along her skin, uncertain and confused.

To trust or not to trust. "I don't know," he answered honestly.

She nodded. She was trembling but didn't back away. "Well, control it, I'd rather not lose a limb today." He breathed, then heaved again. Nothing came up. "We need to move," she said, "That way, out the back." Rion followed her finger and only nodded.

It was broad daylight; there wouldn't be anywhere for them to hide.

Selina slammed open the heavy door, then released him long enough to unfold a cloak from her pack. She fastened it across his shoulders, pulled up the hood, then wrapped her arm around him again.

"No one will find us now," he said sarcastically.

"You're just another drunk guest. The citizens on the streets won't think twice."

The citizens. He squinted against the harsh sun. She planned to try to disappear into the crowd. Perhaps she hoped that would stay his assailant's hand.

"Can you walk?"

He didn't realize how heavily he'd been leaning on her. "I don't know." It felt like the only thing he could say.

She chewed her lip and pulled him forward. Rion's feet obeyed. His entire body was numb now and it felt like trying to walk after one's limbs had fallen asleep. He tried to watch the crowd as they went. If they were attacked, he wouldn't have any choice but to defend himself. And the civilians would be caught in the crossfire.

Each step felt like an eternity. Like his world was spinning through an endless vortex. His stomach rolled again, but Rion held it at bay. Sweat rolled down his face, plastering his hair against his forehead. He wanted to wipe it away but couldn't lift his hand to do so.

Rion found a corner and he wretched again, spitting out bile. Selina rubbed his back and smiled to those passing by, offering comments about him not being able to control his liquor. Most laughed it off. He ignored them.

Selina grabbed his arm again and he only looked up when she opened a familiar door and ushered him inside. The innkeeper rushed to greet them, but Rion's sand rose up to create a barrier. Selina quickly told the male they were fine, using the same line that Rion had simply drank too much and needed some water and rest.

The male offered to bring up refreshments. Rion wouldn't be partaking.

A long, grueling climb up the stairs, then they were in the room.

Selina guided him to the bed and Rion let his heavy body fall onto the mattress, his stomach still rolling.

Selina's feet padded across the rug and wooden floor, the sound rattling through his skull. He tilted his head to watch, anyway. She paused at her pack, holding two vials between her hands.

He wondered if one were something other than medicine and wondered again if she'd been involved in the whole ordeal.

Gods, he'd been so stupid and careless. He knew better. He knew not to get distracted, yet he'd still taken a drink from strangers. He'd still let his guard fall entirely.

Selina finally turned from her bag and paused when she caught him staring. She crossed the room and he noted her scent.

Gods, his head was pounding.

"You need to take this."

He eyed her again, then the vial. The liquid within carried a greenish hue. "That looks as if it'll kill me faster."

"It won't." Truth, as far as he could tell.

"I already took the antidote."

"I saw. But if that's the only thing you opt to take, then you're in for a rough couple of days."

He draped an arm over his eyes, trying to block out the blinding light. "I'll take my chances."

"If I wanted to kill you, I would have just left you there."

"Maybe you don't think they could have finished the job."

She opened her mouth and closed it again, then braved stepping into the sand still circling his body. Rion pulled it away from her feet, still concerned it might strike out against his will.

Her voice was gentle when she spoke again. "I promise I'm not trying to kill you. It'll help with the headache and get the toxin out of your system."

Rion looked at her, then the vial again before finally holding out his hand. Numbers were etched into the glass. He sat up slowly and she moved to help him, keeping one hand on his shoulder.

He popped the cork and sniffed. It smelled terrible. Rion downed the entire thing and eased back onto the bed, praying he could keep it down.

"Give it about thirty minutes to kick in."

He grunted an answer. She went to the fire. Flint struck steel. He turned to find her standing before a small flame, feeding it to life. Every sound was a blasting echo in his skull.

He didn't realize he'd faded off until she placed a mug on the side table and he jolted. Selina muttered an apology and returned to the fire. Rion glanced out the window. Dusk was settling.

He rubbed his temples and sat up slowly. His head, thankfully, had stopped pounding. Rion eyed the mug and though his body shivered, wishing for a warm drink, he didn't take it.

"There's more medicine in the tea," Selina said, eyeing him as he scooted to the edge of the bed. "It'll help with the headache."

He hadn't seen her make it, though she hadn't tried to slit his throat while he'd slept either.

Rion took the mug in his hands and sipped on the nearly scalding brew.

It tasted bitter, as if the leaves had steeped too long.

Rion flexed his fingers, glad to find the numbness gone, then he stood. The dizziness was gone, too.

"What's in that medicine?" he asked, inching closer to the fire. Weak. His body felt so weak.

"It's an old family recipe. I'd have to kill you if I told you."

He smirked. He felt . . . better and not better at the same time. Like all the acute symptoms had been covered up, leaving a dull ache in his bones.

Selina offered him a blanket. He lifted a brow. "I went down the hall when you were asleep. Your magic was . . . erratic, so I didn't risk putting it on you. Sit by the fire, warm up, and make sure you drink the rest of that. There's more if you need it."

Gods she was just as pushy as Saoirse, but . . . he couldn't deny enjoying it just a little.

"Do you want anything to eat?"

His stomach soured at the thought. "Not unless you want the rugs to have a fresh stain."

She grimaced. "Right. I'll make sure breakfast is light then."

They stood in awkward silence for a time, then Rion took the chair beside the fire while she took the one by the desk. An assortment of documents were scattered over the surface along with a page half full of notes.

She scribbled a few more things at the bottom of the page and Rion sipped his mug slowly, letting the warmth coat his stomach.

"I'm sorry." Her voice was soft. Small.

"What for?" His heart beat just a little faster. If she mentioned her involvement . . .

"For announcing you. If we'd just gone somewhere else, none of that would have happened."

"It wasn't your fault. Foley knows I'm here. I'm willing to bet those were his warriors trying to get rid of us before we become a problem."

"You don't think the restaurant staff was involved?"

Rion shook his head, an action he regretted when his neck muscles pulled. "If they were, they were under coercion."

"They're probably hightailing it out of the city." He nodded. "Will you go after them?"

He studied the question in her gaze. "No." She loosed a breath. "But I doubt I'll be dining anywhere else anytime soon. I'd suggest you do the same."

"You're telling me that I'm in a city surrounded by incredible food and I can't partake?"

"Not unless you want to end up in the same position I'm in."

"It's almost worth the risk," she grumbled.

"I assure you, it's not."

"This is going to be torture. It's like dangling alcohol before an alcoholic."

"I'd steer clear of that, too."

She threw up her hands. "Great. No delicious food and now no alcohol. Just tie me up and throw me to the wolves."

"That can be arranged. Foley is quite wolfish."

"I'd rather die." She sighed. "I guess I'll have to wait until the ball. Surely they wouldn't risk poisoning their guests."

Rion watched the fire, feeling warmth return to his limbs. "You've . . . dealt with a lot who've been effected by the poison, haven't you?"

She stopped writing. "I was on the first set of teams sent out. The things we saw . . . let's just say I won't be forgiving anyone involved and will personally make sure they pay for the lives they've stolen."

"I'm not against ensuring they never stand trial."

"Good. They don't deserve to."

He sipped his drink again. His stomach churned. "How long until the body aches stop?"

"Not until morning. If you hadn't taken a double dose of the antidote, you'd be in worse shape. If you were a half-breed, your heart would have stopped in minutes."

"Glad to be Fae then."

Selina refilled his mug twice, despite him claiming he could do it himself. She added more medicine and Rion found himself dozing again.

"You should get some more sleep. We have things to do tomorrow and I need you on your feet."

Rion eyed the bed. "Are you sure you don't want—"

She pointed. "I'm busy, go rest."

He finished his mug, then stumbled back to the bed where he slept harder than he had in years.

CHAPTER TWENTY-ONE

The next few days passed in a blur. They scouted the palace and even got an inside tour, courtesy of Selina batting her eyelashes at guard. The male was more than displeased to learn that Rion would be joining them. She didn't reveal Rion's identity and the guard clearly didn't recognize him.

During the tour, Selina took the guard's arm, much to the male's delight, and inquired about the statues and art. The male was proud to detail every story. It gave Rion time to study their surroundings.

He marked the exits, the stairs, and other guards wandering past, shaking their heads at the one who'd allowed them in. He'd likely be losing his position once the higher-ups caught wind of it.

Selina paused at each statue of the seven gods and bowed. Rion hardly looked at them. They'd done nothing for him in his short life, aside from maybe spare it.

Once finished, the male eyed Rion before asking Selina to dinner. She enthusiastically agreed with a nod and the male puffed out his chest. He didn't seem to notice that she'd never verbally accepted his invitation. Rion almost felt sorry for him. He'd be sitting at a table alone, waiting for a stranger who would never arrive.

The pair went shopping next and wandered the marketplace, weaving between stalls and venturing into store fronts. Some recognized

Rion and cowered, while others offered to dress him in an assortment of finery. He always gave the same answer: They had to impress Selina first.

The female knew her fabrics. She knew her jewels, too. It made Rion wonder if her father and uncle had been merchants at some point in their lives.

Selina purchased food from stalls in passing, and Rion balanced a few of her boxes with one arm.

Some items were scheduled to be delivered later that afternoon. Selina joked and laughed and Rion found himself envious of the way she interacted with the vendors. She acted as though the day at the restaurant had never happened. As if the people who surrounded them weren't all a threat. He wished he could afford to do the same.

But maybe he could. Rion's mind drifted back to the tiny village off the beaten path. A place where no one recognized a Lord because they'd never seen one.

But could a female like Selina tolerate the solitude? If they became more. If she accepted his invitation for a date. A real date where they wouldn't be fighting for their lives—Rion shook the thoughts from his mind. He could think about those things later.

The day of the ball arrived and hours before the festivities were to begin, Selina kicked him out of their room. She claimed she needed privacy and absolute quiet in order to get ready. To say he was speechless and a bit annoyed was an understatement.

Selina had told him to return just before six, then slammed the door in his face.

Thank the gods he'd already showered.

They'd discussed their plans over the last few days. Per Selina's request, they'd arrive late. Not to draw attention, but to avoid the long-winded Fae and their speeches. She claimed if she couldn't eat, there was no point in listening to them.

Rion scouted the perimeter again, marking all the exits they'd seen in the blueprints. He stopped for a cool drink, paying extra attention to the one who served him, then started back.

The innkeeper avoided his stare when Rion entered. He climbed the stairs that led to their room and paused to listen at the door. Her heartbeat was steady and Selina was humming to herself. Rion might have been content to listen to it were it not for the fact that she'd likely heard him trot up the stairs. He knocked once and waited.

"Come in."

Rion twisted the knob and paused on the threshold. His lips parted as he took in the dramatically changed female before him.

Selina stood beside the bed, bag already in hand as if she were ready to walk out the door.

She'd pulled the bulk of her hair back, using glittering floral pins full of diamonds that caught and reflected the light. It drew his gaze to the softly curled strands framing her face. She'd outlined her eyes with kohl again and painted her lips a deep, sensual red.

His gaze traveled lower. Just like her other dress, this one had a slit up one side, revealing her beautiful tanned leg and the silver heels buckled around her ankles. The top, sleeveless and alluring, dipped in a V between her breasts, showing off more skin than he'd ever seen on the female.

Gods above, he wouldn't survive the night.

Rion swallowed hard. Tried and failed to clear his throat. Selina offered a shy smile. Shy, despite the piece of art hugging her body. She spun for him and the ruffles at the bottom of the dress moved as if they were an extension of her body. "Do you like it?"

Like it? He wasn't sure "like" was a strong enough word for the things he felt. He liked her. Liked the way her eyes sparked with excitement. Liked the way she sought his approval. The way she seemed to crave it.

A slim set of silver earrings dangled from her pointed ears and a silver chain dipped toward the space between her breasts, holding a teardrop pendant at the end.

Rion cleared his throat again.

She frowned. "Too much?"

"No, no," Rion forced himself to look away.

He saw her smirk from the corner of his eye. "Well, if I have that effect on *you*, I imagine it'll be fabulously distracting for others. With any luck, they won't even see you coming."

Rion struggled to form a single coherent thought. *The mission, the mission, the mission.* "And how do you plan on sneaking around in something like that?" She'd probably skin someone alive if they got a speck of dirt on it.

"I don't. I'm the distraction. You'll be the one sneaking."

"Can you—" *Get it together.* "Can you move in that?"

She snickered. "Why do you think I always opt for a dress with a slit up the side? It makes running easier. Along with reaching in to snag a blade if I need it."

Rion slammed down any thoughts about reaching into her dress.

Selina stepped back and gestured toward the bed. "I laid your things out. Try not to wrinkle them. I'd like to appear like a nice normal couple not up to anything at all."

He scoffed, then eyed the pressed suit. The smooth black fabric. She'd gone out of her way to ensure they had the best.

Rion eyed her dress again. His gaze traced the low back as she turned to rearrange his belongings. He'd be touching her tonight. Talking with her as they'd done in the restaurant. His mind drifted back to Fernsworth and how he'd acted there. That primal part of him was singing now, tainting his blood with power and instinct.

Control. He needed to maintain control, otherwise he'd look like an ass again and she might not forgive him twice. Her dress shifted, revealing the muscles along her thigh. Maybe he'd outright damn the mission and take her up to one of the private rooms, just to ensure they weren't interrupted this time. Maybe he'd get to see exactly how far she'd allow him to push. Tease her into—

"Come back to earth, Rion."

His name on those painted lips—

"Right. I'll get ready then."

She made a sound of approval and he watched her retreat to the bathroom, claiming she needed to do something else with her hair. She was perfect. A fine wine that had him drunk just from sight alone. Never mind that she smelled divine as well. What the hell was she wearing?

Rion shook his head, but it did nothing to disperse the images flashing through his mind as he stripped of his casual attire and changed into the formal one.

The suit fit snuggly against his chest, yet still afforded him enough room to move should he need to. And he would by the time the night was over.

She waited a full fifteen minutes before inquiring whether he was decent. Not that he would have minded otherwise.

She exited and her assessing gaze roamed over his form. A smile tugged at the corner of her mouth. "Even nicer than last time."

Rion eyed her dress. "What's the plan when we start running?"

"Lose the shoes, tear the dress if need be."

He raised a brow. "I thought you'd be opposed to such things."

"In normal circumstances, it would be an absolute crime, but considering the fate of Brónach hangs in the balance, it's a sacrifice I'm willing to make. I'll just have the tailor fashion me a new one."

"Are you ready then?" he asked.

She nodded. "Let's go tear down a rising revolution."

They exited the inn, biding a blushing innkeeper farewell, and wound their way through the gathered crowd.

The solstice was still a week out, but the Fae had already been celebrating for days. The streets were filled with streamers, flower petals, and discarded waste that the slaves picked up throughout the night.

Everyone wore their finest clothes, but even so, Selina stood out like a rose in the desert. She walked with an elegant stride, her chin high, and eyes alight.

Her heels clicked against the cobblestone path and Rion had to restrain himself from growling at males who stared a little too long. Females, too.

He wrapped one arm around her waist and Selina eyed him before a sly smile tugged at the corner of her mouth. She whispered something about insufferably possessive males.

The guards standing before the palace gate, both immaculately dressed, their weapons glimmering with jewel encrusted pommels, smiled at Selina as they strolled past.

They didn't even look at him.

Rion surveyed the female at his side. She'd promised to be a distraction. And she'd perfected it. Even those who did recognize him didn't linger, their gazes snapping to the beautiful female marching across the marble floor.

No one knew she was part of a two Fae team that planned to tear this entire place apart. Or, at least, the illegal part, which seemed to be a large portion of those in charge.

Selina grabbed the first drink presented to her by a well-dressed slave and downed the contents, loudly smacking her lips afterward. Rion gave her a disapproving stare, but she only smiled.

She eyed the food table near the side wall next, but he held her elbow, preventing her from sprinting straight for it. They'd lived off stall food since his poisoning. She'd complained endlessly.

Inside was just as decorated as the outside, with what appeared to be an indoor garden in the middle of the dance floor. Males and females already spun their partners, swaying in time to the music. It looked like they'd missed the speeches, just as Selina had hoped.

The lights were dim and he kept his magic hidden. Other Fae were gathered in small groups beside pillars or at the edge of the dance floor, watching others with heated gazes that promised an even livelier after party.

Rion was silently grateful they wouldn't be involved.

He searched for Foley in the sea of faces, along with the companions. Rion had spent his time tailing the officials, seeing who Foley worked with. But despite his research, Rion hadn't been able to pinpoint exactly how they were smuggling the poison out.

He eyed the stone faced guards. None were drinking. None took their eyes off the guests twirling around the floor.

Several guards patrolled along the upper balconies and guarded the stairs as well as the side entrances.

No one, least of all him, was sneaking anywhere near the upper levels.

It was a good thing then, that his target lay beneath their feet.

Rion casually took his time strolling through the palace with Selina on his arm. Many greeted her with smiles and compliments, leaving him the chance to look at the new construction that hid the door to the basement.

No guards there.

No door either.

But he'd noticed that little fact during Selina's guided tour. He'd also noticed the slight crease in the wall and the ever so slight color change that indicated a sliding door.

No one would look twice at a servant disappearing through the walls. Old passageways were dusty and full of cobwebs, mice, and other foul things the wealthy wanted nothing to do with.

It was a perfect hiding place.

Rion finally relented and let Selina tug him toward the food table. She ate surprisingly light as he watched the slaves and servants come and go. Rion marked those of a similar build and memorized how they did their rounds.

The guests grew louder, more boisterous and uncaring. Some had started to sway on their feet, drunk from the music and the wine. It was almost time. He'd corner one of the half-breeds in the bathroom and steal his clothes, then take their place among the staff.

Selina huffed and he turned to find her staring. "What?"

"Aren't you going to ask me to dance?"

He didn't have to feign surprise. He hadn't actually expected her to *want* to dance with him. She had plenty of others to choose from. Rion eyed the exposed skin along her back and arms. His jaw clenched. Others who'd be touching the skin he craved.

Rion adjusted his jacket, suddenly overheated. "I'm afraid I was never educated on the steps."

Selina stared at him and upon realizing he was entirely serious. "Are you telling me you don't know how to dance?"

"Yes."

"But you're a High Lord's son."

"Who is hated by pretty much every being on the continent."

"But you had school."

"Only for a few years. Then I was homeschooled."

"And your sister never taught you?"

"She didn't have time and I never asked. It wasn't exactly high on the priority list." Rion had survival to think about. And Caol—well he couldn't imagine Caol teaching him, either.

"Well, that certainly ruins my plan for the evening."

"I'm sure there are others you can dance with."

He expected a sharp retort. It didn't come. She turned away, color staining her cheeks. "Maybe I wanted to dance with you."

His heart skipped and he tried to catch her eye, but she refused to meet his gaze.

The moment was both a heartbeat and a lifetime.

Selina swept her hands over the front of her dress and composed herself. "I'll see you after the . . . events?" she hedged.

He, too, turned away, afraid if he didn't now, then he might damn the mission and see if he could try to mimic the steps of those gliding across the floor. But he wasn't a fool. He knew dancing was like art, it took time to learn. Focus. Dedication.

He inwardly sighed. "You'll know. Keep an eye out."

"Right." Another moment's hesitation, then she was gone, walking through the crowd, swaying her hips and smiling at any who offered her an inkling of attention.

It took less than a minute before a male approached, the lapels of his jacket in perfect order as he gently lifted the back of her hand and pressed it to his lips.

She giggled and Rion forced himself to turn away before instincts drove him to do something stupid.

She'd wanted to dance with him. *Him.* He'd learn, he decided. As soon as they were back in Nàdair, he'd pull Saoirse aside and demand she teach him. Or head to the studio and demand lessons from the teachers.

Rion prowled through the crowd, watching the servant he'd selected as his target. Rion waited, following him at a distance until the male darted for the bathroom. Rion knew it wouldn't take him long, not with how he'd been sneaking drinks at every turn.

Only a servant would dare. Their punishment would be little more than a sharp reprimand or possibly losing their job. If a slave tried such a thing . . . well, he'd seen them killed for far less.

The male barely registered Rion's raised hand as he struck the side of his neck. The male went limp and Rion caught his falling form, preventing his head from hitting the tiled floor.

He stripped the servant of his clothes, stuffed him inside the utility closet, and left his own neatly folded suit on the male's lap.

Rion grimaced at the material he was forced to wear. It was too hot and he'd always hated wearing white. It stained too easily, but the servants were meant to be easily seen, thus the color choice. Rion grabbed the empty serving tray from the floor and slipped out of the bathroom.

He slowed his pace and kept his head down. Guests filled his tray with their empty flutes of wine and glasses of whisky. Some barked a command for more and Rion quietly inclined his head.

The clock had started. Anytime now, the servant he'd left in the closet could be found, then questions would arise and the entire palace would go on full alert. He didn't have time to search for Selina or see if she was dancing with another male.

Rion weaved through the crowd, collecting glasses until his tray was full. He followed the other servants to the kitchens and breezed through the heavy double doors.

The room was bustling and hot and crammed as servants filed in, set their empty trays along a side table and took new ones. Some were filled with alcohol, others small delicacies that made his mouth water. They clearly wouldn't be getting a break tonight. Especially where drinks were concerned.

Rion stepped back to observe, his tray still in hand. To anyone else, he might appear as a new hire. Someone who didn't quite know or remember where things went.

It became clear from the voice ringing above all the others who was in charge. Another male, this one wearing a similar white uniform, but his had some sort of patch in the corner. Rion didn't take the time to study it. Instead, he approached said male, doing his best to appear unintimidating.

The male's sharp gaze locked on him. He looked Rion over then threw his arms up in agitation.

"Someone—" He paused, trying to will a tremor to his voice. He wasn't sure he succeeded. "Someone requested drinks downstairs. They said to bring the ones reserved for the—afterparty." It wasn't a lie, he had overheard someone requesting drinks for an afterparty. Just a different one.

The male's face paled and his voice lowered. "For the governor?" Rion nodded. "You're certain?" Rion nodded again.

The male loosed a nervous sigh, then glanced toward someone in the back. Rion wasn't sure who. He ran a hand through his hair, chewed his bottom lip. Sweat dripped down the back of his neck. "All right. Wait here."

He disappeared through another door and emerged less than a minute later with a tray of bubbling drinks, an entire bottle of amber liquid, and half a dozen empty glasses. A small plate of desserts rested in the center.

"Have you attended one of their . . . events before?" Rion shook his head and furrowed his brow, doing his best to appear concerned by the idea. The male ran his hands through his hair again. "Right. Just keep your head down and do whatever they say. You should be fine." Rion nodded and turned to leave, but the male gripped his arm. "*Whatever* they say," he emphasized. "They have certain . . . tastes." His sympathetic gaze told Rion this male had been subjected to those tastes before. His stomach turned.

Rion made a show of swallowing hard. "I understand."

The male gave him a grim nod, then gestured to follow him back out into the hall. They turned right and went straight for the newly built wall where a staircase had been years ago.

The male touched a side panel and pushed. The wall cracked open and slid to the side.

"Don't touch anything," the male warned. "Just stand in a corner until they arrive." Rion only nodded, then the male closed the wall behind him, trapping Rion in nearly total darkness.

He waited for his eyes to adjust before venturing down the winding staircase. The very one he remembered.

A dim light appeared ahead, followed by another and another. Clearly mood lighting for things he had no intension of participating in.

Rion eyed the flutes and desserts. Others would have likely snuck one, but Rion didn't dare. The gods only knew what strange concoctions Foley and his guests partook in.

Rion shuddered. At least he and Selina agreed on one thing: Neither wanted to be involved with anything that male had to offer.

At the base of the stairs, the walls elongated to reveal a large room with an inviting tone. A lush red sofa sat in the middle of the space with a thick rug laid out before it and two end tables on either side. An onyx coffee table stood atop the soft rug. Someone had already lit the oil lamps and a few dozen candles.

Which meant he didn't have a lot of time.

His eyes roamed over thick curtains, a fully stocked bar, and a small fireplace with smoldering embers that added unnecessary heat to the room. His nose crinkled at the burning incense in the corner, a mixture of ylang ylang and sage.

Rion pulled back the curtains to reveal an uninviting hallway. The air inside was too stuffy for his liking.

He deposited the tray on the bar and studied the space again. Rion briefly rummaged through the small rooms and the desks within, but they were largely unused. One had a single piece of paper in a large drawer. He reentered the main room and began rifling through drawers, knocking on the sides of bookcases and shifting his weight across each floorboard in the event—a creak.

Rion stepped back and shifted his weight again. He stared at the thick rug beneath his feet.

No. It was too easy. Surely they wouldn't put important documents in the middle of the main room. But then, if everyone was distracted and drugged—

Rion moved the table and rolled the rug away. He pulled a small knife from his boot, then pried the floorboard up. Inside, wrapped in a violet cloth, was a small grayish box with a crow etched into the lid.

They couldn't be serious.

Rion popped it open. Inside sat a few folded documents, two pairs of rings, both with a crow emblem, and a series of vials he didn't have any interest in opening.

Rion unfolded the documents. He scanned the list of names and scribbled formulas.

Too easy. It was all too easy and obvious and—

"The look suits you." Rion looked up to find Foley staring down at him, a playful smirk on his face as he scanned Rion from head to toe. The male held a glass of wine in one hand while the other lazily gripped the railing.

Rion stood slowly, papers still in hand. Foley drained the wine, smacked his lips, then studied the empty glass. "Although, I'd place you even lower than the servants. Perhaps lower than the half-breeds, but," his gaze met Rion's again. "A lord on his knees does have a certain appeal."

Rion let his magic unfurl from beneath his sleeves. "Too bad there's not a lord willing."

The male shrugged. "No matter. Ladies are just as pleasant. I'm sure I could coax your sister into submission. I do have a scar to repay her for, after all." Rion glanced to the side of the male's neck and noted the long slender patch of silver skin that poked out from beneath his tunic. Saoirse had indeed given it to him, but she'd also insisted he come quietly. He'd refused.

"I'd keep her alive, of course. No need to waste perfectly good entertainment."

A growl escaped Rion's lips. The rock beneath the rug began to crumble and join the already swirling bits of dirt and debris.

"Now, now, I just had this place redesigned. Please don't tear it all apart." Males and females crept down the stairs, their weapons already drawn and glinting in the candle light. "While I'd love to keep you alive as well, I'm not sure risking the gods' wrath is worth it in the end. Better to be rid of you and earn their favor."

Foley didn't reach for a weapon.

"No plans to take me on yourself?"

The male glanced down at his perfectly tailored black jacket, then his shining boots. "I'm afraid there's a party I need to attend with a beautiful female that has drawn the attention of far too many guests. She's quite pretty, that one. I wonder how you ever landed her." He *tsked*. "It's a shame she sullied herself with the likes of you, though. I would have rather enjoyed peeling that dress off her body."

Rion's entire world froze. He clenched his fists then felt his magic rise. "You lay one hand on her and I'll tear your arm off."

"Hit a soft spot, did I?" The warriors were off the stairs now, circling Rion, waiting for Foley's order. "If you're still alive when I return, I'll have my warriors bring back a souvenir. Would you like a finger? Or a strand of her hair?" He smirked. "Or would someone with your dark tendencies prefer an entrail?" He stepped back and Rion lunged, slamming his magic into and through the three warriors separating Rion from Foley.

Blood sprayed and the others tried to dodge but they weren't fast enough. Rion's hand shot out, but Foley summoned his own magic, tearing the stairs beneath his feet apart as vines rose to block Rion's outstretched arm. Rion shredded the greenery and Foley's eyes flew open wide when Rion's hand wrapped around his throat and slammed him into the nearest wall.

The others recovered and moved, but Rion's magic rose in an impenetrable wall, separating the warriors from their employer.

"Kill me and you'll never find her."

Rion stopped squeezing, slightly loosened his grip, and leaned close, his teeth bared. "Where is she?"

"With a few of my lackeys. As soon as you disappeared, I moved in. It's so easy to drug a female drinking and eating everything in sight. The other guests merely assumed she was too drunk to stand."

Rion growled and slung the male behind him. He crashed through Rion's sand and into his own warriors. Blood filled the air and one cursed, muttering an apology to his companion who clutched a bleeding arm.

Foley scrambled to his feet and his warriors took positions in front of him. Rion barely paid them any attention; his rage centered on the male who'd orchestrated this entire thing. He wasn't lying. Every word that spilled from his vile lips was the truth.

Rion should have known better than to leave her alone. Of course she'd be vulnerable. She was too confident for her own good, almost as if she believed herself invincible. He'd left her to the wolves and had no one to blame but himself.

Rion snarled and the warriors backed up a step, their magic faltering. One female from behind made her move. Vines shot out for him, but Rion's magic reacted faster. Like a viper snatching prey. He turned cold, hard eyes to stare her down and she retreated several steps.

"If any of you value your lives, leave." It was the only warning they'd get.

A few paused, staring. He could tell they wanted to, but something kept them rooted in place. Fine then, if they wanted to serve a male like Foley, then they could die like him, too.

Rion ducked when a burst of roots shot from the ceiling. They impaled the place he'd just been standing and cracked the floor. Rion planted a fist in the male's jaw to his left. He heard a crack, then Rion's magic snatched his neck and twisted. The sound radiated throughout the small space.

Another female jumped for him and Rion planted his fist in her solar plexus before bringing his knee up to her gut. He tossed her to the side and turned for her nearest companion. Rion buried a blade deep in the male's chest. He stumbled back, clutching the area before falling to his knees. Red stained the floor.

Foley backed away, a new sense of fear engulfing him. Another warrior came at Rion from behind. He ducked and let their body sail over his. He reached out with his magic to pull them close, then sliced the male's throat.

It was a short dance, Rion's rage feeding his frenzy as he cut each down one at a time. Selina. Selina was in trouble. Selina was drugged and unable to defend herself. Selina was out there, possibly calling for him—

The last fell and Rion turned to Foley. The male had his back pressed against the bar as if he could disappear into it.

Rion prowled closer.

Foley scrambled for a stool and flung it at Rion. Rion's magic shattered it, sending wood flying in all directions.

"The longer you waste time with me, the worse it'll be for her." He gave a nervous laugh. "She's likely already lost a limb, maybe two if the warriors followed my instructions."

Rion froze. His nostrils flared. "Where. Is. She."

"The thing is, if—" Rion shot a tendril of his magic out. It went clean through the male's thigh, the hole as big as a gold coin. Foley cried out and doubled over, reaching yet not daring to touch the wound and the magic still moving within it.

"Where is she?"

Foley laughed again, hysterical as he tried to breathe through the pain. "You're not going—" The sand clenched around his thigh and began sawing. Foley howled in anguish, then Rion closed the distance and clutched the male's jaw. He tilted his head back and squeezed, forcing Foley to look him in the eye. To meet the gaze of The Demon so many feared.

His magic kept moving, kept cutting. "Where. Is. She?" he bit out again with barely controlled rage.

Tears ran down Foley's face and his lips trembled. "N-North," he choked out. "S-She's n-n-orth, just outside the city. Up the hill th-through the trees."

Rion squeezed and pulled him in closer. "I will count every mark upon her flesh. Every scrape." He squeezed harder. "Then I'm coming back to return what you did tenfold. So you better start praying she's intact." Rion shoved the male and he flipped over the bar backward.

Then he was running. He flew up the stairs and blasted the entire wall away. The crowd screamed and parted and Rion sprinted for the main doors. Guards drew their weapons, ready to intervene, but Rion shoved them aside. He thought he heard part of the marble crack, but he didn't stop to look. Not as panic gripped his heart and spurred him faster.

Those outside the palace fled at the sight of his magic. Outside was dark and clouds hid the moon from view.

Rion's heart pounded in his throat as he raced through the city faster than he'd ever run in his life.

She's likely already lost a limb.

Foley's voice burned through him. It hadn't been that long, he reasoned with himself. He hadn't been gone that long. There was still hope. He gritted his teeth. Had they grabbed her as soon as he'd gone down the stairs, or right after he'd knocked out the servant? He'd refused to find her on the dance floor, afraid his instincts wouldn't be able to handle it. If he'd just *looked*, then maybe—

Rion pushed harder. Foley was dead. As soon as Rion had Selina in his arms, he was going back to tear that male apart piece by wicked piece.

Selina was a warrior, he kept reminding himself as he raced across the open plains. She knew how to handle torture and pain. She'd been trained for it. But—what if they hurt her in ways she'd never recover? If they took her arm, her leg—

Rion had seen other Fae devastated by such an injury. Many were able to recover, and their healers could fashion prosthetic limbs to replace those missing. But there were the occasional few who sank into depression. Those who couldn't cope with losing a piece of themselves.

He prayed he wouldn't have to find out how Selina might react.

Rion sprinted uphill, his magic billowing around his body even as he entered the trees. Darkness surrounded him, an ever present friend.

He scented the males first. Then her. Her blood.

Rion broke through the trees and the sight of her kneeling on the forest floor, her lip busted and body bleeding struck him to the core.

A male stood over her, his weapon raised and Rion roared.

His magic broke from the ground, ripping chunks of earth free before they split and surrounded his body in a spiraling frenzy. The male didn't bother to stop. He swung his blade in a wide arc, aiming for her throat. The earth beneath the male's feet came alive and shot for his arm, wringing the entire limb back so hard, bones snapped.

Rion let the male writhe on the ground, content to watch him suffer in pain.

Selina's tear-filled gaze met his. Her left eye was already swollen shut and he wondered if those beautiful hazy eyes even recognized him from the amount of drugs coursing through her system.

They'd stuffed a gag in her mouth and tied her arms behind her back. Her ankles were bound too and that once beautiful dress was in shreds, barely covering her body.

Gods, had they—

Rion roared again and his magic surrounded Selina, going in to gently tear the bindings from her hands and feet. Her eyelids fluttered and her body tilted, but Rion caught her with his magic, urging that small bit of it to remain gentle. To care for her. He paused to listen to her labored breathing and hated the Fae that had caused it.

A group standing on the opposite side of the meadow drew arrows, some aimed at him, others aimed for Selina. Rion ran for her, ran as if his own life depended on it.

The strings snapped. The arrows flew.

Rion's magic engulfed her completely, forming a thick wall that stopped everything in its tracks.

He missed one aimed for him and it cut across his upper arm. Another whizzed past his leg, barely leaving a scrape. But a third embedded itself in his left forearm, just barely missing the bone. Rion growled at those nocking their second arrows. The earth at their feet bent to his will. It crawled up their legs and their panicked screams filled the air as they tried to jump away and failed.

He crushed their lower limbs, then slid to his knees at Selina's side.

Panic coursed through him as his gaze flickered over her wounds and he wondered where he could touch her. He gently took her swollen face between his hands and tilted it up so that he could look into her eyes. She stared at him, blinking as if she couldn't process the world around her.

"Tell me you're okay," he pleaded. Rion didn't know why he said it. She most certainly *wasn't* okay. Not with her eye swollen shut or the deep cut in her lip. Not with the lacerations across her arms or the bruising he could already see forming along her exposed ribs. They'd beaten her. Blood stuck sections of her hair together from a wound he couldn't see.

Rion's eyes slowly lifted to those daring to circle the pair, daring to draw close to the monster in their midst. They'd done this to her. They'd taken an unarmed female from a party and tortured her. To what end? To discover how much information she'd collected on the rebels?

He was the one with that information, not her. He was the one who'd gone in and—bait. She was the bait to lure him here. The documents had been too easily placed because they'd wanted him to find them. They'd wanted the two to separate.

Foley had been planning this from the beginning. Ever since the day he'd given Selina that wicked smile.

Rion's fists clenched and a familiar burn crawled through his arm where the arrow was embedded. He recognized the sensation for what it was, but even their poison wouldn't be enough to stop him now.

He snarled and two backed away, their gazes flitting between their companions. Their plan had gone awry. Rion snapped the arrow in his arm and wrenched the shaft free. They merely stared in horror.

Then he stood, anger coursing through his veins in a way he'd never felt before.

More Fae emerged from the shadows with weapons drawn and magic poised. They studied him, then the female at his feet.

Rion let his magic crawl up and surround her, completely encasing her in its embrace. Her heart rate didn't change. Either she wasn't afraid or wasn't aware enough to be. He stepped away from the hardened mound and the Fae before him stepped back.

Then Rion unleashed hell upon the world.

He was a frenzy of movement. Bones cracked, blood sprayed, Fae howled in pain as they begged for mercy. He didn't give it.

Rion used their weapons against them. Threw knives and blades and shattered any bits of magic they tried to use.

He wasn't here to fight. He was here to conquer. After what they'd done to Selina, he wouldn't give them a chance to fight back.

The bodies fell. More came. Rion lost count.

Cuts appeared along his skin, but he barely felt them.

Vines wrapped around his feet only to disintegrate seconds later.

Warriors fell as if they were novices.

The night darkened.

Then the world went silent.

Rion's ragged breaths filled the space as he waited, poised.

Someone cried out and Rion's gaze turned to them. He snapped the male's neck.

Another crawled, keeping low to the ground and the very earth he hoped might hide him, swallowed him whole.

Another second. No movement.

He turned, eyes roaming over the scattered bodies. The blood. The limbs.

They didn't move either.

Insects crawled across the bloody grass. A bird ventured close to examine the carnage or search for its next meal.

Someone whimpered and every instinct in his body zeroed in on that one sound.

He scented the air and felt it when she touched that impenetrable wall.

Rion let it fall and the female's scent floated toward him, dragging Rion from the bloodlust.

He blinked a few times, breathed in the blood coated air.

Selina.

She whimpered again.

Then Rion was moving toward her, taking the hand that had

clamped around a fallen blade.

She looked at him again. There. A bit of recognition. And . . . fear.

"It's okay now," he said, his voice too rough and raw from roaring at the warriors who'd done this to her.

Carefully, oh so carefully, Rion tilted her body and scooped one arm beneath her knees before cradling her close. She stiffened and tried to push away at first, then something seemed to come over her. Maybe it was his scent. Maybe it was exhaustion. But Selina curled into his chest and closed her eyes.

Her breathing slowed and Rion was almost thankful.

He stared north and didn't bother looking back.

CHAPTER TWENTY-TWO

ion's jaw worked as he stood vigil beside the tiny window, observing the pouring rain and the door to the inn below. No one entered and no one left.

Rion had stormed through the front door, soaked with blood, and demanded a room. The female at the front desk had run up the single flight of stairs and unlocked a door without question.

Somehow she'd possessed enough bravery to linger and he'd given her a single command before slamming the door in her face. No one was to enter the building. The threat was clear.

To his surprise, the female had delivered bandages, medicine, extra blankets, and clothes and had left them outside the door. He'd placed a bag of coins in their place.

A tray of steaming soup arrived not long after. He took it, but set it aside. He wasn't about to risk eating anything, not with Selina the way she was.

He'd tended to her wounds, far too many, and stripped off the remnants of the dress. Rion clenched his jaw. Stupid. It was so stupid of him to have left her at all.

The bed creaked and Rion's head whipped toward the sound. Selina's eyes were open and she winced as she tried to move.

He was at her side a second later.

She froze.

Her lips parted slightly and her heart rate spiked as she stared at him. Fear. Fear of him, at who else might be in the room, judging from the way her gaze flicked around the area.

He swallowed the lump forming in his throat and slowly seated himself in the wooden chair. He'd wrapped her ribs as best he could, but her breathing was too shallow. Her eye was still completely swollen and a large bluish bruise had bloomed under the left side of her jaw. He'd wrapped her arm too, but couldn't tell if the bones were broken or the muscles simply strained. The entire limb matched her jaw in color.

Selina blinked a few times and tried to breathe in. She winced. "Hi," she croaked. A harsh cough followed and she curled in on herself. Rion went for the water at the side of the table. He'd already threatened the inn keeper and made her drink from it first. Just to be sure.

Carefully and without touching her, Rion raised the glass to Selina's lips. She used her good arm to hold it and took several slow sips.

Selina leaned back into the pillows and looked around the room again. "Where are we?"

Rion shrugged. "Some small village north of Whiteridge."

She furrowed her brow. "And we—" She stopped, seeming to recall the events from last night. "You . . . saved me."

He breathed a sigh of relief and sank back into the chair. "Of course I saved you. Did you expect me to just leave you there?"

Selina shook her head and winced again, lifting her arm to gently prod her jaw. "I didn't see it coming. One minute I was talking and the next—" Rain pelted the roof. She sighed. "How bad is it?"

"I'm not a healer, but I'd venture to guess you have a few broken ribs. The arm might be fractured, too."

Selina reached for the blanket paused upon noticing her exposed shoulders. "You wrapped me?"

He nodded and turned away. "It was dark."

"Thank you."

"There's a shower down the hall when you feel up to it."

"What happened?"

Rion ran a frustrated hand through his hair. "They set us up. The entire thing was a trap. The names on the list aren't even real."

Her brows lifted. "You got a list?"

"Yes, but—"

"Let me see it."

Rion pulled the crumbled parchment from his pocket and handed it to her. He'd looked at it again while she'd been sleeping and cursed himself for not realizing it sooner. There were names, but all of them were from Nàdair. Officials, council members, leaders. Saoirse and Alec. Himself. He ventured a guess that it was more of a hit list than anything. All those who would be against the rebel's taking power.

"What about the formula?" she hedged.

Rion just stared at a loose thread in the thick blanket. "It's probably the same one Saoirse busted him for years ago."

"So we have nothing." Rion clenched his jaw. Selina stared at the list of names again, reading each one carefully before crushing it in her fist and throwing it off to the side of the bed. "At least tell me they're dead."

"Every single one."

"Good."

"Except for Foley, but he'll get what's coming to him."

She lifted a brow. "You didn't kill him?"

"I—" Rion paused and lowered his voice. "I should have. It would have taken less than a second, but after what he told me, I just . . . ran."

She lifted her wrapped arm and draped it across her torso. Her voice was full of emotion as she said, "Thank you, they were . . . cruel." He wanted to ask her so many questions but didn't dare. They were already dead anyway and he was going to kill the one who'd given the command next. "So what's the plan now?"

"You're going to rest," Rion said and stood. "I'll get you something to eat, then we're heading back to Nàdair."

"To hell we are. We still have a mission to finish."

"Not in your condition."

She tried to move and grimaced again. "Fine, I'll rest, but just for a bit."

Rion didn't think she realized he meant for a few weeks, but he didn't push the issue. He ventured downstairs, leaving his sand to block the door and windows. The innkeeper straightened at his approach. She already had water ready and waiting and drank from the cup beside it without being prompted.

Rion wrapped his fingers around the tray. "She needs something to eat."

"O-Of course."

"You'll be tasting that, too. Ensure it's not tampered with."

She swallowed hard and raced to the back, returning moments later with a bowl full of warm broth and fresh bread. Again, she tasted it without prompting.

Selina perked up when he returned. She held her spoon with her non-dominant hand and though it appeared awkward, she made do.

"You were something else out there," she said after a few bites. "The rumors aren't exaggerated after all."

Never mind the fact that he'd been so filled with rage that he could barely remember it all. He'd taken a vial of antidote afterward and given her one as well, just to be sure.

"I didn't think you were lucid enough to know what was happening."

"I remember the image of you running up. I heard everything else. And saw the aftermath."

"I shouldn't have left you alone."

She waved her good hand, spoon between her fingers. One swollen and bruised. "I'm a warrior. I'm trained for these sorts of things."

"It shouldn't have happened, and I won't allow it to happen again." The words were clipped and barely more than a growl.

"We're a team. If we're going to succeed, then that's how we need to function. I'm not anyone's crutch."

He didn't respond. Everything he wanted to say would be laced with emotion and Selina didn't need that right now.

Less than twenty minutes later, the steps creaked and Rion was at the door before they knocked.

Two. There were two at the top of the stairs. He palmed a knife before cracking the door.

The innkeeper stood with another female to her left. He surveyed them, looking both up and down. Neither were armed and the new female carried a large bag at her side.

The innkeeper wrung her hands. "I thought you might need a healer."

Rion let some of the tension fall from his shoulders. The healer looked ready to run.

"No weapons. No magic."

The healer nodded and Rion assessed her again before stepping aside. The female gasped upon seeing Selina and rushed to the female's side. She asked a slew of questions then began prodding Selina's bruised arm.

A sharp wince had Rion moving forward, but Selina waved him off before kicking him out entirely.

He stood just outside the door, refusing to go further.

He listened intently and caught on to the coded conversation regarding Selina's safety. It made a bit of the tension fall from his shoulders. Selina explained how they were on an important mission for the High Lord. Her story made him sound more heroic than he felt Alec would appreciate, but when the healer exited, she looked at him with more curiosity than anything.

"I left medicine on the table," she said, her voice shaking slightly. "She needs to rest for at least two weeks."

"I told you, I'm fine," Selina called from the room.

The healer rolled her eyes, then seemed to remember herself. "She can take the pain reliever every few hours as needed. The other is to help prevent any infection and should be taken once in the morning and once at night."

Her gaze traveled down to his arm. He'd done nothing but wrap it in a crude cloth.

"I could . . . tend to that for you," she offered.

"It's fine. I can take care of it myself." She nodded, but reached into her bag and offered him more bandages and a fresh needle and thread.

"Thank you."

She nodded again. "I'm two doors down if you need me or change your mind."

She walked down the stairs and disappeared out the front door. Rion found Selina with the tray of food back in her lap.

"She said I should shower soon and to call for her when I need my bandages changed."

"I can change them for you."

"You don't have to hover, you know." He opened his mouth to retort, but she interrupted. "You don't have to feel guilty, either. The fault goes to me for being careless."

He was the one who'd been careless. The entire situation might not have even involved the rebels. It could have purely been revenge for what Saoirse and he had put Foley through. Selina had gotten hurt because of his past.

"Care to help me to the shower?" Rion swallowed hard and eyed the blanket covering her. The only thing left on her body, aside from bandages, were her undergarments.

"Sure."

"The robe is over there." Rion retrieved it, then helped her sit up, doing his best to keep his head turned. His face burned and he thought he heard her chuckle as she carefully slipped her arms through the sleeves. She held onto him and Rion helped her stand. Selina pulled the robe tightly around herself and tied the thin rope to hold it in place.

She eyed the door and grimaced after her first step. "Gods, I thought that painkiller was supposed to have kicked in by now."

"She said you could have more."

Selina shook her head. "I want to be able to think and I'd rather not pass out in the shower." She stepped again and her hand reached out to grip the bedpost. Selina cursed and took several breaths. He wasn't letting her suffer the whole walk down the hall. Rion stepped forward and carefully scooped her into his arms. She grimaced once and surprise covered her face.

Rion didn't look at her. "It'll be faster." She only nodded and he carried her down the hall before placing her upright just inside the door to the small bathroom. "There's a stool inside if you need to sit."

"Thank you," she said again, but didn't look at him. Rion tried not to stare at the pink staining her cheeks. She reached out and took his arm when he made to turn. "I'm serious, thank you. Not just for this, but for coming for me."

"I'll always come." She looked up at him and he swallowed hard. "For you. I'll always come."

Her lips parted when he moved a stray strand of hair out of her face. Rion forced a smile, then pulled the door shut before seating himself on the floor outside.

CHAPTER TWENTY-THREE

Selina wanted to be up and moving within a few days, but it came as no surprise to him when a week and a half flew by before she was finally able to stand and walk on her own. Albeit limping.

She still winced when drawing in a full breath, but the healer gave her instructions to walk outside every day. It didn't take long for others in the village to recognize him, especially with his magic a constant swirling storm.

He'd marched right up to the village elder and gave explicit instructions that if anyone entered the village, he was to be the first to know. The male had nodded, his fear nearly palpable as he assured him visitors this time of year were rare. Everyone was busy visiting one of the major cities to celebrate the solstice.

The innkeeper kept her distance, delivering supplies whenever she thought necessary, and the healer stopped by every morning to check on Selina.

Her bruising had shifted to a nasty yellowish color and looked far worse than it had in the initial days. The swelling in her face was gone, thank the gods, but discoloration still lingered around her eye and beneath her jaw.

Rion paced the inn hallway whenever Selina kicked him out and walked the building's perimeter when he needed fresh air. One night, he'd even slept on the roof, with his magic guarding Selina's door, of course.

She was moody, as anyone might be when cooped up for too long, but gods—Rion wasn't sure he could survive another night of her endless demands for perfection.

Food had to be warm, but not too warm. Her sheets needed to be changed daily because sleeping on sweaty ones was only for barbarians, never mind the fact that she showered every night. And the wine, gods, if he heard about the wine one more time he might chuck it all into a fire and force her to go without.

Rion rubbed his temples, then grabbed the tray of food from the counter. The innkeeper left it there every night, and every night she tasted it. The female had even gotten the courage to offer him a smile or two. She never complained, only bowed and offered her assistance should he need anything. Coin definitely went far where courtesy was concerned.

Rion marched up the stairs, listening to the sounds of the night outside. He'd barely closed the door when Selina said, "We need to leave tomorrow."

"The healer said you should take a few more days." He set the tray on the table beside her.

"We won't make it to the rendezvous point if we wait."

Rion handed her a drink. Thankfully not wine tonight. He might have mentioned something to the innkeeper about supplying a different beverage. "What rendezvous point?"

Selina eyed the liquid and made a face. "It's something I developed with my team. We're set to meet on a certain day when we believe the mission should be over. If we don't show up, they'll think things took a turn for the worst."

He shrugged. "Let them worry for a few days. We'll meet them back in Nàdair."

She eyed him. "They won't leave me behind."

"So let them wait."

Selina shook her head. "If I don't come back, they'll head to Whiteridge and raze the entire thing to the ground."

Rion shrugged again. "It's nothing they won't deserve."

"But it'll blow our chances of finding the ones involved."

"We know who's involved and if your team takes them out without realizing who they are, then I'd consider that a win."

"I don't *want* my team to take them out."

Rion paused at her tone and studied her face. "You want to be the one to do it."

She didn't meet his gaze. "I've never failed an assignment, and if it gets back that my team decimated the city instead of publicly executing those involved like we'd originally planned . . ."

"You're worried about your reputation?"

"Yes, yes, I am." She shot him a look when he opened his mouth. "I have worked very, very hard to earn it and it's not something I want thrown to the wind just because I made a stupid mistake."

Rion let the silence stretch between them. "Even if we get there in time, you're still in no shape to fight. You'd only slow them down. Our best bet is to return to Nàdair where I'll secure a new group, probably recruit my sister just to give her the satisfaction, then handle the problem myself."

She grimaced. "I don't want Saoirse involved. If she finds out I failed, she'll never let me live it down. Alec will find someone else for his top secret missions, and my team will be thrown on a list to handle the leftovers."

Rion shrugged. "You won't be out of a job, why would it matter?"

"It matters to *me*," she emphasized. "I don't want to be picked second. I don't want to be mediocre."

Rion sat back and stared out the window. He could see the frustration written all over her face. Selina clenched her jaw. "How long did Alec give you?"

"Two months." Not enough time. Not for her to fully recover.

He sighed and ran a hand through his hair before sitting forward again. "I don't imagine you'd let me and your team handle it while you sit back and take the credit?"

"Why, so my team can question my abilities themselves?"

"I don't think they'd do that. Accidents happen on assignments all the time."

"I let myself get captured. That's hardly an accident."

Rion thought through his next words carefully. "Even if we reconvene with your team, there's no way your body is going to be healed enough to fight. There's nothing you can do about that."

She sighed and her shoulders slumped in defeat. "I'll never recover from this."

"You will. I'll ensure it."

She scoffed. "Careful, you're starting to sound a lot like a friend."

Friend. The word sounded nice, even if it wasn't enough. "I kind of like the sound of that."

Her gaze lifted, a smile at the corner of her mouth. "I think I might actually miss having you around."

His heart beat just a little faster. "I don't have to go anywhere."

Her lips parted and her eyes flickered between his. "Rion—"

"I know we'll have our orders. We're duty bound to Brónach, but it might be nice to . . . meet up in between. When we have spare time. If you wanted."

"Time," she shook her head. "Such a stupid concept for the immortal, isn't it? We're told we have infinite amounts of it, and yet so often it's cut short." Rion didn't know how to respond to that, so he kept quiet. She chewed her bottom lip, an act that was far more distracting than it should be. "We'll meet up with my team and go from there," she finally said.

Rion nodded. "I can have transportation ready whenever you are."

"Give me an hour."

CHAPTER TWENTY-FOUR

$\mathcal{S}$elina showered, ate, then took a heaping dose of painkillers. She was ready in forty minutes.

Rion packed their things and shouldered both their satchels. He'd asked for transportation and the innkeeper had found a merchant already heading for Nàdair. A wagon pulled by a pair of horses was outside the inn in record time.

Rion tossed the male a small bag of coins and told him to head north. Selina could direct him from there.

The male didn't ask questions, he only nodded. Rion shifted the male's cargo to make room for pillows and blankets. He helped Selina settle in, then they were off.

The morning sun beat down on them, but Selina tilted her face toward the warm rays to soak them in.

The little village faded with the distance and a vast countryside spread out before them. Thick grasses waved in the cool breeze and the narrow dirt road was the only thing Rion could see for miles.

The male didn't speak, but it didn't take long before Selina filled the silence.

It started with the weather, then drifted to the Fairy Folk and all the deep philosophies surrounding the Fae and their relationship with the tiny creatures.

Rion mostly nodded while she prattled on, switching topics effort-lessly. Weapons, food, past confrontations.

Even the merchant providing transportation seemed intrigued, if cautious.

Rion inquired about her family and she said they'd once grown pro-duce and raised animals as a source of income, but a great grandfather had rebelled against such a simple life and in doing so had made them rich beyond measure. Her eyes almost sparkled as she told him about the diaries she'd found in her mother's attic. Rion wondered if Selina's rebellious streak stemmed from that very ancestor. Perhaps that's why her reputation was so important. Maybe she felt she had something to prove.

When they approached a fork in the road, Selina pointed the driver west. She took more pain relievers, and Rion handed her a sandwich from their packed satchel.

Selina dozed afterward and slept the afternoon away. Rion watched over her, and the merchant didn't speak.

Night descended and they paused by a river. Rion helped the driver lead the horses to water and brush them down for the night. He mas-saged their legs and the male watched Rion curiously. He bowed and constantly moved out of Rion's way and kept far, far away from Selina. The innkeeper must have warned him not to venture too close.

Rion scattered his magic around the camp before settling for the night. He needed at least a few hours of sleep.

The male cleared his throat. "I can take first watch if you like, My Lord."

Rion shook his head. "Sleep." He didn't want the male awake while he tried to doze.

The male didn't argue. He bowed and unrolled his bedding near the horses.

Selina eased herself onto the makeshift bed and hissed when she laid back.

"Do you need anything?" he asked.

"Not unless you can pull a mattress out of the ground."

He chuckled. "I'm afraid I'm all out of mattresses."

She didn't smile. Selina only watched the stars. She hadn't been as talkative when she'd awoken that afternoon.

"Are you okay?" he ventured to ask.

"No." Rion waited, but she only sighed and turned her head to the side. "Go to sleep, we have another long day tomorrow."

He opened his mouth to speak again, but closed it instead. Perhaps the weight of her failure was getting to her. He'd never seen her brood before, but then again, Rion still had a lot to learn about the female who'd called him a friend.

Rion let himself relax and drifted into a dreamless sleep.

With morning, they ate, strapped up the horses, and were off again. Rion had tried to reassure Selina that everything would be fine, but she'd only grunted at him and settled into her blankets before reaching for more medicine.

She told the male they'd arrive well before sundown.

Rion eyed Selina again. He hated seeing her like this. He'd paint that city in blood and bring Foley's head back as a trophy if that's what it took to make her happy. Maybe they could play the whole thing off. She was his commander, after all. If the strategy was her idea, then she wouldn't lose face.

He'd tell her as much after she reunited with her team. He'd give her the chance to explain everything to them first.

It wasn't until they entered the cover of a thinly wooded area that Selina announced their arrival. Rion helped Selina out of the wagon, then once again, took both their packs and slung them over his shoulders.

She was a bit steadier on her feet now. The limp was nearly gone. He'd overheard the healer mention something about a strained hip. It sent a fresh bout of fire through his veins.

The male stared at them with his brow raised, a question on his lips that he wouldn't ask. Rion merely handed him a few more coins and the male bowed before snapping the reins.

Rion waited until the male was out of earshot before he said, "You're okay with just letting him go?"

"Getting a little bloodthirsty aren't we? You shouldn't kill people who do nice things for you."

"He could tip someone off."

She shrugged. "Even if he did, they wouldn't find where we're going. We still have a hike." Thunder rolled overhead. "And the rain will wash away our scents."

"How long will it take to get there?"

"Roughly an hour."

He grimaced at her limp. "Do you want me to carry you?"

Selina arched her back, stretching the muscles. "I need to walk, just to get some feeling back into my legs."

Rion offered his arm anyway. She glanced at it, as if considering, then opted to use her magic and form a staff by braiding gnarled roots together.

Rion backed away to give her space. Maybe with the mission coming to a close, she was pulling away. Perhaps she didn't really want to meet up in Nàdair. Or maybe it had nothing to do with him and she was simply trying to process how to break the news to her comrades.

Rion prayed it was the latter. The thought of her saying goodbye hit his heart far harder than he wanted to admit.

As promised, roughly an hour passed before the trees parted to reveal a small clearing. His eyes roamed over three Fae standing beside the wide mouth of a cave. One sat on the ground, whittling a chunk of wood while the other two studied the clouds.

A single drop of rain hit the ground, quickly followed by another.

Selina grunted and the three snapped their heads toward the sound. One of the triplets, the most dominant of the trio, jumped to her feet before breaking into a sprint. Another called into the cave, announcing Selina's arrival.

The female slowed at the sight of Rion and bared her teeth at him before carefully wrapping Selina in a warm embrace.

Selina grimaced again and the female pulled back to look her over.

"What the hell happened?" An accusatory glare in his direction.

Selina patted the female's arm. "I was outsmarted."

"Impossible."

Another came up to her side, the female with short black hair. "You found the rebels?"

Selina sighed. "Found, fought, failed."

The rest of her group exited, all lining up at the entrance, but when Seán saw Selina, he too, broke out into a run and skidded to a halt at her side. A murderous shadow passed over his face when he saw her wounds.

More droplets hit the ground and it was the female triplet who said, "Let's get you inside."

Rion followed, even though their gazes told him he wasn't welcome. It was clear from the fires and how their packs were laid out that they'd been here a while. A week, he guessed. He was surprised they'd waited so long. He certainly wouldn't have. Not where Selina's safety was concerned. Selina would have probably scolded him again for not following orders, too.

Though wide at the front, the cave narrowed as they walked inside before splitting off into three separate tunnels. All were carved, he noted, though whoever had originally done so was likely lost to history.

The thirteen of them veered left, all hovering around Selina, whispering question after question. Whatever fear Selina carried about their judgement didn't appear warranted. Her relationship with her subordinates went far beyond that of a commander. It was deeper. Stronger.

They eased Selina into a sitting position on a makeshift cot in the corner. Rion eyed the blankets and scented the space, noting the tang of spice in the air that reminded him of the eldest triplet. The female remained kneeling by the cot. Another brought Selina water while a third procured food.

Seán never left her side. He sat directly beside the triplet. It was as if Rion had ceased to exist.

He leaned against the back wall and crossed his arms. He wanted to be the one fussing over her, but he couldn't do so without drawing unwanted attention. He wouldn't do anything to push Selina though, especially in front of her comrades.

"Tell us what happened," the female triplet said, her voice far more gentle than Rion had ever heard it.

Selina recounted their story and didn't leave a single piece of information out. They turned to him when Selina said his name and their brows raised in surprise. Seán nearly growled when Selina mentioned kissing him during their ruse, but he managed to keep himself composed. It didn't stop him from glaring at Rion for a solid minute. Rion didn't react; he simply met the male's gaze and waited for him to made a decision. It hadn't ended well the last time they'd fought. Not that it was much of one.

The only thing she didn't tell her comrades was about the moment they'd almost shared under the stars. A memory that still had his heart racing as he thought about her hands in his hair and how close he'd been to feeling her lips on his again. He still wanted to kill that blasted deer for its interruption. Then again, maybe it had been a good thing. If Selina had changed her mind afterward, the rest of mission might have proved . . . awkward.

The entire exchange forced her comrades to accept one grating truth: Rion had saved her and he wasn't going anywhere.

CHAPTER TWENTY-FIVE

*U*pon concluding her story, Selina's comrades made sure she was fed before dousing the candlelight. She'd balked, claiming she didn't need to sleep, but the female with short black hair was hearing none of it.

Rion took his leave, though sitting in the cavern staring at her comrades in awkward silence didn't exactly sound appealing. He was still an outcast as far as they were concerned.

Rion peered outside. The rain was light, barely more than a drizzle. Not that he'd care if it turned into a downpour. He had his magic to shield him if he wished it to.

Rion ventured out and followed the strong, clear scent of a nearby river. He freshened up, then settled against a tree to finish off the last of his food reserves.

He leaned his head against the rough bark and peered into the gray sky. She was back with her comrades. Selina was safe, which meant he could finally rest.

Rion's eyes grew heavy and he summoned his magic, cocooning himself in a sphere of protection before letting exhaustion claim him.

RION SLEPT hard and woke well after sunrise. He'd nearly given a squirrel a heart attack when he'd emerged from his cocoon. The critter had run up a tree before turning to scream at him.

He laughed, stretched, and marched straight back to the cavern.

There were two guards stationed at the entrance today. A good thing, considering Foley might be trying to hunt them down. He expected no less from Selina's team.

Rion nodded in greeting, but neither warrior returned it. He inwardly grimaced. If saving Selina wasn't enough to earn their favor—

Despite loathing this presence, none tried to stop him as he veered down the tunnel that led to the single circular room.

Selina's light laughter floated down the hall and Rion's heart warmed with the sound. He slowed his steps and peered inside.

Three of her comrades stood around her with warm mugs in their hands. Selina stood with them, leaning heavily against the back wall.

Conversation halted when they spotted him and the smile that had been on Selina's face faded entirely when she met his gaze.

The female with short black hair slowly reached for her dagger, but Selina stopped her with a gentle hand on her elbow. "It's all right."

The female eyed Selina for a long while. She glanced at Rion, then back again. "Are you sure?"

"Yes, it's fine."

Rion studied the female and her rapid heartbeat. He noted the way she refused to release her weapon. Fire burned through those dark eyes of hers. A deep, burning rage.

The female loosed a breath before jerking her head. All three filed out, their bodies nearly pressed against the wall to avoid touching him.

"What was that about?" Rion asked.

Selina waved a hand in dismissal. "They're just protective."

Rion watched the entrance for another moment, half wondering if the females would return. Selina shifted her weight and grimaced. His attention snapped back to Selina. He eyed her stance and the way she kept her weight off one leg.

"Do you want to sit?" he offered.

Selina shook her head. "My legs were cramping." Her voice turned soft. Disappointed. "We're headed back to Nàdair tomorrow."

"You told them?"

She nodded. "I—" her brow furrowed, then her eyes swam with emotion. Rion felt something in his chest pull. He didn't want her to hurt. Didn't want her to feel anything but joy and happiness.

She looked up then, locking her eyes with his, and a new sort of fear flooded his body.

The air shifted in the small room. It grew heavier. Her heart jolted, and Rion's breath caught when her eyes dipped to his lips. His body.

The mission was over. She didn't need him anymore.

Selina took a limping step toward him and Rion instinctively stepped back, mirroring her motion once. Twice. Particles of dirt floated up between them and she paused.

"Your magic reacts to your emotions, you know." He swallowed hard. "What are you feeling right now, Rion of Brónach?"

His lips parted, but no sound came out. Her chest rose and fell, matching his own as she dared another step closer.

What *was* he feeling right now?

Afraid.

Afraid of change. Of confirmation. Of goodbye . . .

Another step and his back was against the wall. Then she was suddenly so close he could have reached out and touched her.

Selina was breathless as she said, "You liked the kiss." The kiss. The act back when they'd first entered Fernsworth. Then again, after they'd been caught rummaging through a male's desk. It felt like a lifetime ago, yet he'd thought of nothing else. The caress of her lips, the way her body had molded against his. Her intoxicating scent that drove him beyond all rational thought and reason. It had been torture to restrain himself these past few weeks.

She stepped closer. Close enough that their chests were almost touching. She peered up at him from beneath her lashes. His magic danced, pulsing to the rapid beat of his heart.

Selina tilted her head as if still waiting for an answer. The word barely escaped his lips.

"Yes."

It wasn't powerful enough to encompass his feelings. It did nothing to explain the madness that rushed through him from the mere thought of her.

She smiled anyway.

Gods, he wanted her. Rion wanted her more than he'd ever wanted anything in his entire life.

Her gaze slid to his lips once more. "Then kiss me again."

A dream. He'd slipped into a dream and he never wanted to wake. Let this be his eternity. Let this be his life.

Rion dared to lean down and capture her lips in an achingly slow kiss. Her breath hitched and some animalistic instinct broke free of his control.

Rion crushed his mouth against hers and she met his ferocity, matching him movement for movement. Her fingers threaded through his hair, tugging at the strands, and their tongues warred for dominance.

Rion spun her, wrapping one arm around her torso before slowing to press her against the wall. He closed the space between their bodies and only paused when she winced.

His gaze flickered across her face. "Your injuries—"

"I don't care." Then her lips were on his again, consuming him, pulling at every instinct he'd locked away since the first time they'd touched.

Intoxicating hints of vanilla and wildflowers filled his nose, and he moaned into her mouth. Her warm hands ventured beneath his shirt, ghosting over his skin, squeezing his muscles in places he'd always imagined a female might like.

Gods, her touch was like kindling to his blood, igniting his body with flames so bright he was sure they'd take form and consume them both.

Rion let his hands wander over her torso, her legs, her arms, her face, her throat. He devoured that, too. Gods, he loved her neck, the rapid pulse beneath her skin.

Selina pulled on his shirt and Rion only broke their kiss long enough to rip the material over his head before pressing against her again. She could have him. Every bit of him. Here and now if she wanted. He couldn't care less that her comrades were so close. Let them listen. Let that male listen and know who she'd chosen.

His magic still danced around their bodies, caressing her skin in places his hands hadn't yet reached. She hooked one leg around his waist and Rion pressed into her, relishing the friction of the movement. She felt so right. So perfect beneath him. Nothing else existed in this moment but her.

His fangs grazed her throat and Selina moaned, leaning further into his touch.

He had to resist the urge to mark her. It was an old custom most didn't perform anymore. If she'd been at her full strength, Rion might have nicked her skin, just to seek permission.

But not today.

He devoured her neck again with his tongue and teeth, then returned to her lips before blinding white-hot pain tore through his lower back.

Rion roared and arched to try to escape the deep burning sensation. He cursed and gritted his teeth. It struck again, slamming through him before he could collect himself long enough to register where the pain was coming from, who to strike, and where.

Rion shoved Selina away and her head cracked against the stone wall. His stomach soured, dread and despair sinking through him long before he even saw her face.

She wouldn't.

She couldn't.

She'd said . . . nothing. She'd said nothing. All those times he'd mentioned the future, she'd been silent. Contemplative. And he'd quickly covered for her. Because he'd been afraid to hear any sort of rejection.

Every conversation flashed through his mind in rapid succession. The last few weeks they'd spent together. Everything she'd done.

She's manipulative. She doesn't fail a mission.

The rebels. They'd been part of the assignment, but they'd also been a cover. A decoy for the real reason Selina and her twelve were out in the middle of nowhere.

The information. The sneaking in. Had any of it been real?

Rion recalled the way Seán had questioned her. Recalled the male's anger, too. Seán hadn't known. None of them knew, at least not before yesterday. Had she finally filled them in? Was that the reason the pair hadn't smiled at him that morning? Why the short-haired—a flash of pain forced Rion to his knees. He gasped and his palms hit the stone floor.

Breath wouldn't come fast enough.

It had been a ruse. All of it. Every touch was calculated. Every movement thought out.

She'd kept her team in the dark because he would have noticed if they acted differently. It would have given away her plans.

Saoirse had warned him. His instincts had warned him. Selina—he'd fallen, no, leaped for her. She'd been everything he'd ever wanted. To just have someone listen to him. Hold him.

Rion dared to look up and found a warrior standing over him, bloody knife in hand, her magic already crawling from between the cracks in the wall.

She lowered herself into a stance, no longer in pain. Had she told the healer to play along as well? They'd been alone together enough. Is that why the innkeeper had smiled at him? Why others appeared so relaxed? Because they knew, too?

Rion gasped for air. Not due to the physical pain radiating through his back, but because his heart had shattered into a million pieces. He'd trusted this female. Trusted her with truths and dreams. He'd opened himself in a way he'd never done before.

And she'd—

She'd—

"Why?" The broken word was barely more than a whisper. He thought he saw a flash of regret in her amber eyes. Could have sworn he glimpsed a line of silver before she blinked it away and clenched her jaw.

But maybe that was all part of the manipulation, too. Just more ways to throw him off.

His heart beat faster as every image of them fractured in his mind. He'd imagined a life with her. Had allowed his mind to see possibilities he'd never considered. To live as a normal male. To raise a family.

But he'd been cursed by the gods.

Cursed and damned to a life of pain.

The betrayal of his father had hurt.

The betrayal of Caol had hurt.

But this. This was a pain far deeper than any chasm. Bigger than any universe. Rion felt something in himself crack before splintering, falling away piece by piece. The shards moved through his body, sharp and angled, slicing through everything as they went.

"Why?" he whispered again.

"You said it yourself." Her voice wasn't the same. It was darker. Crueler. "I can be quite manipulative when I need to be."

"No." He couldn't accept that it had all been fake. That she'd felt nothing.

Selina cocked her head. "Did you really think someone could love you? A monster?"

He had. And he loved her, even now, as she stood above him with a weapon in her hand. He'd fallen so hard there was no getting up. Fallen for all the times she'd extended her hand and not been afraid.

And none of it had been real.

Rion gasped from the pain making its way through his heart. Like a black snake poisoning him from the inside out.

Maybe her injury had been part of the ruse, too. Maybe she'd planned it right alongside Foley and they'd laughed together at his expense.

Alec. His brother's face flashed before his eyes. Alec had known. That's why he hadn't told Saoirse about the mission. Because too many details and questions would have revealed his true intentions.

To rid the world of the abomination.

Rion pushed up to his feet and stumbled backward. Blood trickled down his skin, coating the waistband of his pants. He just stared at the female before him. Stared at the ruthless look in her eyes.

Selina bared her teeth. "You are an affront to nature and if your father had any sort of backbone, he would have ended you himself."

"You don't mean that." He'd been an innocent child. She couldn't really be willing—

Rion fell back to his knees. It was too much. All of it. The pain. Reality. The truth.

Monster. The word rang through him, whispered by countless voices in his head. People from his past, his present, his future.

Monster.

Monster.

Monster.

Everything happened in slow motion.

Selina moved, her body swift and unyielding as she crossed the short distance. Her movements weren't sloppy or that of a novice. She'd only asked him to teach her as part of the act.

A war cry fell from her lips.

Rion raised his arm and earth shot out to intercept her knife. Selina's magic speared for him then, the living vines and plants as deadly as any blade. She'd had so many other opportunities. But she hadn't been sure of herself. No, maybe that wasn't it at all. Maybe she'd wanted *this*. Wanted him broken and on his knees.

He saw the wicked gleam in her eyes. Saw the way she craved what was before her. It wasn't just about the missions or her reputation. It was about the final act. The breaking. The reveal.

The Selina he'd fallen in love with wasn't real. The warrior angling her blade for his throat wasn't the sweet female who loved shopping and food and expensive trinkets. That had been her mask. One she wore so well, Rion wondered if she believed it herself.

Rion's magic blocked two more tendrils that shot for him, then smothered the small plants crawling through the earth. It all felt different. Her movements. Her magic.

He'd loved a façade.

A root broke from the surface at his feet. For half a heartbeat, Rion wondered what it might be like to succumb to her onslaught. To relent and leave this life while begging the gods for mercy in the next one. Perhaps they'd allow him to atone for the atrocities he'd committed to warrant his current punishment.

Or maybe he'd return just to relive this nightmare all over again.

One look at her face told Rion she wouldn't regret his death. She'd celebrate it. Boast about it until the next big story came along and he was forgotten by the world.

Hot tears streaked down Rion's face and he roared, letting anger and pain fill his body, his soul, his magic. The very mountain shuddered. The cavern walls split, cracking all the way to the ceiling before coming apart, floating in the air around him.

His ears rang and Rion let his rage take over. Screams echoed from within the tunnels. Screams and war cries as her comrades' feet pounded against the earth, coming to assist their leader.

They didn't adore her because she cared. They followed her because of her ruthlessness.

Rion's magic grabbed Selina's body, caging her in a strong vice. She struggled, screaming and roaring and snapping her teeth at him in defiance.

He squeezed and she cried out. Then her face shifted, turning back into the female he'd known for the last several weeks. "Rion," she tried, her voice strained. "Please." His stomach hollowed out, then he snapped her neck.

Something inside him snapped along with it.

Seán roared from the room entrance and vines split through the dirt at Rion's feet. He shredded them without a single passing thought and in the next second, the male's body splattered against the side wall, his head crushed by the Fae sized boulder Rion had thrown in his direction.

If they wanted to be together, they could do it here where their corpses would rot. He hoped their souls did the same.

The sisters came at him next, all three moving as a unit. One went left, the other right, but the center one, the eldest, came at him head on.

In other circumstances, in another life, Rion might have enjoyed their fight. He would have likely dragged it out just to see what the three of them were capable of. But right now—his fists clenched. Right now, all Rion wanted was blood.

Their snarls called to his instincts, and Rion let the ceiling collapse, leaving only a small pocket for his body to safely stand in. He stayed there a moment, listening to the grinding of their bones and their last breaths, before lifting it again.

Only the eldest still drew breath. She choked on her own blood, her chest caved in. The others had their limbs twisted at odd angles. Too fast. It was too fast and yet he wanted to kill them faster. Rid the land of their filth.

He didn't bother putting her out of her misery.

The rest died one at a time. Some cursed him as they went, others passed silently; as warriors were trained to do, fighting until the bitter end.

Caol had tried to teach him to fight without emotion. The male claimed emotion was a distraction. But emotion was exactly what fueled

Rion now. It tore through his body in an angry current, carrying everything he'd tried to hold back.

Like a dam, he'd broken and was ready to flood the land with his rage. He didn't care that it was dangerous or that it might be a crutch. He didn't need to control himself. His enemies were falling just fine with his mind addled. Broken. Shattered beyond repair.

The mountain above him shuddered and the walls cracked. Heavy debris fell, rocking the earth as he limped from the cave. Rion held it all up until he walked beyond the entrance, then turned to watch it all fold in on itself.

Large boulders tumbled down the mountainside, but he shattered them before they got close. Trees toppled over, and Rion broke through the bark, scattering it into a million pieces.

Water gushed out from one side of the mountain, running across the flat ground, searching for another crevice to sink into.

Dust and debris flew up and around his body in a deafening frenzy, then just as quickly, the world fell silent again.

Particles lingered in the air, burning his nose and staining his cheeks. He didn't care that it clung to his tears. Didn't bother wiping them away, either.

Rion stared at the rubble, at the cracks under his feet, then a shuddering breath went through him and he collapsed. Pain returned to his body tenfold as the adrenaline ebbed and he cried out against it, cursing the gods for ever letting him walk the earth.

Every shift of his body hurt.

Everything . . . hurt.

He was nothing all over again. A being left to survive in a cruel world that didn't want him.

Rion roared at the heavens and the thunderous clouds rolling in. It felt as if the sky itself was ready to weep right alongside him.

Time passed. He didn't know how long. The roar in his veins simmered to burning coals, and Rion continued staring at the crumbled mountain.

It reflected everything he felt. He was broken, no longer able to return to his former self. Even if someone miraculously put the pieces back together, it would take a simple shift to bring it crashing down all over again.

The sky rumbled overhead, then the rain began to fall. He tilted his head back to let the cool drops hit his face. Then finally took a deep breath.

Then another.

And another.

He had to get out of here. He needed to go home. Once again, he was running to Saoirse. Without her—

Another breath and Rion forced his aching body to stand. He could handle physical pain. He could get back to Nàdair. So long as he didn't think about—fresh tears rolled down his cheeks, hot and angry.

He deserved this. Deserved every second for being so gullible and stupid.

Rion drew his magic around his body, feeding the frenzied storm even as the rain continued to beat down on his back. He took a single step, caged his heart in steel, and began the long, agonizing trek home.

He wouldn't look back.

His breath was ragged, his heart rate sporadic. Warm rain rolled down his face, or maybe those were more tears.

He grew numb. Cold. But pushed on.

Night and day came and went. His body screamed, begging to stop. To fall. To fail.

His back throbbed, his muscles ached, and his heart bled, and bled, and bled.

He refused to give in, even when waves of emotion overwhelmed him and he wanted to tear the land to shreds. Rion took that emotion and buried it in a deep well within himself.

He would remember. This drowning pain was the direct result of him putting his trust in others.

Images began pouring through his mind. Memories of her.

The first conversation. The first lure. A female who desired the basic comforts of life. Someone who was innocent.

The first kiss, a ploy meant to throw off not only the citizens, but him as well. A taste that would leave him wanting more. And gods, he'd wanted so much more.

Both memories went into the well, falling deep.

Her tugging him around the marketplace, then changing into a dress that was to serve as a distraction. A distraction for him.

The way she'd planned to be caught so she could pull him close, then see how volatile his temper could be. A test to see how she might navigate him.

The attack from the civilians—likely her plan—and the way she'd helped tend to him afterward. To further gain his trust.

The tender way she'd run her hands through his hair. The look in her eyes.

Rion clenched his fists and shoved all those thoughts down, hoping they'd drown and never resurface.

His mind drifted to the party and the way she'd been hurt. The way she'd planned it all so that she seemed worse off than she actually was. The patience. The timing. The planning.

She'd done it all. Just so she could see the look of devastation in his eyes the moment she revealed herself.

He'd never forget that look.

Never forget the female he'd loved either, even if she never really existed.

Rion kept moving. Kept letting his mind cycle through the memories, piecing everything together one small bit at a time. Every word, every touch, every calculated move.

He passed trees, meadows, travelers as they raced from his destructive path.

He ignored them.

Rion's throat burned, begging for water. He vaguely remembered drinking what was left in the water skin hanging from his belt. Then he dropped the water skin and kept moving.

He was done. Beyond done. Never again. He'd never let his heart bleed like this again.

Everyone would just betray him, eventually.

His father. His teacher. His friend. His classmates. The villagers. The staff that had once looked out for him. Each and every person held a knife, just waiting for the moment they could shove it in his back.

His legs finally gave out and Rion's palms scraped against the rock as he hit the ground. A fresh wave of pain coursed through him as he sat there, staring at the very rock he commanded.

A laugh escaped. Grew. Bubbled over into hysteria. Maybe that female would succeed, even buried under a mountain. He wouldn't say her name. He'd already erased it.

His wounds still bled, breaking open as he trudged across Brónach. Rion's vision blurred, but he forced himself up. Sweat rolled down his face, but he could see the redwoods rising above the trees that surrounded them. Calling him. Beckoning him home.

Rion circled around to the side entrance Saoirse had designed for him all those years ago. He blasted through the greenery meant to shield it from view. Maybe he should have second guessed using it. Maybe in his absence, Saoirse had set traps for him too, ready to be rid of her nuisance of a little brother.

No—not Saoirse. She'd always been there for him. Healed him. She'd made a promise to protect him and care for him.

Grief lodged itself in Rion's throat.

So many promises. So many broken.

He didn't remember entering the room. Didn't remember the walk up the stairs or down the hallways. Or whose room he now stood in. He only knew it smelled familiar somehow, safe, maybe, if anywhere was safe anymore.

His magic kept circling, kept close to him, ready to protect.

"Gods, Rion, what the—" He knew that voice. Rion turned slowly, the figure nothing more than a blur as it ran toward him.

His heart rate spiked. Was it her? Had she somehow escaped the mountain? Slender fingers wrapped around his wrist, but Rion smacked the hand away.

"Don't fucking touch me," he screamed, his voice hoarse as he stumbled back into a dresser. It tilted and he fell with it. A vase shattered, cold water covered his hands, and his magic billowed out, reaching for the individual.

No, no, he couldn't do that—he knew them—knew the scent— he—he—his body collapsed and Rion collapsed with it, everything shaking with uncontrollable sobs.

One person. That's all he wanted. Just one person to understand his soul. His mother. She would have understood. He needed her. They all needed her.

"Rion." The voice again. So soft and gentle. Coaxing. He looked up, but his vision wouldn't clear. They moved slower now, crouching as they crawled forward, one arm outstretched.

"It's Saoirse."

Saoirse. His sister. She still cared, right? She wouldn't—his shoulders shook again and his voice broke. "Saoirse?"

That gentle hand touched him again. "I'm here." He let her wrap one arm under his shoulder. He didn't like it. Didn't trust the touch. Any second now—Rion cried out in pain as she pulled him to his feet. "I'm here," she said again and led him toward the bed.

Rion fell onto his stomach and his sister cursed when she pulled his shirt up to examine his wounds. His head was too heavy to lift anymore. She left and returned moments later. Perhaps she'd put an end to him. Maybe she'd been waiting for the perfect opportunity as well.

Something warm dabbed across his back and he arched off the bed before sobs tore through him again.

He'd killed her. He'd killed her. He'd killed her.

That beautiful smile was gone. The sound of her laughter nothing more than a memory.

No, she'd deserved it.

Didn't she?

"What happened?" Saoirse voice was soft, welcoming as she cleaned the deep wounds.

"I thought she wanted more," he replied weakly. He was as pathetic as they came. "She promised—she promised—" Rion couldn't finish. He didn't want to.

"Is she dead?" Rion nodded, still clenching his fists. He could scent Saoirse's anger through his haze. It burned through the room like wildfire. "Good."

No, it wasn't good, but he didn't have the strength to argue. Maybe Saoirse would have killed her if he hadn't. He'd never know.

All Rion knew was that his dreams for a different life had shattered. Fate had once again intervened to ensure his misery.

Saoirse pressed a cup to his lips. "I need you to drink this."

He didn't pull away. Rion took the bitter liquid and swallowed.

Maybe this would be his undoing. A painless end.

His body stopped shaking.

His mind stopped racing.

Saoirse cut the shirt from his body and carefully eased it out from beneath him.

"I tried," he whispered, but his lips had gone numb. He wasn't sure Saoirse heard him. "I wanted it to be different. I wanted—I wanted—"

Oblivion dragged Rion down, down, down until he knew nothing but the sweet caress of darkness.

CHAPTER TWENTY-SIX

Saoirse

It had taken her hours to stabilize him. She'd called in every healer across the city, explained his injuries, then had led the five who claimed they could heal such extensive wounds right to her brother.

They'd balked at the sight of him, but she'd threatened to maim their hands if they refused. Or if he mysteriously died under their care. She didn't care if the demand was unreasonable, or if Rion might die anyway. She'd do everything in her power to keep him alive.

Saoirse watched their every move. Only one had tried to use their magic in a way that she'd deemed threatening.

They'd left without an appendage.

From there, the others worked tirelessly.

The medicine she'd given him kept Rion sedated.

None were sure he'd live.

She'd kept her tears at bay, even when they advised her to say her goodbyes.

Saoirse refused. Rion was strong. Her little brother would pull through. He had to.

When there was nothing more to be done, the healers left her with strict instructions to keep his wounds clean and change his bandages often. They said if he made it through the night, then he'd live with nothing more than a few scars on his body. He'd lost a lot of blood. And if the blades had nicked his organs, then he'd bleed internally. From the position of his wounds, it would be a miracle if they hadn't.

Saoirse prayed.

It was a long night. Saoirse stood vigil the entire time, watching the rise and fall of his back as he lay on the blood-soaked sheets.

She didn't bother cleaning it up. Not yet. She wouldn't risk jostling him and undoing what the healers had done.

Saoirse didn't know exactly what had happened, only that Selina, the viper, was involved. She'd told Rion not to let her get to him. Saoirse could only imagine the things that female had done. Said.

Her heart ached for her little brother and the pain he'd endured. His last words stabbed through her heart.

I tried.

He'd fallen for her. Fallen hard and yet he'd still managed to kill her. Other males hadn't been so fortunate. Saoirse should have done it herself years ago.

Rion woke a few times but was hardly lucid. He muttered under his breath and she carefully coaxed him into drinking the medicine left by the healers, along with as much liquid as she dared force down his throat.

Saoirse rubbed her hand over her face and glanced out the window to watch the first traces of dawn illuminate the sky.

If he makes it through the night . . .

He'd made it, which meant he wasn't bleeding internally, at least. She'd prayed to the gods all night.

Saoirse stood and removed her little brother's boots. She cut away his pants and tended to other small wounds, wiping away crusted blood and dirt. His magic had fallen still when he'd gone unconscious.

Small bits of color had returned to his face, though his eyes were both still black and sunken in.

Saoirse draped a fresh sheet over his body and cut away the blood-soaked ones, still careful not to jostle him too much. She'd clean the bed once he was talking again.

Rion muttered in his sleep, the words indecipherable, but she could feel the heartbreak in them.

Saoirse stood and stared down at her little brother. She'd known who Selina really was, but it was Alec who'd assigned her. Had their older brother arranged the whole thing or had Selina been working of her own accord? She needed to find out.

Her gaze shot toward the door. Saoirse had commanded her second, Fin, to stand guard. He was one of the few Fae she could trust. He'd never failed her, but could she risk leaving Rion in his care?

Caol had promised, and yet—

Her jaw worked and Saoirse pulled the door open. Fin turned, then bowed. The two warriors who followed his command bowed lower.

"Is there something you need?"

Saoirse didn't invite them in. She just stared at him, studying the male who'd vowed to serve beneath her. She glanced back at her brother again. "I need to see Alec." Her mind was at war with itself. All it would take was one bad decision and Rion would be torn from her forever.

"I'll see to it that no one enters this room."

She turned back. "Will you?"

He bowed again and placed a hand over his heart. "My loyalty is to you, My Lady."

Saoirse clenched her jaw and lowered her voice to a near growl. "If anything happens to him, you will pay for it with your life." She turned to the other two and met their gazes. "All of you will pay for it. Your families will pay for it, too. I'll destroy your entire lineage if anyone so much as steps a foot in this room and you don't intervene."

One of them paled, but Fin nodded in understanding. "Understood, My Lady. I will guard him as if he is one of my own."

She sniffed the air, searching for any hint of deception. He'd been loyal since the day he was stationed at her side over fifty years ago. He'd never stepped out of line, and he'd saved her life on more than one occasion.

Saoirse gave him a final nod, then locked the door and marched down the hall. She found Alec seated in the throne room, pouring over maps and documents. The council sat with him. She was supposed to be here, too. These meeting were always of utmost importance.

Today it didn't matter.

Everyone looked up at the sound of her boots thudding against the marble floor. "Leave us," she commanded.

None hesitated. Alec didn't even bother looking up as they scrambled from the table. "That was an important meeting," he said in a bored voice.

Saoirse clenched her fists and stood at the bottom of the three stairs that led up the raised platform. She was already shaking as she said, "I want you to look me in the eye and tell me you didn't command the assassination of our little brother."

Alec didn't move. "He's no brother of mine."

Her blood heated. Blazed. "He is our blood. Our responsibility."

"Not anymore."

"Why?" She threw up her hands. "Because of a prophecy? What did he do before his magic appeared? Nothing!"

"And yet, when it did appear, he killed our father." Alec didn't raise his voice. He didn't speak as if he felt any emotion at all.

Saoirse just stared at him as if he were a stranger. Her brother. Alec was her brother too, and yet, ever since their mother's disappearance, he'd morphed into someone else. He wasn't the same male that had taught her how to ride horseback, how to hold a sword, or control her magic. Maybe she should confess everything right here. Admit that she'd been the one to cut down their remaining parent.

But if she did that, there'd be repercussions. Rion was injured; she couldn't risk being detained.

Her voice was cold and lethal as she said, "You will never touch him again."

Alec finally looked up. His face reminded her so much of their father. "Last I checked, I was the High Lord, not you."

Saoirse didn't back down. "If you *ever* raise your hand against him again, I will make you regret it."

He stood to his full height and his lips pulled back in a snarl. "Is that a challenge, Saoirse?"

She scoffed. Laughed. "You're worried about your throne? How low have you fallen to think I'd want the stupid thing?" She stepped forward, her magic tingling beneath her skin, begging for freedom. "Leave Rion alone, or I'm out."

His gaze hardened. "What do you mean *you're out?*"

"I'll leave."

He smirked at that. "And where would you go?" He turned his attention back to the maps spread across the table. As if her threats were nothing more than a child throwing a tantrum.

"The human lands. The western continent." She shrugged. "Maybe I'll find another continent below the southern isles."

"Don't be dramatic."

He reached for a pen and Saoirse exploded. Magic fed the seeds stored in her sleeves and the greenery raced through the air and hit the table so hard it slammed against the back wall and shattered. Alec's maps and documents went flying, floating through the air.

"You will not touch him again."

Her brother growled. "Go cool off before you do something foolish."

She met his unflinching gaze. He was so much like their father that it hurt to look at him sometimes. But he wasn't their father and he didn't control her.

"Enjoy your lonely reign, My Lord." He grimaced at the title and tone, then she sketched a bow and pivoted on her heel.

"I'll see you in an hour," he called to her retreating form.

No. He wouldn't.

SAOIRSE RETURNED to Rion's room and thanked Fin upon finding Rion safe. Fin was happy to report that Rion hadn't stirred. She almost wished he had, just so she'd know he was okay.

Saoirse began planning. She sent a slave to pack her belongings. Just a few things. It would be a few days before she could move Rion. Until then, she'd remain here and watch over him.

Once he was back on his feet, Saoirse would pull a few bags of gold from the vault. It would carry them over for a time. Afterward, she could take various other jobs, as could Rion. It would be a different life. A simpler one where she wasn't responsible for an entire country. The thought was almost refreshing. Her only regret would be lacking the resources to continue searching for their mother.

But their mother had been missing for years. Rion was right here in front of her, and she'd face hell itself before she let anything happen to him.

Maybe she'd leave a letter for Alec explaining what really happened to their father that night. She could hide it in one of his books. Even if it took years for him to find it, one day he'd eventually know the truth.

Saoirse invited Fin into the room and quietly explained her plans. He vowed to remain at her side until she found a safe place to settle.

She knew Rion would object to leaving, but she'd find a way to bend him to her will. She was fed up with everyone hurting him. Caol had almost been her breaking point. Alec's involvement—she clenched her fists. Damn him to hell.

Saoirse remained in the room with Rion for another three hours. A light knock on the door indicated her slave had finished packing. She'd told the half-breed to leave the two bags by the door. One for her and one for Rion.

It would be . . . fun, she supposed, to wander different parts of the country.

Another knock had the hairs on the back of Saoirse's neck rising. She took a relaxing breath, then crossed the room and pulled the door open.

Alec stood on the other side, leaning against the back wall with his arms crossed. He eyed the bags by the door, then her. "You didn't show for the meeting."

"And?"

His jaw flexed and he swallowed hard, the only bit of emotion he'd allow himself to display. "You're really leaving."

"That's what I said."

"I didn't think—" He loosed a breath and ran a hand through his hair. "For him? You'd really give up your country for him?"

Her second and his underlings looked like they'd rather be anywhere else. They didn't move.

"I'm not giving up anything. One of my siblings wants to murder the other, what do you expect me to do?"

"You know the ancient texts just as well as I do. Probably better. He should have been put down as soon as his magic showed up."

Saoirse growled. "Well, I guess Father failed then, didn't he?"

"*You* failed," he seethed. "You were right there, you should have been the one to do it. He killed everyone in that room."

"And how old was he when he did that?" Saoirse questioned. "Tell me, Alec, do you think you could stomach killing an innocent child?"

"Sometimes sacrifices are necessary."

"Says the one who re-homes orphans. Or did you forget your own decree? Have you turned so cold-hearted that you'd have killed our little brother yourself?"

Alec clenched his fists. "I would do what is necessary for my country."

Saoirse just stared at him. "You disgust me."

"Do not treat me like the enemy here."

"You are my enemy." He flinched. "Everyone who tries to hurt him," she pointed toward the bed, "is my enemy. I don't care how close we are or what we've been through. If you come after Rion, I will put you down."

"You'd kill me?"

"How about we not find out?"

Alec growled. "If you keep—"

"Do not threaten her." Saoirse spun to find Rion sitting at the edge of the bed, his feet on the floor, bent forward as if he intended to stand. She ran into the room to put a hand on his shoulder, hopefully to hold him down. If he tried to fight right now—

Alec followed her. "Or what," her elder brother spat. "Plan to kill me, too?"

"If fate demands it."

Alec glared at him, his gaze drifting to the bloody sheets on the bed.

Saoirse stood between them, ready to intervene should Alec strike out.

"I never thought I'd see the day when my own sister stood against me."

"Neither did I," she said quietly, still keeping one hand on Rion's shoulder. "Go rule your country, Alec. I'm sure you'll find another adviser to fill my place."

"I could have you tried for abandonment."

Her gaze turned cold as she met Alec's stare. "If you send anyone in here to put me or Rion in chains, you'll discover exactly how ruthless I can be."

"You wouldn't kill your own people."

Saoirse bared her fangs at him. "Try me."

Alec opened his mouth to speak again, then decided against it. He glanced between the two of them. Locked eyes with Rion, then Saoirse. His jaw worked. "Fine."

"Fine, what?" she demanded.

"No one will touch him and I'm giving you a one month leave to sort your shit out."

"I want your word."

Alec huffed. "I already said—"

"Your word, Alec. I'll settle for nothing less."

He met his sister's gaze. "You have my word. I swear I will never send anyone after him again, directly or indirectly." He sighed and his tone softened. "Now will you stay?"

She glanced back to Rion. "I'll think about it during my leave."

Alec nodded, stared at them again before pivoting on his heel and marching down the hall, his guards in his wake.

CHAPTER TWENTY-SEVEN

Rion pulled the towel down his neck then flung it onto the bed before slipping on his black pants. He stretched his arms overhead, feeling his taunt muscles lengthen. He'd just finished a round of morning exercises and determined himself fully recovered from his wounds.

Rion twisted in the mirror, staring at the fresh scars seated just above his hip bones. One on either side of his spine. His jaw clenched at the memory, but he refused to dwell on the emotions attached. He'd done enough of that in the last few weeks.

Thankfully, Alec never returned to his door and though Rion had told her to go away a number of times, Saoirse was a thorn in his side, constantly fussing.

She didn't miss the way he flinched away from her touch. She'd asked about it, but he'd refused to answer. Touch felt . . . strange now. As if it were an invasion of his person.

He hated it. Hated that Se—Rion pushed her name down, grabbed his shirt, and pulled it over his head. He tested his magic. It had never failed him. Not once. Magic was something under his control and it would be the only thing he'd rely on from this point forward.

If Brónach wanted to treat him like a monster, then a monster is exactly what he'd become.

Rion buckled his belts and slid his freshly sharpened knives into place across his torso. A sword dangled at his side. More knives rested in his boot and against his back. They were the friends he'd carry with him. They were his only allies.

Saoirse still had her second stationed outside his door. The male bowed upon seeing Rion, and Rion let his magic glide over the mosaic rugs, dancing at the male's feet, daring him to lash out. Saoirse had assured him the male wasn't his enemy. Rion knew better than to believe it.

When Fin didn't react Rion moved on, marching down the long hall.

Everyone backed away when they saw him coming. Some pressed their bodies against the walls while others slipped through unlocked doors.

He snarled at any who dared to meet his gaze and something strange in him relished their fear. Let them cower. They deserved nothing less. These were beings willing to murder a youngling for nothing more than being born different.

If they wanted to see a real monster, all they needed to do was look in a mirror.

How many innocents had come before him? How many younglings had suffered as he had?

Rion clenched his fists. None. Because none had survived the people who had claimed to love them.

The thought sickened him and sent his stomach rolling.

Brónach. A city of strength, yet one founded on abhorrent traditions. Maybe it would be better if the city fell. If he himself tore it apart from the inside out.

Maybe he should be the one to do it. Eventually.

Rion's heavy boots echoed in the halls as he kept walking, then shoved the throne room doors open without pause.

He hadn't stepped foot inside since his injury. Hadn't seen his brother, either.

Alec pretended he could control everything. Everyone. It was time he learned otherwise.

Alec's nostrils flared upon seeing his youngest sibling. The guards reached for their weapons but didn't draw. Saoirse sat across from the High Lord, but Rion didn't look at her. He wouldn't bring his sister down with him. She didn't deserve that. He'd tuck her love away in a velvet box and save it for the next life.

"Why are you here?" Alec demanded, barely restraining the hate in his voice.

"I'm healed," Rion said simply. "I'm ready for another assignment."

Alec's jaw ticked. "Your last one failed."

"I seem to remember encountering . . . a scheme that derailed me."

Alec stood slowly, assessing Rion's body and the magic dancing at his feet. "You won't be assigned further missions."

Rion cocked his head and glanced around, meeting each face one by one. The council's fear burned his nose, something he used to find unpleasant. "Really? Do you have duties for me to attend to here?" A small smile spread across Rion's face. "Perhaps I'll start attending council meetings. After all, I am a Lord." He met Alec's gaze again and his voice turned lethal. "Or do you plan to stop hiding behind your puppets and take me on yourself?"

"Rion." Saoirse's stern voice was a warning. He didn't look at her. He wasn't a child anymore and didn't need her protection.

She didn't need him weighing her down.

The scent of Alec's magic sparked in the air and small tendrils of greenery poked out from beneath his sleeves. Likely all deadly. Rion knew Saoirse utilized deadly plants to make killing easier on the battlefield.

"It's a pity Selina didn't finish the job."

Rion knew the mention of her name was meant to rile him, but Rion only smiled. "Pity indeed. She didn't even put up much of a fight in the end. Tell me," he dared a step forward, forcing Alec's guards to draw their weapons. "Did your warriors find their bodies beneath all that rubble, or did you leave them there to rot? Rotting would be preferable."

"You killed an entire unit of our best warriors."

Rion shrugged. "They violated the code of conduct which states comrades aren't to engage one another in combat while on assignment. Last I remember, that same code allows the victim to defend themselves by any means necessary.

"Besides," Rion continued. "Let's not stand on false pretenses. We all know I was their real target. *They* were the ones who failed." Rion pulled at his magic, letting it rise up and around his body. "And rest assured, if you try to repeat such events, the next group will also fail. So let's make this easier for everyone. You'll pretend to control me and save face with the masses, and I'll put my skills to use in the field."

"I could exile you," Alec threatened. Saoirse's head shot toward him, a retort on her lips, but Rion responded before she could.

"Could you?" He tilted his head toward Saoirse. "I don't think losing our sister is in your best interest." Alec growled. Rion gestured to an empty chair. "Should I sit? Discuss strategy?"

"You won't take one more step into this room."

Rion took two. The guards summoned their magic. Vines and plants snaked around their forms like living creatures.

"Did you know that the security in our villages is—how do I phrase this—lacking? I'd love to know the name of the lazy individual responsible. Or how about the ones in charge of training said warriors? Have you checked in on them?" Rion made a show of eyeing the guards. "If someone were to attack Brónach from the eastern coast, rest assured they'd sweep across the continent with ease."

"Don't act as though you saw enough to make an informed decision."

"I saw enough and I was disappointed. Father would be downright insulted."

"Shut your mouth. You don't have a right to speak about my father."

Rion made a show of flicking a piece of dust from his sleeve. "Send me to deal with it and I'll be out of your hair, but," Rion said, his tone dangerous. "If you assign anyone to get close to me again, I'll kill them on the spot."

"You can't go alone. We have rules for a reason."

"Those rules no longer apply to me," Rion said. "And if you try to force the issue, I'll make sure I'm solo by the end of it." The two males stared one another down. "I'm done," Rion said simply. "If you want me dead, then you'll have to step down from your pretty little throne and do it yourself."

Alec stepped, but Saoirse jumped to her feet, grabbed her older brother's arm and placed herself between her brothers. "Enough. If he wants to address security issues, then we should be grateful for his assistance."

Alec growled at her. "He has no love for this country. He's more likely to sabotage our outposts than reform them."

"Only if they're too incompetent to follow orders." Rion tilted his head again. "Or have you forgotten everything you were taught in school? Or perhaps Caol's teachings were wrong? Have the warriors of Brónach grown soft?"

"We cannot afford to lose perfectly good warriors."

Rion shrugged. "If they'll go, I'll send the lazy ones back for more training. If not, well, I can't help what happens to them."

"I've noticed it, too," Saoirse said and Alec turned to her. "We've been receiving complaints from several villages. It's time someone looks into it." She turned back to Rion without waiting for Alec's response. "Start with the northern most villages and work your way down the coast. When you're finished, return for a reprieve and further orders."

Alec's nostrils flared. "You are not the High Lord."

"You're right. I'm your advisor, and I'm supposed to handle such things so you don't have to. We have one of our strongest—"

"He is an abomination and doesn't—"

Rion took another step toward the throne and the guards backed up, closing in around Alec and Saoirse.

"I know, I know," Rion said, waving one hand in annoyance. "I should be eradicated from the earth." His voice lowered. "But that's not going to happen if I have any say in the matter." Rion stepped away. "Sit back and relax Alec, I'll go handle your problems for you."

His brother growled, but Rion ignored it, pivoted on his heel, and marched from the room. He headed for the library first and requested an updated map of the coastline. The librarian was trembling when he returned with a large rolled up document. Rion studied it, made a few notes, then proceeded to the kitchens. The staff there scrambled from his presence. Rion simply helped himself, then returned to his room for his pack. No reason to remain in Nàdair. There was work to be done.

"Wait," Saoirse called. He huffed. He'd almost made it to the city gates. Rion turned to his sister and she slowed to a walk, eying the pack slung across his shoulder. It was heavier than the ones he'd carried before, packed to the brim with food and medical supplies. Whatever he needed in order to care for himself. No one was going to do it.

"You shouldn't provoke Alec like that in front of everyone. It makes him look bad."

Rion scoffed and turned to walk away. Saoirse reached out to grab his arm, but he caught her wrist and held it in the air between them. Her eyes were wide and he inwardly kicked himself when silver lined her eyes.

He released her and turned away. "I'll be back."

"The trip could take you months." Her voice was too soft.

Rion clenched his jaw, hating himself. "Then it will take months."

"Will you write?"

"You'll get regular reports."

A long silence, then she straightened. "I demand them weekly."

Rion dared to glance at her again only to see anguish written across her face.

"I don't rightly care what happens to Alec, but you should know there's a traitor in the council."

"Who?"

"He wears a gaudy ring with a crow on it. Deal with him before I get back or I'll do it myself."

Rion didn't wait for her response as he exited the city. He wouldn't look back. It was better for her this way. She'd threatened to leave for him but he couldn't let that happen. He wouldn't let his sister sacrifice anything else.

The guards shrank away from his presence. They feared him. Everyone did. Their views were solely based upon an ancient prophecy. No one had heard from the gods in centuries. Sometimes Rion wondered if they even existed.

He shifted to an easy jog until he was well beyond the border of redwoods and the trees beyond.

He had a purpose. A mission. A target. And he'd accomplish his task with the same precision he'd always used. By the time Rion was done, the world would know Brónach as a ruthless, unyielding nation once again.

He just had one thing to settle first.

CHAPTER TWENTY-EIGHT

Rion hadn't told anyone he was traveling south rather than north. They didn't need to know. Not until he'd finished. They'd hear the news, and if Alec wanted to confront him about it, then he could seek him out along the coastline. He wasn't asking for permission. Not for this.

Rion paused at inns along the way, throwing coins at the innkeepers and warning them that if they valued their lives, they'd keep their mouths shut.

No one dared to confront him.

Days later, he stood outside Whiteridge's gates. He walked the same road, saw the same guards. Only this time, Rion wasn't entering their city with the intent to be civil. This time, he'd come to raze it to the ground.

The guards charged, their magic ripping free. Rion didn't change his pace, he merely raised one hand and crumbled the ground beneath their feet before wrapping it around their torsos. They screamed and their fear burned his nostrils. Growling, Rion threw them into those familiar white pillars, cracking the thick marble columns all the way to their tip.

Their hearts still beat. He could kill them. But he left them to suffer instead. He had another target in mind.

Foley. The one who'd been working with Selina and had planned

Rion's demise from the first moment he'd stepped into the city. Maybe even before.

Rion prowled the streets, tearing up the cobble stone as he went, dismantling the road and vendors stands. The civilians screamed and covered their heads, fleeing. A few tried to fight and Rion shoved earth down their throats and left them to choke on it.

Warriors wearing the city's sigil appeared in the road before him, all standing shoulder to shoulder, their magic and weapons out as they waited for his approach. The palace stood just behind them, sparkling in the summer sun. Heat rose up from the cobblestones, giving the large yard a hazy look.

It was the gemstone of the city. A beacon of hope for all who dwelled here and for those who hoped for a different life under a different monarch. It had stood for centuries as an impenetrable fortress.

Shame that it would all be nothing more than rubble come nightfall.

The guards charged and Rion danced around their movements. He didn't bother with his knives, not when the warriors threw their own. He formed a wall of earth around his body and their blades sank deep. Rion exploded his magic and sent those blades right back to their owners. Some blocked the strike. Others didn't.

They fell one at a time. He twisted around their bodies, breaking arms and crushing legs. When he finally drew his sword, heads hit the ground one after another. He wasn't in the mood to play with them.

The road cleared and Rion continued prowling toward the door, hoping Foley sat just inside, screaming demands for his warriors to put a stop to Rion's advances. He smirked at the thought. He wanted Foley afraid, if only to savor it before his end.

Rion stepped one foot inside the palace and the entire room collapsed around him. He caught it, of course, then threw the heavy pieces away from his body.

Inside, more guards stood at the ready. But they weren't as confident as the first group. Their legs and bodies were shaking, their weapons trembling in their grasp.

"Where is he?"

They lunged and Rion cut them down. Blood coated the once pristine floor, the statues that depicted the Fairy Folk and the gods. Some Fae tried shifting into their animal forms, hoping to surprise him from behind.

Rion crushed their smaller bodies with little effort.

A broken wing sat to his left, poking up at an awkward angle. A shattered jaw sagged from a wolf to his right and the creature whined before shifting back into his Fae form. He gripped the loose bones, tears of pain spilling down his face.

Rion didn't put him out of his misery, either. If he remained in the building, he'd be dead soon, anyway.

One male had fallen onto his backside and attempted to crawl away from Rion's approach. Rion grabbed the male with his magic and yanked him forward. The male cried out and his teeth chattered.

"Where is he?" They all knew who he meant.

"I'm right here," a familiar voice called. Rion's gaze rose up to the second balcony. Several warriors flanked Foley, all wearing grim, angry expressions.

Rion threw the male and his head hit the floor with a sickening thud. He tore at the marble, cracking it in all directions.

The male *tsked*. "No respect for the arts, I should have known a mongrel like you wouldn't know how to cherish beautiful things." Rion didn't respond. "How did things turn out for your little girlfriend?"

"I killed her myself."

Foley clicked his tongue and surveyed his nails. "Pity. She was such a pretty thing and was so confident in her plans. I had hoped to play with her a bit myself. I don't suppose you got the chance?" He raised a brow as if in question. Rion still didn't respond. The male huffed. "Well, I'm afraid we don't have all day. Some of us have important meetings to—"

Rion launched himself to the second level at dizzying speeds. Foley's words caught in his throat as Rion dug his fingers into his windpipe.

The warriors stationed to guard him tried to reach their employer to no avail.

Rion's fingers dug deeper. Particles of earth held Foley's hands at bay, just to ensure no more plants ended up beneath his skin. Tears ran down the male's red face. It shifted to purple, then Rion crushed his windpipe. Rion stared at him for a long minute then dropped his corpse. He severed the male's head for good measure.

Chaos and screaming surrounded him as the warriors beat against the wall he'd created.

Rion spit on Foley's twisted face. "I don't have time, either."

There would be time to savor kills later. Right now, he was here to make a statement. To tell the world that he was to be feared. If they didn't want to love him, then they'd know his name another way. They'd cower at his presence. Whisper that The Demon had arrived. None would dare to even speak his name.

The warriors were nothing. They were mere gnats attacking a bear. He shook them off, killed most, and let the smart ones flee.

Rion walked over cooling bodies and headed straight for the ballroom. His gaze roamed over the vast space before settling on the door to the basement.

He ventured down, taking an oil lantern with him.

Fae jumped to their feet at his approach. One male wet himself.

Rion snapped all three of their necks.

A slave stood in the corner, their clothes torn and tears staining their face. Rion rummaged through the dead Fae's pockets with his magic and threw a key at the slave's feet.

"Free yourself. Search the rooms and free the others, then get out of the city."

The slave nodded and ran, not even bothering to cover himself. Rion ventured toward the back rooms where he found three more slaves. Two male, one female. He snapped the chains and told them the same. Free the others, then flee.

Rion's gaze wandered over the office and the records that would likely prove useful to Saoirse and Alec.

Then he decided he didn't care. He took an oil lamp from the corner and shattered it across the desk. Flames spread, papers curled up, turning from brown to black. The oil dripped onto the floor and after a few moments, the wooden desk caught as well.

Rion backed out of the room, leaving the door open, then did the same to the next room and the next.

When he emerged back upstairs, there were slaves running toward the doors, shrieking at the bodies scattered across the floor.

Rion listened carefully. He heard the crackling flame below. Heard the screams outside.

He searched for heartbeats and ventured into one room at a time. He found a pair of children cowering in a closet. Children of the nobles, if their clothes were anything to go by.

He didn't smile at them, but he wouldn't be like the rest of the people in this gods-forsaken land. He wouldn't kill a child just because of how they'd been born.

Rion broke the window, grabbed the shrieking children with his magic and carefully deposited them on the ground below.

Once he'd cleared the rooms, Rion returned to the ballroom. His magic crawled beneath the mosaic tile of the floor. It cracked, splintering and stretching from one wall to another.

Portraits fell from the walls, the frames cracking when they hit the ground. Statues toppled over, shattering against the ground. Rion grabbed the pillars that held everything up and ripped them away one at a time. The massive structure shuddered, cracked, then collapsed in on itself.

Rion shielded himself from the crumbling roof and yanked another pillar from its place. Then another, until everything began folding in on itself.

Then Rion walked out, pulling at the already fallen structure as if he were wading through water. He emerged to find two dozen Fae standing outside, their weapons drawn and magic out.

The wind shifted, carrying the dust away long enough that he could make out their faces.

Rion counted them one by one. "I will give you one chance to walk away."

They tightened their hold on their weapons and charged.

Rion's magic exploded. He didn't hold back. He'd done that long enough. He was free to just be. To exist.

He'd thought freedom meant retreating to a secluded place in the country. He'd been wrong. Freedom was being able to walk wherever he pleased. To experience life the way everyone else did. Freedom had never tasted so good.

He wouldn't walk the land fearing he was too much anymore. Too much for people. Too much for the gods themselves. They'd either accept him or fall at his feet. He'd carve out his own purpose even if he had to do it in blood.

Rion moved with their magic as if in a dance. An elegant symphony of blades and snapping bones. He pivoted on his feet, unleashing everything.

Music. It was music to his ears. Maybe he'd finally lost his mind. Something within him had certainly changed, snapped, shifted. Whatever it was, he liked it and the euphoria that followed.

Rion threw every blade on his person, sinking them deep into tender flesh. He never missed his mark.

By the time he was breathing hard, a smile covered his face.

The once perfect yard was bathed in blood and limbs and gasping Fae. He was coated in it too, the blood and gore.

The remaining warriors backed away, glancing at one another. Rion stepped forward and they all scrambled back. A strange silence settled over the area as he waited.

"That's it?" he challenged. "You're done?"

One male broke from the group and charged. Rion grabbed the male's foot, severed the limb, then shot a spear of earth straight through the male's chest.

The others stared in wide-eyed horror.

Rion tasted blood at the corner of his mouth. He didn't remember the hit or the reasons for the slight cuts along his body either.

Another step forward and Rion growled between his teeth. "Run."

They gaped. Some stepped back. "Run," Rion repeated. "And if you ever rise against the crown again, know that I'll find you."

Two turned and sprinted away, their arms flailing in an almost comedic manner. After a moment's hesitation, the rest followed.

Rion turned back to the crumbling palace and crushed more sections, just to ensure it would never rise again. Then he turned to the city itself. To the residents gathering their families and loading anything they could carry onto horses and wagons.

It was next.

Rion slammed the door open to the nearest building. A female screamed and tears ran down her face as she curled further into the corner of the darkened room. A small bundle in her arms cried out and his heart froze.

Kill them, a voice whispered in the back of his mind. *They'd do the same to you.* Rion backed away, as if pulled from a drunken haze. The female shook with uncontrollable terror, clinging to that bundle as if she could protect it with her body.

He'd planned to tear the entire city down. Each and every building. But if he did that . . . Rion glanced down at the child. An innocent being who had done nothing of consequence in the world. He thought about the life it would have. How it might not survive if the mother couldn't provide adequate shelter. Or find food.

His resolve weakened.

"I'm sparing this place for you," he said, then stormed away. Rion tore the gates apart as he left the city and started northward, back to his original assignment.

This would be his life now. Nothing more than one mission at a time.

THE CURSED FAE AND A FATAL MISTAKE

CHAPTER ONE

aoirse slammed her mug of ale down on the table and called for another.

"She's got you beat. Give up before you fall over."

The male seated across from her had turned a shade greener. He eyed the twin pair of mugs between them. Saoirse took hers and sat back, sipping at the foam. His eyes watered, then he pushed his mug away and raised both hands in the air. "I submit."

A chorus of applause went up and another male slapped Saoirse across the back. Coins were exchanged and bouts of laugher filled the tavern.

She only smirked. "I warned you."

The male burped and she scooted her chair back, just in case the dozen and a half tankards didn't stay down. "You're not Fae," he accused. "You're some creature created by the gods to make us lose money."

Saoirse lifted her mug. "To a fabled existence, then."

More laughter echoed behind her, then conversations resumed. Saoirse tilted her head back, enjoying the pleasant warmth flooding her body. She'd probably had a little too much, given the fact that she had a meeting with Alec and the elders at sunrise. He'd scold her, but what was life without a little fun? Saoirse crossed her boots and sipped from her mug again.

A voice drifted toward her, too loud for him to be sober. "I hear The Demon is headed back this way. Shall we set something up?"

Saoirse tilted her head toward the male. "Leave it alone, Vaz."

The male's golden hair fell over his face as he sat back in his chair. "Come on, you can't honestly still feel sorry for him. I understood when he was a kid, but after everything he's done just this past decade alone?" The male shook his head.

Another chimed in. "I've lost count of the kills. That male is on an absolute rampage, and no one wants to do anything about it."

"Watch your tone," Saoirse warned.

The male snapped his mouth shut, but Vaz wasn't done. "He's coming back from one hell of an assignment. He'll be tired. He won't expect it."

"He will," Saoirse countered. Her voice lowered. "He always does." And gods, her heart ached to even think about it. Sure, he'd secured their borders, but the cost had been astronomical.

"You could join us. He won't expect *you*."

The buzz she'd been enjoying vanished entirely, eaten away by the adrenaline now coursing through her. Saoirse sat up slowly, set her mug on the table, then glared at her childhood friend. "Stay away from him."

He didn't back down. Vaz never did. Her second, Fin, intervened and clasped Vaz on the shoulder. "Come on, let's not ruin the night already. I still need a few more drinks before you get us kicked out of yet *another* place with halfway decent alcohol."

They'd been thrown out of five in the past two years.

Vaz loosed a sigh and leaned back in his seat. "All right, all right, call for another round. Saoirse can pay for it."

She didn't drink another drop, her gaze locked on Vaz for the rest of the evening. He never gave up on something that easily. The barkeep supplied bread, and Saoirse used tomorrow's meeting as an excuse to sober up.

She chewed her lip. She'd probably have to follow Vaz home, just to make sure he didn't do anything stupid. She couldn't lose Rion, but she didn't want to lose Vaz, either. She'd lost enough friends as it was.

Friends and her little brother's companionship. She'd give anything if he'd just talk to her again. Play a game of chess. Go for a walk. Anything.

NIGHT HAD fallen long before Rion made it back to the city. The forest was quiet. Peaceful. A welcome home. Mostly.

He marched straight through the main gate, keeping a trained eye on those who hid within the treetops in both their animal and Fae forms.

Most didn't challenge him anymore. Not after he'd felled their comrades. Likely brothers and sisters. They'd all thought they could win.

They'd all been wrong.

These days, his magic never left his side. He was a constant brewing storm, which made most avoid his company.

It was a . . . secluded life. Occasionally, he'd crave conversation. Occasionally, he'd show up to a tavern with his hood up and magic nowhere to be seen. But he never lingered. Not when he knew how those males and females would react upon discovering who sat amongst them.

The four Fae stationed to guard Nàdair's gate reached for their weapons. He smirked when he scented their magic and quickly squashed the seedlings that were answering their call.

It drew the guards up short, forced them to back away as he strode toward the city he called home. Such a strange word to label a place where everyone wanted you dead.

The streets were quiet, most having already retired for the night. A few drunks stumbled from taverns, bidding their friends farewell. Others leaned against walls, where they'd likely wake in the morning. The weather was pleasant, at least. Winter's chill was still far off. The changing leaves bathed the forest floor in a mixture of oranges, yellows, and browns.

He'd always enjoyed this time of year.

The stars twinkled above and the moon was nearly full, helping to illuminate the dimly lit streets.

The setting was peaceful. Serene. Nights like tonight were one of the many reasons he chose to return under the cover of darkness, if only to enjoy the city for a few brief hours without interruption.

A shuffle in the dark alleyway to his left made Rion pause. He studied the shadows, then a sliver of movement drew his attention to the ground.

A black and white cat dug through the trash, pulling out leftover scraps. The small creature froze and watched him with one paw raised. Its green eyes reflected the streetlights, and the two stared one another down before more movement shifted Rion's attention.

A Fae sat against the outside wall farther back, his head hung forward as if he'd fallen asleep. Rion scented the air. Not a Fae, a half-breed. He heard the faint click of metal, then noticed the chains. A slave. Either a runaway, or one who'd been discarded. Nàdair had programs in place to keep them off the streets. The slave would likely be picked up come morning and transferred to a new owner if their old one couldn't be found.

A shred of sympathy rose from the depths of his darkened soul. They were as trapped by their circumstances as he was. Escape would only lead to death.

Rion clenched his fists as he studied the male. Thin. So impossibly thin and frail. There should be rules in place. Safeguards to prevent owners from mistreating their slaves.

They had heartbeats and drew breath just like anyone else, and yet horses were treated better.

Saoirse had once protected him when Rion couldn't defend himself. Maybe that's exactly what the half-breeds needed. A Saoirse to save them, perhaps guide them to a new life.

He sighed. The only thing that stood in his way was an entire country and their ridiculous beliefs. The continent had been built on slavery. It would take nothing short of a miracle to end it.

But Móirín had. Many Fae had balked at the High Lord's command. Most had labeled him a sympathizer. Others questioned his sanity and whether he'd grown too soft after finding his mate.

A slight scuff of boots against the cobblestones drew Rion's focus away from the half-breed. His eyes scanned the road, then Rion cursed and he leaned back just in time to dodge a knife aimed at his throat.

Plants broke through the cobblestones at his feet and reached for his legs, but Rion's sand ground them to dust.

He leaped back to avoid a barrage of knives, then cursed again when another set flew at him from behind.

Rion rolled across the ground and jumped back to his feet, drawing his own weapon to block a blade aimed at his heart. A sharp sensation pierced his left shoulder and Rion roared at the shadows.

A male voice barked a command.

He was home. Home and yet once again, Fae from his own country were trying to kill him.

Rion gritted his teeth, then a blade sank deep into his thigh. An unbridled rage pulsed through him then.

He hated this. Hated always having to keep his guard up. Hated *them*.

Rion's magic rolled across the ground like a wave, and he caught several hidden bodies in its clutches. They growled and snarled and fought.

It took less than a heartbeat for Rion to crush their bones, rendering their legs useless. Howls of pain filled the air, then a roar of fury followed from another alleyway.

Rion turned to find a male charging him head on with his sword drawn. Stupid, really, but Rion allowed him to get close. Allowed their swords to clash, too.

Anger flashed behind those dark, unfamiliar eyes. Emotion had taken over. The male swung his blade again, throwing too much of his body weight into the thrust. Rion scented the alcohol on his breath as he parried the weapon and flung it from the male's grasp. The blond-haired male resorted to using his fists, seeming to disregard the magic at his disposal. Rage blinded him. Rage and intoxication.

Rion took a blow to the face, then another to the gut. He relished the pain. It was the only thing that eased the torment he carried day in and day out.

The male drew a blade and sliced it across Rion's arm. Another strike came too close to his throat.

At one time, Rion had considered letting another take his life. But that part of him was long gone. Buried. Dead. If they wanted him, they'd have to be strong enough to claim him.

Rion planted a knee in the male's ribs and shoved him to the ground. Rion drew his sword and lashed out, relishing the feel of his blade cutting through another's flesh.

The male struck at him again and Rion returned the blow. Again and again and again. They moved and clashed and danced.

His warriors rejoined the fray, likely violating their commander's wishes to take Rion down one on one. He caught them with the loose particles floating through the air. The sand raced up their legs, wrapped around their torsos and arms, then dove down the warriors' throats.

The male lunged at him again, rage renewed, but Rion tackled him, wrestled for dominance, then pinned the male to the ground. The male spit in Rion's face, snapping his teeth as he shouted obscenities and cursed him to the deepest level of hell.

Rion had heard it all before. Heard the other words, too. Monster. Demon. Abomination.

Rion slammed his blade through the male's chest and twisted. A soft gasp, then the male fell limp. Rion stood, sucking down breath and tilted his head up to the stars. A brisk wind picked up, hitting the blood and sweat coating his skin.

He wiped them away, smearing droplets across his cheeks. It didn't matter, he'd clean up once he was back in his room. He'd receive a letter from Alec tomorrow demanding he answer for the deaths of those left in the street.

But Rion would simply throw it away. Just like he had all the others.

A near silent gasp had Rion pivoting toward the alley, ready to defend himself yet again. The feline was gone, but the half-breed stared at him with wide eyes, frozen to the spot. Rion wasn't even sure he was breathing. Rion's lips parted. He'd forgotten the male was there, caked in his own filth, and he'd just seen . . . a monster. He'd just seen a monster.

Rion's gaze traveled over the bodies at his feet. The half-breed's horror-struck eyes followed and for a split second, guilt washed through him. This male had already been through so much and he'd had to witness this, too.

Rion took one step toward the male, and the half-breed scrambled back. A sob escaped his too-thin frame, and Rion halted. Moments ago, the male might have accepted his offer, but not now. Not after what he'd just witnessed.

Footsteps echoed off the pavement, coming in fast. Rion pivoted again, ready for another group to strike out. He lifted his magic. Adjusted the grip on his sword.

Saoirse skidded around the corner, one hand braced against the wall, chest heaving, and froze when their eyes locked. She wore her casual attire today, a simple pair of slacks and a shirt. She always carried at least one weapon. Today, it was a set of knives in her belt.

She surveyed him, then her gaze dropped to the male at his feet. He expected her brows to furrow. For her to reprimand him for not holding back, as she'd done so many times before.

A sharp intake of breath told him this was different.

His sister gripped her chest, then stumbled forward, one arm outstretched as if she could reach the male from where she stood.

Fear engulfed him.

Rion stepped back, his heart thundering as Saoirse crossed the short distance and fell to her knees, landing right in the puddle of the male's blood. He watched her caress the male's face, then her fingers reached for his neck. A broken sob tore from her throat when she didn't find a pulse.

Saoirse draped herself over the body as if she could protect him, then an anguished cry escaped his sister's lips.

Rion stepped back. Stumbled.

Saoirse.

She clutched the male's tunic so hard her knuckles turned white. Her shoulders shook, rising and falling as despair tore through her body.

Rion's breath came faster and pain speared through his heart, ripping open the emotions he'd buried for the last decade.

Saoirse.

A door cracked open nearby. Someone stepped into the blood-soaked street. Rion looked at his hands. At the blood coating them, then back to his sister's shaking body.

She shifted, trying to sit up, then Rion ran faster than he'd ever run in his entire life. He couldn't face her. He couldn't bear to see the same look on her face that so many others had given him. He could take being called a monster from everyone else. But if Saoirse looked at him that way . . . Rion's heart lodged in his throat. He couldn't—he couldn't—he—

Rion rounded the next corner and collided with another body. Both went to the ground, rolling, and the Fae cursed, turning on him in anger before realizing who he was.

Fear. Always so much fear. Rion scrambled back to his feet and kept running. His leg throbbed. The small cuts and lacerations across his body burned. But he couldn't stop. He needed to get as far away from the city as possible. As far away from her.

Saoirse. Had he finally done it? Had he lost her forever? Why hadn't he ever considered it before? She'd grown up in Nàdair. She'd trained, gone to school, had friends and a life outside of him. How many others had he taken from her? How many friends had he forced her to bury?

And gods, what if that male had meant more? What if—

Rion bolted through the same hole in the redwoods he always used to escape. His leg twitched and Rion stumbled again, but he forced his body up and kept running. Ran from Nàdair. Ran from the responsibility and anger and rage that had driven him for the last decade.

Gods, he really was a monster.

RION KEPT going and only stopped long enough to bind his leg. He limped across the open plains, pushing southwest until the sun rose in the sky.

Dry tears caked his face and his throat was raw from screaming.

Pain. There was always so much pain no matter where he went. And now Saoirse . . .

Rion clenched his fists and slammed one through another tree. His knuckles were already bruised. He was certain one had cracked, judging from the swelling.

He didn't care.

It wasn't until the sun began its descent in the sky that Rion collapsed next to a slow-moving river. He dropped his head in his hands, pulled at the strands of his hair, then rubbed his face.

Rion stared at the water for a long minute, watching leaves lazily drift downstream. He crawled toward the edge and splashed water over his face, clearing away the blood and dirt.

The sound of Saoirse's sobs tore through him again and Rion clenched his shirt in one hand, right over his aching heart. He gritted his teeth, trying to force the tears back.

He'd messed up this time. She'd never forgive him, and he honestly couldn't blame her.

Hearing her scream had broken something else in him. Something Rion hadn't even realized he'd been clinging to. Despite pushing her away for the past several years, Saoirse was the only thing he'd had left. She'd never lost faith in him. Even after his ruthless treatment of the border villages, she'd always stood by his side.

But now—Rion took a breath and tried to steady himself. Could he handle it if he'd lost Saoirse, too? The answer was obvious.

Maybe now she'd join the others in plotting his demise. Hell, maybe she'd hunt him down herself.

Rion cleaned his wounds and spread a salve over the worst two before binding them with a clean cloth. He finished the last of his food, then stared at the small fire.

Gone. It was all gone. His home. His sister.

They were the last things he had to define himself. They were the only connections he had to his mother. He was a vagabond, left with only the wide wilderness to claim.

Rion sat there, thoughts ringing through his mind until shadows stretched across the land. Perhaps he should go to the northern continent after all. That's where Saoirse had originally planned to hide him. He could wipe his hands clean of Brónach and Alastríona forever. No one would know him there, and no one would hunt him so long as he steered clear of the humans.

There was also the continent to the west. None lived in the wild lands, or so the Fae claimed. He could also try traveling south and jump between the islands. Maybe he could even convince an explorer to sail east, discover a new continent altogether, if any existed.

But something kept Rion from pursuing those options. As if the land itself called to him, begging him to stay. He didn't understand it, he only knew he couldn't leave. This was his home, whether he liked it or not.

Rion thought about his mother and, for the hundredth time, wondered what she'd think of the male he'd become. Her opinion probably wouldn't differ from others. She'd see her youngest son as an abomination. A disappointment. If there was one being in the world Rion wouldn't fight, it was her.

Rion suffocated the fire, then spread his legs out, content to watch the last rays of the sun dip below the horizon when the mountain in the distance caught his eye.

It loomed above the land. A silent reminder that even the Fae had something to fear. Rion studied the ominous trees. It was a dark place, a forbidden stretch of land where the Dark Fae were rumored to run wild. A forest full of monsters.

Monsters like him.

The great mountain peaks separated Móirín from Brónach. Neither country claimed them as part of their territory. Fae didn't go there. Fae died amongst those trees, left by the creatures that prowled beneath the ancient boughs.

But maybe that's where he belonged. Somewhere where the world couldn't find him. Where they'd forget he ever existed. He'd vanish and become nothing more than a whispered fable. Or maybe they'd let the memory of him slip away altogether.

Rion snapped a stick between his hands, then stood and shouldered his pack again. He glanced back once more at Nàdair. To those familiar trees that rose high above all the others. A pang of longing echoed in his chest.

Then Rion turned away and began the long trek toward the forbidden mountains.

CHAPTER TWO

Rion stood at the edge of those ominous trees. He peered up into the thick boughs, closed his eyes, and absorbed the strong pulse of magic that seemed to leak from the roots. Ancient.

He'd researched, but Rion had never found anything about the forest's origin. It had been dark and forbidden since the day the Fae arrived on Alastríona's shores. Perhaps the magic was a direct result of something their ancestors had done. Maybe they'd dabbled with something beyond their control and kept it from the history books to hide their failure.

Rion gazed up and down the stark line that separated the smaller trees from the looming giants before him. Not as tall as the redwoods, but still menacing in their own right. He glanced between the trunks. Thick fog rolled along the ground, kissing his boots and disappearing. A line. There was some sort of magical line here, but he couldn't explain it. He hedged a guess no one could.

Adrenaline pulsed through him and his magic reacted, rising up to surround his body with a comforting embrace.

The trees almost seemed to reach for it. For him.

He should have feared the darkness, but Rion stepped beyond that line and walked inside.

His boots were silent against the moss underfoot. The trees creaked and groaned, almost as if they were speaking to one another. He listened, but the normal sounds of birds and scurrying creatures were absent. It was as though the forest were observing him, curious about the creature who'd dared to enter its territory.

Minutes later—and to his utmost surprise—the Fairy Folk appeared. They danced between the trees. Dozens upon dozens of them. Rion paused to watch their carefree nature. They weren't cautious like the ones in Nàdair. They ran and played freely. They almost seemed to be buzzing, as if excited about his arrival.

One landed on his shoulder and kicked its little Fae-like feet back and forth. The action reminded Rion of a youngling before the solstice. Its skin resembled the bark from a tree and a smile spread across its tiny face.

"You're certainly lively today." It chirped, then pushed off, its nearly translucent wings fluttering to keep it afloat.

Others joined it, buzzing through the air in zigzag patterns, chasing one another without a care in the world.

Rion smiled at them despite the pain in his heart. He didn't understand. This place brought death, and yet the sacred Fairy Folk flew through the trees and scurried across the forest floor without fear.

Maybe this was their home. The one place they didn't have to hide. But he'd never heard of the Fairy Folk hurting anyone. Looking at the creatures, Rion wasn't even sure they possessed the ability.

No, there were darker things responsible. Did the Fairy Folk coexist with them, or avoid them altogether? Were the Dark Fae a threat to them?

Instead of walking farther, Rion collapsed against the trunk of a large tree and propped his arm up on a gnarled root. His heart was heavy, his energy spent.

Saoirse.

Rion clenched his jaw. He hated the anger that had driven his every step. Hated that it controlled him more often than not.

But here, just sitting amongst the trees, watching the Fairy Folk running back and forth, that anger was gone somehow. As if someone had carved it from his soul. If not for his aching heart, he might have even felt at peace.

He could use some peace. The last decade had been . . . the opposite. He'd secured every major outpost in Brónach. The minor ones, too. The guards stationed at each one now took their jobs very seriously. So many had lost their lives, choosing to fight rather than relinquish their titles. Some had willingly resigned, but not many.

Once word spread, the rest of Brónach began cleaning themselves up for fear of The Demon's arrival.

It had hardly seemed like a decade. He'd drowned himself in work. When he wasn't visiting villages, he made his way to Whiteridge, just to inquire about their current state. Everyone ran from him, and the Fae male who'd taken on the responsibility of governor refused to look Rion in the eye. His bookkeeping was always immaculate, which made reports easy.

No one challenged him. No one attempted to rebuild the palace.

Rion had rooted out every single manufacturer of the poison and ensured those creating it paid with their lives. There would be no trials. No public executions. They knew who was coming for them.

He'd eradicated the problem in less than two years. Attacks on smaller villages ceased altogether. Not that he received any credit for it. That went to Alec.

Rion sighed and rested his head against the tree trunk. His mind drifted in and out, reliving pleasant dreams and wicked nightmares. Whenever he jolted awake, Rion found the Fairy Folk still dancing and playing. He wondered if they slept at all.

HOURS LATER, Rion stood and stretched his stiff body. It was still dark and his leg throbbed, but Rion forced himself deeper into the forest and up the steep slope of the mountain. Curiosity was his driving force. To know whether the monsters were real. To know if he belonged among them.

He continued for days, treating his wounds, watching the shadows, and enjoying the company of the tiny creatures that followed him wherever he went. They brought him small gifts, leaving folded leaves full of salve and a crown of flowers beside his boot whenever he slept.

He wasn't above putting the flowers on his head, especially when they chirped in delight. He figured it was the least he could do for the medicine they provided. It did far more for the pain than the ones made by the healers.

The dark creatures rumored to prowl the forest didn't make an appearance. Or maybe they were just as frightened of him as the Fae within Brónach. Just his luck. Even sinister creatures were too afraid to challenge him.

Rion sighed and paused at the sight of a glittering patch of sunlight leaking through the canopy. He studied the area. A stream wasn't far off. The land was flat, though he could certainly shift it if need be. He was far from Nàdair. Far from everything.

An idea sprang to life. Perhaps . . . perhaps this was where he was meant to be. Isolated, sure, but . . . a new home. He could build a new home with his own two hands. Maybe it wouldn't be permanent. Maybe he'd never truly find his place in the world. But here. He could do it here. No assassins would dare enter the forest. No eyes would watch him with absolute hatred.

Rion surveyed the area again. Caol, as loathe as Rion was to think about the male, had taught him how to build. They'd worked on the cabin together and had once rebuilt the entire back shed after a storm. He'd taught Rion how to construct fires and how to hunt for food and find clean water.

He didn't need slaves or servants to bring him anything. Rion didn't need anyone to survive.

He started a fire, no longer fearing if it drew anyone's or anything's attention, then set to work.

Rion used his magic to cut down trees and haul stones from the nearby river. He laid the foundation in two days. The walls only took him one, and by the end of the week, Rion finished the roof.

He was finishing the fireplace when the ground shook beneath his feet.

Rion stood, his magic circling his body in a frenzy. The atmosphere shifted, the animals scurried away, and the ground shook again.

Something big was coming.

The hairs on the back of his neck rose, and Rion separated himself from the nearly built cabin. He stood beside the outdoor fireplace, the setting sun at his back, and waited for the monsters to arrive.

The earth beneath Rion's feet shook again and he fed his magic through the ground, letting it stretch toward those rumbling footsteps. Rion nearly gasped at the size of the creature. The weight. It was definitely bigger than anything he'd ever encountered.

The Dark Fae. It had to be one of them.

Rion didn't move. He merely stood, waiting like a statue to finally glimpse the creatures the world avoided.

The beast's steps slowed. He could hear its chuffing breath now. Rion's magic swept across his shoulder, as if it might whisper details to him about the strange creature in the forest.

Then the Fairy Folk emerged.

But they weren't running. They popped their little heads out of the ground and hidden tree hollows with tiny reeds in their grasp. An ethereal tune started. It grew louder, rising through the trees and taking the buried pieces of his soul with it.

Rion gazed up into the canopy and saw the glow around their hands. The slight halo of magic that surrounded their frail bodies.

The Dark Fae emerged then, casting a looming shadow over the tiny beings at its feet. Rion sucked in a breath. It towered well above his head, but not as tall as his imagination's creation. Bark-like skin covered its wide body and bright blue flaming eyes studied him. Neither moved for several heartbeats.

Long, branch-like fingers stretched from both hands. The Fairy Folk continued playing and Rion finally understood.

If someone were to stumble upon this creature, they'd see claws. If fear consumed their thoughts, they might assume the mouth to be full of jagged teeth. But this creature didn't have teeth at all, just an uneven jaw shaped as if it had cracked under pressure.

The being opened that jaw and a long groan escaped, reminding Rion of the trees when they refused to bow to the wind. Rion let his magic settle. He watched the Fairy Folk dance and sing.

Then Rion stepped forward. The tree-like Dark Fae didn't move. Rion stepped again until he'd closed the distance, then peered up into those piercing blue eyes that looked like tiny living flames. "You're not here to kill me," he said, not as a question, but as a statement.

Because the Dark Fae weren't dark at all. This one wasn't, at least.

They were misunderstood.

Just as he had been.

Rion placed a hand on the creature's leg and the Dark Fae reached down, grazing Rion's shoulder with those branch-like arms. As if to provide some semblance of comfort.

A mountain full of monsters.

Home.

The Cursed Fae and Freedom

CHAPTER ONE

Rion adjusted the pack around his shoulders and marched toward the main gates of Nàdair. He didn't summon his magic or reach for his weapons. He'd felt strangely at peace for the last few decades. Like the rage that had once consumed him no longer prodded the edge of his subconscious.

His head tilted up to stare at the barren redwoods surrounding a home he'd nearly forgotten. A place where his childhood memories dwelled. His heart clenched when those memories resurfaced, one after another.

His mother. Saoirse. His childhood friends and all the battles he'd survived over the years.

He knew returning would dredge up those memories. He'd prepared himself for the blow.

The guards didn't react to his presence and Rion didn't expect them to. Not after how long it had been since he'd last set foot in the grand palace halls.

Decades.

Decades to himself where he rarely ventured beyond the mountain's protective borders.

Loneliness occasionally crept in, and Rion allowed himself to visit an inn where he played games with complete strangers who wouldn't recognize him.

Every now and then, someone's eyes would widen and that familiar fear would sweep in, then Rion would vanish, returning to his secluded life among the ancient trees.

Saoirse looked for him.

He heard her name on occasion. He'd almost run into her once, but he'd managed to outpace her.

At the time, Rion hadn't been ready to face his sister. He'd been a coward then.

But he was ready to face her now. Or maybe that younger part of himself just didn't care anymore.

The harsh winter wind cut through the trees, and Rion found himself thankful for the pelts wrapped around his body. He'd learned to live off the land. To use what nature provided to ensure his survival. His hair was longer now, stretching down to the middle of his back. He should probably cut it if he planned to rejoin society. Not that he expected society to welcome him back.

What the citizens across Brónach didn't realize was how much Rion had intervened in their affairs over the last several years. Or maybe they did. He'd heard whispers about himself, too. A Demon that entered the battlefield only to vanish like a wraith.

He'd burned various secret hideouts and dispatched rebels who tried to rise against Saoirse and Alec. He'd even killed the male in Whiteridge who'd taken over the governor's role. He'd warned him.

He hadn't lived in seclusion at all. He'd lived a life at war. One where he kept to the shadows, never taking credit or seeking praise. He rarely used his magic in those moments, choosing instead to hone his skills in combat.

But it had all grown . . . boring. He needed more. He needed to communicate. For someone to know who he was, even if they feared him.

He needed to see Saoirse. Just to know she was all right.

The guards let him pass, and the first few civilians only backed away due to his wild outward appearance.

Then the whispers started, followed by the wide, shocked gazes of those who put the pieces together.

Warriors stiffened, reaching for both their magic and weapons. Some ran straight to the palace, no doubt to announce his arrival.

One warrior blocked his path, weapon drawn and eyes wild. Rion's magic rose then, ready to protect, but no longer beyond his control. No, with time he'd coaxed it into submission. Something about the mountain's magic had fixed whatever had been wrong with him. As if pushing something back on its axis.

"Let's not spill blood on my first day back."

The male visibly shook. "You killed my brother."

Rion sighed and his magic jerked. A familiar irritation returned. A foreign thing buzzing in the back of his mind. "Stand aside."

The male lunged, a war cry falling from his lips. Rion's particles shot out and grabbed the male. The magic held him suspended in the air for a few minutes before Rion threw him into the nearest vendor stall. Wood cracked and gold trinkets flew, scattering through the dirt. The merchant didn't move. Rion just kept walking.

He heard the male rise, but others grabbed his arms, holding him back.

Rion ignored them.

He wanted a warm shower, whether in his old room or in the barracks, he didn't care. He wanted normal clothes and he wanted a purpose. Something to do that his name could be part of.

Another trio—two males, one female—confronted him before the palace gates. Rion made quick work of them, throwing their flailing bodies to the side as if they were little more than nuisances. He didn't kill them, but they'd wake with headaches and a few broken bones.

The guards inside the palace backed away as he strode down the halls.

Rion eyed the familiar paintings. The vases and floral decorations that came with the winter solstice so near. He inhaled the sweet evergreen fragrances that reminded him of his childhood.

Rapid footsteps sounded down the hall, and Rion paused when

Saoirse skidded to a halt in front of him. The two stared at one another, her mouth gaping and shoulders heaving as if she'd just run from the other end of the palace.

Rion's lips parted. Saoirse's green eyes scanned his body from head to toe. He hadn't seen his sister since the night he'd killed her friend. He'd been afraid to confront her then, and if he was being honest with himself, he was afraid to confront her now.

But he missed their conversations. Their games. The way she'd joke and treat him as if he were anyone else. Rion opened his mouth to greet her, but a dozen Fae guards raced from the other end of the hall. Their commander shouted an order, then the guards surrounded his sister, their weapons drawn and aimed at the new threat in their presence.

Him.

Rion eyed the males and females, then with a sinking gut, met his sister's gaze.

"Rion." It was a million questions in a single word. But despite the longing, Rion turned away and headed up a narrow staircase toward the third floor. He felt that familiar pain bloom in his chest. The reminder of why he'd begun pulling away from her in the first place.

Because the people looked up to her. They relied on her to make sound decisions, and if she were caught with The Demon, then she could very well lose everything.

So Rion tucked her away in his heart, went to his room, and prepared to face the world once again as a creature of the night.

CHAPTER TWO

oise from the gathered crowd echoed off the ball-room's marble walls as the dancers bowed to their partners, then stood face to face, readying themselves for yet another round on the floor.

Some flitted between partners while others stayed with the ones they'd walked in beside. Rion memorized every face. He'd been back less than two weeks and had already thwarted a dozen attempts on his life. He'd killed half of them and left the other half in the dirt. They'd all be seeking a new profession once they woke. *If* they woke.

He sipped from his drink, the amber liquid burning his throat. Rion crossed his ankles, his back pressed against the wall farthest away from the food tables. He didn't want to deal with anyone. Here, in the darkness, they simply avoided him.

Rion eyed the bottom of his glass. He'd poured it himself from a bottle hidden in his room. He should have brought the whole thing down. He supposed he could always find an unopened one in the kitchens.

Alec had already planned the celebration before his "untimely arrival," as his brother had so kindly put it. He didn't need words to know Alec wasn't happy. He'd probably thought his little brother long dead. Likely hoped for it.

Rion eyed the guests of honor. They'd emerged victorious in a skirmish to the north involving a rogue group from Pádraigín. The small port city usually kept to itself, but its citizens had been stirring lately. Rion imagined they were likely tired of their boring life at the edge of the continent.

He eyed his glass again. It wasn't his concern. Even if he got involved, it wasn't as though Alec would throw a celebration in *his* honor.

A male's rough voice rose above the crowd, drawing several gazes. Glass shattered, skidding across the polished floor, then Rion watched the male slap a half-breed across the face. The slave barely reacted to the hit. Blood leaked from the corner of the female's mouth, but she bowed and quickly began collecting the shards with her bare hands.

The scent of her blood filled the space as glass cut across her palm. The male kicked her in the stomach, then stormed away. She curled in on herself, sucking down breath.

Anger clouded Rion's vision and those who'd dared to step close quickly moved away. He stared at the slave. The half-breed. Then at the surrounding Fae who sneered at her in disgust.

She kept picking up the glass.

Half-breeds hadn't asked to be born different. Their parents had made that decision for them. Some were love matches, as forbidden as they were, but most resulted from a human female's unfortunate encounter with a disgraceful male.

Rion couldn't fathom ever forcing a female, human or no.

The gods allowed the half-breed's conception. Just like they'd allowed his. And the gods also tolerated their mistreatment. Just as they'd always turned a blind eye to his plights.

Rion continued watching the slave. Another took her place, the two barely nodding to one another in a silent language they'd developed to survive.

He followed her as she weaved through the crowd, carefully balancing the tray of broken glass. He followed her again through the set of double doors.

She didn't notice him, and Rion remained silent as he watched her deposit the glass in a trash receptacle before tending to her hand in the sink.

Moments later, she fetched a pair of tweezers from a side drawer and began picking at the tiny shards embedded in her palm.

The female winced, then cursed. A foul word Saoirse had scolded Rion for using in his youth. The memory brought a smile to his face.

Rion took all of two steps before the female whirled around. He didn't know whether she'd scented him or heard his footsteps.

Her eyes widened, then she hit her knees before pressing her head to the tiled floor. His smile faded.

"I-Is there something I can do for you, My Lord?"

He debated leaving. Perhaps he shouldn't interfere. It had been centuries and no one else ever had. But he was so tired of the gods not taking responsibility for the beings they'd created. He was tired of seeing so many suffer.

"How would you feel about freedom?"

The female didn't lift her head. Tales of his reputation had spread far and wide, even beyond Brónach's borders. He'd done some traveling to other countries. Visited their major cities and villages.

Everyone knew The Demon's name.

But he'd never laid a hand on a slave.

"I am your slave, My Lord." Technically, she was. Every slave within the palace walls was to answer the Lords and Ladies first.

Another slave entered from behind and quickly turned around. Rion watched the door. He couldn't disclose his plans here, not if he wanted to keep them from Alec and the council.

Rion weighed his options and for the first time in a long while he felt his heart lighten with something he dared to call hope.

He was known as a monster, but he could become so much more. And he could use the shadows to do it.

If the world didn't want to give him a purpose, he'd give himself one.

"I want you to finish cleaning your hand, then meet me outside the door."

"I can finish later if it pleases you, My Lord."

He grimaced. "I don't want blood everywhere. Clean your hand and bandage it well."

"Yes, My Lord."

It took the female less than five minutes. She entered the hall, glanced around, then headed straight for him, her head bowed and eyes averted. Rion asked for her hand and inspected it thoroughly before turning toward the door.

"Follow me."

No one looked twice as a slave followed Rion outside the ballroom and down the hall. He scented her fear and prayed she'd agree to his spur-of-the-moment plan.

Rion led her to the study and held the door open to gesture her inside. He checked to be sure no one had followed before closing it behind him.

The room was . . . foreign. He hadn't stepped foot inside since the last night he and Saoirse had played chess together. It had been decades. His sister had kept it mostly the same. She'd replaced a few pieces of furniture, and their old chess table stood in a corner with a layer of dust covering the glass pieces. Pain blossomed in his chest anew.

Rion swallowed it down and turned to face the half-breed. Her pulse was racing.

Rion clenched his jaw. "For the sake of clarity. You're not here for . . . entertainment." Her gaze lifted a bit. "I'm not interested in such things." Tension seemed to fall from her shoulders.

Rion pulled out a chair and set it before her. "Sit, if you'd like." She eyed it for several long seconds, then obeyed. Rion separated himself and stood on the opposite side of the room. He craned his head to listen, just to be sure no one had snuck up behind them.

"Freedom," he began. "How far would you go to obtain it?"

The female looked at him, opened her mouth once, then closed it. "I don't understand, My Lord."

"It's not a trick question. I want to know how far you'd be willing to go."

The female fell silent again. She looked at her hand, flexed her fingers, and winced from the pain. Rion let her think, but she was quiet for so long that he wondered if she'd answer at all.

Then finally, in a voice so soft he could barely hear it, "As far as I need to." She glanced up at him through her lashes, fear written plainly across her face. "I'd do anything, but only if my family came with me."

"Children?" he questioned.

She shook her head. "I was . . . permitted to marry, although we've been," she chewed her bottom lip, "hesitant to have children. But I have two sisters and three nephews. I could never abandon them."

"And if I said you wouldn't have to?"

She looked up then, daring to meet the blazing gaze of The Demon of Alastríona. "What do you want in exchange?"

"Nothing."

Her lips parted again, but no sound emerged. She looked back at her hands, to the chains around her wrists. "I don't understand."

"I'm offering you freedom. There's nothing to understand."

"But why?"

He sighed and looked toward the closed window and the gray sky beyond. "I've never owned a slave." He felt her gaze on him again. "And maybe I'm just tired of the concept."

"Won't the High Lord be angry?"

A smirk played on his lips. "That's part of the fun."

"But he'll figure it out, won't he?"

Rion shrugged. "Eventually."

"What will you tell him?"

"You ask a lot of unimportant questions for someone being offered the chance at a new life."

She straightened, that fear returning, but something else lined the scent, too. Something like excitement.

"I don't want the others punished."

Rion clenched his jaw. It was a valid worry, especially with what he'd seen in the past. It was one of the many ways owners kept their slaves in check, using their friends and family against them.

"I'll tell them you annoyed me enough that I took it out on your family."

Her voice was too soft again. "Many believe you would."

"Many believe a lie." She shifted, uncomfortable, yet curious enough to keep listening. Most slaves had never known freedom. "The choice is yours."

She chewed her lip again, thinking, likely running scenarios through her head and remembering the consequences of those who had tried and failed in the past.

"Where would we go?"

"To Móirín. Levea is lovely in the spring."

CHAPTER THREE

The female, Cara, had asked a hundred questions and apologized a hundred times. How long would the journey take? How would they obtain provisions? Where would they sleep on the journey, and how would they sneak past the guards? Would Levea welcome them in or turn them over to be tried as runaways?

Rion found himself impressed with her attention to details. Cara was a planner, able to think through serious situations carefully. She'd help the others adjust and steer them all toward a better life in Levea.

He understood her need for information. The slaves didn't trust anyone, least of all the Fae. Their lives would be in his hands. He was a Lord. If he was caught stealing slaves, the punishment would be minimal. But runaways and their families would be put to death. Most were tortured in front of their peers, just to reiterate the consequences of trying to escape.

She needed time. Rion gave her a month. By then, the snow would have melted along the mountain pass and the journey wouldn't be as treacherous.

It also afforded Cara enough time to convince her family of his sincerity. He could only imagine what her husband would think. He'd be the first to find out and would probably look at his wife as if she'd lost her mind.

Rion spent the time securing provisions. He ran small packs to the mountain's edge one at a time, stashed water in various locations, and prepaid for a room in a village they'd eventually pass through.

He prayed everything would go according to plan.

The month came and went, then Rion stood before two dozen frightened half-breeds in a secluded garden room on the outskirts of the palace. They watched him, eyes wide and uncertain. Five looked ready to outright sprint back to their rooms.

With the late hour, the children slept in their parent's arms. None were older than five. If they woke before Rion got them out of Nàdair, he'd have a problem on his hands.

Rion pulled a pair of bolt cutters from his bag and offered them to Cara. She extended her wrists, body shaking, and Rion easily cut the chain from the shackle. He needed to keep those on for now, just in case they were stopped by any guards along the way.

Rion went down the line and iron chains hit the ground one after another.

"Is everyone ready?" Most didn't respond, but Cara nodded. Rion gestured to the packs lining the walls. "There's enough food to get us to Levea. Grab one and keep quiet until we clear the forest. We won't stop until dawn."

Three picked up their packs and slung them across their backs. Rion listened to their rapid heartbeats as they readied themselves for the long journey.

The others merely stared, still weighing their options.

"Stay if you want," Rion said. "No one is forcing you."

"This is madness," a male whispered and backed away. His gaze flickered to Rion, then to Cara. "Don't you see? He's going to take us out there and get us all killed."

"And what possible motivation would I have?"

"What motivation do you have for setting us free? What do you get out of this?"

Rion clenched his jaw. He could have told the male any number of things, but those truths were too close to his heart. Too deep to explain to a stranger. Instead he said, "Nothing." The others still hadn't moved. "Again, the choice is yours."

The male backed away, but Cara stepped toward him. "It'll be okay. We'll all be together."

He shook his head. "I can't—I saw what happened to—" he cut himself off. His throat bobbed. "I can't go through that."

"You won't," she tried again, but the male was still backing away.

"Are you going to sell them out?" Rion asked, his voice harsh.

"Never. I won't say a word, but I can't—" He choked and tears fell. "I'm sorry."

The male turned and darted down the hall, his footsteps too loud for Rion's liking. Rion waited for others to follow, but they all turned to Cara, as if waiting for her response.

"Can you trust him?" Rion asked. He hadn't scented a lie, but one could always change their mind.

"Yes." Cara's voice was full of sadness and longing. "If I could just have a minute—"

"There's no time," Rion interrupted. He peered through the glass. "We move in three minutes."

A tear escaped down her cheek, then the half-breed steeled herself and grabbed a pack. The rest followed suite.

"We're ready."

Rion peered outside again. The guard stood. "Move fast and silent." He opened the side door and a crisp breeze flew in, carrying with it the scents of the night. Rion's eyes adjusted to the darkness quickly. He prayed the half-breeds' would as well.

Rion crept through the rose garden with hurried steps. The half-breeds followed, Cara leading the way.

Her resolve settled the others. Rion only wished it had done the same for the male that'd fled.

He had a right to be afraid, of course. He wondered what Rion stood to gain by setting them free. He was worried Rion had some sinister motive behind his kindness. Rion would have likely thought the same if he were in the male's position. But the prospect of freedom seemed to outweigh the fear for the rest of them.

Freedom for themselves and future generations. Freedom from a lifetime of beatings and fear and being told they were worthless.

A small chance was better than no chance at all.

Rion surveyed the area outside the gardens, then gestured Cara to run across the street. He stood in the middle, watching and listening in case the guards came back early. One of the children whined, but the male holding them quickly put a hand over their mouth and shushed them back to sleep.

Their hearts raced, Rion's right along with them. He didn't know what he'd do if someone found them. Would he kill the individual just so they wouldn't sound the alarm? Would he blatantly tell the Fae he was taking the slaves for his own use? They'd scent a lie, sure, but they'd likely just assume Rion was going to kill them anyway.

Rion remained alert and prayed he wouldn't have to make the decision.

They were panting before they reached the small hole in the trees. Each walked through one at a time, almost holding their breath, as if waiting for something to yank them back.

Rion was the last out. He nodded to Cara and pressed a finger to his lips. There were still patrols out here, but with their hoods up, the slaves looked like any other group headed out on an assignment. So long as the guards didn't venture too close, they wouldn't know the difference.

Less than an hour later, they broke from the forest surrounding Nàdair. Rion didn't let them stop, and the half-breeds didn't complain about his pace.

Their hearts had been racing the whole time, but out here in the open beneath the light of the full moon, he caught a few smiling faces. One paused to glance back, likely bidding farewell to the only life she'd ever known.

Rion locked his gaze on the mountains in the distance. If they maintained a decent pace, they'd arrive in the village before tomorrow afternoon.

Freedom. He wondered if this was as close as he'd ever come to tasting it. He glanced at the younglings, all still nestled in their parents' arms, and decided that any consequences he might face for his actions would be worth it. They were worth it, and if he could spare even one from a life lived in chains, then perhaps his existence wasn't so damned after all.

CHAPTER FOUR

The children needed more breaks than he'd anticipated, but none complained the way noble born younglings always seemed to. They ate whatever they were given and walked as long as their parents pushed.

Rion threw the shackle keys to Cara. "Magic can be volatile when it's contained too long. Make sure to stand back when you remove the iron."

"But we're half-breeds," she said, a question in her gaze.

"Half human," Rion replied, "but also half Fae. You, in particular, should be wary."

She glanced down at her shackles, studying the metal as if she could imagine the vines unfurling from beneath. "We still have a ways to go, right?" Rion nodded. "Then I'll wait." She pocketed the key. "What's a few more days after a decade of wearing them?"

It was nearly dusk when they finally arrived in the small village. The half-breeds pulled up their hoods and Rion marched straight to the inn, ignoring those who stood along the streets. Most ducked away from his advancing form.

The female inside gestured him up to their prepared room and Rion laid another pile of coins on the table. "I need adequate, warm food." He jerked his chin toward the half-breeds. "I don't need them fainting on me."

She nodded, counted those with Rion, then disappeared through a back door.

The slaves followed him up a narrow staircase. It wasn't until they were in the room that Rion grimaced. He definitely wouldn't be sleeping in the small space alongside them.

They stood in the middle of the room, huddled against one another, eyeing Rion as if he held all the answers. It was then that he realized they'd never been free to make their own decisions. This was their default. To wait for orders.

"As far as I'm concerned," he started. "From this moment forward, you're free." They blinked and shuffled their feet, glancing at one another in uncomfortable silence. "Food is on its way. Light a fire if you want. The shower is down the hall. Just don't leave this room for anything else. We don't want to draw attention. If you're questioned, just tell them you're on an errand from me."

"They'll know if we're lying, though," a female said, her voice timid.

Rion sighed. "Fine, I command you, as a favor to me, to see to your needs, then to rest for the evening."

He reached for the door, but Cara asked, "What will you be doing?"

"Sleeping," was his only reply before Rion exited the room and went to the roof.

He ate the food he'd packed for himself and listened to the half-breeds in the room below. The innkeeper knocked on the door and delivered hot meals as promised. One tray after another filed in.

The children laughed, delighted by the assortment. The adults gasped in awe, as if they'd just been given a delicacy. They'd probably never even eaten a decent meal. Judging by the male who'd owned them, it wasn't a far stretch of the imagination. Rion almost wished he was in Nàdair just to see the male's face when he woke and realized two dozen of his slaves had vanished overnight.

The half-breeds grew more comfortable by the minute. Whispered conversations started followed by giggling from the children and slight reprimands to keep their voices down.

He heard one pad toward the window and move the curtains aside to glance out. Cara, more than likely, though he wondered if she was looking at the village or for him.

The children settled down until they fell silent, their slow deep breaths filling the space. The adults followed one by one.

Rion laid back and folded his hands behind his head. They still had a long way to go, but perhaps today the half-breeds had tasted enough freedom to push them through the forbidden forest. Perhaps they'd remember instead of trying to run in fear.

He could only hope.

CHAPTER FIVE

It took two days to reach the forest's edge and another few hours to arrive at the entrance where he'd hidden their packs. They'd run out of food and Cara had voiced her concern for water.

Rion simply told her he had everything sorted.

But when he stepped into the forest, a hushed silence settled over the group. They stopped following.

"We're going inside?"

Rion turned to the male who'd asked the question. He saw the fear all over his face and saw it in the way his hands tightened around the strap slung across his shoulders.

"We're going through. There's a valley that will make crossing easier." He eyed the younglings and watched as they craned their heads back, trying to see the tall peaks that reached for the clouds. "We'll exit in Móirín territory. I'll stay with you until we reach Levea. They welcome refugees at the main gates."

The male eyed the ominous trees. "What about the Dark Fae?"

"What about them?"

"Aren't they—shouldn't we be concerned?"

"Would you rather turn back and face the wrath of your former owner?"

"There are children with us," a female spoke up, her voice tentative. "If we have to run . . ."

"The Dark Fae won't be a problem. Not with me around."

"ARE YOU sure about this?" Cara had let the first shackle fall, but hesitated on the second.

"You'll be fine. You're away from the others, and I'll stop your magic if it gets out of hand."

"How are you so sure I even have it?"

"Because you possess more qualities of the Fae than the humans. I'm willing to bet long life and impressive hearing aren't the only things you inherited."

Cara swallowed hard, but excitement coursed through her as she inserted the key and turned. The shackle hit the grass, and the fresh scent of budding flowers and evergreens wafted through the air, as if a strong breeze came from somewhere within the female.

The ground beneath her boots began moving. Plants emerged at her feet and Rion stepped back as they grew to her knee, then past her waist. Their leaves unfurled and flowers emerged, reaching toward the night sky.

Her eyes shone with unshed tears as she watched the magic react. Not volatile, as he'd expected, but calm and nurturing, as if her body was ready to let that magic flow for the rest of her life.

She smiled at him then. Genuinely smiled, and he couldn't help but return it.

"You're really freeing us."

"That's what I said I'd do."

"But you're following through. You don't know how many," she wiped a tear from her eye. "So many lies. We've been told so many lies."

"I know."

Rion stepped to the edge of the small cliff, no more than seven feet up and the female looked down with him, smiling in triumph. Her family clapped for her, clearly delighted.

"Those in Levea will help you learn to control it. They'll help the others, too."

It might have been smarter for her to wait until she'd entered Levea, but Rion had wanted to see her magic himself. Just to see if it was really possible for a half-breed to have it. He'd told her to wait to release the others, just in case.

"We'll reach the other side tomorrow. We've crossed the border, so you won't have to hide anymore."

"What stops Móirín from just shipping us back? Aren't they Brónach's ally?"

"Yes, but the High Lady has a very strong opinion on the matter. She doesn't approve of slaves. She's the reason slavery was outlawed in the first place, and she's made her stance well known."

"But the laws—"

"Don't apply here. Those in Brónach believe that if they lose their slave, then it was something either ordained by the gods or their owner was careless. They'll only pursue the matter for a week before they forget all about it."

"And purchase more," she finished.

Rion didn't try to deny it. There was always a surplus of slaves.

"Thank you," she said. His lips parted at the sincerity in her eyes. In her voice. "We never thought—" she shook her head. "Whatever your reasons, thank you."

"You're welcome." She kept still. Waiting. Rion wanted to say more. He wanted to invite her to sit with him. To talk as if they could be friends. But a familiar wound rose to the surface, reminding Rion of a long buried heartache.

He clenched his teeth. "I plan to do this again. Would it be too much to ask for you to inform whoever needs to know?"

Her eyes widened. "O-Of course not."

After a breath he added, "If I'm to continue this work, then I need to remain anonymous." She opened her mouth to protest. "If word gets back to Brónach, to Alec, well, I'm not exactly sure what would happen."

His brother would make his life a living hell.

"So you go down in history as nothing more than a monster? That hardly seems fair."

"My life hasn't been fair since I was very young."

"I'm sorry," she clenched her fists. "It's—what you're doing, it means a lot to us. It will mean a lot to the others you help as well. If there's anything you ever need, even if it's just a place to rest, don't hesitate to reach out."

Her hand extended and Rion eyed it. His jaw ticked, emotions warred, then he stepped away. "I'll keep it in mind."

Hurt flashed across her features. "Sorry," she whispered.

Rion hated the guilt wading through him. "It's not you. I've . . . let's just say some lessons were learned the hard way."

She nodded. "Well, the offer still stands." He looked at her then, to the gentle smile on her face. The sympathy in her gaze. "And maybe someday, you'll find someone worthy of your trust."

"Maybe." He doubted it. With a final look, Cara started down the steep hill to join the others. He watched her. Watched her family as they congratulated her and marveled at the magic leaving trails of flowers wherever she went.

He was a shadow above them. A dark guardian.

A forest sprite emerged from the moss at his side and sat down, stretching its little rooted feet out as it leaned back on two spindly arms. One smooth finger touched his.

Rion raised a brow at the creature, but it just sat there as if it knew Rion needed the company. Rion didn't pull his hand away.

Trust. He rolled the word over his tongue. He doubted he'd trust anyone ever again. But he'd help those who couldn't defend themselves. He would free the oppressed. Because when he was a child, he would have given anything to have a stranger look at him as if he were something more than a monster.

Chapter Six

o one in the palace questioned Rion's absence. If anything, his return was just a grim reminder of his existence.

The noble that had owned the slaves sent guards to search for them, but after a week he gave up and simply purchased four more. Four slaves who, Rion overhead, were doing the same amount of work as the others. Fewer mouths to feed meant more money in the noble's pockets.

Rion clenched his fists and found a way for the male to disappear less than a week later. Nàdair's guards found him on the bank of a river, drowned. Some thought he'd done it himself, to escape some sort of financial obligation.

Only Rion knew the truth, and he'd made sure that male knew, too. Rion had relished the taste of his fear.

Two weeks later, Rion escorted another group to Levea. But unlike Cara, they weren't as trusting. Half of them backed out. Only four achieved freedom. But four was better than none. Another week flew by and Rion freed seven.

Ten more at the end of the month. A couple with a young child the week after.

He stayed at different inns. Covered their tracks and always left on different days of the week.

Whispers of someone stealing slaves floated through the halls, but no one looked at him twice. Nor did they question when he declared he wasn't available for long missions.

Saoirse began eyeing him, watching him at odd hours of the day. She never said anything and only nodded when she caught him leaving the slave district. She knew. She had to know, but she never turned him in. Maybe secretly, she wanted them freed, too.

He'd only been caught by a guard once. Rion had promptly grabbed the chains of the three females and made a show of dragging them along. The Fae guard had wisely kept his mouth shut and ducked from view.

Less than six months went by before other rumors began circulating. Too many had seen him conversing with the slaves and assumed he was killing them. It made the slaves wary and all refused his offer for two months.

Rion caught another noble beating his female slave in the middle of the hall. Blood leaked from her face as she begged the male for mercy.

Rion snapped. He'd struck from behind and cut the male's head from his body. It had landed with a heavy thud against the carpeted floor.

Alec had been furious, but something in the slaves shifted after that moment. Rion tried again, using Cara as a way to gain their trust, and two dozen agreed to follow him through the mountains.

Dusk had just begun to settle and Rion turned to watch the tired faces of the half-breeds as they climbed the final hill. "Not much further," he promised. He knew they were exhausted, especially the older one, but he needed them to cross the final stretch tonight. He had an assignment to get to and—Rion paused and scanned the forest. He scented the air but kept his magic in check. He couldn't risk those in Móirín learning his identity.

Rion backed away and the half-breeds stood at the top of the hill, leaning against trees as they struggled to catch their breath.

He checked his hood, just to be sure it covered his features and stepped back again. Móirín was here.

"You're safe now," he whispered to the male who led the current lot. "They're here."

"W-What do you mean, what do we—"

"You don't have to do anything. They'll take you in."

A female emerged from the trees with two others flanking her sides. Their magic floated through the air, but she raised her hands, showing them she wasn't armed.

Rion stepped back again. The former slaves watched him, ready to flee at his side.

"Are you the one responsible for liberating the slaves?" a light voice asked. The scent of heavy waterfalls and sweet lilies drifted from her.

Rion nodded.

"I am the High Lady of Móirín." His lips parted. *Shit. Shit, shit, shit.* If she revealed him to Alec— "The High Lord of Brónach inquired about whether we've received any refugees." Rion held his breath. "I sent him a letter telling him we haven't seen any."

A letter. Fae could lie in letters. But if Alec ever confronted her personally—

"My husband asks where they're coming from, but I've refused to answer, though I'd venture to guess he suspects." Another step. "The half-breeds you've brought also refuse to reveal your identity, but I'd like to know who's responsible for their salvation."

Rion glanced back toward the mountain. Was he fast enough to outrun the High Lady? Possibly. He only had to make it to the mountain's edge. Once he disappeared within the trees, she wouldn't follow.

"It's better if you don't know," he said, keeping his voice low.

"I won't turn you in," she promised. "I've wanted to liberate the slaves from our neighboring countries for years, I just—"

Rion stepped back. "It's better this way."

Moonlight filtered through the canopy above and shone on her pale face. "For whom?" she questioned.

Another step. "Everyone involved."

"You could rest here," she offered. "I could arrange lodging. Supplies. Whatever you need."

Rion shook his head. They might not even welcome the slaves any-more if they knew who was responsible. "Just help them."

Rion waited for The High Lady to glance at the frightened slaves, then he broke into a run, sprinting through the night as fast as his feet could carry him. She didn't pursue. Neither did her guards. Even so, Rion didn't slow down until he was safe behind those ancient trees.

Rion had never imagined the High Lady herself was the one guid-ing the former slaves through Levea's gates. She cared. Truly cared what happened to them.

Thereafter, The High Lady of Móirín was always waiting for him. He tried to change the times and dates, but the female always had senti-nels on watch. She was just as proficient as he was. Maybe even more so.

He found supplies littered throughout the forest. It put the slaves at ease, especially when they learned who'd left them.

Rion never spoke to her again. He couldn't risk it. He remained a silent liberator and quietly watched the slaves shift from prisoners of Brónach to citizens of Levea.

CHAPTER SEVEN

ion's brow furrowed, staring at his brother as if the High Lord had completely lost his mind. "Care to run that by me again?" He couldn't believe the words that had just come out of Alec's mouth.

Alec didn't even look at him as he repeated. "I want you to kidnap the High Lady of Móirín."

"Over land?"

His brother studied the glass of wine in his hand. Tilted it so the liquid caught the nearby candlelight. "Can you do it?"

"You'll be breaking a centuries-old treaty. Are you really willing to go to war?"

"I thought war might entice you." With anyone else, Rion wouldn't have hesitated. Hell, he'd rather kidnap the High Lord himself than ever lay a hand on Lillian.

"What do you want me to do? Sneak in and steal her from right under the guards' noses?" He'd studied the city. He could probably figure out a way in but . . . he couldn't do that to her.

"As fun as it would be to watch the High Lord scramble afterward, no. I've received reports that she frequents the outskirts of Levea and often only has a few guards as her escort. She's made herself an easy target."

Rion clenched his fists. *He'd* made her an easy target. "Why is this so important?"

"We need access to the river. It's necessary, and negotiations aren't going well. Things have taken . . . a bloody turn, as I'm sure you're aware." He was. Their two countries had been on the brink of war for the better part of five years. It had started with petty squabbling, of course, then someone had wound up dead and neither party wanted to admit fault.

Alec met his gaze. "You're not to harm her under any circumstances. If I know Lillian well enough, she'll try to negotiate on her husband's behalf." He sipped his wine. "There's a safe house along the edge of the border." Alec pointed to a folder on the far table. "The details are in there. Hold her and wait for further instructions. Once the High Lord complies, we'll release her and be done with it."

"And if he doesn't?"

"She's his mate. He will."

Rion hissed through his teeth. He knew why Alec had picked him. Because if anything went wrong, then Rion would be the one to blame. Or so Alec hoped. Rion had never known his brother to be stupid before, but this—Rion clenched his fists. This wasn't how one worked with their allies.

"When?" Rion asked.

"In two days. I've assembled a tea—"

"No." The word was out before Alec could finish his sentence.

"This isn't like—"

"I don't give a damn," Rion interrupted again. "The answer is no. Whoever you need to send can arrive afterward. I go alone, or you can find someone else."

"You're refusing?"

Rion crossed his arms. "It's within my right."

Alec watched him carefully and after a moment, leaned back in his chair. "Fine. They'll arrive afterward, but they have a specific job to do. I'd appreciate it if they returned intact."

Rion didn't smile. "You tell them to keep their magic and blades to themselves and there won't be a problem."

Rion grabbed the folder from the desk and pivoted on his heel before marching from the throne room.

Shit.

Shit.

Of all the Fae he didn't want to encounter. She'd been trying to uncover his identity for years. Less so now that she had younglings of her own, but still, she'd never relented. If he got anywhere near her, she'd catch his scent and know exactly who'd been dropping slaves at their gates.

She was a High Lady. Rion wondered if his brother had forgotten exactly what that meant. What it had meant for their mother. To fight her would likely shake the very foundations of Levea. And alert everyone in the city.

He'd need another way to get close to her. Rion just wasn't sure he liked the idea.

CHAPTER EIGHT

tupid. That one word had been echoing in his head since he'd left the borders of Nàdair. Now he stood with his cloak pulled over his face, leaning against a tree just outside the main city of Levea. A place he'd often dropped off slaves.

Maybe he'd get lucky and she wouldn't show up at all. Maybe she was too busy with her younglings, reading them stories, baking them sweets, whispering the same fairy tales his mother had so often whispered to him.

Alec was a fool. The only thing kidnapping the High Lady of Móirín was going to accomplish was inciting a war. The prospect didn't sound . . . terrible under any other circumstances. But with her—he sighed and shook his head again.

Stupid.

Things had been complacent too long. The warriors were restless, seeking conflict where there wasn't any. Sure, they had their occasional skirmishes along the borders, but it wasn't enough. They needed a reason to fight. Desired it, even. Perhaps they were similar to humans in that regard.

Peace. It was always within their reach, yet never attainable. Maybe it had nothing to do with the myth about a queen for which they'd been searching for millennia. Maybe she and the gods had abandoned them because they couldn't solve their own problems.

Rion stared through the trees. He studied the city and the crisp waters that had always called to an internal part of himself, as if beckoning him home. He watched a lone figure emerge from the gates and gritted his teeth.

Damn Alec to hell.

RION CURSED himself for the hundredth time as he stared at the iron bracelets around the High Lady's wrists. He'd lit a fire in the safe house and had draped a blanket over her torso and legs.

Now he leaned against the mantle, waiting for her to wake.

It had been too easy. He'd caught her warriors off guard with his magic and before any of them had realized who was attacking, he'd knocked them all out cold.

Rion grimaced at the bluish bruise on the back of Lillian's neck. He hadn't meant to strike her so hard. She'd turned on him and he'd just reacted, afraid to let anyone from Móirín put their hands on him.

Now, the High Lady sat in a wooden chair, her hands secured to the arms with ropes. Her head lolled to the side at an awkward angle.

He ran his hand through his hair and hissed through his teeth. He should have refused. He should have run to Saoirse and told her about Alec's idiotic plan. Now it was too late.

Rion eyed the iron bracelets again. He couldn't stomach the shackles. It was a risk, especially when they could be easily removed, but . . . this was Lillian. She'd likely never hurt a thing in her life. Putting the heavy metal around her wrists had just seemed . . . cruel.

Rion stared back into the flames, still debating whether he should just release her and disappear when her breathing changed.

He froze, waiting. Her eyelids fluttered open and she blinked a few times, groaning as she lifted her head and tilted it from side to side. Regret and guilt flared through him.

The High Lady of Móirín absorbed her surroundings. Her heart sped as realization of her predicament spread through her, but panic didn't settle in. Not yet, at least.

She pulled at the ropes holding her in place, then her eyes landed on the blanket. The bracelets. Then finally him.

The pair stared at one another across the dark room, neither moving. She took him in slowly, from the blades strapped across his waist to the sand shifting at his feet.

Her nostrils flared as she scented the air.

"I won't hurt you," he said quickly. Not that he expected her to believe him. "As soon as Alec gets what he wants, I'll release you and we can forget this ever happened."

Anger pulsed from the female. She scented the air again, opened her mouth, likely ready to call him every foul name known to their language, then hesitated. She sniffed the air again. studied his face. Rion's heart skipped.

"I know you." Her voice was soft. Surprised.

He shrugged and turned away. "Most do."

"No." She shook her head. "I *know* you." She adjusted in her seat, as if trying to get comfortable. "You're the one who's been liberating Brónach's slaves."

"I don't know what you're talking about." The scent of the lie floated between them. He only said it for those who might be listening nearby. Alec always had spies everywhere. Even in Móirín.

Lillian followed his gaze outside and seemed to understand. But to his utmost surprise, she relaxed in the chair.

"Interesting choice of . . . restraints," she commented.

Rion didn't meet her gaze. "I didn't like the alternatives." One of Alec's slaves had given him a bag full of iron shackles. Rion had chucked it into the nearest river. "You're a High Lady. You shouldn't be in chains." Rion only knew about the bracelets due to his mother. She'd often worn them to control her visions when they got out of hand.

"The thoughtfulness is appreciated." She observed the room again, from the single door to Rion's right to the lack of furniture save for a moth-eaten mattress in the corner. It looked more like a prison cell than a safe house.

"Could I request some water?"

He should have said no, especially considering where she was from, but Rion pushed off from the wall and grabbed his canteen. He poured a bit into a cup before approaching.

Lillian didn't balk at his magic; she simply stared at it, as if curious. Without touching her, Rion lifted the cup to her lips and tilted it back slowly. He returned to his place by the wall once she'd finished.

"Is this about the land?" she finally asked.

Rion ran his hand through his hair again. "My brother seems to feel this is the only way to obtain it."

She sighed. "I almost had my mate convinced to hand it over last night." She shook her head. "When he discovers I've been taken—"

"I know." Rion had never viewed the High Lord of Móirín as a gentle male. Alec had spoken to him before. He knew his mannerisms and yet he'd still done this. "Alec will probably try to cast the blame on me in the end."

"He's done that before?"

"Not to this extreme." If Alec was able to convince the High Lord of Móirín that Rion had acted of his own accord, the male could likely demand Rion's life in exchange for peace.

Alec would be more than happy to oblige.

"You're upset with his decision."

"It's a common occurrence."

A small smile tugged at the corner of her lips. "Is this what I have to look forward to when my daughters come of age?" Rion didn't respond. "Though, I suppose your relationship with your siblings is somewhat strained due to—" she paused. "Circumstances beyond your control."

"You could say that."

She eyed him, watching, evaluating. "The slaves still protect you, you know." Rion turned to her. "All these years and they've never once given you up. No name, no description. Nothing, no matter how much I beg." She studied his reaction, but Rion kept himself still. "That first group," she continued. "The female leading them. Cara. She's much older now, but still runs things in her segment of the city. She started her own business. I thought you'd like to know. She opened a tea house and has three beautiful children."

Emotion welled in Rion's throat. "Why are you telling me this?"

"I thought you should know how much of a difference you've made. Many, not just Cara, have children of their own. Some aged, others didn't, but they all live very different lives now. Their children live very different lives."

They were free. Because of him.

"We don't have to continue this, you know." He turned to look at her. "I can tell my husband this is all just a big misunderstanding."

"I'm sure he'll listen."

"He will to me." The shift in her tone had Rion straightening. He had to remind himself that Lillian wasn't just any female. "I'll tell him the truth. About who you are and what you've been doing. He won't hold you responsible."

"And what do you want in return?"

"For you to come live with us."

His head snapped up. "What?"

"You're an outcast in Brónach, are you not? I've heard the rumors, and yet I see a very different male before me."

"You don't know what I've done."

"I do. I'd venture to say I know more than most, given my position. I know about your trips to the border. I know how you've defended your people in secret. I know about the slaves."

"Do you also know how many people I've killed in the process?"

"Are we going to start judging one another by the amount of blood on our hands? Because I believe I have a few centuries on you."

Rion looked at the female, then to her hands. "I can't imagine you have much." He didn't mean it as an insult and thankfully she didn't take it that way.

She smirked. "Not in recent years. Not with my girls. But rest assured, I've seen my fair share of battle. My mate and I even fought alongside your parents at one time." Rion's heart skipped. "Our countries are allies, Rion of Brónach. There's no reason we can't remain as such."

"What about the ancient texts?" he whispered.

"They're stories. Let them stay stories."

"You don't believe?"

"I find it very hard to believe a male would risk everything—his reputation, his home, and his life—to free others if he was nothing more than an abomination."

"Not everyone will share in your beliefs."

She shrugged. "They don't have to."

"It might discredit you as their High Lady." It was the whole reason he'd steered clear of Saoirse for so long.

"I've ruled our country for centuries. One incident isn't going to change the people's view of me." Rion's jaw worked. A new life. He could start over somewhere. And Saoirse would know exactly where he was. She wouldn't have to worry.

"What do you say? We could liberate the rest of the slaves in Brónach together."

"Alec won't release them."

"Maybe not at first, but we could set things in motion. I'm certain your sister will join us in the movement." Rion couldn't speak for her. Saoirse had always owned slaves, but she'd never mistreated them. She often punished those who did.

"She might, but you should know, the warriors of Brónach are looking for a fight. There's already been blood spilled."

"No permanent damage has been done. We can work toward re-kindling our alliance. Perhaps we've been isolated from one another too long, especially with a new High Lord in place." She sighed. "My mate and I should have pushed harder for meetings. Perhaps the fault lies with us." She nodded, as if confirming something to herself. "We'll see to it. We can make political statements, sentence those who have gone without proper punishment for their crimes. Maybe even change a few more minds about you. The former slaves will step forward. They'll help you."

"No one from Brónach is going to listen to a former slave, and Alec is just going to be pissed you didn't return them."

"But the citizens of Levea will. You forget, we have half-breeds and humans here who were born free."

"And Alec?"

"My mate and I can deal with him. He's young. I'm confident he can be swayed." Rion wasn't so sure. "Nothing happens overnight. It'll take time, but we can start. You and I can begin making changes for those who can't stand up for themselves."

Change. The entire concept seemed too good to be true. To think the key to changing things could very well be in the hands of the female he'd been avoiding for years. A High Lady from a neighboring country.

"Even if all this works out, there's still the fact that I stole you in the dead of night. I'm not sure your mate will be willing to forgive."

She shrugged. "Then I guess you two will have to fight it out." He blanched. "Not to the death, of course. I'll be there to intervene if it comes down to it. Maybe you'll get off with a right hook and that'll be the end of it." He couldn't tell if she was joking or not.

"And you?" he asked. "Are you willing to forgive so easily?"

A flame flickered behind those blue eyes. Eyes that reminded Rion of the rivers circling their beautiful city. "I will do a great many things for the sake of freedom. And to be fair," she eyed the bracelets around her wrists, then the blanket still draped over her body. "You did make an effort to ensure I'm comfortable." She rolled her neck and winced. "Mostly."

Rion grimaced. "I'm sorry for striking you. You surprised me and I thought—well, you're a High Lady and I didn't exactly want to be crippled for the rest of my life."

"Smart on your part."

Rion stared out the window, watching the swirls of snow drift by. If Alec had any spies listening in, then his brother would know of his involvement with the slaves soon enough, anyway. He sighed and ran a hand through his hair again.

"Just . . . give me a minute."

"I'll be here."

Rion eyed her and smiled slightly at the humor in her tone. She was serious. About everything.

He walked into the small bathroom and splashed water on his face before leaning against the counter.

Freedom. Not just for the slaves, but for himself. A chance to be something more than just a feared weapon.

She was a High Lady. She had the authority and power to declare him anything she wished. And if the former slaves vouched for him, too . . . could his actions have ensured his own freedom? Would he get the life he'd always dreamed about? To be able to interact with others and walk the streets without worrying about his safety?

He splashed more water on his face, then looked into the old mirror hanging over the vanity. Rion studied those familiar eyes. The eyes of his mother.

If he ever saw her again, would she be proud of him? Could he make her proud by doing this?

Rion used his sleeve to wipe the moisture from his face and jolted from a loud noise in the main room. He sighed. She'd promised to be there but hadn't promised not to escape.

Rion pulled his magic around his body, just in case, and opened the door.

The entire world he'd just fabricated shattered before his eyes.

He ran, moving faster than he ever thought his body capable, and slid to his knees at Lillian's side.

Her wide eyes locked with his and he cupped the long slice across her throat with one hand.

"No," Rion breathed the word, praying he could make it true. "No, no, no."

Blood leaked from between his fingers and spilled out onto the floor. She reached for his face, for the tears forming, but her hand fell limp. The light faded from her eyes. Rion ripped her bonds away and pulled her against his chest, still clutching the fatal wound along her throat.

Less than a second. A heartbeat. A breath. That's how long it had taken for the hope in his heart to shrivel and die.

The fleeting plans were gone. A new life for himself and others. Gone.

Her final breath left her lips, then a collective gasp sounded from the open door. Rion glanced up to find three of Brónach's warriors peering inside. They looked at his hand, the sand snaking across the floor, the dead female in his arms who was meant to be his charge.

Fear filled the entire cabin and they backed away, staring at one another as if they didn't know what to do next.

Rion looked down at Lady Lillian, then used his other hand to close her eyes. His body shook with rage and grief, but Rion forced himself to focus. He scented the air. Someone had managed to sneak inside. Somehow, they'd gotten past his guard. He hadn't heard a thing.

There weren't footprints and they hadn't bothered to leave the knife.

Rion tried to calm the blood pulsing in his ears. He scented the air again—there. It was faint. Just a trace of shadow. Another minute and he might have missed it altogether.

Fiadh.

A shadow weaver.

Rion breathed it in again. Male. He hadn't bathed in days and he smelled too much like flames and the mountain to be anything else.

Rion committed the scent to memory, carefully laid Lillian's head against the floor, and stood. Rion was going to kill him. Kill and torment the male who'd dared to intervene.

A choked gasp had Rion spinning to face the door just in time to see a wall of ice barreling toward him. Rion jumped back, but deadly spikes followed his every move. He stumbled into the nearest wall and a shiver went through him when a roar shook the land itself.

The High Lord of Móirín had come for his mate.

A frozen spike buried itself in Rion's arm and he winced. Water gathered around the male's body, rising in a wave so tall it nearly touched the ceiling.

Rion didn't waste time. He shattered the wooden planks of the wall behind him and jumped through, narrowly escaping the icy torrent chasing after him.

The High Lord roared again, this one full of pain and longing. Rion watched him fall to his knees at Lillian's side. Saw him caress the female's cheek with shaking hands, then bury his face in her hair as he drew her body into his arms.

Ice coated the floor beneath the male's knees, the magic rapidly spreading to the walls and ceiling.

He looked so . . . broken at that moment. Not like a High Lord, but like a male who'd lost the one thing that rooted him to the earth.

Half the guards charged Rion, their own fury written plainly across their faces.

Gods above, what had he done?

Rion had taken her. He'd made her vulnerable, then he'd left her and she'd become an easy target.

Now, there was nothing to be done. No conversation he could have that might ease the situation.

Rion retreated, refusing to fight back.

The ground beneath his feet shuddered and Rion knew the High Lord was coming for him next.

He turned and ran straight for the mountains.

Alec hadn't wanted a war, but a war was exactly what had just been started.

CHAPTER NINE

The wooden table shattered against the far wall, then Alec pivoted, magic flaring as he shouted, "I told you not to touch her!"

Saoirse stood in the middle of the room, her body between her two brothers as if she was a shield.

"Do you have any idea what you've done?" Alec roared.

Rion had walked through the throne room doors without bothering to wipe Lillian's blood from his hands or clothes. He'd intended to explain the situation, but as soon as Alec saw him, he'd begun screaming, pacing, circling the throne as he rubbed his temples and ordered everyone from the room.

"Why didn't you consult me first?" Saoirse nearly shrieked. "You've just plunged us into war."

Alec snarled at their sister. "He," he pointed a finger in Rion's direction, "just plunged us into war."

"Dead or alive, the High Lord of Móirín wouldn't have forgiven you either way. What were you *thinking*, Alec?" Saoirse's gaze drifted to Rion and her lips parted as she beheld the blood on his hands. She just stared, as if she didn't quite believe her little brother could be capable of such a thing.

"You did this on purpose. You did it to undermine everything we've

"

tried to build. Do you want Brónach to fall? Or is your problem solely with my reign?"

Rion could have said a million things. He could have attempted to explain himself. Perhaps Saoirse would have listened, but Alec, Alec had made his own decisions. So instead of the truth, Rion quirked a wicked smile. "At least now you have the land you wanted." Rion waved an arm. "Hell, you can invade Móirín and lay claim to more if you wish."

Alec flashed his teeth. "I should have killed you years ago."

"I'm right here," Rion snarled back. "Take your shot."

Alec's magic twitched and he stalked forward, shaking the jacket from around his shoulders. Saoirse stepped between them, but Alec didn't pause. He didn't so much as look at her as he glared at his brother.

Rion's magic wrapped around his body, preparing for a fight to the death.

"Enough, you two." Neither male backed down. Saoirse stepped toward Alec again, but a tendril of his magic shoved her to the side hard enough that Saoirse slammed into the desk.

Then his brother lunged. Rion didn't see the knife until he raised his magic to block Alec's strike. Particles of sand ran down Alec's arms and Alec's magic burst from his sleeves in a rapid frenzy that forced Rion to jump away.

Alec didn't let him get far. Rion drew his own dagger and his brother's blade locked with his own. Their magic burst above their heads. Around their bodies.

Saoirse screamed from the sidelines.

Rion refused to turn away or back down. He grabbed Alec's wrist, intending to wrench it backward, but Alec shifted, forcing Rion to shift as well to keep his balance. The two pushed against one another, grappling for dominance as they stood mere centimeters apart.

"Mother would be ashamed of what you've become," Alec spat.

Rion saw red and before he could rein himself in, his magic exploded, shoving Alec back hard enough that the male tripped on his own vines and hit the marble steps hard enough that something cracked.

Rion didn't care. He closed the distance, ready to plant a fist in

Alec's pompous mouth, but Saoirse jumped in front of her older brother. She reached for the greenery in the room, snaking it around herself and her sibling. She lowered her body into a fighting stance even as silver lined her eyes.

Alec still hadn't gotten up.

Rion stopped. He studied Saoirse and the way her hands shook. Her throat bobbed, then one tear slid free.

A mountain of regret followed. He thought he'd locked it all away, but at the sight of that single tear, the box where he'd stored his sister's love burst open.

Memories of all the times they'd laughed together rushed to the surface. Times with their mother. Times when he was a teen and she'd come to his rescue when no one else had.

Alec slowly rose to his feet, something like surprise written across his face and—if Rion hadn't imagined it—a tinge of fear.

Rion kept his gaze on Saoirse, watching as she made a decision that would alter the course of his life forever. If she attacked—

Thick emotion welled in his throat. He'd gone too far. She'd once stood between him and Alec. Now the tables had turned. He was the villain in her story.

Rion stepped back. Saoirse didn't relax.

"Leave," Alec growled.

"Send me to hold the front line and I will."

"Why in the seven hells would I do that?"

"Because I've never lost a battle. And I can guarantee I won't lose this war."

The Cursed Fae and Hope

CHAPTER ONE

Rion stormed through his camp, rage coursing through his veins. He ran his tongue over his teeth, tasted blood, then used what was left from his water skin to cleanse his mouth. He snarled at those who dared to even meet his gaze. They quickly turned away, scurrying behind tents.

Rion wiped his bloody hands over his tunic only for it to smear from more that had soaked into his clothes.

He hated every single one of them. He ought to just be done with the entire camp. Wipe it off the continent and give Móirín an easy win. It would be better than dealing with it himself.

But if he did that, he'd wind up right back in Nàdair's palace. He'd been in the field for almost a decade. Returning to a life of comfortable pillows and prattling nobles wasn't appealing in the least.

A warrior exited his tent right in front of Rion, and Rion snarled at him. The male bowed at the waist, his gaze averted. Rion had no way of knowing how many were involved in the most recent attempt on his life. Probably all of them.

He'd barely stepped through the gate when they'd lunged. A dozen of them. It was always the same story. A group, usually the young, would band together, certain they could outsmart him. None ever succeeded, though a male had gotten a good hit in, hence his bleeding gums.

They'd been a savage lot till the very end, coming at him until none could stand. Even the last hadn't faltered.

A lot of good it had done them.

Rion marched up the small overgrown path to his cabin and slammed the door open. The magic circling his body entered first, always searching corners and shadows for any who might try to press their luck.

The grains paused. A fluttering heartbeat met his ears, then her scent flooded his nose. It sent his blood racing. Raging all over again, but in a different sort of way.

He spotted the female in the far corner of the room, staring at him with wide frightened eyes. Rion bared his teeth at her. He knew the scent of his enemy better than anyone.

Rion stepped into the cabin, eyes roaming over her face, then her body. He noted the scars around her wrists, the absence of shackles that were supposed to accompany a slave.

But this female wasn't a half-breed.

He waited, daring her to move, to summon the magic he'd encountered on the battlefield so many times before. Females were just as strong as males, and usually more cunning.

She didn't so much as blink. The female just stared at him with piercing blue eyes. Eyes that stripped him bare and dug down to feelings and secrets he'd hidden from the world.

For a moment, Rion forgot his anger. For a moment, he was breathless and reeling. For a moment, his pain vanished entirely.

Rion knelt, clasping his hands together as he studied the female before him, suddenly more curious than angry. Something . . . pulled him toward her. An invisible hand he couldn't explain. For the first time in years he wanted to touch someone, pull her up from the floor and trace her face. The pulse in her throat.

His magic moved instead, always separating him from a potential threat. She lowered her head to the floor, exposing the back of her neck. Her wrists were already turned up.

Pure submission.

It sent a thrill of delight through him. So many others had done it before, but her—his blood sang for it.

Sand reached her hands and crawled up her arms, wrapping around her fingers and wrists. Coaxing. Teasing. Demanding.

Her scent was intoxicating. A lethal drug begging him to taste it.

Mine.

The word pulsed through him. His blood pounded in his ears. Her heartbeat quickened. She was *his.* His prey. A beautiful fawn trapped in his grasp.

A low animalistic growl rumbled through his chest and his sand dared to venture beneath the poor excuse for a dress. It traveled up her torso, wrapping around that slender neck.

A sob escaped her lips and the world stopped. Cracked. Whatever trance he'd been under shattered as Rion came back to himself, driving instinct and desire back to the far recesses of his mind.

Ice coated his veins and something in him screamed that this was *wrong.* So very, very wrong.

He stood and reined his magic in, struggling to control it for the first time in decades. Rion stared at the female. Her shaking body. Her breath trembled and guilt overwhelmed him. He hadn't felt guilt in a long time, either. Rion hated the feeling and the way it sat heavily on his chest.

This female, half-breed or no, was a slave. Had been for several months. Possibly even years, if the scars across her wrists were anything to judge by.

She'd disguised herself, letting others believe she was nothing. Useless.

Why?

Rion wasn't sure why he wanted to know or why he cared, but the curiosity was already eating away at him as if it were a parasite. Curiosity was dangerous.

Perhaps she was part of another ploy from the warriors in his camp. Maybe they'd figured out what she was and put her in his service with the hopes that she'd eliminate him herself.

Cowards.

Rion stared at her for another long moment, then marched to the small bathroom and slammed the door shut. He listened as he pulled off his clothes and piled them on the floor.

The female didn't move.

He should have killed her, but he'd never been able to bring himself to kill a slave.

Rion worked his jaw and splashed water on his face before retrieving a cloth to wipe his body down.

He'd wait. Feel her out. If she proved herself innocent, he'd run her to the edge of the mountains and point her home.

If she didn't—

A spark shot through Rion's body as he recalled those cerulean eyes. Something deep in his body had come to life at the sight of them. Like she was the song he'd been trying to find his entire life.

That word echoed through him again. He didn't understand it. He didn't know what it meant or what he'd do about it. Rion only knew he liked the way that word tasted on his tongue.

Mine.

Acknowledgements

Now that I've spent three books with the character, I can honestly say that Rion is by far, one of my favorites. I love everything about him and you readers seem to feel the same. Therefore, I wrote this book for you. If you've read book one, you knew everything in these pages, but I needed a way for you to experience his pain and really feel the depth of his character. Sorry, I'm not taking any therapy bills at this time. So my first thanks goes out to my readers because without you there wouldn't be a story at all.

To all the authors that have shared their journeys, accomplishments, cover reveals, special editions, and so much more. Just know that they helped keep this little author going before she was full time. Even now, I watch those success videos and tell myself, "One day soon." Especially you Emily Blackwood. I've been watching from the beginning and following you every step of the way.

As always, a huge thank you goes out to my husband for being my support person from the very beginning. You've read every draft and given feedback that polishes my crazy scattered ideas into a finished manuscript.

And last, but certainly not least. A thank you goes out to Story Wrappers for making this incredible cover art and to Dawn Jonckowski for catching the mistakes that always seem to slip through the cracks.

Author Bio

J.E. Reed is the #1 bestselling author of The Fae of Alastríona series. Reed loves writing magical stories full of love and adventure and she believes everyone deserves a happy ending.

Reed currently lives in Ohio with her husband, her son, and an orange tabby cat who, she is certain, used to be a Viking in another life. Her latest series has enabled her to pursue a full-time writing career and she plans to bring readers more heart-wrenching romance.

Visit Reed's website at www.jereedbooks.com
Follow her on Instagram: @jereedauthor
Follow her on Tiktok: @a_writers_quill
Follow her on Facebook: @J.E.Reed.author